A MATTER OF PHILOSOPHY

For a long time I thought and studied on the problem, and it wasn't until almost twenty-four hours later that I come up with some thinking that made sense to me. I had a friend, an ex bank robber turned professional gambler and saloon proprietor, who had a philosophy I'd never paid much attention to. Wilson Young said a man had to get himself a cardinal rule and live by that rule and never violate it. If a man did that he would never find himself getting upset by the minor details and nuts and bolts of life.

Of course, Wilson's cardinal rule was to never loan money to a stranger on a moving train. But there was some truth in it. Laura and I had gotten so tangled up with the nuts and bolts of everyday life we'd gotten to where we didn't know an ace from a deuce.

The ace was our marriage. I went to hunt up Charlie in his cabin. The hour was late and he was asleep, but it didn't matter. I gave him three thousand dollars and told him I was going to Jefferson on the next day's train and he was to tend to matters.

As I was getting up to leave, Charlie said, "Fetch her back, Mr. Grayson, even if it has to be at the end of a lariat rope."

I wrinkled my brow. "I wish it could be that simple, Charlie," I said softly. "But I greatly fear that it won't."

Praise for Giles Tippette's The Duel

"This well-written story, told entirely in Warner's intriguing voice, remains flawlessly true to the characters and jargon of the code of the American cowboy. The people and the love story are compelling, and the horse lore is entertaining."

—Gerry Benninger, *Romantic Times*

Books by Giles Tippette

FICTION

Warner and Laura*	China Blue
The Duel*	Wilson Young on the Run
Mexican Standoff*	The Texas Bank Robbing Company
The Button Horse*	Hard Luck Money
Tombstone (Novelization)	Wilson's Woman
Slick Money*	Wilson's Revenge
The Horse Thieves*	Wilson's Choice
Cherokee	Wilson's Luck
Dead Man's Poker	Wilson's Gold
Gunpoint	The Mercenaries
Sixkiller	Austin Davis
Hard Rock	The Sunshine Killers
Jailbreak	The Survivalist
Cross Fire	The Trojan Cow
Bad News	The Bank Robber*

NONFICTION

I'll Try Anything Once: Misadventures of a Sports Guy
Donkey Baseball and Other Sporting Delights
Saturday's Children
The Brave Men

*Published by POCKET BOOKS

GILES TIPPETTE

WARNER AND LAURA

POCKET BOOKS

New York London Toronto Sydney Tokyo Singapore

An *Original* Publication of POCKET BOOKS

POCKET BOOKS, a division of Simon & Schuster Inc.
1230 Avenue of the Americas, New York, NY 10020

ISBN: 0-671-87160-9

First Pocket Books printing June 1995

10 9 8 7 6 5 4 3 2 1

POCKET and colophon are registered trademarks of Simon & Schuster Inc.

Cover art by Dennis Lyall

Printed in the U.S.A.

For Betsyanne

1

Laura

"I guess if I ever expect to have a son I'm going to have to get myself another woman to have it with."

In one breath my husband had accused me of being barren and then used that accusation as an excuse to commit infidelity. The shock of the brutal remark was like being hit in the face with a bucket of cold water, followed by the bucket. For a moment I was speechless. By the time I could regain my composure he'd walked out of the small morning room where we normally had breakfast, through the kitchen, and outside. I heard the screen door slam and his boots clumping on the back steps, then deafening silence.

I was not really surprised that a showdown of a kind had come. I was only surprised that it had taken such a blunt and irrevocable form. The subject of having a child had been between us for the last couple of years, taking on a greater and greater sense of urgency as we'd grown older. I was thirty-six and so was Warner—Warner Grayson, my husband. Thirty-six was late for a woman to be carrying a baby and Warner and I both knew it. We had been together for seven years, four of them married. Or a little better than four. Back when we met Warner had somehow gotten the idea that I was two years older than he. I'd never bothered to straighten him out on the score because it was, in his eyes, one of the few advantages he had over me. Though I am not sure that being two years younger than anyone, woman or not, is necessarily an advantage.

But Warner was a young horse breeder in those days, of fairly moderate means. Against the general run of young men in their own businesses, he was doing quite well, and was known far and wide in south and west Texas as one of the best horse breeders to be found. By the time I met him he had graduated from general work and cattle horses to high-quality traveling animals and short-track race horses, mostly Morgans and quarter horses.

His condition, however, didn't compare to mine, as I was quite wealthy, thanks to an inheritance from my deceased husband, John Pico. John and I had been married less than a year when he'd been killed by Mexican horse thieves. He had foolishly run out in the open to fight against a dozen guns. His end had been quick. I did not love John Pico and had married him with the understanding that it was a marriage of convenience for me. What I wanted for a wedding present was a horse ranch stocked with very high-priced Andalusian stallions I could use to do some experimental breeding, looking to improve the cattle horse. Curiously enough it was because of that same raid by the Mexican banditos that I met Warner, who had been victimized by their depredations as well. He, however, was intent on recovering his stolen property. He trailed the bandits into Mexico, wiping them out, not only recovering his own animals but my six Andalusians as well. I had been swept off my feet by the uncharacteristically serious young man. He was handsome, he was obviously fearless, he was ambitious, and he was not bashful about his knowledge of a woman's body. I had been taken with him from almost the first, but even more, perversely, when he'd returned my stallions. He had claimed one of the Andalusians as a reward for recovering the rest. I hadn't wanted anyone else to have control over the scarce breed and I'd offered him two thousand dollars instead for the horse, which I called Paseta. He had surprised me by turning down what to him must have seemed a considerable amount of money, probably more than he'd ever seen in his life. But he had further surprised me by seeing the possibilities in the Andalusian as a road horse and had said he'd just keep the horse instead. I'd asked him to throw in with me and run my ranch. He'd only laughed and said he already had a ranch a hundred fifty miles north, near Corpus Christi, and that I was welcome to bring along my other five Spanish purebreds and go in with him.

He was audacious, if nothing else. I had, in the end, leased my Andalusians to him in return for a portion of the get from the breeding of the Spanish stallions to Morgans and quarter horses to produce an almost perfect traveling horse. I had even moved to Corpus Christi from where John Pico had bought us a ranch down on the border near Del Rio. I had built myself a large house there overlooking the bay and, at first, had only visited at Warner's ranch. Of course, in time, I began to stay for one night and then two and then more.

Warner's feelings of inferiority toward me were chiefly because of my family. I was from old, wealthy stock in Virginia and he was an orphan who'd been raised by his grandfather and then left to make it on his own when the old gentleman died when he was fifteen. My ancestry went back two hundred fifty years in Virginia. Warner could barely trace his own back three generations, let alone centuries. It had made him feel uncomfortable and ill at ease and, perhaps, slightly inferior. I had seen that when we went back to Virginia on a horse buying trip. He had mostly been silent and slightly withdrawn, and he could not be drawn into a conversation that didn't involve horses. He had been ready to leave from the first day we arrived and it had been plain to see that he was uncomfortable. He had accused my family of being a bunch of snobs, of which I was one and most likely the ring leader. On the contrary, it had been he who had been the snob but, of course, he couldn't see that.

That had been four years before, when we were in the process of starting up the ranch in Tyler where Warner intended to raise Thoroughbred racing horses. He considered them the cream of the horse business and the only way to make big money. But buying sufficient land in east Texas, along with establishing a ranch house and the necessary pens and outbuildings, had been beyond his means. Certainly buying the blooded brood stock and stallions was out of his reach on his own. He reluctantly brought me in as a full partner and I think that was the beginning of the trouble. When he had to recognize my money, had to take my money, had to give up his individual dream in order to recognize a part of that dream, the trouble took seed and began to grow.

Oh, we always fought, right from the first day we met. My strawberry blond hair was a fair warning to anyone that I was of an independent nature and planned to remain so. Warner knew that, but he thought he could break me to halter; a mistake he kept making over and over.

We were married at the end of that trip to Virginia, but it didn't stop the trouble between us. I was too high bred and I had too much money and both of these were sins in Warner's eyes that I could never be absolved of.

He never knew how much money I had and swore that if I ever told him he'd leave on the spot. The fact was that my former husband had left me over a half a million dollars and I had increased that to almost three quarters of a million on the day that Warner had made his insulting remark and then walked out.

In the early days of the Thoroughbred breeding ranch I had, from time to time, put in amounts to keep the operation going. Each time that had been necessary the toll had been obvious on Warner's face and in his attitude. It was almost as if it were a direct reflection on him, on his failure to do it on his own. For me to try and smooth it over by reminding him that we were husband

and wife was of no avail. If anything, that seemed to make it worse after we were married. It was one thing to let down your partner by being undercapitalized; it was quite another, in Warner's eyes, to let your wife down. He took the hard going very hard. Not knowing how much money I had, he would act as if an infusion of ten thousand dollars into the business was an enormous sacrifice on my part. In reality it was nothing, but, in his stubborn pride, he wouldn't let me tell him that.

Phoenix, my maid, came in and interrupted my reminiscing. She didn't come all the way into the morning room, just stood there with her hand on the swinging door to the kitchen, looking at me with a worried and sorrowful frown. Phoenix had been with me since I'd built the house in Corpus. She was a coastal Negro and she wasn't sure about these colored folks up in what she called plantation country. She was almost forty years old, she'd been born free and had had some education, and a pretty good opinion of herself. She asked me if I wanted anything else.

I shook my head, glancing beyond her into the big kitchen, half hoping to see Warner suddenly come in through the back door to apologize. It was probably just as well that he didn't. As his words continued to sink in deeper and deeper I got more and more angry. I asked her if Mr. Warner had gone on out to work.

"Yes, ma'am. I mean I reckon he has. I seen him saddle up his horse an' ride on off. You sho' I cain't git you somethin' else? You didn't make much of a breakfast. Got some apple pie go mighty good with yo' coffee."

I shook my head. What I wanted was a drink, but I wasn't going to let Warner have the satisfaction of driving me to drink. I said, "Thank you, Phoenix, but I couldn't eat a thing."

"You know you ain't got to worry 'bout stretchin' yo' clothes. You slim as a young girl. I do believe you don't eat mor'n a bird, Miss Laura. What clothes you want me to lay out fo' you today?"

I had forgotten I was sitting in my robe. It seemed very

late in the day, considering what had happened, but it was hardly eight o'clock. I said, "I don't know yet, Phoenix. Don't you worry about it. I'll look after it myself. I may be going into town. I don't know."

"You be wantin' me to go with you?"

I hesitated. "No. It won't be necessary."

She frowned deeper. Phoenix was a great one for style and the proper appearance of decorum. She said, "Now Miss Laura, that ain't right. Lady like yo'self ain't supposed to be goin' 'round town without someone to tend to you. You can't be goin' in stores an' such by yo'self."

I half smiled. If she only knew how close I was to being on my own. The nineteenth century was rapidly drawing to a close. It was beginning to appear that my marriage would close before the century did. I said, "Don't concern yourself, Phoenix. If I go I'll take you with me."

Her face softened a little. She was a large, big-boned woman but she still had a delicate way about her. Like many of the Negroes raised along the coast she was light skinned. She had a gold tooth that I had bought her and it was her pride and joy, but it wasn't much in evidence. I knew that she was aware there was trouble between me and Warner. Just how much she'd heard I didn't know. She said, "Onliest trouble with marriage is, a man got to be involved. An' that's a fact!"

I had to smile. Her husband was Albert, our coachman and man of all work about the house. If ever there was a husband who'd been broke to saddle and bridle it was Albert. She scolded him like a school child and I'm certain he was more afraid of her than of either Warner or me. I said, "You go along now, Phoenix. I'll be going upstairs in a moment or two. See to it that the cook makes an extra-special lunch. You plan it. You know what Mr. Warner likes."

She just glowered at the mention of his name, but she nevertheless went back into the kitchen without another word, letting the door swing shut behind her.

I sat there pining for the days when Warner and I

fought on equal terms and then went to bed and made up. We fought a lot, but we also laughed a lot. It seemed as if it had been forever since we'd actually had fun together. Warner had gotten so serious. He worried about everything. If I even looked as if I were going to ask a question about the business he'd say, "What's the matter? Worried about your money? Think I'm spending too much for that last brood mare? That's the way this business goes and you shouldn't have gotten into it if you were afraid."

And there was nothing I could say to reassure him because I—we—couldn't talk about my money, either the lack or the abundance.

I think that was the reason having a child was so important. I think a child would have bridged the gap between us, made us more one, made us a single entity that would have soothed Warner's pride.

I suppose this question answers itself: How do you go on loving someone and living with them after the brutal and fatal words are said that make it impossible to go on together?

Or perhaps: How do you accept the pain of such words, together in an untenable coupling, or separately?

Warner had always assumed I was at fault in the business of conception because I had been married to John Pico for a year and had never been pregnant. I never told Warner that John Pico had suffered an injury as a young man that precluded his ever being a partner to sex. A shotgun had discharged accidently while he was climbing a fence and injured his vital parts beyond function. He had explained that to me when he proposed our marriage partnership and it had been the clinching argument. I could have been married to him without love, but I couldn't have been his wife in the truest sense.

I had never claimed to Warner that I was a virgin. He hadn't expected it. I'd been a married woman. But my experience had been very slight and I had taken most of my cues from Warner in matters of technique and style. The passion was my own and came quite naturally.

In some of our arguments, without giving my own position away, I had asked just how many children he, Warner, had fathered. It was a question bound to cause him to sull up and end the argument.

Still I sat there in the morning room with a cold cup of coffee in front of me, his words still ringing in my ears. I just sat. For once in my tempestuous life I didn't know what to do. The son of a bitch had cut me to the quick. Warner had done something I had never thought him capable of—he had fought dirty. It was as if I had been a cripple and he had kicked the crutch out of my hands.

I sat there feeling guilty. I knew better, but he'd worked it so that I actually blamed myself for something I wasn't even sure was my fault.

The idea of having a child had never been a formal issue between us. Before we were married we had worried that it would happen. Then, after our vows, we'd abandoned the so-called rhythm system and waited for nature to take its course. As time went on we became a little more concerned, but never to the finger-pointing stage. I knew that Warner would feel much more secure once there was a child to tie us together closer than any words said by a minister could do. He made his accusatory statement about a son, but that was the first time the sex of the child had been mentioned. He just wanted a baby. He only said son to make it sound as if I were depriving him of an heir. More dirty fighting. It was a side of him I'd never seen and one I didn't particularly like.

I suppose it was the visit of my sister, Lauren, and her husband, the famous ex bank robber, Wilson Young, that had started the water to a boil. They had been married three years and they had a two-year-old boy. There was clear evidence right in front of Warner that such a commodity could be had. A son. Warner took more delight in playing with him than did Wilson Young, who looked a little overwhelmed by the idea of being a father. He even confessed that robbing a bank was nothing compared to the care and handling of an infant.

They stayed a week and Warner started in before their carriage was out of sight. Now his remarks were becoming pointed and they all pointed at me as the failure. I didn't bother to mention that since my sister had a baby, it was strong evidence that the fault might lie with him. I didn't mention it because it wasn't what he wanted to hear. He was frustrated and angry and growing more so with every week.

As I sat there thinking I became aware of how dim the room was. The morning room had big windows on the east and it was our custom to draw the inner drapes that were made out of gauze to keep the sun from blinding us when it first rose. But now the sun was well up and I'd made no move to pull the curtains back. I got up and did so and then stood looking out the tall windows at the back of the ranch. There was activity around the two big stable barns, horses being led in and out and a few being brushed and curried and smartened up. Down a ways at the blacksmith shed I could see our farrier shoeing a colt. They weren't really shoes, just thin plates that would help shape the hoof. You did that with Thoroughbred race horses. Every part of them was so important and so vulnerable.

As was I, I thought. Finally, I decided I had to bestir myself. I couldn't sit in the morning room for the rest of my life and no matter how many times I went over Warner's words they still came out the same.

I went upstairs, took off my robe and gown and began to dress. I saw my naked form in the full-length mirror that stood by my dressing table and it was not without pride that I regarded myself. I hoped that Warner remembered it, because it might be a long time before he had use of it again.

And then I was not so sure. I sat down on the bed in my undergarments, wondering what I should do. Even the bed was a sharp reminder of him. The mattress was an outsized ticking of eiderdown that Warner claimed was too soft, that he was going to wake up some night smothered to death. To please him I placed, on his side, a thin, hard cotton pallet of the type put on cots. It made for a two-tiered look once the bed was made, but it had pleased him. However, when our lovemaking turned a shade acrobatic the pallet did a rough job on my back.

I sat there feeling bad and sad and lonely. Finally I began to feel the first stirring of anger. The son of a bitch. I'd rather he'd punched me with his closed fist than said what he had. He had called me barren. It was the same as if I'd said he had no testicles or that his penis was of no value to me, and he had added to that by giving notice of infidelity.

Well, I would not stand for such treatment from anyone, let alone a man who was supposed to love me. I listened to a noise I heard downstairs. It was a door slamming. I was suddenly afraid that it might be Warner coming back. Before I had been afraid that he would not come to apologize. Now I was worried that he would. I didn't want his apology. What I suddenly realized I wanted was to get away from him. I got up quickly and went to my closet and took down a dress. Then, just as quickly, I threw it to the floor. It was a bright yellow frock with a low-cut bodice that was one of Warner's favorites. I didn't want him to see me in that and think I was wearing it for his benefit. Instead I chose a severely cut, dressy blue gown of wool and cotton that gathered at the throat with a clutch of lace. It was ankle length and I chose a pair of slippers with a medium heel to go with it.

I knew Warner had been greatly worried about the progress of his racing stable. Our first crop of colts was two years old and they were due to begin serious training for their debut the next spring. It was now September. Warner had only six or seven months to get them ready, but he was not satisfied with the look or the performance of any of the horses. They had yet to be run at speed with a rider in the saddle, but that didn't matter. Warner could look at a horse and tell what that horse could do, and if our first crop didn't look right then you could bet that they weren't right, that they would not be able to hold their own against horses from the other racing stables. So far as I knew, ours was the only racing farm in Texas, and at only sixty miles from the Louisiana border, we were only barely in Texas. The other stables were in the traditional acreage of Virginia and Tennessee and Kentucky and Louisiana. It was from these farms that Warner had bought the basis for our own bloodline. Many were the nights he sat poring over his registry books and saying, "I should never have bred that small Virginia stud to that big mare out of Kentucky. It was a mistake and I knew better. And look what I got. A waste of ten months and a colt with no chest and damn little in the way of driving hams. I don't think I've done anything right so far."

I would give him that. I would allow him the worry and the agitated state of mind about making his dream come true. But he overlooked the fact that it was partly my dream too. I had originally been drawn to Warner by his uncanny ability with horses, and the breeding farm was as much a part of me as it was of him. In fact it had been I, when Warner had first started talking about racing bluegrass horses, who had pointed out to him the poor quality of the coastal ranges. The land had been leeched of its goodness in millenniums past by salt water, and the quality of the grass showed it. I knew from my girlhood that Thoroughbred colts had to have big pastures to run and gallop and play in while they developed their lungs and the muscles they'd need later as runners. But they needed good grass for that. You can't keep a Thoroughbred colt up and fed on corn and hay. It will never develop. You could do that with the quarter-horse racers we'd been breeding because they only race up to four hundred yards, but true Thoroughbreds ran at distances of a mile and over.

Warner had not wanted to leave Texas. I didn't either, as I had grown accustomed to the place and liked the high pitch and speed of the life style. Texans felt anything was possible and they didn't drag their feet making a deal. If they liked you, they were your friend and the devil take your enemies.

The Tyler area had finally furnished us with the kind of grass that Warner felt we had to have. It was a little hilly for my taste, but it was blessed with an abundance of clearwater lakes and stately groves of pine and elm and oak. The climate was moderate, if a shade on the warm side, but weather was something you got used to if you lived in Texas.

So Warner had sold his ranch outside of Corpus Christi and I had sold my ten-room house on the bluff overlooking the bay and we had gone into business. Thus far we had sunk about one hundred thousand dollars into the venture. I had put in eighty-five thousand and Warner had put in what money he had, along with his expertise.

And that, I decided, was the problem. His expertise, as far as I was concerned, well outweighed the money I had contributed. But I could never convince Warner of that. We hadn't been married when we'd gone into partnership and all he knew was that he'd taken a woman's money and now it was at risk. I think that rode him night and day, not that he might fail at the business, but that he would fail and fail me at the same time. I honestly believed that he had come to resent my contribution so much that he had inquired among several of his wealthy friends about buying me out. When I first got scent of it I was incredulous and then I was angry. I made certain he understood that as his partner, not his wife, I had no interest in selling my share and while he, as my husband, might be seeking a buyer to protect my interests as his wife, his partner was telling him to go to hell.

As I said, I gave him that worry and that anxiety. But I did not count it as cause to throw into my face the vilest accusation a husband could make to a wife. If a man is not of a temperament to handle a business without letting it affect his home life then he should eschew such endeavors and work for wages and let the other man worry.

I stood in front of the mirror, fastening an ivory brooch to the lace at my throat. I heard another noise.

For a moment I stood stock still. But after a moment I didn't hear the distinctive sound of Warner's boots and I relaxed. But in that instant, I knew what I had to do. I whirled on my heel and went out of the bedroom and down the stairs. Phoenix was in the dining room dusting. I said, "Phoenix, never mind about that. I want you to go upstairs and pack my clothes."

She had her hair done up in a bandanna. She had wavy hair, not at all nappy. She was quite a handsome woman except for her size. She said, "Now you be talkin', Miss Laura. How many them clothes you want I should pack?"

"All of them." I said.

She stared at me. "*All* of them?"

I frowned at her. "Well, not all of them. But we are going to be gone for some time. Get the cook to help you."

"Is I goin'?"

"Of course you're going."

"What 'bout Albert?"

I frowned again. I was moving so fast I was bypassing some decisions. I sighed. I said, "Yes, I think he'll have to go, too. You can tell him to hitch up the big carriage."

It was beginning to dawn on her that this wasn't going to be just a weekend excursion. She said, "Yes, ma'am. And right quick. I'll git that worthless Albert movin' fust." She went off grumbling about the curse of needing a man from time to time.

I went into the parlor and poured myself a brandy. I was a strong woman but I was even a little startled at the boldness of my action. I was about to leave my husband. So far as I knew no woman in my family had ever done such a thing. I tossed the brandy down and then walked to a rear window to look out into the horse lot. There were men working with horses, but Warner was nowhere in sight. Now that the decision had been made my greatest fear was that he would come back and attempt to interfere. The next time he walked into the house I wanted him to find it vacant of my presence. I started back upstairs to pack my jewelry. As I moved I became uncomfortably aware that I was rushing into an action that might very well change my life. Warner was not a man who took being backed into a corner very well. I might be compounding the damage to such an extent that there could be no reversal. But at that moment it didn't matter. I felt I couldn't stay in that house an hour longer and certainly I would not share his bed again, not as matters stood. I hastened my part of the packing, urgency making my hands fly. I was leaving without the slightest idea where I was going to stop.

Even though it was September there was no hint of fall in the air. The air was heavy and hot, the only breeze coming from the motion of the carriage as we rode over the red clay road toward the town of Tyler some five miles from the ranch. Phoenix sat across from me fanning herself with a cardboard fan that had a passage from scripture in the midst of a sunset on one side with the words The Primitive Baptist Church at the bottom. She was wearing a lavender dress that was a little too heavy for the season, and she was paying for it. Beside her and beside me on the rear seat and on the floor of the carriage was piled our luggage, mostly mine, but some for Phoenix and Albert. Albert was up on the driver's seat, a short, plump, pleasant Negro man of about forty years of age. He was wearing a derby hat and his best Sunday-go-to-meeting clothes. I didn't know what Phoenix had told him, but he'd shown me not the slightest curiosity. He acted as if it were an everyday matter to just up, bag and baggage, and change locations. Phoenix and Albert had not come as a pair. He was a country Negro that she had met when we'd come to Tyler. He was much more dark skinned than she and it reminded me to sometime ask Phoenix why coastal Negroes, as a rule, were so much lighter skinned.

But right then I had much more pressing matters on my mind. We had gotten away before Warner returned, but Charlie Stanton, Warner's foreman, had come to me, much troubled, to inquire if he might know what was

happening. I'd simply told him to ask his boss. Charlie
was such a good natured and conscientious young man
that I hated to give him short shrift. I could see he was
dying to ask where I was going with such a load of
luggage, but was too well mannered to do so. I finally did
him the favor of saying that I was going on an extended
visit to Virginia. He accepted that, though I could tell he
was much troubled. Charlie didn't like trouble in his life
or the lives of those he cared about, and I was sure he
could see trouble in my method of leave-taking.

Telling him that I was going to Virginia was as good an
answer as any. It would be what Warner would think.
Which only proved how little he knew me. If he thought I
was going to run home to my family he had another think
coming. Virginia was the last place I'd go. I ended up
telling Charlie to take special care of my Andalusians
and then I mounted the carriage and Albert clucked to
the splendid pair of bay horses and we drove away.

Now we were only a mile or two from town and I still
had not formulated a plan for our immediate future
accommodations and general form of living. Tyler was
more a village than a city, being only about two thousand
strong in population. The principal industry of the town
was sawmills. There must have been four or five, and
trains were constantly roaring out with loads of lumber
cut from the heavy pine forests. But sawmills, while
necessary to the fundamentals, did not attract the type of
genteel society I intended to live amongst. So while I had
no intention of staying very long in Tyler I would have to
be there a sufficient time to think my position through,
make plans, and then carry out those plans. That meant
that we would need a place to stay. There was only one
hotel of any consequence in the town and it was far from
meeting my needs. It didn't even have indoor plumbing,
and it certainly wouldn't have a suite of rooms to
accommodate me. The more I thought of it the more I
decided that my first stop should be at the bank. The
president was an enterprising man named Robert
Quince and I was one of his principal depositors. I

thought he would find it in his best interest to assist me in any way that he could.

Phoenix said, with just a catch of worry in her voice, "We sho' done got away from that place, Miss Laura."

"Yes," I said.

"We done showed that man, ain't we." But she didn't sound as sure as she had that morning.

"Oh, yes."

"Gonna come home an' find the bird done flown. Yes, ma'am, bird done flown clean out the coop. Ain't that right, Miss Laura?"

"Yes." I was thinking about what I'd say to Mr. Quince.

Phoenix was silent for a short while. Then she said, "What you gonna say to him?"

We were going through a wall of pine trees, the forest opening just enough to let the road through as we drove around a curve. I brought my mind back inside the carriage. "What?"

"What you gonna say to him?"

"Who? Say to whom?"

"Mr. Warner. That's who." She was fanning harder.

"When?"

She stopped the fan. I could see that the scripture printed on it was a verse from the Gospel of Luke but I couldn't quite make it out. She said, "Why, when he come lookin' for you."

I gave her a severe look. She was still supposedly my employee and not some cousin whom I told my deepest secrets. I said, "Phoenix, I do not know what you mean and I don't think you do either. There is nothing I need to say to Mr. Grayson."

She started up with the fan again and looked away. I heard her mumble something, but it was too indistinct for me to hear.

"What? I didn't hear you Phoenix."

"Nothin', Miss Laura. Nothin'. Jest makin' comment to my own self."

"What was your comment?"

She was making the fan fly. She said, "Oh, I maybe noticed wadn't ever'day we up and took off with ever' stitch of yo' clothin'. I thought it might be noticed. Might need some sort o' explanation."

"Phoenix, you are a busybody and you know that is wrong and a sin. You have no idea what I'm doing."

She mumbled something else.

"What?"

"Nothin'. I was jest wonderin' if *you* did. Know what you was doin'."

"That'll do, Phoenix."

We had come out of the woods and were entering Tyler. It was a pretty enough little town except everything was made out of lumber. There wasn't a bit of brick or masonary to break the monotony. And even that wouldn't have been so bad if white hadn't been the prevailing color. It seemed every building, church, residence, or business was painted white. The only relief was the lettering of signs over stores and in store windows, and that was nearly all black. Tylerites did not appear to me to be a very imaginative people.

I said, to Phoenix, "Tell Albert to stop at the Eastland Bank."

"Where we goin' to stay, Miss Laura?"

"Not at the bank, if that is what you are worrying about."

We pulled up in front of one of the more respectable looking establishments and I got down as Albert helped me onto the boardwalk. I bade him and Phoenix wait with the carriage.

Mr. Quince saw me at once, as well he should. Warner and I had three accounts. The principal one was the ranch account in the amount of some eighty thousand dollars. Then there was the household account, a piddling sum of some several thousand dollars used for small, everyday purchases. But, besides that, I had a personal account of approximately twenty thousand dollars. Warner knew nothing about that account and didn't want to know since it made him almost ill to know how much I spent on clothes.

Of course the majority of my money was with a banking establishment in Houston where I kept a little over six hundred thousand, most of it in government bonds paying a tidy six percent. It was all reachable quickly by bank draft or money wire.

Mr. Quince was young for his position, appearing to be on the springtime side of forty. He ushered me into his office and got me seated and then went around his desk and placed himself. He was balding on top and was a little plump, but he was pleasant and businesslike enough, though I had never had cause to test his acumen. He inquired how he and the bank could best serve me.

I wasted no time. Coming into the bank I had realized that I was still in love with Warner, but I didn't love him at the present time. In fact I despised the bastard. Because of that feeling I had no intention of protecting his reputation in arranging what I wanted. I said, "Mr. Quince, I find myself in a position of needing suitable accommodations in town for what might prove to be a matter of days or weeks or even months."

I could see his interest perk up. He said, "Oh? Has something happened at your ranch? Not a fire I hope."

I leaned forward and said, in a level voice, "The reasons don't matter, Mr. Quince, and I don't want to discuss them. All I want to know is whether the bank might own or have foreclosed on a dwelling that might be suitable for me. Certainly there is nothing at the hotel that would do as accommodations for me and my servants."

He stared blankly at me as if trying to comprehend what I was talking about. He knew I had a home—he'd been there, at the ranch. Now here I was talking about another one. Finally he said, "I'm not sure I understand, Mrs. Grayson. Is this, uh, something you want to rent or buy? Some small place for when you might wish to stay in town for a few days. If you want to rent the bank couldn't help you. We don't deal in that sort of property."

I didn't know if he was being intentionally dense or not. I said, patiently, "Do you or do you not, Mr. Quince, have a relatively small house, but one with all the conveniences, that I could buy. I am not going to come to the bank to rent a house any more than I'm going to go to a real estate company to deposit money. But I do know that banks very often have to foreclose on properties and they like to dispose of them as quickly as possible. Now, my question is a simple one. Do you have anything in the foreclosure line that I might be interested in?"

It soaked in and he began to think. He finally said, "There is a very nice little cottage just at the north edge of town. Virtually new. It was built for the manager of one of the sawmills but then, ah, well, let's say he found reason to take his family and move. It has indoor plumbing and there are four rooms not including the bathroom. Has a very modern kitchen and a stable with sleeping quarters and a carriage shed."

"Is it furnished?"

He was still puzzled, but by now he had understood I wasn't going to explain my actions or my plans. He said, "Why, yes it is, as a matter of fact. The house and furnishings were financed together."

"How much?"

He hesitated, trying to get his feet under him. He made a harrumph sound, as people do when they are trying to buy time to think. He said, "Well, Mrs. Grayson, I'd have to look that up."

He knew to the penny how much he had in the house and what he planned to get for it, but I was willing to go along with him. I said, "Then why don't you do so?"

When the banker came back into his office he settled himself and said, trying to sound casual, "Mrs. Grayson, we can let you have that house for four thousand dollars. It should do you ideally as a place to stay when you want to come into town for a few days. It has a maid's room that I forgot to mention and your coachman can sleep in the stable."

To me he sounded as if he thought he were doing me a favor. Or at least he wanted me to think that. As much money as I had, why quibble over a few hundred, perhaps five hundred dollars. I said, "What was the length of the original loan, Mr. Quince?"

He looked startled, as if surprised I'd concern myself with such matters. It had taken Warner quite a time to find out I was a better businessman than he was. He said, "Why, uh, ten years I believe. Something like that."

"Fine," I said. I stood up to let him know I was making my one and only offer. "You have already received the front money, which you kept of course. I'll give you two hundred more down and pick up the payments. If that is satisfactory you can have the papers drawn up."

He looked flabbergasted. He said, "But Mrs. Grayson, I honestly couldn't let it go so cheap. I—"

"Mr. Quince," I said crisply, "you probably loaned five thousand dollars on the house originally, of which you took five hundred down. Then you've enjoyed over a year of payments. Anything over three thousand dollars is profit on top of profit. Make up your mind. It's my only offer."

He was still looking off balance. He said, "But you haven't even seen the house."

I said, "I don't need to, Mr. Quince. You are not a foolish banker and it would be a fool of a banker who would put a major depositor into something she would be displeased with. There are other banks."

He got quickly to his feet. "My dear Mrs. Grayson, I'm willing to accept your price, but I hope you realize this little house can in no way compare with your residence in the country. I mean—"

"Oh, I don't expect it to," I said. "Just as long as it is clean and functional. I do not intend to use it that much. Draw up the papers."

He ducked his head in assent.

I said, picking up my purse. "You have people employed for keeping your bank presentable. I want you to send them over with my maid and coachman immediately to make the house spick-and-span. I am going to sit in this bank and wait. When it is ready for me to occupy you may come there and I will sign your papers and give you your money."

He said, "Uhhh . . ."

"What?"

He looked embarrassed. He said, "Should the warranty deed be in your name and that of Mr. Grayson?"

"It should be, Mr. Quince, in the same name that my personal account is in. Does that answer your question?"

He nodded slowly, full of gossip. "Yes. Yes. Thank you, Mrs. Grayson."

2

Warner

I had no more gotten to the colt barn, fifty yards distant from the house, when I realized with a sinking feeling that I had perhaps gone too far. The last words I flung at her had been hurtful words, harmful words, and words she didn't deserve. If I'd had a lick of sense about me I'd have turned on my heel and gone straight back and begged her forgiveness.

But the anger and frustration were still up in me and I could not bring myself to do it. Many are the folks who think of me as calm and levelheaded and not one to go off half-cocked or let his mouth overload his situation. But these people are mistaken. All my life I have only shown people what I've wanted them to see of me and, in that, I may have been far too careful. Perhaps Laura had come to see the other side of my face as no one else ever had, not even close male friends like Wilson Young and Justa Williams. I was known as a man who didn't rattle, who never lost his temper unless there was a purpose for it, a man who was always on top of the situation, cool of head and steady of eye.

That of course was all bullshit. What I was was a man

who'd been flung on his own too young and who'd been struggling to get out of his own mire from the beginning. I had one real talent: I was a whiz with horses. I knew what a horse was thinking and what he was going to do even before the horse himself knew. I could get horses to perform beyond their own expectation. I could make a horse run faster than he was supposed to and I could stop a horse from acting up with nothing more than a look or a quiet word.

I was not, however, so gifted with people. So, for people, I played a role. It was not always easy, but it was easier than letting down the bars. Not that I ever played anyone false, I simply never let them get too close to me.

Except for Laura. I had the misfortune to finally discover love in the person of a strawberry blond, beautiful, willful, stubborn, fascinating, sexual, argumentative, tender, loving, wildcat of a woman who was born independent and would die untamed. And I had the ignorance and reckless disregard for our common good to make the worst blunder of my life with the one person who meant the most to me.

I even knew why I had done it. Before I was fairly in the colt barn I had worked out exactly what had caused me to throw those amazing words in Laura's face and it had nothing to do with me wanting a son or our seeming inability to have a child. I had hit back at her because she had money, money that was financing my attempt at the big time in the horse business. And because that made me feel inadequate as a man, I, meanly and viciously, wanted to make her feel inadequate also. As a woman. And what better way to hit out at a woman than to go straight to the core of her being, her ability to be a mother. It was just chance that children had not come along. Hell, I hadn't even known if I was ready for them. But the weapon was handy so I took it and struck.

Standing there, I could not believe I had done what I'd done. I could not believe that I could sink so low. But there it was. I'd done it. I'd let worry and pride and manly convention cause me to act so bitterly and angrily that I had spoken words I had not meant and that were at cross purposes with my true feelings.

The words rang in my head like a gong. ". . . have to get myself another woman . . . !"

God in heaven knew I didn't want another woman, wouldn't have another woman, and could never love another one.

Work was going on all around me in the colt barn as hired hands were taking different colts out to the working ring to give them training on a lunge line. I could hear the sound of Charlie Stanton, my young foreman, giving them orders in his quiet, authoritative voice. Right then if anybody needed work on a lunge line it was me. A lunge line was a colt's first introduction to discipline and it was intended to let him understand that there were things he could do and things he couldn't. It was intended to get him used to working within the bounds of certain limits.

But it was too late for me. I had already jumped the fence and raced off into desperate pastures. I had eaten too much loco weed, I'd lost my head, I'd cut loose and was now about to run wild until I finally realized that what I had mistaken for firm footing was actually quicksand.

I walked back out of the colt barn and looked toward the house. I longed with all my heart to go as quickly as I could to Laura and to beg her to forget the words I'd said. But I knew better than that. She would be angry, probably more angry than I'd ever seen her, and with good reason. The only thing I would accomplish by going back so soon would be to allow her to lash me with that anger. It might have the effect of helping it to run its course faster, but it might also cause her grievance to be deeper set in her mind.

I stood there, studying on the matter, trying to think of the best angle of approach. It was difficult because I had no past circumstance to compare it with. I had never committed a transgression of such a magnitude, so I had no way to calculate how long it would take her anger to subside to a point where she might accept my apology. I walked on down to the next barn, still thinking. These were the stud stables, currently occupied by twenty-four stallions, of which ten were blue-blood Thoroughbreds, all bought with money that Laura had put into the partnership.

I decided that perhaps my best course was to allow her to think I was still upset and angry and that I still considered her at fault. If I felt that way then I obviously would not want to be in her company. Maybe, I thought, the wisest course would be to absent myself for enough time to let her get over being mad and maybe she might begin to think she needed to do a little apologizing herself. I knew that she was expecting me back through the door at any moment. I knew that because I knew she knew me better than I knew myself. If I didn't show up for a good little while she might even go to worrying. Supposedly, she loved me the same as I loved her. We didn't talk about such things much, but we'd been together for a good long while and there had to be a reason other than horses and fights and sex.

I walked over to the box stalls where the original Andalusians were kept. They, after all, were what had brought Laura and me together. There were only four left out of the original six. One had broken a leg and had to be destroyed and one had died of screw worms. I absently patted the forehead of the one that Laura called Paseta. I had never broken her of the habit of naming work animals. To me they were the bay gelding or the Andalusian with the white fetlock or the little jumpy quarterhorse. They weren't pets like old Spot the dog. But she still insisted on personalizing them and, as a result, grieved all the harder when something happened to them.

Paseta was my horse. He was the one I'd taken as my reward for returning her the rest of her property. I think it was the idea of my taking Paseta back to my ranch outside Corpus that had caused Laura to follow me there.

I'd accused her of it on more than one occassion but she'd simply told me not to be silly. She'd said she'd moved her operation to make use of my skills. "What skills?" I'd asked her. She'd blushed and said, "Why your horse handling skills, you big oaf. What did you think?"

Standing there, idly rubbing the stallion's ears, I let my mind wander back to that time when I'd stopped by her ranch on the trail of the banditos. I'd just survived three days on a waterless alkali flat where they'd left me to die, and I was burning with revenge. She couldn't believe I was going after the same Mexican bandits who'd killed her husband. And not only going after them, but crossing the Rio Grande and going into their country. She'd thought I was crazy. Looking back, I wasn't too sure I wasn't still a little touched from the three days of sun. I wondered if I would do the same again. I doubted it. It had been almost eight years before and a man can learn an awful lot of caution in eight years.

And caution, right then, was what I expected I'd better use with Laura. The game had turned very dangerous and I didn't think it was going to be improved by anything I could say.

I had a friend in a town about fifteen miles away, Overton, who'd been trying to get me to come over and look at a quarter horse stud he had. I really wasn't much interested in breeding the short-distance race horses any more, but this seemed like an ideal opportunity for such a visit. The man claimed the stud would change my mind about Thoroughbred breeding, and he was for sale cheap. Well, hell, I was always ready to buy a good horse, no matter what breed, if the price was right, because I knew I could turn a profit. People expected to pay more for a horse they got from me because they knew the animal would be the real goods.

Without giving myself more time to think about it I opened Paseta's stall door and led him out and then got him bridled and saddled. He was still the finest road horse I had ever ridden and we still used the Andalusians to breed that type of horse for the few customers I still had in that line.

I guess that was one of the first things that impressed me about Laura, besides her looks. She not only knew about the Andalusian, but had gotten John Pico to import six of them as a condition of their marriage. The Andalusian was the granddaddy of all the hot-blooded horses including the Arabian. In appearance Andalusians looked like Arabians except they were bigger and stronger, but they had the same graceful curved neck and dainty legs and feet and deep liquid eyes. And there never was a breed of horse with better manners or gentler ways than the Andalusian. The particular one I was saddling up had saved my life when I had gone off my head from the sun and he kept going and finally found us water.

I wasn't certain I was doing anything outstandingly smart, but when the horse was saddled and ready I mounted and rode out of the stud barn and around to the training ring where Charlie was working. He came over to the high, smooth boarded fence and said, "Yes, sir?"

Charlie had been with me for eight years and here he was, all of twenty-five years old, and the chief horse handler on one of the biggest horse ranches in Texas. He was a tall, lanky young man with sandy hair and big ears and an innocent face, who didn't look much older than when I had first hired him. He was my foreman for the simple reason that he had damn near as much talent with horses as I did. Given time and what he'd learned from me he'd probably end up a better horseman than I'd ever been.

I spent a few moments giving him instructions on what colts I wanted worked and what I wanted done with them. It was just routine stuff. Charlie would have done it with or without instructions. He had ten men under him and he was as good a hand at working men as he was with horses.

He said, nodding at Paseta, "You goin' somewheres,

Mr. Grayson?" In eight years I had never gotten him to where he'd call me by my given name. "No, sir," he'd answered. "Not so long as I'm workin' for you. This way it keeps it clear who is the boss."

"I'm going to take a little ride, Charlie." I looked back toward the house. "Got a little business down the road." I hesitated for a second. I said, "If Mrs. Grayson happens to ask after me you just tell her you don't know exactly where I am."

He looked up at me with that innocent face of his. "Well, I don't, do I?"

"No, you don't. And we'll keep it that way." I turned Paseta away from the fence and eased him up into a slow canter. I glanced back at the house again as I rode, but there was no sign of Laura. For a mile or so I rode east, as if I were heading for some pasture we had in that direction. But directly I hit a little clay road I turned off to the right, to the south, on a general route that would take me to my friend's ranch. As I left him, Charlie wore a troubled look on his face, as if he wanted to ask me why I didn't want Laura to know where I was going. I could understand that troubled look. It matched my own mood inside. As I rode I wondered if Laura had been watching for me out a window, perhaps from our upstairs bedroom. But I had to put such thoughts out of my mind and harden my spirits if I were to carry out my plan of turning the tables. I had to somehow work my way up to a plateau where I could say some healing words that might be believed. There was, unfortunately, the complication in any apology, that Laura might think I was making it in order to preserve the ranch. That was the hell of the problem of her money. It got in the way of everything, even my own true feelings that might be misunderstood. It caused me to wish she'd been penniless when I met her and dependent on my rise in fortune for her own. Out loud I said, "Damn! Damn! DAMN!"

Paseta cocked his ears back at me as if to say he didn't understand. I couldn't have agreed with him more.

I found my friend at home at his ranch outside of

Overton. He was glad to see me and informed me I'd arrived just in time for lunch. He was an older man than I, about fifty, and a good horseman and an honest fellow. His name was Mack Gordon and I'd been doing horse business with him for at least ten years.

We went into his comfortable house and had a drink of whiskey and then sat down at the kitchen table, where his cook served us a meal of barbecued beef and beans and canned tomatoes. There was cornbread on the side and soft cider to drink.

Mack had lost his wife some two years before to the lung consumption. I didn't know if it was because of the keen loneliness I was already feeling for Laura, but it seemed that he talked an extraordinary amount about how much he missed his wife.

"Twenty-two years," he said. "Twenty-two years we was together and I guess I got to taking it for granted. Same way a man does a good horse. You never miss the good you've got until it's gone. I tell you, Warner, I'd give everything I had, have, or ever hope to have for just one more day with her. Just enough time to make sure she knew how much I cared for her."

Lord, how that made me squirm in my chair. I'd ridden fifteen miles just to have a knife twisted in my chest. I said something soft and comforting like, "I'm sure she knows, Mack. I imagine she never doubted it for a moment."

Mack was a stocky fellow, at least six inches shorter than my six foot two inches. He had muscular forearms and bulging shoulders and a big, balding head, but now I could almost see a sign of tears in his eye. He said, in a funny kind of husky voice, "That's the hell of it, Warner. The very day before she went down with the fever I give her hell for goin' into town and buyin' a buncha clothes I couldn't see she had no need for. Bonnets and hats and such. Pretty thangs. You know." He stopped and got control of himself. After a moment he went on, "Hell it was a kind of automatic reaction on my part. We'd more than plenty of money by then. She'd gone through the

29

hard times with me. She'd done without. Done without a hell of a lot more than she'd done with, I can tell you that. But there she was, happy as a lark with all her new things and I come in—" He stopped and shook his head sadly.

I could not believe the ill turn of my luck. If destiny had set out to guide me to a merely morose place it had failed. It had delivered me to the worst possible place. I strangled down a mouthful of beef and said, "Hell, Mack, life is like that. You never meant nothing by it. We all say things we're sorry for later."

He looked up at me. "Of course I never meant it. I come in mad about something else, one of the mares had gone down and lost a colt she was carrying. Hell, I don't even remember what it was. But I was mad about something and there she was, humming and gay, and I just busted loose. The Scotsman in me come to the fore. I asked her if she thought I was made out of money? Did she buy the store out? And on like that until she started crying." Mack looked down at his food and shook his head. "I knew I was wrong the minute I said it. And I meant to tell her so, meant to tell her to get whatever made her happy." He poked at his plate with a fork. "Next day she come down sick and just kept getting worse and worse. I never did get the chance to tell her I hadn't meant what I said. It somehow just got lost in the shuffle, busy as things got when we seen how sick she was."

I said, with my own sick feeling in the pit of my stomach, "I'm sure she knew, Mack. I'm sure she understood."

"Yeah, but it would have made me feel better if I'd of got the words out before it was too late." He looked around the kitchen and then glanced through the door to the rest of the house. "She was just a little bitty woman. I never knowed how much room she took up. God, it's mighty empty around here with her gone."

I sat there. There was nothing I wanted to say. But I

was seriously wondering if I hadn't better get on my horse and get home as quick as possible.

Mack looked up, putting a cheerful note in his voice. "But you don't want to hear all that. I've just been kind of down in the dumps today. Don't let me pull you down. How are things with you and that mighty pretty wife of yours?"

My plan had been to make a good visit with Mack, staying overnight with him if he invited me. But I didn't calculate I could stand, in the frame of mind I was in, to listen to him lament the loss of his wife when it appeared I was on the very precipice of losing mine. I figured, then, to take a quick look at his horse and then go into Overton and stay the night there and make my way back to the ranch sometime the following afternoon. I judged that would allow about the right amount of time for Laura to cool off if she was going to cool off.

But in the afternoon, after we'd looked at the quarter horse stud Mack was interested in selling me, things got considerably lighter and I took him up on his offer to stay the night and have a good talk.

The stallion came to nothing. He was what we called a slant. A slant was an accident of heredity. The stud himself was a magnificent animal and, at four years of age, would have been perfect breeding stock. The horse had size, he had plenty of speed, and he was a joy to ride. But he would not produce any more like himself. There was nothing in his bloodline, either on the dam side or the sire line, to suggest that he was a continuation of excellent breeding. Even going back several generations and tracing his lineage through the maze of different sires and dams in the papers that Mack had, it was obvious the stallion was an accident, a lucky joining and mingling of various and diverse little odd lots of blood that had all got together and produced him. But the accident would stop with the stallion. Slants didn't produce what they were. They just passed on the second-rate conditions they should have inherited in the first place. You could mate Mack's stallion with the best mares you could find and all the colts would be referred back to their grandfathers and their great grandmothers and so on.

I looked the papers over in Mack's office while he sat in the kitchen drinking coffee. When I came out I just gave him a sour look and sat down and poured myself a cup. I said, "You don't think much of me, I see."

He gave a little laugh. "Hell, Warner, it was just a prank. Wanted to see if you were still as sharp as ever."

"I ride fifteen miles and you try to unload a slant on me. Shame on you, Mack."

"Aw, hell, you needed to get out. I was curious if you still knew anything about honest horseflesh after all the time you've been spending with those bluegrass bluebloods."

"What are you going to do with him? Make a damn fine cutting horse if you geld him."

He gave me a wink. "Oh, I ain't going to remove his equipment. Everybody ain't Warner Grayson. I'll sell him as a stud and get two thousand dollars for him."

I laughed. I said, "You old fraud. I'm going to spread the word you're a damn thief and a cheat."

"Hell, yes. But I'm damn good at it." He slammed the tabletop with the flat of his hand. "Let's drink some whiskey and tell some lies. Maybe play a little heads-up poker. I'll get your money one way or the other."

It was good that we stayed up late because I had a difficult time going to sleep. Lying there, my thoughts played my breakfast exchange with Laura over and over in my mind. No answers came, no easy outs. All I knew was that I felt swept along by a current of trouble stronger than gravity. I could lose it all, I thought. I could lose the marriage, I could lose the ranch, I could lose what little I had come to think of as happiness. Of course, the loss of Laura as my wife did not automatically mean the end of the ranch. We were legally partners, married or not. It was just that I wouldn't want the ranch without her.

I awoke with the sun, feeling creaky and worried. The

taste of the previous night's whiskey was not pleasant in my mouth and even repeated brushing of my teeth and gargling with salt water didn't remove it. I finally went down and had breakfast with Mack, who didn't seem to be feeling any better than I was. We were a subdued pair. The artificial light, from both the kerosene lamps and the whiskey, was extinguished and we were back to the cold light of day. Mack still had an empty house and an empty bed and I was tied to a stick of dynamite with the fuse cord already lit and sputtering.

I got away at mid morning, calculating my time so that I would arrive a little after noon. I had visions of Laura looking out the window with the lunch hour approaching and wringing her hands and worrying. I could just imagine her saying to Phoenix, "Oh, now I am getting worried. I thought surely he'd be back by lunch! He must really be angry. Oh, I should have gone after him yesterday morning when he walked out."

It all sounded very fine and possible as Paseta stepped along at a lively canter, going down a road lined on both sides with growths of pine and oak. In a month the oak leaves would begin to turn and the weather would become cool enough so that we might light a fire in the fireplace of an evening. That was pleasant, sitting around a fire with Laura, both of us having an after-dinner drink and her listening as I talked about what had been accomplished that day. And then there was always the prospect of going upstairs together and the mood being just right and having that exciting kind of lovemaking that only she could make happen.

That brought a slight pang to my heart. Love and money aside, the loss of that part of Laura would be a difficult commodity to replace. Certainly, I had never experienced another woman like her and I was not exactly a novice when it came to having a sampling here and there.

Finally the road crossed one that ran northeast toward Tyler and I cut up it for a mile and then turned Paseta off the road and through some woods and then broke out onto my southeasterly pasturage. I had—rather Laura and I together had—approximately ten thousand acres. It was not all together, not continuous, but all of my pasture was within a mile and a half of the ranch headquarters. I had been in the process of negotiating to buy some tracts of land that would connect up my acreage but it was difficult to reach a price with the owners because the land was timbered and they expected me to pay a price not just for the land, but for what the timber, in time, would fetch. It made for some hard bargaining, as I didn't know anything about the lumber business and had no desire to learn.

I went loping toward the big house. I couldn't see anyone stirring, but that was not surprising. What wranglers there were about the headquarters would be in the cook house eating their lunch.

But what I especially didn't like, even from a distance of a quarter of a mile, was how still the ranch house looked. It didn't seem to have any life within it. There was no smoke rising from the kitchen chimney, there was no sign of anyone passing by a window. It looked uninhabited. My stomach started to slowly move its way up to my throat.

I rode into the stallion barn, unsaddled and unbridled Paseta, gave him a quick rubdown with an empty feed sack, and then turned him out into the little adjoining corral where there was hay and oats and water.

I had shaved that morning at Mack Gordon's, borrowing his razor, but I kept running my hand over my cheeks as I walked toward the back door of the house. I hadn't taken a change of clothes and I hadn't had a bath so I didn't reckon I looked my best. I felt strangely self-conscious as I mounted the kitchen steps and let myself in through the door.

The kitchen was empty in that way that a place is when it is deserted. It doesn't matter how long a place has been deserted, five minutes or five months, there is no mistaking the feel. You can go away from a place you intend to come back to and stay away a year and it will not feel deserted when you first step back into it.

But that kitchen felt deserted. And standing there, not a foot inside the door, I could sense the same feeling from the rest of the house. I started to call out, but I knew it would do no good.

I walked slowly through the kitchen, pushed through the swinging door, and went into the morning room. The curtains were drawn and it seemed unusually dim. Maybe it was my mood. I stood there looking at the table where scarcely twenty-four hours before Laura and I had been having breakfast. It had started like any other of a thousand mornings. Then something got said and then something else and then the level of acrimony on each side gradually began to rise. I stood there, trying to reconstruct the tangle of the conversation in my mind, trying to figure out when it had tumbled toward the edge of the cliff before it finally fell over and careened on down and down and down. I took my hat off and wiped my brow with the sleeve of my shirt. It wasn't as if it had never happened before. We'd had some real bell ringers through the years.

Except somewhere, at some point, this one had changed and gone too far. I had not just volunteered the ugly words I'd said to her. Surely she'd given me cause. Surely I wasn't such a brute that I'd rip out at her like that without *some* provocation. But then I didn't know. I'd been so bemused of late, worrying about the ranch, worrying about the crop of colts, worrying that I'd made the biggest mistake of my life and Laura's money.

Without much hope I passed into the hall that separated the parlor from the dining room and turned up the stairs. As I climbed I listened for any sound. The house was like a dead man. I reached the landing and opened the door to our bedroom.

It did not take more than a cursory examination to see that Laura was gone. I opened closet after closet and cabinet after cabinet. Except for a few empty hat boxes the room was devoid of her apparel and personal items. I shook my head and went over and sat on the side of the bed. Someone had made it up neatly before the exodus. I looked at it, noting the slight rise my pallet made on my side. Well, now I could have any kind of ticking I wanted. I wouldn't have to worry about the mattress being soft enough for Laura. Only had to please myself.

There was a bottle of brandy on a sideboard and I stepped to it and had a quick pull straight out of the jug. It burned, but other than that it didn't seem to have much effect.

After a while I went down the hall to the small room Phoenix occupied at the end. I pushed the door open. The room was as bare as Laura's. For some reason the sight of Phoenix's room brought it fully home to me. I'd been halfway hoping that maybe she'd just gone off in a huff to some nearby town, as I had, and had hid her clothes in Phoenix's room. But they weren't there and neither was her maid. Taking Phoenix told me that she meant to stay wherever it was she'd gone.

Going down the stairs I heard a slight sound. With hope rising I hurried down the steps and burst into the morning room. It was Jambalaya, our Negro cook from Louisiana. Jambalaya wasn't her real name, but that was what she was called. She was busy polishing the tabletop in the morning room. She was short and dark and on the plump side. She was a good cook, but she was not the fastest thinker on the ranch. I said, "Jambalaya, where is Miss Laura?"

She shook her head, slowly. "Dey all gone."

"Who? Where'd they go?"

"I don' know 'bout that, sir. But she an' him an' Miss Laura, they done took off in de big carriage."

"Him? Who?"

"Oh, Albert an' 'course Phoenix."

"Albert drove the big carriage?"

"Yes, suh. 'Spect he had to. Load they wuz carryin'."

"Miss Laura took a lot of her clothes?"

"Reckon she took 'em all. Dat Albert wuz haulin' 'em down from de upstairs for de longest. You be wantin' somethin' fo' yo' stomach, Mr. Warner? Somethin' to eat?"

I sat down in a chair at the oblong table she'd been polishing. Laura and I ate most of our meals off it, even supper from time to time, though Laura called supper dinner and dinner lunch. I was getting to where I'd been starting to do it myself. There was a sideboard right behind me and I reached back and got a bottle of whiskey and a glass. I poured myself out a drink and then looked at my watch. It was just coming one o'clock. I said to Jambalaya, "No, I'm not hungry. But I want you to go out to the barns and tell Mr. Charlie that I want to see him."

She looked a little surprised. It was not the sort of errand she would ordinarily be sent on, out to the barns around all the horse handlers. She was a kind of shy, uneasy woman who jumped at the slightest noise. I could see from the look on her face she didn't relish going out there around all those rough men. I hated to ask her to do it, but, right then, I didn't feel like having to talk to anyone and, as soon as I showed myself, there'd be half a dozen men with twice as many questions wanting to know what I wanted to do about this horse or that or would I come take a look at Shiro's Luck and see if he wasn't clicking his heels. I said, "Just go a little way out there and yell out for Mr. Charlie. Tell whoever answers that I want to see Mr. Charlie up here at the house. Now run along, Jambalaya, and maybe you can fix me a steak in a little while."

She went, but unwillingly. It didn't matter. It would take her awhile, which was just as well. I needed to get a couple of drinks under my belt before I talked to Charlie. And the idea of eating was silly. The only thing I was going to be able to get past that lump in my throat was whiskey.

But Jambalaya was back sooner than I thought with

Charlie Stanton. She held the swinging door open as he came through and said, to me, "What you want wid yo' steak, Mr. Warner?"

Charlie was looking at me keenly. I was pretty obviously doing something I didn't do very often, sitting with a bottle of whiskey in front of me in the middle of a working day. I said, to Jambalaya, "I'm not ready to eat yet. Never mind about doing anything in the kitchen. Just go take a nap. I'll call you."

She gave me a bewildered look, but let the kitchen door swing to. I heard her go into her little room off the kitchen and close the door. Charlie was still standing there looking at me. I gestured toward the other end of the table. "Sit down, Charlie."

He took one of the carved wooden chairs that Laura had ordered from somewhere, spun it around and straddled it backwards. "What's the matter, boss?"

Hell, I felt like someone had died, and if I'd answered him honestly that would have been what I would have said. I didn't bother offering him a drink. Charlie drank very little and he would only have taken a drink during a workday at gunpoint. I said, "Tell me everything you know about when Miss Laura left and how she left. Tell me everything you saw. Tell me everything she said."

He was a moment in answering. He had a cud of chewing tobacco in his cheek, which made quite a bulge in his long, lean face. He leaned a little ways out of his chair and aimed a spit of tobacco juice at a cuspidor set against the wall. Then he wiped his mouth with his forearm. He said, "We got trouble, boss?"

I said, dryly, though I didn't feel very humorous, "Not unless we are both married to my wife. Now tell me anything you can."

I could see from his eyes that he knew that matters weren't right. He didn't know the details, but he could see by my face that something was way out of kilter. I'd told him the previous morning not to tell Laura anything about seeing me leave or where I was going and then he'd seen her leave. Or at least I had to figure he'd seen her leave. Getting off an expedition the size of what Laura's must have looked like, he'd had to have been blind and deaf not to have known something was happening. He said, "Boss, all she told me was that she was going for a visit to Virginia." He shut his mouth and then started to open it again and then closed it. Finally he said, "Going for a visit. To Virginia."

I helped him out. "And then I come along beforehand and tell you not to tell her I've ridden off."

He looked down at the middle of the table. "Yeah, that didn't sound right. None of it sounds right. But it ain't my business."

I took a drink of whiskey. "The welfare of this ranch is your business and I'm part of this ranch."

"The biggest part," he said. He looked clearly unhappy now. "So we got trouble?"

"How much gear she take with her?"

He whistled and shook his head. "I don't know if I can describe it, boss, but the springs of that carriage was near to flat. She had several of them big trunks and all kinds of valises and suitcases. Damn near wasn't room for her and Phoenix to sit in it, overloaded as it was."

I let out a slow breath. Finally I said, "Yeah, we got trouble, Charlie. I know you don't want to hear about my problems, but they could turn out to be yours as well. It might be I'm going to have to be away from the ranch for a time. For a good while, maybe."

I could see him wince. It was the worst possible time, what with us finishing out the first crop of colts with the hope of running some of them in meets next spring and summer. It was unfair to drop that kind of responsibility on a young man like Charlie, no matter how capable he was. He couldn't do my job and he and I both knew it. If the colts measured up it would be to my credit because of the way I had arranged their breeding. If they didn't it would be because Charlie had failed in some part of their critical training, training that, by all rights, was my duty to oversee. But he didn't say anything about that. He said, quietly, "You think you might have to go on that visit with her? Sickness in the family?"

He was offering me an easy out, but I couldn't take it. I said, "I reckon she's a little put out with me, Charlie."

He looked somber. He had been as close to us as family for a lot of years. "I'm real sorry to hear that, Mr. Grayson. Shame that folks sometime have to get cross-wise of each other. Specially man and wife."

The odd thing was that Charlie was due to get married right after the first of the year. He'd been courting his girl long-distance style for over four years. She was in Del Rio, right at the Mexican border, which was where Charlie was from. But her daddy wouldn't let them get married until Charlie could prove he had a steady job and two thousand dollars in the bank. He'd had the steady job for a long time, but it's kind of hard to build up that kind of bank balance working for wages. The year before I'd offered to put the amount that Charlie was lacking in his account, but he wouldn't hear of it. He'd said, "No, sir. Her daddy might not ever know, but I would. And if that's what it takes to get his daughter I'll work at it until I meet the requirements."

Charlie was that kind of a man. I wished him a trouble free marriage, but I didn't believe there was such a thing.

I said, "What time did she get away yesterday?"

He thought a moment. "Well, I can't be sure, Mr. Grayson, but I'd reckon it was between ten-thirty and eleven. I didn't look at my watch, but it was another good hour to the noon meal."

I shook my head. "They didn't seem to waste much time getting started."

"Wasn't much more than an hour and a half, two hours after you rode off."

I nodded. "Virginia, huh?"

"Yes, sir. Least that's what she said."

I glanced up at him. There was a doubting tone in his voice. "You getting at something, Charlie? You don't think she went to Virginia?"

He looked uncomfortable. "Mr. Grayson, I ain't got no business talking about my boss's personal affairs."

"Charlie, tell me what you think. You don't think she went to Virginia, do you?"

He shook his head slowly. "It's just a feeling, Mr. Grayson. But, no, I don't. Not yet."

"Why not?"

"Albert."

"What about Albert?"

"He ain't come back yet."

"So?"

He shifted and spit before he answered. He said, "Mr. Grayson, if she was going to Virginia she wouldn't take Albert with her. Phoenix, yes, but not Albert. All she needs Albert for is fetching and carrying heavy loads. Once she's on the train they got help to do that for you. And in Virginia her folks would have plenty of hired hands. So since Albert ain't come back, and he's had time if she went into town to catch a train yesterday, I got to figure she ain't on no train for Virginia."

I thought about it for a moment. It made a lot of sense. I said, "But how do you know that Albert would come straight home? What makes you think he wouldn't fall off and get drunk?"

Charlie shrugged and smiled. "Three reasons. You, me, and Phoenix. He's scared of me. He's mortally afraid of you. But he's terrified of Phoenix and she would tell him to get straight home and get the horses and the carriage back safe. He's a good hand, boss, and he wouldn't pull a stunt like that."

"And she wouldn't take him to Virginia?"

"What for? Would you? Who'd bring those matched bays home? That's a thousand dollars worth of horse flesh. Mrs. Grayson is going to see to those horses, you can bet on that. She wouldn't leave them in no livery stable to be found. We'd have heard about those horses by now."

I had to agree with him. He hadn't said, "No matter how mad she is at you she'll see to those horses," but I'd added it in for him. That was the clue. If the horses weren't home then Laura either hadn't gone to Virginia or else something had happened to Albert.

I leaned back in my chair and sipped at the whiskey for a moment, thinking. Maybe her hurtling off to town like that was her way of throwing my words back in my face, walking out on me. Walking out, but not too far.

The only problem with that argument was that she'd taken the bulk of her clothes. She wouldn't have done that if she was doing a showy bluff. Or would she? If she didn't take her clothes and other stuff it would be clear to me she was coming back. You didn't bluff in a thousand-dollar game with a ten-dollar bet. Well, I thought, every dress and every pair of shoes and every earring or bracelet she'd taken was going to cost me a pound of sweat to work my way back into her good graces. I said, "Charlie, this is one time I wish you didn't work for me." I sighed.

He gave me a puzzled look. "How come, boss?"

"Because I need someone to talk to right now and it ain't good business to talk to your employees about your personal tangles. You and I have been close for a long time, but there are just some things a man ought not to talk about."

He nodded. "I can see that, Mr. Grayson. I reckon you can understand now why I never would call you by your first name."

I had to laugh. "You were smarter than I was about that, Charlie. It's a good practice. Someday you'll have your own business, your own ranch, and you'll be a success at it because of that kind of thinking. But—" I shook my head. "Right now it don't help me a damn bit."

"You thinking on going into town today?"

I shook my head. "I don't think that would be the smart idea, Charlie. Don't you reckon that is what she is expecting?"

He frowned slightly. "Well, I ain't nowhere near the expert you are when it comes to the fair sex, but—"

I burst out laughing, a little bitterly. "Me? An expert

with the fair sex? Hell, Charlie, I'm in trouble with my wife! That ain't got nothing to do with the fair sex, as you'll find out soon enough. How much you got in the bank now, Charlie?"

The switch in subjects caught him a little off balance. He had to think for a second. "Uh . . . a little over eighteen hundred. I ought to have it all by the first of the year if I cut it close."

"Don't worry about it. I'm going to give you a two-hundred-dollar bonus for the extra work you'll have to do while I get this straightened out."

He blinked doubtfully. "I wouldn't want you to do that, boss."

I changed the subject back. "You'd go in today? Not wait until tomorrow?"

"Well, if my girl was as close as town—" He shook his head and took the cud out of his cheek and dropped it into the spittoon. "I know I got to give this up pretty soon. She don't care for chawin', not even a little bit. But, yessir, I'd be on that road right now. What if Albert was to come wheeling into the yard this afternoon?"

I rubbed my jaw, feeling the stubble. I needed a shave. I said, "Believe me, Charlie, that's what I want to do. Go right now. But that's the very reason I'm going to sit tight." I got up. "I'm going to take a bath and get cleaned up."

He half smiled. "Case *she* shows up?"

"Something like that. Listen, come up and eat supper with me tonight. Maybe we'll play some kind of cards or something. You don't have to drink but you can at least watch me. Ain't a good habit a man gets to drinking alone."

"Yes, sir." he said. He got up.

"I'll see that you earn that bonus." I started for the stairs. I could hear him going out behind me. I reckoned I didn't have to explain to him that I didn't want to be alone in that big old house, especially that first night.

* * *

I got off for town by ten o'clock the next morning. Since I wasn't sure how long I'd be gone I'd taken time to go over several days' work with Charlie and get him lined out on the overall progress I was looking for from the ten main colts we were trying to get ready.

Riding in, my mind kept going over and over what I was going to say to Laura. I felt pretty sure she'd be at the hotel and since there wasn't but one big one her selection was pretty narrow. We wasn't much known there, being seldom in town, but Tyler could be a hard place to hide. There were a couple of other small hotels, places she wouldn't be caught in disguise, and about two boarding-houses. If she had any friends there it would be news to me. We hadn't made any as a couple and she had never talked about meeting anyone that interested her. Laura was a shade on the snob side and she had already passed judgment on the cultural aspects of Tyler. She'd said, "It's fine if you like to talk about lumber, but how long can you discuss shiplap and two-by-fours?"

I knew the manager of the hotel casually and he happened to be on the desk as I came into the lobby. I had not quite decided how I'd go about asking after Laura without giving it away that there was some reason I didn't know where she was. Obviously I didn't want anyone to know there was trouble between us. I didn't like people knowing my business anymore than anyone else enjoyed being gossiped about. So I kind of casually slid up to the desk and exchanged greetings with the manager, a man named Dennis Mabry. I said, "Dennis, can you tell me where my wife is staying?" I of course meant what room or suite she was in. But he just gave me a blank look and said he hadn't the slightest idea.

I had been so sure she would be at the hotel I was taken aback for a second. I said, "You mean she's not staying here? At the hotel?"

He shook his head. "Not that I know of and I'm pretty sure I'd know because we ain't half full."

I was so confused I didn't know what to say. I finally mumbled out some story about she'd come into town to shop and had mentioned she'd be staying over. I'd just assumed she'd be at the hotel.

But he shook his head. "She's not here, Mr. Grayson."

"Are you sure? She might have registered under another name. But she'd have her maid with her and her carriage and team would be in your livery stable."

He looked at me queerly. "Mr. Grayson, I've seen your wife and the lady is not staying at the hotel. The only female guest in the place is the wife of a drummer who is selling ladies' ready-to-wear to Hobson's Dry Goods store. And there's no carriage or team in my livery."

There was no pretense about my perplexity. I said, "Well, where in hell can she be? There's not another hotel in this town she'd go in."

"Maybe she's staying with friends here in town."

"Yeah," I said, nodding, even though I knew it couldn't be so. "Yeah, maybe you're right. Maybe she told me and I wasn't listening."

Mr. Mabry said, cheerfully, "You want to watch that. A man can get in trouble that way."

It sent me back out on the street not at all sure what to do next. It was closing on eleven o'clock and I mounted my horse and went down to the train depot. I went inside and up to the single ticket window they had and asked the passenger agent if he'd sold a ticket to a Mrs. Grayson, a Mrs. Laura Grayson. Either to her or to her Negro maid.

The old man behind the grille shook his head. "Nawsir, shore ain't. Fact of the bis'ness is I ain't sold no tickets to no females this morning. Or yesterday. Only Negro customer I've had was a man. Been real slow. Seems like folks don't want to go nowhere right now."

It left me scratching my head. Just so I could say I'd left no stone unturned I even rode by the two shabby hotels and the two boardinghouses. There was no carriage at either one of them and no place to hide one if there had been.

Finally I stopped at the bank. I needed some cash anyway and I thought maybe Robert Quince might have some news of her. I asked to see him, but he was out. I took the opportunity, though, to cash a check for four hundred dollars on the ranch account. That was another jab in my side about Laura. I needed her signature to write a check for five hundred dollars or more. The funny part about that was that it had been done at my insistence.

And now she was gone and the most money I could draw in any one day was four hundred and ninety-nine dollars. It was going to make it hell to run the ranch that way. We had some part-time help clearing pastures and they'd need to be paid as well as the regular hands. If I was forced to go hunting for Laura I was going to need some cash to leave Charlie. The way things were looking it might turn out we'd need his eighteen hundred dollars to keep the ranch going and he'd have to put off his wedding.

I stood outside the bank, standing on the boardwalk, thinking, wondering if Laura realized what kind of a financial lurch she'd left the ranch in or if she knew and didn't care. But that wasn't like her. She might well hate me by now, but she still cared about the horses we'd been raising. I stood there looking up and down the street, wishing Quince would show up. He might know where Laura could be traced or perhaps she'd come by and made some adjustment about the accounts.

But there was no sign of him and the teller in the bank, an old maid woman named Watkins, had been vague and not much help at all.

Finally I mounted up and took a kind of roving look around town. I had no earthly idea where Laura was and no idea where to look, and I had asked after her to everyone I could think might know. I'd even gone to Hobson's Dry Goods, thinking maybe she'd gone in there to pick up some little item or another, but they hadn't seen her.

When there was nowhere else to look or anybody to ask I wheeled my horse and started for home. During the ride I couldn't help thinking that maybe there was a chance she'd been on her way home and we'd somehow missed each other. It was a hope, but it didn't last five minutes once I got to the ranch. Charlie had seen me coming and he came walking into the stallion barn about the time I dismounted. I left the unsaddling and care of my horse to a hired hand and walked up to the house with Charlie. He'd come in the barn with a hopeful look on his face, which I'd misinterpreted. He'd thought I was bringing good news and I'd thought he had some. Didn't take long to straighten that part out.

"No, sir," he said sorrowfully. "Ain't been no sign of nobody. Not Miss Laura nor Albert and the team."

We went in the house and sat down at the morning room table. Jambalaya popped her head out the door and asked if I wanted something to eat. I said, fretfully, "No, and damn it, quit bothering me!"

Charlie gave me a look. It was understanding, not disapproving.

I said, "I know. Ain't no use taking it out on the help. It's not her fault."

"No, but I can see how it might make you a little snappish."

I pulled a look. "That might be what got me in this mess, Charlie."

"We all get a little that way from time to time. You didn't pick up no scent of her?"

I reached back to the sideboard and got the whiskey and a glass. "Not a smell." I said. "She can't be staying in Tyler. There's no place where she could get a room that I didn't check. And they haven't seen her at the train depot. She hasn't bought a ticket."

He sat there looking thoughtful for a moment.

I looked at him. "What?"

He wrinkled his boyish brow. "What if she didn't stop in Tyler? What if that was a little close and she wanted to work you a little to see how serious you was?"

He was already starting to talk like a married man.

"All right. I could see her doing that. But where the hell could she go? Ain't much more than one-saloon towns close around."

"Athens," he said. "That's only twenty-five miles on to the west and it's nearly twice the size of Tyler. Or maybe Marshall to the east, though it's fifty miles and the roads are none too good."

I had heard her speak of Athens. She'd said she'd heard it was far advanced in culture over Tyler. And she was a great one for culture, though I wasn't actually dead certain I knew what she meant by the term. I said, "Athens is a thought. But could she make it? In a carriage? Before dark?"

"Why shore, Mr. Grayson. Let's say it's a little over thirty miles from the ranch here, going by way of Tyler. And it's a good road from Tyler to Athens. One of the best in this part of the state. You remember that matched team is Andalusians bred to pure Morgans. That pair can go all day at six or seven miles an hour, eight if you want to push them. She could have been in Athens within five hours after she left here. And she could have gone around Tyler so that nobody even laid eyes on her."

I had given Charlie the job of scouting around for more and better pasture, so he was more familiar with the country than I was. I sat there thinking for a moment. I could just imagine Laura doing such a stunt. She'd probably figured I'd come after her, if for no other reason than the business about needing two signatures on the ranch checks. But even more than that she'd want to make it as hard on me as she could, make it hard just to find her to say some words that she'd make me say a number of times before she accepted them as an apology.

I said, thinking out loud, "Wonder what time it is?"

"Going on for four o'clock, Mr. Grayson. You wouldn't want to start out now? Not if you was going to take Paseta. He's already done a good fifteen miles today."

"You think Athens?"

He shrugged. "Well, 'course I don't know. But it sounds likely for a lady of Miss Laura's persnickity tastes. And the railroad runs through there. It's the closest town of any size she could make in one day."

I called out, "Jambalaya."

She put her head through the door. "Fix me something to eat. You want something, Charlie?"

He shook his head.

"What you be wantin', Mr. Warner?"

"Steak and eggs. And in case I forget I want you to pack me some vittles for the road tomorrow. I'll be leaving early so I want my breakfast by six."

"Yes, suh." She disappeared back into the kitchen.

Charlie got up. I said, "Wait a minute." I dug into my pocket and pulled out the four hundred dollars I'd gotten at the bank. Besides that I had several hundred more around the house but I figured to need that traveling. I handed him the money. I said, "You might have to pay off them hands that are clearing brush before I get back. That ought to be more than plenty, but it will leave you some for emergencies."

"You got any idea how long you'll be gone, Mr. Grayson?"

I shook my head. "I can't be gone too long. End of the week is payday and I've got to be back for that. What you've got there won't pay the regular hands. And there'll be other bills. I'd guess four or five days. However long it takes."

He nodded and looked at me in that serious way of his. "I wish you good luck, Mr. Grayson."

"You better wish us both good luck. Might not be a ranch if this thing can't be patched up."

"I got faith in you, Mr. Grayson. There ain't never been nothing I've seen you run up against you couldn't handle. From outlaws to Thoroughbred horses."

I said, grimly, "What about wildcats? You ever seen anybody successfully gentle a wildcat?"

He leaned against the kitchen door. "I'll see that your horse is ready in the morning."

"Keep a tight rein on the place, Charlie. I'm off chasing strays."

He smiled and pushed through the kitchen door and I was left alone with the whiskey bottle and my thoughts, neither one of which was much comfort.

3

Laura

The cottage was almost exactly as I had imagined it would be, including its coat of white paint. It did not have a white picket fence around it, but the small yard and neat flower beds were all ready to receive me. By the time I arrived, Phoenix and her helpers had my wardrobe in place and were ready for me. The little house would do for my purposes. It looked like what it was, a place a man making two or three thousand dollars a year would buy for his wife—complete with nondescript furniture. That she had left him, suddenly, Phoenix had already confirmed. The exact reason was not known but Phoenix was pretty certain it had to do with drinking or gambling or him running around with ladies of low repute. Didn't it always?

I had eaten lunch in the hotel, but it quickly became obvious that we had set up housekeeping without pot or pan or a single item of groceries or food or liquid refreshment. We were also without eating utensils, tableware, pillows, pillowcases, or bed clothes of any kind. Nor were we in possession of a number of other articles, such as soap and towels and items necessary for daily living. I immediately gave Phoenix two hundred dollars and sent her and Albert into town to rectify the situation. It was an amazement to me the odds and ends you took for granted in your day to day living and never gave them heed until you reached out your hand and found them missing. That afternoon, for instance, I was going to take a bath and put on a complete new set of clothing. It was then we discovered that my hosiery and other silk undergarmets had not been packed. Phoenix was beside herself and was all for directing Albert to hitch up the carriage so she could return to the ranch that instant and return with the missing items. I prevented her since I feared that Warner would be there by then and might follow her back to town. I was not yet ready to deal with him. Consequently, I sent Phoenix back to town to do the best she could in the ladies lingerie line, though I had scant hopes for what might be found in Tyler.

But it didn't really matter that much. We were not going to be long in the east Texas town. It might have seemed extravagant to buy a house you were only going to occupy for a week or less, but such was my mood. Besides, I would have been surprised if I did not end up making a profit. The payments on the house loan were forty-two dollars a month. Rather they had been. Mr. Quince had been charging the previous owner eight percent per annum. When I read the papers I pointed out that I would not pay more than four percent and if that didn't suit him I'd take my money out of his bank and move it elsewhere. He was only too happy to oblige and that brought the monthly note down to thirty-five dollars.

Knowing that I wasn't going to remain in Tyler was one matter; deciding where I was going to move was another. I had decided that I would stay in Texas. That limited my choices immediately. I could not live in a small town. I had to reside in a place of some culture, where the necessities of life could be obtained without having to send to Europe for them. As a result, I kept running the bigger cities through my mind. I did not care for Houston, nor Dallas for that matter. They were large, but they were rough and vulgar and growing at astonishing rates. There was San Antonio, but its Spanish influence was so pronounced as to smother every other cultural aspect. Austin was the capital but it was full of politicians, and if there was one thing I despised more than a card cheat it was a politician. I toyed with the idea of returning to Corpus Christi, but that struck me as retreating in defeat. No, Corpus was out. So were Laredo and any other town on the border.

I thought of New Orleans even though it was in Louisiana. If I made an exception to leave Texas it would be for New Orleans. I had visited it several times and found the style of the antebellum south still very much alive and even prospering under New Orleans' natural French influence.

But ever since we had moved to east Texas, the name of one small city kept cropping up. Jefferson. Jefferson, Texas. From all that I had heard it was an unusual town. In the little more than four years we'd lived in Tyler I had always meant to visit it. It was only seventy miles away by rail. But Warner, naturally, had shown no interest and I'd simply never gotten around to making the trip by myself, although ex president U.S. Grant had visited there, as had the celebrated English playwright and poet Oscar Wilde. Even as I surveyed our new, cramped quarters it was lurking in my mind.

Phoenix was not happy with our new environs. She felt the cottage was not a proper abode for a lady such as me nor, therefore, by extension, for her.

"Mighty small doin's," she said, looking around the rooms. "Mighty small. Ain't room to cuss a cat, you ask me."

I did not bother to tell her the situation was entirely temporary. Sometimes Phoenix tended to take more on herself than was her place. I seldom scolded her but I did, as a lesson, exclude her from my thinking.

She said, "You take a look at this furn'ture, Miss Laura? Ain't fit fer common folk, let alone quality. I ought to git Albert to chuck it out the back door and set it a-fahr."

"Where would you get more, Phoenix?"

She gave me a blank look. "Why, at the sto'."

"This is what the store in Tyler has to sell. If you burned this up we'd have to sit on the floor."

She made a helpless gesture with her hand. "But that furn'ture in the big house. That quality business. Where'd that come from?"

"That had to be shipped in. Some of it came from as far away as Chicago and New Orleans. You remember some of it came from my house in Corpus Christi?"

It did not placate her. She was definitely unhappy and not at all sure we'd made the right move. She said, "You seen that kitchen, Miss Laura? How I 'spose to cook in that little dab of a place? I 'spect you didn't fetch along the cook, did you?"

"No, Phoenix. You are the cook. Just as you have been before."

She grumbled a little and started to turn away. Then she turned back. She said, "Maybe Mr. Warner done been punished enough. I reckon he's sick to his soul from worryin' 'bout you. He's a fine man, Miss Laura."

I gave her a stern look. "Go start lunch, Phoenix. And I don't want to hear another word about this house or the furniture or, especially, Mr. Grayson."

But Phoenix had reminded me of something else in speaking of Warner and the ranch. Of the three accounts we had in the bank, one, the big ranch account, required both our signatures on checks for amounts over five hundred dollars. My own account, of course, needed only my signature. Our household account could be used with either signing. But the ranch account required us both. It had been Warner's idea and he had insisted on it. I'd thought it was foolish and would cause needless delays, but he was determined to have it that way. I understood why. The money had come from me and he felt guilty about it, too guilty just to put his single name on it. He wanted me involved so it would not seem so much that it was him alone using a woman's money. It was just misplaced pride, false pride, and bad business at that.

Still, there it was. It occurred to me, since I would not be available, that I had three choices. I could simply leave matters as they were and let him try and squirm his way around that. But I knew that was foolish. It could well be that he would miss an opportunity or that it would harm the ranch in some other way. I did, however, take some mean pleasure in visualizing him going into Mr. Quince and trying to convince him that we had meant to change the procedure before I'd left to visit relatives only we had overlooked it in the rush. Mr. Quince would say, "Oh, gone to Virginia to visit relatives, has she? Does she always buy a town house before she does that? A furnished house?"

It made me smile, the thought of it, but I knew I could never do it. The second alternative was to go by the bank and have my name taken off the account so that Warner would have complete freedom.

I thought about that and even smiled at how astonished and humbled it would make Warner feel. He would think, She did such a magnanimous thing after what I said to her. What a cad I've been.

Yes, I thought about it and I would have done it if I'd been some kind of saint or a complete angel. But I was neither, and I had no intention of giving Warner absolution and freedom. What I determined to do was go down the next day and instruct Mr. Quince that, in my absence, he would be the cosigner of such checks as needed to be drawn. I was going to further instruct him that he was to be precise in drawing from Warner a full accounting, in detail, of just how and why the money was to be spent. Further, I was going to give him an address where I might be reached by telegram once I'd settled on my destination, and he was to wire me at that address about any amounts he questioned or any expenditures he felt were not absolutely necessary. I intended to pay him a small personal stipend for following my instructions.

The arrangement, I calculated, would eventually cause Warner to dread going to the bank and would give him cause, on each occasion, to regret his hasty and brutal words. As I said, I was not a saint and did not expect to become one.

Jefferson, from all that I could learn, was a very unusual town. It was the furthest inland river port in the south and southwest. An unusual occurrence had caused it to come into being and then to flourish well beyond any reason. Most river trade was confined to the Mississippi and those few tributaries that were large enough to accommodate the big riverboats. The Red River that lay between Texas and Louisiana was just such a tributary. However, once it left the Mississippi at New Orleans it began narrowing and shallowing up so that it was barely able to serve Shreveport, a struggling town in western Louisiana.

Jefferson lay to the northeast of Tyler, very near the Louisiana border and some twenty miles from Gaddo Lake, into which flowed the Red River. By a freak of nature a log jam had occurred on a bayou above Jefferson causing the bayou to back into the lake and provide a broad, navigable stretch of water to the lake and then on beyond. It even had the salutary effect of widening the Red River at Shreveport, allowing paddle-wheelers to travel to docks they had never been able to reach before. As time went on the log jam lengthened and lengthened until it was judged to be five miles long and a permanent fixture. This had all happened some twenty years before and the upshot had been to transform Jefferson from a sleepy little country village to a booming, racing river port whose population swelled with every passing day.

I knew very few people in Tyler, none more than to say hello to, but by diligent questioning I was able to discover that Jefferson was a small city of some thirty thousand inhabitants and that, culturally, it was the match of New Orleans or Charleston or even Richmond, Virginia. It was said that steamboats unloaded goods and treasures from all over the world on Jefferson's docks and left loaded with cattle and cotton and all sorts of other important commodities, such as lumber and pitch and pecans. I was told there was an opera house there and that the finest traveling theatrical troupes regularly made Jefferson part of their route. The wife of the passenger agent for the railroad, who had been there several times, said that a woman could find the latest fashions from Europe and that it was nothing to see Belgian lace or Irish wool or even styles from Paris, France.

Of course everyone in Tyler was quick to point out to me that the place was dizzyingly expensive and that while it might do for a visit one either had to be rich or crazy to live there. I was informed it was also full of the worst kind of adventurers and speculators that one could imagine, especially the men. And the women who plied their trade there, well, my informants usually blushed and were unable to go on.

It sounded exactly like what I was looking for. I determined to go and investigate the place without delay.

By the time I'd made up my mind to make a trip to Jefferson, several days had passed. I had mystified Mr. Quince by my instructions as to his duties as a cosigner, Warner had not made an appearance or sent word, and Phoenix had not reconciled herself to the little cottage. My announcement to her that I was going to entrain for a place she'd never heard of threw her into a dither. She thought we had been independent enough and that it was time to go back to the comfort of the ranch. The idea of putting more distance between us and it, and especially going to some strange locale which possessed heaven only knew what kind of dangers, was almost too frightening to contemplate. Still, I couldn't go alone. Women of quality and means did not travel unattended. It was unseemly. I had spent most of my life doing whatever the hell I pleased and not worrying what anyone thought, but I was rather enjoying the role of proper, if estranged, lady. I also expected it to ward off any unwelcome attention from gentlemen who might perceive me as an easy mark.

The cottage was part of a neighborhood on the edge of town. The houses were quite separated from one another, some by as much as a hundred yards, but on the third day two of my neighbor ladies came to welcome me. They brought fresh bread and cake and I had Phoenix make coffee. I wasn't sure that they knew who I was but just the fact that I was a woman alone in a house in such a small town was reason enough for a visit to gather gossip material. We talked for an hour and even though they offered me a wealth of openings to explain my situation I managed to evade every trap. Toward the end one of them, almost perspiring with the chore of getting a definite answer out of me said, "I'm sure you can use a man's hand around the place for the odd chore. Shall I send my Abner over to help you settle in?"

I smiled nicely and said, "Oh, that won't be necessary, though it is so kind of you to offer. But my coachman is very handy with tools."

That stopped them. They had not reckoned on a coachman. I made myself even more mysterious by constant references to the ranch and wondering how it was doing while I was taking this sabbatical in town. Finally I asked if there were a decent hairdresser in the town and that left them looking at each other. Not only did they not go to someone to dress their hair they didn't know anyone who did.

But they were nice women with just a little more curiosity than was good for them. I did, however, find out what had caused the house to suddenly become vacant. The sawmill manager that had been occupying it with his family had cut part of his hand off and had been sent back to the company headquarters in Houston. His company had persuaded the bank, in the person of Robert Quince, to return his down payment. I'd made a mental note to take that up with Mr. Quince in the future.

On the subject of Jefferson the ladies were thrilled and excited and claimed it was wicked enough to rival Sodom and Gomorrah. Mrs. Ross, a kind-faced lady who was about my age but looked much older owing to steady childbearing, put her hand to her mouth and giggled. She said, "Ooooh! You'll never believe what happened to me there. You know about it, Irene. Of course this was a few years back."

Irene said, "You mean when that man . . ."

"Yes!" Mrs. Ross put out her hand, palm forward. "You would never imagine. I was walking along the street, on my way to shopping. And this dandy in a pinchback suit and a derby hat fell right in step with me and, and, and—" She started giggling.

Her friend finished for her. "You'd never believe it," Irene said. "This man, in broad daylight mind you, put his *hand* on Rose's *hip* and says, if you can imagine, 'How 'bout it, kiddo?' Just like that! Did you ever?"

I wanted to laugh, but I shook my head. "Laws, what is this world coming to. Right there on the street!"

"I'm just lucky Abner wasn't around. Lord knows what he'd have done."

They loved to talk about Jefferson, and as frightening and wicked as the place was it appeared that they went there every chance they could. Irene explained it. She said, "There are just some items, proud as we are of Tyler, that you can't buy here." She'd leaned forward. "Feminine matters, you understand. And they have a proper doctor for ladies there."

Mrs. Ross said, "And it's such a nice train ride. And not at all expensive. Of course I wouldn't want to live there, but it is a sight to go down on the wharves and see them unloading them boxes and barrels from just everywhere. But you better be forewarned. That town never shuts down. They got gamblin' dens and drinkin' dens and—" she leaned forward and lowered her voice, "—and dens of iniquity, if you know what I mean."

Phoenix, of course, had been listening at the kitchen door and had heard every word. She looked grim when, after my new neighbors had departed, she said, "That Thomas Jefferson place sounds like where we don't wan' to be. Place sounds jus' plumb full o' wickedness. Man comes up to the lady on the street an' puts his arm 'round her waist an' says, 'How 'bout it, kiddo.' Huh! An' her plain as a mud fence. No tellin' what happen to a beauty like you, Miss Laura, in such a hell hole."

Phoenix had always had a flair for overstatement. I said, "We are going there tomorrow. You and I."

She looked horrified. She said, "Oh, Miss Laura, you cain't mean it! Say you are joshin'. Besides, Mr. Warner might come lookin' this way any time now. Won't do fo' us to be gone."

I gave her a flat look. "Phoenix, stop acting silly. There is no danger. Those women were just talking to give themselves a thrill. And I do not want to hear you mention Mr. Grayson's name again. You certainly seemed happy enough when we left the ranch."

"That," she said, apropos of nothing, "was then. This here is now."

"What is that supposed to mean?"

"Never you mind," she said, nodding as if she knew something. "They is things helped by doin' an' they is things that ain't."

That was her way. She liked to make wise-sounding pronouncements with no basis in fact or logic. I said, "Send Albert to find out what time the train leaves for Jefferson. If there is more than one I'd like to leave as soon after lunch as possible. Albert will not be going."

"Yes'm." She did not look happy. "I'll do it, but my heart ain't in it. I know one thing—we go up to that sinful city I'm gon' carry my Bible wid me in my purse."

I said, "Well, if it is that copper and leather bound volume I gave you it ought to make a formidable weapon."

I myself carried a little 32-caliber derringer in my bag that I was not too happy with. It was too small a gauge and it fired only two bullets. I determined to better my armament so, when Albert had the team hitched to the carriage, I rode with him downtown and sought a gunsmith's shop. The shopkeeper seemed embarrassed and ill at ease. It was obvious from his actions and the stares of his few other customers who were lounging around that they weren't used to women in such an establishment. I explained to the gunsmith that I wanted a small gun, one that I could carry in my purse, but I wanted more shots than a derringer and a larger caliber. My request seemed to strike the men in attendance as humorous. I turned around to where two ill kept men were slouching back in a corner and chortling. I gave them a long look. They gradually quieted down. I said, "Tell me, what wages do you draw for making public fools of yourselves?"

They opened their mouths in unison and gaped. I didn't care. I was tired of the atmosphere that restricted women to territory selected for them by men.

Finally one of them found his voice. He said, "You wouldn't be talkin' so smart, lady, if you wadn't hidin' behind yore skirt."

The gunsmith had placed a small, snub-nosed five-shot revolver made by Smith and Wesson on the countertop before me. Ignoring it, I said to the rude man, "You appear to be hiding behind several layers of common dirt. Allow me to get this revolver loaded and then you and I can step out into the alley and see which is the best protection against a bullet, a skirt or dirt."

There was a small smattering of laughter from several others, but the man I'd addressed just glared at me. He was sitting amidst a small pile of shavings from the stick he'd been whittling. They were all around the chair he was seated in. He looked no different, nor was he dressed any differently, from the other loungers, he had simply opened his mouth at the wrong time. He said, "Pshaw, lady. Them's mighty easy words for you to spout, you knowin' I ain't gonna swing fer pluggin' no woman."

I said, "All right. Then let us step out and shoot at a target." I reached in my purse and took out a hundred-dollar bill. It was my habit to carry at least five hundred dollars in cash money on my person. I said, "If you are so certain you are a better shot, then match my bet and we'll quickly see who should be in a gun shop and who shouldn't."

Even as I was doing it I was ashamed of myself. The poor man had probably never before seen a hundred dollars at one time in his whole life. I could afford to lose, he couldn't. And I also happened to be an excellent shot.

He sat there, his peers watching him in anticipation. Finally he hung his head and got up, folding his pocket knife as he did. He waved a hand in my direction. "I wouldn't want to get near no woman with a firearm in her hand. No tellin' who's liable to git kilt." He put his knife in his pocket and went out the door still holding the stick he'd been whittling.

It was quiet in the shop. The gunsmith cleared his throat as if to return my attention to the gun he was showing me. I wasn't ready. I looked at the other three men, still holding up the hundred dollar bill. I said, "The bet is still open in case any of you other *gentlemen* might care to chance your luck." I tapped the top of the glass display case. "Of course, if we are to shoot at a mark, I will want a longer barreled weapon than this belly gun I'm presently contemplating." I said it to make sure they understood that I knew about guns and that the longer the barrel, up to a point, the more accurate the weapon.

None of them would look at me. Finally, one by one, they left their rockers and cane-bottomed chairs and filed out of the shop. I turned back to the owner. I said, "I hope you will forgive me. It appears you have lost some customers on my account. I'll be glad to make it up to you if you can put a value on what they might have bought."

The gunsmith was a pleasant looking man with a balding head and a pot belly. He wore rimless glasses and sleeve garters. He laughed. "Ma'am, I reckon I owe you the apology. That bunch hangs around in here until I get fed up and sweep them out. I can see how surprised they was to see a lady like you come in to grace this place. But they ought to have had better manners. I reckon they will in future." He looked down at the little snub-nosed revolver and then at me. He said, "So you knew this is what we call a belly gun. I reckon, then, you want something you can get at in a hurry and that will do more damage than a derringer. I'd recommend this gun. It's made by a good outfit known for quality work and it's a .38 caliber, which will do some damage. I'm sure I don't have to tell you it ain't accurate much over ten feet."

"I understand that. What is your price?"

My purse was open on account of my taking out the hundred dollar bill. The derringer was inside, in plain view. It had been a present from Warner and was silver chased. It was a beautiful little gun, but not what I needed. The smith said, "Well, if you were to pitch in that derringer I'd swap even."

I smiled slowly. I said, "I'm certain you would, Mr. Aikens." I assumed it was Mr. Aikens. That was the name on the outside of the shop. "But I don't want to part with the little gun. Besides, you and I both know that the derringer is worth considerably more than the Smith and Wesson."

The gun cost thirty dollars and I bought a box of shells for three dollars more. While he wrapped my purchases, Mr. Aikens said, "You wouldn't happen to be Mrs. Grayson, would you?"

I admitted as much.

He smiled. "Then that explains it. I reckon those loafers got off mighty easy. I do some trade with men that work out at y'all's ranch. I understand that Mr. Grayson is the second-best shot on the place."

I smiled thinly. "Don't believe all you hear, Mr. Aikens. Mr. Grayson does not pay much attention to target shooting. However, he becomes a different breed of cat when the guns come out for real."

He nodded. "I understand that, but you'd be amazed the number of folks who don't." He tapped his glass-top case. "Well, since I got you in here, is there anything else I might show you?" He pointed to a long revolver just in front of him. "This is that new Colt. Comes in a .44-caliber model. This is the one that has the floating firing pin so you can load all six cylinders without fear of one going off and blowing your foot to smithereens." Then he realized what he was saying and chuckled. He said, "Or your purse. I was talking like you wore a pistol strapped around your waist in a holster like some man."

"If it suited my purposes I would. Thank you, Mr. Aikens, and good day to you."

"You call again, Mrs. Grayson. We won't have no more trouble with them clabberheads like we done today."

I went outside and got into the carriage. Albert had already been to the depot and purchased tickets for me and Phoenix. We were to leave on the one o'clock train the next afternoon. As he handed me my change Albert said, in his unnaturally high voice, "You sho' you don't wan' me to go 'long, Missy Grayson?"

I spoke a little sharper than I meant. I said, "No, Albert. We may be women but we are not completely helpless."

In most of what I had heard about Jefferson the Excelsior hotel had more often than not been mentioned. It had at one time been the private home of a cotton planter who had used it as a town house for himself and his family. But when Jefferson turned into a cosmopolitan center he had sold the house and it was revamped into an exclusive hotel and dining room. It had, at first, been fairly small, but as the town grew, so did the hotel until it was known far and wide as an inn that could rival hostelries of any major city. It maintained an exclusive clientele by means of its prices which, according to those who couldn't afford it, were exorbitant, and which were never mentioned by those who could. All agreed, however, that it was the plushest and most comfortable hotel to be found in most states and a place where the wishes of the guest were satisfied, if humanly possible.

That afternoon I got off a telegram to the Excelsior advising them of my arrival the next afternoon and requesting a suite for myself and a room for my Negro attendant. It was, unfortunately, the custom, even in an enlightened age, to billet colored servants separately from ladies' maids who happened to be white. It enraged me, but Phoenix had long since explained that there was no use exercising myself about the matter because it couldn't be helped. She claimed not to be disturbed by this rank unfairness.

Though I knew that the Excelsior was where the former president of the United States, U.S. Grant, had stayed with his party, I was surprised to learn that the management had built a special wing to accommodate the president. As it turned out the wing was not completed by the time of Grant's arrival, but I was most favorably impressed to learn that the attempt had been made. It was a sign that the people of the hotel, and perhaps the town, did not shilly-shally but believed in getting things done.

There had still been no word or sign of Warner. I did not know if I was relieved or disappointed.

Phoenix and I spent the night before we left for Jefferson going over my clothes and accoutrements and accessories. Clearly I wasn't going to take my whole wardrobe, but I did want to take enough so that I would be presentable whatever the occasion. Sometime around midnight we reduced my apparel to two large trunks and four other large pieces of luggage, along with some smaller bags. Phoenix was able to accommodate herself with two large valises.

I said, "I hope I'm taking enough, Phoenix."

Phoenix, who was sweating and frustrated said darkly, "I jest hope the railroad train can pull it all."

All that was left was the matter of the bank and giving Albert his instructions. I anticipated some curiosity on Mr. Quince's part, but no trouble. Albert, however, was a different matter and I instructed Phoenix that I wanted her to give him a good talking to before I gave him his orders. I said, "I want you to impress on him that he must do exactly as I say and he is not to drink while we are gone. I know he will be lonely here by himself, but it is important that he follow orders. Make sure you have his attention, Phoenix."

Her brow got stormy. "I scare the liver out that man. Don't you worry, Miss Laura. He do what he told an' you ain't got to worry 'bout him drinkin' no whiskey. I'll make him believe I'll smell it wherever I am an' then back I come and *wham!* He do right. Don't you fret about that."

Before we went to bed Phoenix gave the rooms of the little cottage a disdainful look and said, "Even if we be goin' into the midst of sin and wickedness in that town you is set on goin' to, least we gettin' out this chicken coop. Ain't fit, Miss Laura, lady yo' quality livin' place like this here."

Of course it was not Phoenix's place to make such comments, but I had long ago given up reminding Phoenix of her place. Phoenix's place was wherever she decided it ought to be.

I was in Mr. Quince's office by eleven-thirty the next morning, wearing a soft green linen traveling suit. I had eschewed a hat as just something extra to keep up with and had Phoenix put my hair up and secure it with a jeweled comb. Without telling Mr. Quince any of my personal business I gave him his instructions as to how checks were to be handled on the big ranch account. When I was through he stared at me, almost in disbelief. He said, "Let me get this straight," and then proceeded to practically repeat word for word what I had told him.

I nodded. "If you will undertake that service I will be most gratified."

He blinked for a moment. Finally he said, cautiously, "Will this arrangement be all right with Mr. Grayson?"

Of course the man didn't know that it was my money, though he might have guessed by the sum I kept in my personal account and by the fact that, when the accounts had been set up, and set up by him, the money had come in the form of cashier's checks on Corpus Christi banks in my name. But, he was, after all, a man and so was

Warner and Warner's precious ego had to be protected at all costs. I said, "I'm certain it will be, Mr. Quince. The dual signature was Mr. Grayson's idea. He believes it is a sure protection against the counterfeiting of a check by a fraud artist."

Mr. Quince nodded emphatically. "To be sure, to be sure."

"But since I am going to be on this extended trip we will require another signatory. Who better than the president of our bank?"

He nodded again with equal vigor. "Oh, yes, oh yes indeed." Then he stopped and frowned. "But there is one small item I don't completely understand. You'll forgive me, but it seems to defeat the purpose of my authority."

"Wiring me for confirmation of amounts of one thousand dollars and over?"

He nodded slowly, warily. "Yes. Does Mr. Grayson know about that?"

I smiled sweetly, imagining the first encounter Warner would have with the stipulation. "Oh, yes," I said. "He knows about that." I took a piece of paper out of my purse with the name of the Excelsior hotel in Jefferson on it. I pushed it across the desk to him. "Until further notice you can wire me at that location."

He looked at it. He said, "I was under the impression you were going to Virginia to visit friends."

I stood up. "In time, Mr. Quince, in time." I took a step toward the door and stopped. I said, "By the way, Mr. Quince, my whereabouts are to be known to no one else. And that includes Mr. Grayson."

He looked up, staring. I could see the wheels of juicy gossip turning in his head. "I don't understand."

"But you heard me?"

"Oh, yes."

"Then all you have to understand is that I would hate to draw my money out of your bank, but I would."

I left him staring after me as I exited his office. At the cashier's window I drew a cashier's check for a thousand dollars out of my personal account and then went outside to where Phoenix and Albert were waiting in the carriage. It was twelve noon and time to be getting to the station. It was going to take Albert more than a few minutes to get my luggage up on the passenger dock where it could be taken aboard the train.

We had made a sort of lunch before we'd left the cottage. It was really a late breakfast, but it would do us until we reached Jefferson. It was no more than a two-hour ride. While Albert was manhandling the trunks and valises, Phoenix and I went and sat in the waiting room. I had a good view of the town through a big window. It was strange. I had never felt or noticed that much about Tyler, but I suddenly had an awful sinking feeling of loneliness, as if I were about to be homesick. Homesick? For what? I couldn't explain it, but there it was. I was already homesick for a town I barely knew. It made no sense.

About ten minutes before the train was due in I gave Albert his orders. He stood listening gravely and nodding his head. I told him that he was to go back and occupy the cottage and take care of it. I gave him three twenty-dollar bills. I said, "That is feed for you and the horses. I want the horses exercised every day, but you are not to do it in town. I do not want you making a spectacle of yourself. Now I understand that Phoenix has already warned you about any drinking of whiskey?"

He nodded his head vigorously and rolled his eyes in her direction. "Yes, ma'am, yes, ma'am. She done give me the straight of that."

"And you are to tell no one where I have gone to. That especially includes Mr. Grayson."

He looked astonished. "Mr. Warner? He come 'round an' ast me an' I ain't 'spose to tell him? But he de boss!"

I shook my head. "You work for me, Albert. Be sure you understand that. You are not to tell him where I have gone to."

He looked puzzled for a moment and then said, "Well, fack o' the matter is, Miss Laura, I ain't all that sho' where y'all goin'. You wrote on that piece of paper I was to git tickets to there, but I don' know where that is."

"I forgot you can't read, Albert. Did you keep that note I gave you?"

He shook his head slowly. "No, ma'am. Was I s'pose to?"

"No. You've done fine, Albert. Now, I'm entrusting you with the care of the little cottage and the possessions I've left there. There is one more matter. You must come every day to the telegraph office here at the depot in case I have a message for you. I may well want you to come and join me when we are settled." He started to say something, but I stopped him. "The telegraph operator will tell you what it says."

He was still looking pained. "But what is I to tell Mr. Warner, he come 'round askin' me 'bout you?"

"Tell him that you don't know anything and that I gave you orders not to say a word. He will understand and respect that."

He shook his head slowly. "I hopes so, Miss Laura. That Mr. Warner ain't no gen'lman I wan's git crosswise of."

At long last, the train arrived. Phoenix gave Albert his final orders, having to do, no doubt, with the dangers of drinking, and I didn't imagine she was referring to what the alcohol did to your stomach. We boarded and, after a spirited discussion with the conductor in which legal action was mentioned several times by me, Phoenix was allowed to ride with me as my attendant rather than back in the degrading Jim Crow car. It amazed me that such practices continued in the modern and up-to-date times we lived in. But, then, if it weren't for the Negro, who would the white trash have to look down on?

Shortly after we pulled out of the station at Tyler an odd thought crossed my mind. I was thinking about Warner, naturally. Nothing in particular, just odd thoughts and images flitting across my mind. Not too long after we were married I'd asked him how it was that men came to refer to women's breasts as knockers. He had been driving me in the buggy at the time. We were on our way to a distant pasture to see a new mare. He answered off-handedly while he tended to his driving. "Oh, it's an old expression. It means that a lady has such a fine set of breasts in shape and size that they will knock your hat off. Or knock your socks off. Whatever. It's like when you see something really fine, like a beautiful view or a horse, and it makes you gasp in amazement."

"Oh," I said. "I thought maybe it meant they stuck out so far they knocked things off the table or whatever."

"Naw." He laughed. "Breasts that big wouldn't be interesting to a man. They'd belong in a sideshow." He went along for a second and then suddenly turned to me and said, in what I could only call a distressed voice, "Where did you ever hear an expression like that? What sort of men would use that language around you?"

I explained that I had overheard the expression some years before quite by accident and had always wondered what it meant. I assured him that it had never been said to me.

He gave me a troubled look. "That's not the sort of thing a lady should know about. Especially when that lady is my wife."

I did not say anything further because the subject seemed to excite him so. But, thinking on it, I realized that it was illustrative of the problems we had been having of late. During our early years together such a question would have gotten nothing more out of Warner than a laugh and the statement that I shouldn't worry about the term. By that he would have meant that I had breasts that were on the smallish side. "More than a mouthful but not quite two hands full," was the way he had once described them.

But since we had been married it was as if he could not abide the idea that I had had any sort of life before him. I was to be crystal pure, ladylike, modest, and obedient. I was to be the perfect wife and mother, spitting out babies on command, and swallowing down any ideas of back talk.

It was in that instant that I realized that I was not on the train only because we could not have a child. That was just one of the manifestations of the trouble that lay between Warner and me. There was a great deal that had to be settled between us before we could be happy together. It was strange, as I thought about it, because it sounded as if we'd been two strangers who had married in haste. In point of fact, that was the case even though we had more or less lived together for over three years. But once the minister said those words Warner began to look at me in a completely different light and I was expected to reflect that light. If my money and his attitude toward money were added to that it made for a well nigh impossible situation. With a shiver I looked out the window as the landscape passed and wondered if the load wasn't too great to be borne. I still loved Warner but I didn't know if we could live together. It might well be that I would end up as only his business partner.

The flurry of thoughts brought a sinking feeling inside me, a feeling of loneliness and desolation. But then I straightened myself in the seat and firmed up my mind. I was going to a new town. I would see the beginning of that and handle matters as they arose. Curiously enough, it was an attitude that I had learned from Warner Grayson.

4

Laura

I was much taken with the outward appearance of the Excelsior hotel. As the carriage that brought us from the depot pulled up in front of it I was conscious of a southern style of charm and elegance that I had not really seen, outside of New Orleans, since leaving Virginia. The hotel was on Front Street, very close to the river, as it was called, though it was really a bayou. Just down from the hotel were the wharves and docks. As we passed I saw several large Mississippi stern-wheelers sitting elegantly at their moorings like so many plump matrons settled down for afternoon tea. The wharves were simply teeming with activity, with stevedores moving huge bales and crates of cargo both on and off the big boats. Almost from the moment I stepped down from the train I felt an electric pulse in the air. It was as if the town were saying, "This is a going concern and if you can't keep up you'd best get out of the way." I found the whole experience exhilarating and I could see why my neighbors at the cottage in Tyler thought Jefferson was fast and wicked. I liked the hustle and bustle of the waterfront, situated as it was so near the front of the elegant hotel.

The Excelsior was a long, two-story, whitewashed brick building with a high, flat roof and many chimneys riding up out of its slate top. The windows on both floors were wide and appeared to be at least six feet high. One would not feel cooped up in such light and commodious surroundings. The front of the hotel ran one full block. The carriage driver pointed out as we neared that the new wing made an L at the western end of the block and ran back north for a hundred yards. The eastern end already had a wing running to the north, so the two wings gave the hotel a U shape. The driver said there were a courtyard and garden in the middle of the U. I was prepared to be fascinated by the place. My one worry was whether or not they would accommodate Phoenix. If not, then I would have to take accommodations where they would. It was not without cause that I was concerned on that score. Most small towns in the south were still so bitter about the War that they were blind to the necessity of a lady's maid living close at hand. Some of them had even gone so far as to build second-rate quarters some little remove from their main hostel and call that cooperating with madame's wishes. How, I had asked on many such occasions, was I supposed to summon my maid in the middle of the night if I needed her? Walk across an open field in my night dress?

I had made a scene, to Warner's chagrin, on more than one occasion at such so-called traveler's hotels. And since I anticipated being at the Excelsior for some time I intended to make sure there was a clear understanding between me and the management.

The driver of the hired carriage drove in under the spacious portico that roofed over the entrance to the hotel. He was a husky, middle-aged man who was less than thrilled with the extent of my luggage. Fortunately, there was a porter at the depot to give him some help, but he made it clear that he wasn't going to attempt the heavy trunks by himself. "Lady," he said, "You're one fare to me and I've got my back to think of. I got an Irish wife and three chi'rrun an' I ain't leavin' go of my health for this one job."

I assured him that there would be help at the hotel and that he would be well compensated for his trouble. Once he stopped and it became obvious he wasn't going to dismount and open the carriage door for me, I let myself out and stepped down. I bade Phoenix wait and went in through the ornate doors of the hotel.

The lobby was impressive and I was pleased to note that, though it was furnished with pieces of both the French and the English style, the two breedings of furniture were not mixed but placed in charming individual groupings. It gave an intimate and elegant touch to the spacious lobby.

Looking beyond the desk, which was just off a wide set of stairs, I could see through some open double doors into a commodious and well appointed dining room. My immediate impression was that the hotel would do. It would do very well indeed.

I went to the desk, which was manned by a young man in a high, starched collar and a foulard tie. His sideburns were long, which seemed to be the fashion among the dandies. He was all attention as I came up. I announced myself and said that I had wired in advance for a suite for myself and a room for my colored maid.

He was the soul of accommodation right up until we came to the part about a room for Phoenix. That, he said, would be impossible, as they did not house Negroes under the roof of the hotel. He said that space for her could be found at a boardinghouse down the street. I had been expecting it and I immediately rapped on the top of his desk with the ivory handle of my umbrella and demanded at once to see the manager.

It startled him. I do not think he was used to ladies suddenly rapping on the top of his desk, especially with such force. I said, evenly, "Young man, I have heard this story one more time than I care to hear it. My maid is of no value to me unless she is at hand. Now, I wish to see the manager and I also wish to have my luggage brought in from the hack that is currently under your portico."

He stammered out something about not being sure if the manager was in. I rapped again with my umbrella, which startled him all over again. There were several people in the lobby and they turned to look at the commotion. It was what I intended. I expected to be heard when I spoke and I was going to start in this hotel as I intended to finish. I said, "You find the manager. And I will not take kindly to being kept waiting. Now, get about your business."

He disappeared through a door behind the desk and I laid my umbrella on the countertop and turned to survey the scene. I was pleased to note that the people in the lobby who were looking my way were not staring in disapproval but with interest at how I should make out in dealing with such a slowpoke. I was also pleased to note that the men as well as the women were universally well dressed, including one slim man with a hawklike face who was wearing a well cut five-button Prince Albert coat. As he smoked his cigar from the chair where he was sitting his eyes seemed to study me with considerable interest. I felt myself coloring and turned aside to look up the broad stairway to my immediate right.

The desk clerk appeared through the door and, holding it open, asked if I would accompany him to see the manager, who did happen to be in his office. I thanked him courteously to show that I could do without the umbrella rattling when I was treated graciously. I felt the meeting with the manager would be a very important one because I had determined, from almost my first sight of it, that the Excelsior was where I wanted to make my fortress while the trouble with Warner was resolved.

Mr. Charles Morgan, who proved not only to be the manager of the hotel, but also one of its principal owners, was a man of courtly and elegant look. He was dressed in a velvet-fronted morning coat with a ruffled shirt and a string tie. Had he not comported himself with such casual elegance and grace he might have been taken for a dandy. He was not a large man, perhaps a size or two smaller than Warner, but he had an impressive air about him that seemed to enhance his stature until he seemed bigger than he was. He rose as I entered and put out his hand. I thought he intended that we shake, but he used the gesture as a device to take just the tips of my fingers and guide me to a gilt, padded chair facing his. It was done very smoothly; he did not even come around his desk, yet I felt very well received. He nodded at the clerk to leave and then seated himself. He said, "Mrs. Grayson, let me say what a pleasure it is to have such a lady as you as our guest. Now . . . how may I better assist your stay with us? I understand you wired for a suite for yourself and that you need accommodations for your maid. Is that correct?"

I nodded, doing it with a little flip of my head that I know showed off my neck, causing it to arch backwards as I finished the nod, and gave me a view of my subject over my high cheekbones. "That is correct, Mr. Morgan, and may I say how much I appreciate your seeing me so quickly."

He leaned back in his chair, a little twinkle in his gray eyes. "Mrs. Grayson, does my finely tuned ear detect a foundation of Virginia in your speech?"

I could feel myself coloring again. I thought I'd been too long in Texas for it to be detectable, though I heard a sound in his speech that stirred memories. "Why, I suppose you might, Mr. Morgan. I am originally from Shelbyville."

His eyes twinkled more. I at first placed his age at somewhere beyond forty, but now I was not so sure. His rich brown hair was touched with gray at the temples, but his face was unlined and his hands had felt strong though soft. He said, "Horse country. I am originally from Virginia, but yours is a part of the state I felt particularly drawn to. Well, this only adds unexpected pleasure to my immediate delight in making your acquaintance." He suddenly frowned slightly. "Grayson? Grayson? I have heard that name and I have heard it in connection with horses. Is there one?"

I was immediately confused. I did not want to get so quickly into my marital state or my present circumstances. I said, a little awkwardly, "My husband, Mr. Warner Grayson, and I own Grayson Farms, which is situated some eighty miles southwest of here. We have begun a bluegrass bloodstock operation."

He tapped his desk with the flat of his hand. "That's it! Exactly. I was flabbergasted when I learned that we were to have a sure enough Thoroughbred racing stable in these confines. Well! This is indeed an honor, Mrs. Grayson. The one thing I have missed in my time in Texas has been the race meets with the Thoroughbred runners stretching out for a mile or a mile and a half and the grandstands all done up in colorful bunting with the ladies no less splendid. My friends have never been able to draw my interest to these short races, these quarter-horse races that are over in the blink of an eye."

I was very glad that Mr. Morgan and I seemed to be finding so much in common, but we had wandered far from why I had come to see him. I didn't want to become so friendly that I would lose my determination. I said, hoping to steer the conversation away from the subject, "Well, you must understand, Mr. Morgan, that we have not yet begun to race. Our colts will not be ready until next year, in the spring."

He suddenly smiled. He had a thin, intense face which was not overly handsome, but was not displeasing. He said, "And you'd like me to quit talking about horses and get to your situation. Is that correct?"

I nodded and smiled slightly. "I'm afraid so."

He leaned forward and crossed his hands on the top of his desk. "Mrs. Grayson, my clerk has told me of the predicament." He lifted his hands and let them fall. "What can I say? We do not allow colored guests in the hotel and—" He held up his hand as I started to speak. "I understand. You would not view her as a guest, but as your maid. I understand that and, if we were anywhere else but in Texas, where ladies don't seem to have personal maids, it would be no problem." He sighed. "Unfortunately we are in Texas, where ladies don't seem to have personal maids, at least not colored ones. And your maid would be sleeping under the roof of the hotel and moving about it just like any other guest." He smiled. "What would you have me do, put a sign on her that announced her as your maid?"

I could see the worst was happening. Here was a man who sincerely wanted to help me, but he was powerless. I could not expect him to make an exception for me that might bring the wrath of the town around his ears. "But what if she is not seen as mingling with the guests, but acting as a servant? She does not have to enter and leave by the guest doors. You have Negroes working here. I've seen them."

He smiled sadly. "Mrs. Grayson, we have no separate entrance for the servants. And all the people who work here wear uniforms. You will see that your upstairs maids wear one type of livery and that the waiters in the dining room a different kind." He shook his head. "I'm afraid it cannot be, Mrs. Grayson, as much as I would like to have you as a guest of the hotel. We would find accommodations for your maid, but they can't be within the confines of the hotel proper."

I sat back, thinking. I said, "You have an unfinished wing of the hotel. I believe it was built for President U.S. Grant's visit."

He nodded. "It turns on Front Street and runs for half a block. Strictly speaking, however, it is not a wing to the hotel, since the downstairs floor has been made into several small shops and a café. Only the upper part was meant to be finished into several rooms with one big suite."

"Why was it never completed? I understood there was plenty of time before Grant's visit."

He got a slightly roguish look on his face. "Let us say that certain of us took a more vested interest in the hotel in order that the great conqueror from the North shouldn't leave another mark on the South by having a wing of my hotel named after him."

I gave him an amused look. "Still bitter after all this time, Mr. Morgan?"

"No, not really, Mrs. Grayson. It is only that I prefer to name the parts of this hotel according to my own tastes. But had the president stayed there it would forever after, in legend and common usage, been known as the Grant wing. That was a circumstance I chose to avoid."

I was still confused on one point. I said, "But why hasn't it been finished since?"

He shrugged. "Money, for one thing."

I looked around his office. I said, "You don't exactly appear to be in serious straits, Mr. Morgan."

He smiled. "I'm not. Neither is the hotel. We have forty rooms and suites now. It is more than sufficient for our needs."

That made me frown. I said, "I find that hard to believe. Your hotel is famous all over this part of the country. It is a sought-after luxury."

He nodded. "That is the key word, Mrs. Grayson. Luxury. We cater to a certain clientele who want and can afford the best. This is a rapidly growing town, a busy town, a booming town. A town with plenty of money. But very few of the people here want our particular brand of hospitality. There are any number of good, respectable hotels that fit most of the needs of the people who visit here." He leaned forward. "Mrs. Grayson, if, in your telegram, you had inquired as to price we would not have answered."

It made me laugh. I said, "Why, Mr. Morgan, you are a terrible snob."

He bowed slightly from the waist. "Quite guilty as charged, Mrs. Grayson. But we still haven't solved your problem. You may have to content yourself with lesser accommodations or house your maid at some distance."

I was about to answer, but just then there was a quick knock on the door and the desk clerk stuck his head in. He said, with a quick glance at Mr. Morgan, "Pardon me,

Mrs. Grayson, but the hack driver is becoming quite impatient. What shall I tell him?"

I opened my purse and took out two ten-dollar bills. "Give him one of these and then split the other between two of your porters and have them bring my luggage in and put it somewhere convenient."

The clerk glanced at Mr. Morgan. "Shall I have it taken to the Rose suite?"

I answered for him. "That has yet to be determined, young man. Just have it brought in and ask my maid to wait outside. Or find her someplace comfortable."

Charles Morgan was twirling a pencil in his fingers when I turned back. He said, "Have you come to some decision?"

I stood up. "Yes. I'd like to see that wing."

"It's not finished, Mrs. Grayson."

"I'd like to see how unfinished it is."

He got up, laughing slightly. "I must say, aside from being our most attractive guest, you are certainly the most unpredictable."

The wing was just off the corner of the west end of the main building. We entered through a locked door and were immediately in a spacious area that could serve as parlor or ballroom or whatever anyone could desire. Out of this room a door opened onto a wide porch that looked out over the inner courtyard. The porch itself, which was railed and decorated with wrought iron in the New Orleans fashion, acted as a hallway to the other rooms that occupied the wing. There were four in addition to the apartment at the end, which, owing to the size of the receiving room, could be made into a very commodious apartment of three or four rooms.

I could see the pipes myself but I asked Mr. Morgan if the plumbing was in. "Oh, yes, indeed," he said. He pointed upward. He said, "You can't see it from the street because of the false facade that makes the roof seem to slant. Actually it is flat over most of the hotel and supports a very large cistern or reservoir, which provides us with running water. We are able to raise hot water from a boiler in the basement through steam power. And, of course, you can see that the gas for lamps and for heating is in place. A fireplace was planned for this room, I believe." He looked around. "Ah, yes, there is the base of the chimney."

I walked over to one of the windows in the big space that still waited to be divided into several rooms. I could see down on the street below and, by looking to my right, see the wharf and the steamboats. Standing on a balcony outside one of the huge windows I could watch the business of the whole town.

Of course none of the rooms had been wallpapered or furnished. But, except for the partition walls in several places, most of the structural work was done. And the view from the long porch into the courtyard was spectacular. It had a beautiful viewing pool and casually placed tables and chairs and was dominated by several huge cypress trees that were liberally bestowed with hanging moss. It was the very vision of southern gentility.

Mr. Morgan and I stood in the middle of the big room. He said, smiling, "I suppose you are now satisfied that the place is not quite habitable."

I said, slowly, "How much would it cost to finish, Mr. Morgan? This apartment and the rooms down the wing?"

He frowned. "Mrs. Grayson, may I inquire what your motives are? So far I haven't even discovered how long you intend to stay with us as a guest. Might I know that?"

I said, carefully, "I can't give you an answer to that right now, Mr. Morgan."

He studied my face for a moment as if searching for some sort of answer. He said, "I see."

"Shall we go back to your office? I'd like to make you a proposition and see how well it sits with you. I noticed a stair descending at the end of the porch near the last room of the wing. Does that staircase exit onto the street?"

He had been about to lead me through the door. He stopped and frowned. He said, "There's a gate there. It exits through the gate. Mrs. Grayson, you have my curiosity mightily engaged. Perhaps you'll answer a few questions for me before we go much further."

"In your office."

When we were seated, with the door closed at my request, I said, "Can you at least give me an estimate of the cost of finishing the rooms and making an apartment out of the large space?"

He chuckled softly. "Mrs. Grayson, I hope you are not thinking of buying it. I hardly believe we could sell a wing of the hotel. That wouldn't seem quite right somehow."

I waited.

He looked up at the ceiling and thought for a moment. Finally he took a pencil and scribbled some figures on a paper. After a moment's hesitation and a sigh, he said, "The best I could say, in round numbers, would be about twenty thousand dollars. Of course that doesn't include furnishings. The hardware is in all the rooms, including the one you call an apartment, that is, the basins and taps and bathtubs and commodes and other fixed appliances. But, yes, about twenty thousand."

I said, "I heard the clerk mention the Rose suite as intended for me. Is that your best?"

He nodded slowly. "One of the two we think of as our most luxurious. There is a seven-foot bathtub in the Rose suite and the fixtures are gold plated. The bed sheets are silk, for instance."

"And what is the cost of that room? I am not asking to see if I can afford it." I smiled.

He smiled. "That room is let for forty dollars a night or two hundred for a seven-day week."

It was about what I had expected. I sat quietly for a moment, doing some mental calculations. I said, "I have a proposition for you, Mr. Morgan. A business proposition involving your hotel."

He leaned forward slightly. "That is somewhat surprising, my dear lady. And somewhat abrupt. I don't believe you have been under this roof quite an hour yet."

"Nevertheless," I said. I put my hands together at my breast. I was very conscious that Mr. Morgan had been scrutinizing me as something more than a prospective guest of his hotel. I did not mind. I was not a woman who was too foolish or too proud not to take advantage of my endowments. Men certainly used all of theirs to their best advantage, whether it was expertise with a gun or a handsome set of shoulders or a head for figures and calculations. I said, "Mr. Morgan, I propose to pay for the immediate completion of your west wing, including having the best apartment designed to my wishes. You set an estimate of twenty thousand dollars on such a project. Very well, I am more than ready to underwrite the cost of finishing the apartment and the other four rooms. As to furnishings such as curtains and rugs and furniture, I am willing to underwrite that cost as well, with the understanding that they would remain my property."

He was looking at me with his mouth slightly agape, surprise and disbelief on his face. He said, "My dear Mrs. Grayson, you astound me. Whatever are your intentions?"

I said, "In return I would be willing to pay a lease of four thousand dollars a year for the whole wing for the period of five years with an option for another five at the completion of the initial period. Any time I am not in residence and any time rooms are unoccupied you would be free to rent them, with sixty percent of the revenue coming off my lease."

He sat staring at me.

I calculated that the apartment should rent for at least fifty dollars a day when I was not using it and it should be reasonable to expect to rent it at least one hundred days a year. That would return three thousand dollars a year to me against my lease. The other four rooms should produce another five thousand dollars easily. That would net me six thousand dollars per annum and would pay for my lease and, in five years, pay off my initial outlay of twenty thousand dollars. In addition, I would have free lodging for both myself and Phoenix during that period.

Mr. Morgan said, "You are quite serious."

"In my purse, Mr. Morgan, I have a letter of credit from the Houston Trust Bank. It is in the amount of one hundred thousand dollars. In the morning, as soon as the banks are open, I will put that letter on deposit and you may begin work at once."

He shook his head slowly. "I must say that you have certainly taken me aback." He paused for a second. "May I know, Mrs. Grayson, why you would want to take on such an endeavor?"

I smiled sweetly, but there was no sweetness in my voice. "This is business, Mr. Morgan. Do my reasons matter?"

He studied me. "I'm not sure. I'd like to be completely certain of the latitude of this proposal. May I ask if you are acting for your husband?" He suddenly flinched slightly. "I hope I have not offended. You're not a widow, are you, Mrs. Grayson."

I shook my head. "No. Mr. Grayson is alive and well as of three days ago."

"Are you acting with his knowledge?"

I frowned. "I really don't see what that has to do with our discussion, Mr. Morgan. I have independent means, as well as an independent spirit."

He nodded. "The latter is certainly evident, my dear lady. But I am still intrigued by your interest. Is this to be the new headquarters for the Grayson Thoroughbred stable, or just a branch office?"

In truth I could not tell Mr. Morgan why I was making the proposition. I certainly hadn't planned it. I had known about the unfinished wing and after asking about it I had asked to see it. At some point, I had done the rapid mathematics of the plan and made the offer. I didn't know if I was doing it so I would be more independent of Warner, or if I wanted to be associated with such a beautiful place, or if it was nothing more than a way to find an accommodation for Phoenix under the same roof with me. The middle reason was probably involved, but I think my main concern was to get around a stupid and unfair custom. Of course there was also the fact that I expected to make money off the deal, just as I would make money off the house I'd bought so quickly in Tyler. Thinking of that almost made me smile. Apparently there was nothing like leaving my husband to bring out the real estate urge in me.

In answer to his question I said, "Mr. Morgan, this business is completely independent of my husband. That is all I can tell you on the matter. However, I should point out that if we strike a deal, that wing will be under the control of Mrs. Warner Grayson and my maid will occupy that end room by the stairway, where she can enter and exit without disturbing either your staff or your guests."

He suddenly put back his head and laughed out loud. When he finally stopped, he looked at me and said, "Damn, Mrs. Grayson, if I don't believe this is all about a room for your maid. I have met some unusual people in my life, but you may be among the most delightful. And the most surprising. And the most audacious." He looked away for a second. "And the most strikingly beautiful, if a single man may make such a remark to a married lady."

I made him a curtsey from my chair, a symbolic one. "Married or unmarried, a woman never takes amiss having her vanity confirmed."

He laughed with delight. "You are a credit to Virginia, ma'am. An absolute credit." He stood up. "But I think we had better see to getting you settled. I fear your poor maid must think you have been swallowed up in this big, white edifice."

I stood also. "I should not expect an immediate answer to my proposal?"

"I have a partner to consult with, Mrs. Grayson. He is a minority partner, but a partner nevertheless. I expect I owe him that."

"I'm sorry. I'm the impatient type."

He held up a finger. "However . . ." He smiled. "Your audacity has at least carried one part of the field. I will immediately give orders for the necessary furnishing to be put in that last room of the *Grayson* Wing and I will have one of our engineers make sure that the room has functioning gas and water." He gave me a little bow. "Your maid will be allowed to move in this very evening."

I clapped my hands with delight. "Oh, that is wonderful of you, Mr. Morgan. I am ever in your debt."

"The Rose suite is very near the door that leads into the west wing—or the Grayson Wing, I must remind myself. No more than ten yards along an inner corridor. So she will be able to attend you day or night. Will that be to your satisfaction?"

"It is most grand hearted of you, sir."

He gave me a keen look from behind his desk. In a slightly tentative voice he said, "Would I be presumptuous if I asked you to dine with me tonight?"

I hesitated. It must have been plain on my face that I wasn't sure it was proper. I said, "Oh, Mr. Morgan, I wouldn't want to take you from your duties. I—" I was floundering and it must have been obvious.

He put up a hand, smiling very nicely. He said, "Please, Mrs. Grayson. I propose only that we meet over a meal as two possible business associates. We'll dine in the hotel. I will meet you there, if that would be to your taste."

I suddenly felt very silly. If the situation with Warner hadn't been what it was I'd have accepted without a second thought. But with that troubling rift with my husband looming just under my thoughts it hadn't seemed fair or right or something. I said, "Of course, Mr. Morgan. I didn't mean to give the impression I wouldn't enjoy such an occasion. Will you have time to confer with your partner before tonight?"

"Possibly." he said. "Possibly. Shall we fix a time? Say, eight o'clock?"

"That should give me plenty of time to recover from my trip and get on some decent clothes."

He stopped as he came around the desk and stood very close to me. I was aware that he was taller than he seemed and that there was a powerful presence about him. He had an aura that gave a completely different impression from the smiling face he turned on me. I thought he was a man who could be very dangerous if he chose. I had an idea that he had not always been a hotel keeper. There was something about the soldier in the way he carried himself, straight as a board, but with a casual confidence. He seemed small because he was fine boned. Close, now, I could feel that he was a very powerful man, and more than just physically. He did not frighten me, but he did pique my interest.

I had been so busy and involved since we'd reached Jefferson that I had scarcely thought of Warner, since we had been on the train. It was an odd sensation when, for so many years, he had occupied the majority of my thoughts. Whatever was to be done or how it was to be done or when it was to be done were lines of thinking that had always included Warner and needed either his opinion or his permission. And now I was suddenly making major decisions without a thought to whether he might care. It was an amazing transformation and might have made my knees tremble if I had not been still so angry with him.

I missed him, though. A thought would rise to my lips and I would turn to locate him and give voice to the thought only to find that he was not there and was not going to be there. I had grown very accustomed to his presence and it was a shock to suddenly be so alone again. In a way I had surrendered my independent spirit to Warner and now I found it difficult to regain it as a natural part of my makeup.

I was conscious that I was dressing very carefully. I chose to wear a fairly daring gown that was off the shoulder with a wide vee neck that showed more than ample cleavage and displayed my small waist. Helping me dress, Phoenix said, "Lawd, Miss Laura, these here look like yo' huntin' clothes. Who you be going after?"

Of course I had not told her very much about what transpired while she waited so patiently outside with the luggage. The room had flabbergasted her and she was still convinced I had worked some kind of miracle. She said, "Does the white folks know what they got under they same roof?"

She, even more than I, was aware of the racial injustice that was abroad, but I think she took it better than I did. I had arranged for her supper to be sent up to my suite where she would stay until I returned and went to bed. All in all, it looked as if the arrangements were going to turn out most satisfactorily. I still didn't know, however, why I was committing myself to what seemed like permanent residence in Jefferson. Had I given up on Warner? Was there no way for us to reconcile? Were he and the ranch now in my past? Was I, as I was undoubtedly giving Mr. Morgan the impression I was, available?

They were difficult questions. I did not have any answers.

But they must have been troubling Phoenix, because, as I prepared to go downstairs, she said, a little frown on her face, "Now, Miss Laura, you got to remember that us is still married. Mr. Warner done made hisself a mistake, but we gonna let him get over it. Shoot, we don't need to be playin' up to the manager of no hotel. We quality! Yes, ma'am. And don't you forgit it."

She had reminded me of my morals and my fidelity and I let her get away with it. Phoenix had a way of speaking that took you off guard. You didn't realize she had overstepped her bounds until she had, and by then she'd hurried on to some other portion to be served, usually dessert, so that you were so thrown off by the sudden ladle of honey that you forgot the reprimand she deserved. The worst of it was that she did it wilfully and consciously and she knew that you understood and connived in allowing her to get away with absolute sass.

* * *

He was seated at a table in the far left end of the room. I saw him almost immediately as I came into the dining room, even though it contained at least twenty tables, ten to a side. As I walked down the middle of the room, he rose and waited for me. I was aware of heads turning on either side of me, mostly men's. In a conscious gesture that I could not seem to break myself of I unhesitatingly lifted my posture and tilted my head back just slightly. The gesture thrust my bosom forward and exposed more of my front. Not that my gown needed any help. It was of a pale yellow, simply cut, and made of the finest silk. I was wearing a shortened single strand of pearls that went perfectly with the ivory and white lace fan I was carrying. My gown was ankle length and each step exposed the tip of the white patent-leather slippers I was wearing.

As I neared him I could see that Mr. Morgan was wearing a white linen suit complemented by a light tan silk vest and a four-in-hand tie of the same material and color. They went very well with his light golden complexion and his dark hair. When I reached the table he extended his hand and once again guided me to my chair with the tips of my fingers. I thought it a very pretty gesture.

He had seated me so that I was facing the entire restaurant, giving me the best vantage point in the room. His back was to the wall, and I was thus placed nicely on his left rather than across the table from him. His first words were, "I think it is unnecessary for me to compliment you on your appearance as that has already been done by every pair of male eyes in the place. And the few female eyes that allowed themselves the luxury of envy."

I smiled, though I could feel myself coloring. I said, lightly, "Mr. Morgan, do you always talk so to your prospective business partners?"

He pretended to give the matter some thought. "Now that you mention it, Mrs. Grayson, no. But then I have never had a business partner who looked like you. Champagne?"

There was a bucket of iced champagne already waiting.

I nodded and he looked up. Instantly a waiter was at our side, pouring the sparkling French wine into flute glasses. He made a toast to mutuality, which I believe I never heard of before, and then we drank. It was a wonderful wine. I had not seen the label, for the wine bottle was wrapped in a white napkin, but I knew that it was a vintage year. Apparently, Phoenix had given her hunter lecture to the wrong party.

He said, "I've taken the liberty of selecting the menu for both of us. I hope you don't think that too presumptuous of me."

"Not at all. I rather think you know the chef better than I."

He laughed and made a signal and a waiter came forward with a screen and blocked us off from the rest of the dining room. Mr. Morgan said, "I think I've been a good sport and shared you long enough with the rest of the diners. Now I intend to have you all to myself."

I said, "My, I wonder what Mr. Grayson would think of that?"

It bothered him not in the slightest. He said, "I'm sure he would do the same. I'm sure he has done the same."

That made me smile. Poor Warner. The idea of creating an intimate dinner in the midst of many would never have crossed his mind. My smile was a trifle on the sad side. But I said, in Warner's defense, "Oh, yes, for himself. But he is possessive. I must warn you, he is the most possessive of men." The man threatened to go looking afield in search of a woman who could give him a son.

Mr. Morgan said, "I hope you have no aversion to shellfish. Oysters."

"Oh, no. On the contrary."

"Good, because we are going to start with a dish I think is unequaled anywhere. Our chef calls it oysters flambé. The raw oysters are allowed to steep in apricot brandy for several hours. Then they are brought to the table in a chafing dish, a dash of pure spirits is added, and the concoction is set aflame here at the table.

Scallions and mushrooms are added just prior to the cooking as well as a dash of lemon juice to cut any sweetness that might have remained from the brandy."

"It sounds marvelous."

"I think you will enjoy it. For an entree we are going to have southern fried chicken, except the chicken is boneless filets of white meat served in a cream sauce. Along with that we shall have garden vegetables."

"It sounds a perfect menu."

"Ah, but for dessert we are to have cherries jubilee. Have you ever had that concoction?"

"I can't say that I have."

He smiled. "You will not be disappointed. I brought my chef in from New Orleans. He is worth the exorbitant salary he commands." He nodded his head toward the screen, indicating the rest of the dining room. "Out there are a few souls who are asking their waiter why there are no prices on the menu. My policy is—if you have to worry about the cost of eating here, you can't afford it."

"Mr. Morgan, I have to tell you once again, you are the most frightful snob!" I picked up my champagne glass and toasted him. "I find it very refreshing. By the way, your first toast was to mutuality. That was rather strange. Whatever did you mean by it?"

He smiled easily. He appeared a very cocksure man. "Why, nothing, dear lady. Only that we should discover many mutual interests."

"Does that mean we are mutually interested in my proposal about the wing?"

He sat back in his chair. "That's a subject I think needs more exploring, Mrs. Grayson. I think I am going to need to know more about your plans."

I started to speak, but just then the waiter arrived with the chafing dish. He set it on a stand by the table and, with a flourish, lit the contents. After that we became preoccupied with the dinner and did not speak more of business until after the dessert.

Finally, we were sitting with coffee and brandy and I was wishing my gown were not quite so tight waisted. I

said, as I stirred cream into my coffee, "I don't understand what my intentions have to do with a straightforward business proposition. Whether I am here or not
here shouldn't matter to you in the least."

He inclined his head toward me in a gesture that
somehow seemed intimate. "Ah, but that is where you
are wrong, Mrs. Grayson. Your presence or absence is
going to bear great weight in my decision."

"I don't understand why that should be."

"Perhaps if I told you a little about myself you might
have a better idea. My motives are not necessarily those
of other men. Sometimes I do things that are contrary to
what would appear logical."

I looked at the screen, which was covered in silk and
bore some sort of oriental design. "Then please tell me."

Mr. Morgan surprised me when he told me that he was
forty-five years of age and that the greatest disappointment of his life had been that he couldn't make a career
out of the army. "I was enrolled at Virginia Military
Institute as early as they would have me, which was at the
age of fourteen, when I had received sufficient tutoring to
pass their very strict entrance requirements. But then, of
course, came the war." He said it with such a bitterness
that his whole face changed, growing hard and angry. "I
was not able to get into the fighting until the last year and
then only by disobeying orders and posting myself to a
regiment that was in the thick of it." He smiled. "I was
audacious and I was a very young second lieutenant. All I
can say for that brief career was that I didn't get anyone
killed."

At the conclusion of the war he attempted to return to
VMI and take up his studies once again. "Of course by
then it was in Yankee hands." I could see him grit his
teeth. "The professors and instructors and the comman-
dant were Union officers. But I forced myself to suffer it.
I would learn all I could from them. I would subjugate
my pride for the sake of a better future." He sighed.
"Unfortunately, I discovered that I could not stick it. I
was able to last a year and then I had to leave. I never

graduated. However, it was not wasted time. I learned a great deal about the enemy and about his ideas of Reconstruction. I was able to put those to good use in the years to come by knowing how to bypass and use their very own methods. It allowed me an advantage in any matters concerning the Yankee bureaucracy, which was damn nigh strangling the South."

The waiter came to pour us more coffee. Mr. Morgan waited until the man had left. "I am not going to bore you with many details, but suffice it to say that I prospered in cotton and timber and any sort of perishable goods that needed to be moved by rail or by steamship. I was what you might call an expediter. Because of my knowledge, businessmen would come to me to make a thing happen. It paid well. I came here three years ago because I could see the possibilities and because Texas was not so overrun by the Yankees as Virginia." He paused and looked at me. "You know, of course, that the Old Dominion will never be the same."

I nodded. He was a very passionate man on the subject.

He leaned toward me. "I hinted at this before, Mrs. Grayson, but I bought this hotel because they were about to build that wing in honor of General Grant." He sat back. "I still think of him that way rather than as President, but it is a small matter."

I was taken somewhat by surprise. "You bought an entire hotel to stop them from building a wing for Grant?"

He nodded slowly. "You know, of course, that they took General Lee's estate at Arlington and turned it into a cemetery. Did you think I'd pass up a chance to insult the man who had done that?"

I could do little more than look at him. I'd been about to take a sip of coffee and I just sat there like a dolt with the cup halfway to my mouth. Finally I returned it to the saucer. I gained control of my surprise. "As interesting as all this is, Mr. Morgan, I'm not sure what it has to do with my proposition."

He said, arranging himself comfortably sideways so that he was facing me, "Just this, Mrs. Grayson. I could very easily afford to finish that wing. Your proposition is a fair one, though I can see where it is weighted in your favor and how you arrived at your figures. But two years have gone by and that wing has not been completed, obviously because I didn't much care. I enjoy being a hotelier because it allows me to appear a gentleman without a great deal of work. I enjoy dealing with the class of people my establishment attracts. I'm not sure I would enjoy it as much if it were bigger. You think me a snob because I charge high prices. I charge high prices to keep the volume down. Everyone would like to stay at the Excelsior. But I don't want everyone to stay here."

Now I did take a sip of coffee. "I don't see what that has to do with me."

"Mrs. Grayson, the only reason I would be willing to lease you that wing is if I could be certain of your presence a good portion of the time. Do I have to make it simpler or is that plain enough?"

"I'm a married woman, Mr. Morgan."

"My given name is Charles. I wonder if you would consider calling me that?"

"Not in the foreseeable future."

He laughed. "Yes, you are a married woman. You are married to Warner Grayson, a man who is justifiably famous across Texas because of his ability with horses. You have a Thoroughbred farm some eighty miles from here with what I would presume to be very comfortable quarters. Yet here you are in Jefferson making plans for a residence that would have to be viewed as something more than temporary. I find that very curious."

"You're implying I've left my husband." I was aware of his eyes, which were gray, boring into me. It was very easy to understand why I felt an aura of power from him. He was a very powerful man with fixed ideas of what he wanted and how to go about getting it.

"I'm not implying anything, Mrs. Grayson. But here you are and your husband is nowhere around. I find it difficult to believe that you've come on ahead to make a nest for him to rest up from the work of horse breeding. I would imagine he has difficulty finding an hour to call his own, let alone time for a vacation in Jefferson. That leaves the question of what you are doing here."

I almost shivered. He frightened me. He was so powerful, so magnetic. I would never have believed that I could be attracted to another man, not once I had been with Warner six months. I wished mightily for Phoenix's presence. She would put in plain language what I should do. She would say, "Miss Laura, you gatha yo' skirts 'bout you an' march right on out of there. Get plumb on away from that man."

But Phoenix wasn't here, and if I couldn't handle this mild flirtation I wasn't the woman I thought I was. I drew my head back slightly. "Mr. Morgan, let me acquaint you with some facts. I consider myself a lady of culture. However, for the past two years I have been stuck out in the pine woods giving help and comfort to my husband while he undertakes to put a new enterprise on its feet, an enterprise that you are correct in assuming requires almost all of his time. If you had thought further you might have realized that it is I who needs a rest from the horse farm. And that, as simple as it is, is what I am doing in Jefferson and why I would like to secure proper accommodations for myself for the near future. I am assured that Jefferson is full of the type of society I will enjoy. For that reason and that reason alone am I here and making you this proposition."

He studied me for a long time without blinking. Finally he took his napkin out of his lap and dropped it on the table. "Sadly enough," he said, "until better information surfaces I am forced to believe you. I rather hoped you had left Mr. Grayson."

I ignored that. It was too close to the truth. I said, "Knowing what you do, how do you intend to treat my proposal? Or do you still have to discuss it with your partner. If you have a partner, which I doubt."

"Oh, no. You are wrong there. I have a partner who

owns twenty percent of the hotel. I gave him that to take off my hands a wife I married in haste."

I was amazed again. "You—you had a wife you traded for an interest in your hotel?"

"She would divorce me only if there were an eligible marriage waiting. She's in society here, you see." He gave me a dry smile. "So much for the Jefferson culture you spoke of. He would marry if there was a continuing remuneration. Presto. I traded a full-time, meddlesome wife for a know-nothing minority stockholder."

I would have laughed if almost anyone else had been telling me the story. I said, "But what is to keep him from accepting the stock in the hotel and then divorcing the woman, who would then look to you?"

He frowned slightly and looked past me for a second. Finally he shrugged. "Fear, I would expect."

"Of you or of her?"

He smiled. "Does it really matter? So long as it is effective?"

He walked me to the foot of the stairs in the lobby. To go farther would have not been proper. He said, "Thank you for an exquisite dinner."

"Isn't that what I am supposed to say?"

"I wasn't speaking of the food." He bowed over my hand and took a step backwards. "I'll give you my decision concerning your proposal within forty-eight hours. Meanwhile, anything you need for your comfort or convenience will be provided. Goodnight, Mrs. Grayson."

"Goodnight, Mr. Morgan."

I went up the stairs with a great deal on my mind. Suddenly I missed Warner very badly. I wondered if I had done too good a job of covering my tracks, because I feared it was imperative that he arrive soon.

5

Warner

If Laura had ever set foot in Athens in her entire life I
could find no trace of it. Not of her, nor Phoenix, nor
Albert, nor even a pair of matched bays and a gilt-and-
black carriage. I had asked the sheriff, his deputies, every
banker in town, every hotel manager, the proprietors of
every conceivable boardinghouse, the passenger and
freight agents for the railroads, the telegraph operator,
the clerks and manager of every mercantile, grocery, and
dry goods store, as well as every livery and every feed
store. I had even commissioned a crowd of boys, at fifty
cents a head, to scour every barn, stable, corral, and
carriage house for a span of matched bay horses. If she
was in the town she was doing without groceries, without
shelter, without money, and without feed for her horses.
There were four cafés and one restaurant in the town
where Laura could have eaten. No one even remotely
answering her description had been in. There were two
cafés that catered to Negroes. Neither Albert nor Phoenix had been in either one. The sheriff had finally told
me, "Mr. Grayson, I don't know the circumstances and
you don't seem to want to talk about them, but we don't
get many strangers here and I can guarantee you that if

an elegant lady in a proper carriage with two black servants had come to town I would have heard about it."

I spent two days looking through the town for her and in the end I had to agree. I stayed over for a second night because I had nothing to rush home for. The next morning I saddled up and rode sadly and worriedly toward Tyler. I could not for the life of me figure out where the woman had got to. Naturally there was always the thought in the back of my mind that she could have had some accident or been the victim of road agents. It was unlikely, but it was still a possibility. It did nothing for my state of mind.

It was early afternoon when I rode into Tyler. I headed straight for the bank and dismounted and tied my horse. If Quince wasn't in I'd simply have to wait for him and try and get something straightened out about the ranch account. Laura was gone, but she might come back and in the meantime I had to keep the ranch running and I couldn't do that without being able to get at the money.

I had never felt so frustrated in all my life. I was not a man who shied from problems or conflicts, but, damn it, I wanted them to be the kind I could face, the kind I could confront, the kind I could get my hands on. I simply didn't know how to handle mysteries or situations where a man couldn't do anything, right or wrong. I had patience. Anybody that spends his life working with animals learns patience first thing or he doesn't do well with animals. You can't see inside a horse's head and he ain't going to tell you what he's thinking, but you can pick up little signs by the way the horse acts or reacts. But, hell, you can see the damn horse. There ain't a man alive can handle or train a horse he can't lay hands on and can't even catch a wiff of. And that's exactly where I was. The only thing I could figure to do was go in the bank and somehow get a bundle of cash, leave it with Charlie to run the ranch, and head for Virginia to where Laura's kin lived. She might not be there, but she communicated with them. I knew that for a fact. I might not be very welcome, but I was going to where her family lived and I was going to camp on their doorstep until they told me where she was. After that I would see what it would take to get her back home. Whatever it was I was going to do it.

I went into the bank and Robert Quince was in. He got up as I came in his office and we shook and I sat down. All during the ride from Athens I'd been wondering exactly what I was going to say to the man. I couldn't come out and say my wife has run off and I don't know where she is. I couldn't say she was sick at home or off visiting. I was unwilling to lie and I wasn't about to tell the truth. I said, "Robert, I've got a little problem here. It's basically just a matter of procedure, but I need to change an account around a little."

Right then he surprised the hell out of me. He said, "You must be talking about the ranch account, about it requiring two signatures. Well, that's all right. It's all taken care of."

I stared at him. I think my mouth was hanging open. I said, "What? How'd you know that?"

"Why Mrs. Grayson was in and made the arrangements. She said she was going to be gone. I'm to be the second signatory."

I was still staring at him. I had been in this self-same bank five days earlier. Or six. I was starting to lose track. But I had been in this bank and no one had said a word to me about Laura having been in. True, Quince hadn't been there, but the god damn tellers had. I said, "Exactly when was this? When my wife was in?"

He wrinkled his brow and looked up at the ceiling for a second. "Let me see . . . It was the morning of the day she left. I'm almost certain of that. What is today, Friday? It would have been Tuesday. Yes, Tuesday."

"The day she left?"

He looked at me, blinking. "Yes. The day she took the train."

I had never much cared for Robert Quince. Oh, he was a good enough banker, but he always seemed too full of himself. He was always dressed as if he were expecting company and I had never seen him without a pair of gloves near to hand—dress gloves—or with a hair out of place. He was always shaved and always smelled of cologne and his vests were always too damn shiny. But right then I planned to play him very carefully. "So you are to sign, or countersign, the checks I write on the ranch account?"

He nodded. "Those were my instructions, yes."

I said, "Well, I'm going to need about three, no, make that four thousand dollars right now. In cash. Some large bills, but a number of ones and fives and tens."

He wrinkled his considerable brow again. "That's quite a sum of money, Mr. Grayson. May I ask what it's for?"

I leaned forward very slowly, as if I were having trouble hearing. "What?"

"I said I'd like to know what you need such a large sum for."

I sat back in my chair and regarded him in amazement. "If I heard right, it sounds as if you are presuming to interfere in my business. But since you are a banker and a smart man I know that can't be right. So there's got to be some other reason for you to ask such a damn fool question. What is it?"

His face went crimson. He said, "Here now, Mr. Grayson, you've got no call to talk to me like that. I'm merely carrying out Mrs. Grayson's orders."

"You are not going to compound your foolery by telling me that my wife ordered you to interfere in my business?"

He was looking nervous. He said, trying for his dignity, "I know what she told me. I was to act as cosigner. The function of a cosigner is to make sure the funds requested are for a legitimate reason. There is no foolery in that."

I put my hands on my knees. "Quince, you are on very dangerous ground. You don't know one fucking thing about the horse business and I do not believe my wife would have given you the slightest authority over the ranch funds."

He was flushed half out of his chair. I could see a vein throbbing in his temple. He said, hotly, "I am not used to being called a liar, sir!"

"Fine. Prove you're not. We'll send a wire to Mrs. Grayson and get the straight of the business." I gestured. "Just write out the wording of it. Nothing could be more fair than that. Put it any way you want to, except make it clear that I believe there has been some misunderstanding. You write it out and I'll take it down to the telegraph office right now. We could have an answer in two or three hours."

His eyes were still hot, but he sat back down. "Fine," he said. "And I will expect your apology with her return wire."

"You'll get it if what you say is true."

He pulled over a piece of paper and then took up a pen and dipped it in an inkwell. For a moment he held the pen poised over the paper. He glanced up at me, then put the pen down and leaned back in his chair. "I don't think this is a very good idea, Mr. Grayson."

My instincts had been right. He knew where she was but he was under orders not to tell me. That left him two alternatives: he could tell me willingly or he could tell me unwillingly. The only difference between the two was the physical inconvenience to himself if he chose the latter. I said, "Robert, I find myself in a hell of an embarrassing position. I'm sure you can guess what it is. You can get me out of that situation by just going ahead and putting down where you were going to send that telegram. I don't want to have to say the words. I'm sure you can understand that. So please don't make me ask."

He gave me a stony look. If his heart had not been in his attitude before, it was now. He had himself a piece of work and he was absolutely relishing it. He was really going to humiliate me, make me admit I didn't know where my wife was, make me admit she had left me, run off, absconded from our marriage. I'm sure he had always felt my slight disdain for him, but he'd wanted the money in his bank and he'd had to take it. Now he could pay me in full.

Or so he thought.

He said, "I'm sorry, Mr. Grayson, I can't help you."

"You mean you won't help me."

He leaned forward and put his forearms on his desk and laced his fingers together as bankers always do when they are going to tell you no. I don't know why bankers do that particular gesture, but I knew I'd seen it more than several times. He said, "Mr. Grayson, I am going to ignore your previous insults and state my position so you will not misunderstand. I am under instructions from your wife and I intend to abide by those."

"I'm going to ask you one more time to write an address on that piece of paper. That's all. Do that and I'm out of your hair and you'll have that apology."

"I have told you I can't do that."

I frowned at him. The son of a bitch was starting to irritate me something fierce. With a little heat in my voice I said, "Look here, Robert, you are a god damn banker and that's all. You got no business mixing in between a man and his wife. Who the hell do you think you are?"

He said, as prim as he looked, "Nevertheless, Mr. Grayson, I have my duty to Mrs. Grayson, who is a depositor as well. She has asked that I keep her whereabouts to myself. I intend to honor that instruction."

I stood up. I took a step to his desk so that I was towering over him. I said, "Then I reckon I'll be taking my money out of this bank. Mr. Quince, get your ass up and go close out all my accounts. I'll take the money in cash. And you better have that much."

He sat there looking well satisfied with himself. "Mr. Grayson, I can not close out your accounts. Not without another signature. The only account you can draw on is your household account and that one—" He reached behind him and got a big, red bound ledger book and turned pages in it until he found the right one. "That one, as of today, has a balance of eight hundred sixty-three dollars and fifty-five cents." He looked up. "Do you want to cash that one out?"

I sighed. "You will have it the hard way, won't you, Robert? Now I know that you are not from Texas and I am allowing for that. In Texas, there are certain parts of a man's business you just don't get in. What is between me and my wife is just that, between us. As for the money, in Texas a man and a woman hold everything in common in a marriage. That's law. Whatever I got she also has got and vice versa. So I don't need your say-so or anybody else's to take my money out of this bank. I don't like you very much, Robert. Never have. I always wondered why that was before, but today I see the reason. You are a pissant, Robert. A pissant. You look like one, you talk like one, and you act like one. I do not mean to be insulting, I'm just telling you in case you might want to try a change for the better. So, now you either write out where my wife said she could be reached or you go get my money. All of it. All three accounts."

He had gone a little pale and sweat was starting to glisten on his long forehead. "Mr. Grayson," he said, and I could hear a little tremble in his voice, "I am going to have to ask you to leave my bank. Don't make me have you thrown out."

The man never ceased to amaze me. I leaned forward. "I just gave you two choices. You didn't take either one. Now we are going down to see the sheriff."

He leaned back further, trying to get away from me leaning over him. "I'm not going anywhere with you, Mr. Grayson."

"Yes you are," I said. "You are illegally holding my money and I'm going to take you down to the sheriff and have you explain it to him. I reckon he is going to take my side. I doubt if the sheriff cares for you anymore than I do."

"The sheriff has no authority to make me release funds to you."

I smiled. "Probably not. But that ain't the point. You see, Robert, while you and I are in his office arguing about the matter it is going to get heated. You are going to tell him that my wife instructed you to cosign my checks and I am going to call you a liar. I'm going to say that you made the whole thing up."

"You would be lying!" He wiped at his forehead. The man was getting nervous.

"I know that and you know that, but the sheriff won't."

"What makes you think I don't have a witness."

"Because I know my wife and she would have wanted as few people to know about her affairs as possible. That's why you don't have a witness."

He stared back at me and then swallowed so that his Adam's apple bobbled. "It still won't get you the money."

"Robert, Robert," I said, as if I were talking to a child. "It ain't the money I'm after. Ain't you figured that out yet? Now, what is going to happen is that, as I say, we are going to get to arguing and things are going to get a little hot. And you are going to say something, or I'm going to claim I thought you said something that was a pure insult. And right at that instant I am going to hit you in the face with my fist as hard as I can. Now Robert, I am bigger than you are and take my word for it, I can hit pretty damn hard. I figure to break your jaw that first lick. But if I don't, while the sheriff is separating us and helping you up I'm going to get in another lick and I figure for certain that one ought to do it. You are pretty fine boned and a little light in the yoke so I don't think it's going to take much to break your jaw. You ever seen a man with a busted jaw, Robert?"

He was looking at me with his eyes getting wider and wider. The kind of talk I was making was not the kind usually heard in a banker's office. It was way off his range. "He'll arrest you and I'll file charges."

I gave him a pained expression. "Naw, Robert. Hell, this is Texas. You don't arrest men for getting into a fist fight. Ain't enough jails to go around. But you never told me if you've seen a man with a busted jaw. Have you?"

His eyes were fixed on me. He made a tiny shake with his head.

I said, "Well, since you never have, let me explain it to you." I motioned up toward my mouth with my finger, baring my teeth as I did. I said, "See, they got to wire your teeth together to keep your jaw still so the bones can knit up. Course, that closes your mouth tight so you can't eat. What they got to do then is the dentist pulls one of your front teeth so you can run a suction tube in there so you can take in some milk or something. Ain't a real pleasant way to get your dinner. If you're lucky and already missing a tooth, the dentist don't have to pull one, which I understand ain't no picnic when you've got a broken jaw. You missing a tooth? Raise up your lip and let me see."

He said, and now his voice was shaking, "I am not going to the sheriff's office or anywhere else with you. You're a crazy man."

My face went hard. I said, "Oh, yes you are, Mr. Robert Quince. This is mighty serious business with me and I will have that address out of you or you will wish you had never heard my name." I walked around his desk. As I came up to him he swiveled around in his chair to face me, drawing back as if I were going to hit him right then and there. "Listen Robert, I don't think you understand this. This ain't no kind of little children's game we are playing here with rules and politeness and all that. My marriage is at stake here. For some reason you know where my wife is and I don't. I don't like that. I don't like having to say the words but you finally made me. We've had some trouble that has got to get straightened out. But I can't straighten it out without getting the chance to talk to her. So this is very serious business, Robert, maybe the most serious you ever dealt with in your life. Right now I got one thing on my mind and that is finding out from you where she is. And you can bet every last dollar that is in this bank that I am going to find out before it is all over. I don't know what kind of shape you'll be in but you will tell me. Now let's go see the sheriff. I'll drag you there if I have to."

For a moment he seemed frozen, as if he couldn't move and would ever move again. Finally, very slowly, he turned back to his desk, scooting his chair forward as he did. He picked up the pen, dipped it in the inkwell again, and then scribbled a few lines. He held it out to me, his face tight and white, his lips compressed. His hand was trembling so badly that the paper fluttered as if it were in a wind. I reached out and took it and looked down at the lines as I walked back around Quince's desk to the customer side. Jefferson. I thought to myself that I should have guessed. More than once I had heard her mention the place and its "culture." She was a bug on culture. I'd never known anyone to use the word quite as much. But then, she was from Virginia so I reckoned it was just something they grew up thinking about. When I'd visited up there they'd certainly talked about it enough. I had never been quite sure what was meant by the word, but I had been assured by Laura that I didn't have any so I needn't trouble my head over it.

Quince said, sullenly, "You have caused me to break my word, Mr. Grayson. I hope you are satisfied."

I glanced up and gave him a pleasant look. "I'm sorry Robert, but there couldn't be no other way for this. You should have told my wife when she asked you to keep a secret that you weren't about to get mixed up in family business. I'm glad it was only your word that got broke."

He said, stiffly, "I wish you would leave my office."

I glanced up again. I was still trying to make out the name of the hotel. Mr. Quince's handwriting had been none too steady. "I still need the money, Robert. In fact, you better make it five thousand, three thousand in big bills." I stared at him, waiting. His mouth worked for a second, but he didn't say anything. Finally he got up and went out the door of his office. I folded the paper and put it in my pocket. The day I'd come to town she had still been somewhere close. Where that was I didn't know, but the reason the ticket agent at the depot didn't remember her was because she hadn't bought her ticket by then and hadn't boarded the train. But where in hell, I wondered, could she have been? All three of them. And a team of horses. Did she know someone out of town she could have stayed with that I didn't know? Hell, it was too big a mystery for me.

Robert Quince came back into his office. He marched straight to his chair and sat down stiffly. It appeared his bent dignity had not come straight yet. He said, "You can pick up your money from the cashier. You still have to put your name on the withdrawal. I have also instructed the cashier that in future all accounts will require only your signature. Now I wish you'd get the hell out of here and never come back. I no longer want you as a customer of this bank."

I sighed. "Aw hell, Robert. Don't take this so hard. An hour or two from now you will have cooled off and got your banker's head back on and you'll kick yourself from here to breakfast if you let a good customer get away."

"Good customer! God damn bully is more like it. I never want to see the sight of you or any of your tribe."

I laughed. "Nevertheless, Robert, I'll give you time to think it over. By the time I get back from Jefferson we'll all have forgotten about this little incident." I turned for the door.

He let me get almost out before he said, with some satisfaction, "You'll not get her back, you know. She bought a house right here in town."

I whirled around. "What? What are you talking about? What house?"

He gave me a tight little smile. "Not so happy to hear that, are you? Yes, she bought a house from the bank. A nice little cottage. Bought it the first day she got into town. Saturday, I think it was."

I was dumbfounded. "I don't believe you."

"Would you like to see the sales contract? She's as big a bully as you are. Beat me down four full points on the interest. Bought it furnished and then insisted I send people over to have it cleaned up so she could move in immediately."

I shook my head, slowly. That woman was sly as hell. She'd figured my every move in advance and then taken steps to foil me. All the time I'd been running around Tyler she'd be sitting right under my nose. For all I knew she'd seen me riding around like a chicken with its head cut off. I said, "I'll be damned."

Robert Quince puffed himself up. He thought he was upsetting me. "Still don't believe me? Your Negro servant, the man, is still living over there. Take a ride by. You'll see your carriage team and your carriage."

"Where is it?"

He jerked his thumb. "Not a quarter of a mile from here. On the northwest side of town. The houses are scattered, but it's a spanking white little cottage. Four rooms."

I laughed. "You think Laura, Mrs. Grayson, bought that to live in? Hell, Robert, she needs four rooms just for her clothes. That was her hideout. But you watch. She'll find a way to make a profit off it. Much obliged, Robert. And don't feel like you broke your word. It was given under the influence and that don't count."

"What influence?"

"A very willful woman's influence and that's stronger than one-hundred-fifty-proof rum. Good day to you, Robert. Stay out of family disputes."

I didn't have much trouble finding the place, mainly because the carriage was sitting outside the carriage house. As I neared I could see that Albert was working around it, giving it a good washing. Just beyond, in the little holding pen, I could see the span of bays standing quietly. I almost laughed out loud at the size of the cottage and Quince citing it as the reason Laura wasn't coming back to me. Hell, Laura couldn't have got along with herself in a place of that size, let alone if anybody else were there, even if it were only Phoenix. As for the cost, I figured she had jewelry she was careless with that had cost more than the little frame dwelling. It was the kind of place a wage hand lived with his young wife while they were still so close they could have slept together on a long pillow.

I rode into the yard and around the house. Albert glanced up, started to go back to what he was doing, and suddenly realized he'd recognized me. He was holding a big sponge in one hand and working out of a bucket of soapy water. He dropped the sponge in the bucket and wiped his hands on his overalls. He got a big smile on his face as I came up to him and stopped. "Why, look heah, heah Mr. Warner. How you be, suh?"

"Hello, Albert. What the hell are you doing here in town when you've got work back on the ranch."

He looked bewildered. He said, "Why, Miss Laura she done tol' me to stay right here at this house and look after matters. She got a bunch o' clothes an' stuff in dere. She give me strict instructions."

I said, "Well I'm giving you stricter instructions. You load her clothes up in the carriage and then hitch up the team and get on back to where you belong."

The confusion was plain on his face. He said, "But, Mr. Warner, she tol' me 'specially to stay right c'here. I suppose ta go up de telegraph office ever' day see if they is word she be sendin' fer me. She was most exact what I was to do." He looked worried. "An' Phoenix, she tol' me, too." He swallowed. "I most near scairt of that woman."

I stepped down out of the saddle and dropped the reins. I said, "Who hired you, Albert? Who pays your wages?"

"Why, you does, suh."

"Then who you reckon is the boss?"

He thought about it for a moment, turning it over and over in his mind. He said, "Well, looked at it like that, I reckon you be de boss."

"Then get busy doing what I told you."

He still looked worried. "What 'bout Miss Laura? An' mos' specially, what 'bout Phoenix."

I had to smile. "You don't have to worry about Miss Laura. So far as Phoenix goes, well, I don't know what to tell you, Albert. Don't you reckon you could whip her in a fair fight?"

He showed me a lot of eye white. "That jes' the thang, Mr. Warner. That woman don' fight fair."

"I'll keep you safe, Albert. Now finish up with the carriage and start loading it."

"Dey's some furniture in dere. What 'bout that?"

I opened the back door and looked in. I said, "Leave it. Maybe we'll get lucky and somebody will steal it. Just you make sure you don't miss any of Miss Laura's clothes. Then we'd both be in trouble."

For a moment I stood just inside the door of the little house, looking around. It felt strange knowing that Laura had been there no more than two or three days past. It seemed I could almost detect a faint aroma of her perfume. It fairly made me ache inside, missing her. I felt as if I had a hole in my chest where she had once been. I had never been a demonstrative man so far as a lot of hugging and kissing, but I sure would have paid a lot for the chance to change right then and there.

I came out to find Albert putting away his bucket and sponge. He said, "Mr. Warner, had I ought go to de telegraph office today?"

I shook my head. "I'll go for you, Albert. You just get on back to the ranch and report to Mr. Charlie. I'm heading that way myself and you might tell him so. I might even catch up with you on the road." I stepped into the saddle. "Now you get busy."

As I rode away he was already starting into the house to bring out a load for the carriage. I may not have Laura back, I thought, but I was heading the current in that way, at least with some of her clothes.

I went by the train depot and verified that, indeed, Laura and Phoenix and an immense amount of luggage had gone to Jefferson. The ticket agent said there was no way he would forget the lady because he was fairly certain it was the most baggage he'd ever seen in his life belonging to one person. He said, "I was working the Dallas station when that English actress, Lillie Langtry, come through on her American tour and she didn't have half that much gear."

After that I took time to eat a late lunch and then to go by the feed store and put in an order for the next month. We didn't buy horse feed by the sack, we bought it by the boxcar and I let the feed store make a small percentage off us for hauling it out to the ranch. I could have bought it directly from the feed mill, the quantity we dealt in, but it made for good feelings all around to give my custom locally and saved me the trouble of taking hands from other work to come and get the feed.

My immediate plan was to go to the ranch, give Charlie some money and get him lined out, and then figure to be back in Tyler the next day and take the train for Jefferson. I was going down the road at a pretty good clip, thinking about it, when a sudden thought sprung up and struck me right between the eyes. I suddenly pulled Paseta down to a slow walk, a maneuver that made him swing his head back and forth to show he didn't care for the gait. But I didn't give a damn what bothered him, I was suddenly bothered by my own business. I had been thinking I would just throw a couple of clean shirts and maybe an extra pair of jeans in a valise and set out to fetch Laura home. But it had suddenly occurred to me, thinking about packing for the trip, that she might be more than a two-shirt job. In fact, from the way she was acting, I might not own enough clothes to see me through the chore of working her around and getting her started for home. The very qualities I had always admired in Laura were now the very qualities that were likely to give me the most trouble. When somebody is working in tandem with you, you are glad to see that they are tough and independent and able to look out for themselves and able to be a help to you. But when that large rock is no longer in the right place and must be moved, ah, then the very strength and solidness you once depended on becomes a hindrance to your happiness.

I pulled Paseta up and sat there, in the middle of the road, thinking. Was I wise in rushing right after Laura? She'd only been in Jefferson a couple of days and wouldn't even have settled in yet. She would have been so busy with making herself a nest that she wouldn't have had time to give me much thought and certainly not to miss me. I wondered if I shouldn't use time as my ally. It was clear I hadn't used it wisely up to the present point. I sat there in a quandary while Paseta champed at the bit and made it clear he'd like to be moving along.

Finally, I shook my head and urged the horse on. I needed to sit down in a chair with a glass of whiskey and a smoke and stare out a window for a time. I had enough difficulty trying to figure out how an ordinary person thought and would react; I doubted that I had a chance in hell with Laura.

It was late in the afternoon by the time I got to the ranch. I left my horse in the barn and went on up to the house. I saw Charlie briefly at the barn, but told him I didn't have anything to talk to him about yet and I'd send for him when I did. Jambalaya waylaid me when I went into the house and tried to get me to eat something, but I said I wasn't hungry. I didn't tell her I'd eaten in town because that would have hurt her feelings. I said I'd maybe want something in a couple or three hours and that contented her. I imagine she thought I was pining for my wayward wife and was too heartsick to eat. She informed me that "that man" was back, meaning Albert, and I thanked her and went on upstairs.

I took a position by our bed. There was a rocker nearby and I pulled it over to the window and sat down. The nightstand on my side was near to hand so I could have an ashtray and a bottle of whiskey with a glass. I got myself settled and lit up and poured myself out a drink and started staring out the window. It was a good view out the back of the house. I could see all the barns and the training rings and see several of the nearby pastures where we were keeping the year-old colts. The younger colts, the ones that had been born the past spring, were kept up with their mothers in big corrals that were not quite visible from my vantage point. It was a pretty impressive sight and represented no small investment.

At that thought I felt a little twinge inside and I wondered if maybe that was the burr that lay between Laura and me, that it was mostly her money that had financed the project. I had put up some money, not a fifth of what Laura had invested, and a lifetime of knowledge. To her credit, Laura had always insisted that mine was by far the more valuable contribution, but I had never left off feeling strange about using a woman's money. The partnership had been created before our marriage and it had bothered me then. I had thought I would feel different after we were married, but that hadn't been the case. If anything I had driven myself harder to somehow force the farm to start paying off as soon as possible. I had been worried about our first crop of colts, the horses I would be sending to race meets beginning the next spring and early summer. I guess they could have been world beaters, but in my eyes they came up short of what I was hoping for. Charlie said to me once when I was worrying, "My sainted aunt, Mr. Grayson, we got some good horses here. You done a hell of a job of breeding. We can't run them hard yet, but they are timing out on the gallops."

But, apparently, nothing could keep me from worrying and, like a spectre, there was Laura every time I came back in the house. Not that she ever said a word. Never by tone or voice or gesture had she shown the slightest concern. Her faith in me was complete. At least so far as my being a horseman went. And even that made me angry. Hell, she should have questioned me, should have worried along with me. God damn it, it was mostly her money. What did she think I was, a magician? Hell, I wasn't even allowed the luxury of the possibility of failure. I was Warner Grayson and any horse I touched automatically became a winner.

It was too much of a burden. Didn't she realize I was human? Didn't she realize I could fail, that I might not be able to produce? She hadn't produced a son had she? She—

I stopped thinking right there because the argument was starting to come back to me. I took a long drink of whiskey and stared out across the land. I had started the fight and I had finished it. In the middle we'd both fought, lashing out viciously without the slightest idea of why we were fighting. Our only intention had been to cause each other pain. I could now see where the problem lay. I just didn't know what to do about it.

I sat there until dark came, until the moon rose. Finally I became aware of Jambalaya at the door. She said, "Mr. Warner, you got to eat yo'self somethin'. It's mighty late."

I nodded and got up. "Go start me a steak and whatever you got to go with it. I'm going to shave and take a quick bath and then I'll be right on down."

For a long time I thought and studied on the problem and it wasn't until almost twenty-four hours later that I came up with some thinking that made sense to me. My friend the ex bank robber turned professional gambler and saloon proprietor, Wilson Young, had a philosophy I'd never paid much attention to. Wilson said a man had to get himself a cardinal rule and live by that rule and never violate it. He said that if a man did that he would allow the small change to take care of itself and would never find himself getting upset by the minor details, the ribbon clerks and the other nuts and bolts of life, that could make a man forget what was important. Wilson's cardinal rule was to never loan money to a stranger on a moving train. He said that he'd made the rule ten years before and had never broken it and he'd drawn considerable strength and self-satisfaction from the philosophy.

He said, "It gives you a firm foundation of self belief to know you are strong enough to carry through on one main principle. Not only does it give you a firm operating base, but it improves your vision so you don't confuse the aces with the deuces."

Of course, that was just some of Wilson's droll sense of humor, but there was truth in it. Laura and I had gotten so tangled up with the nuts and bolts of everyday life that we'd gotten to where we didn't know a deuce from an ace.

The ace was our marriage—the firm foundation we needed as an operating base. But we'd violated the principle of our marriage and as a consequence we'd gotten twisted up and forgotten what was important.

I didn't know if I was going to be able to explain that to Laura or not, but I got up at the exact moment I came to that conclusion and went to hunt up Charlie in his cabin. The hour was late and he was asleep, but it didn't matter. I gave him three thousand dollars and told him I was going to Jefferson on the next day's train and he was to tend to matters. I said that I would let Albert drive me in in a buggy so we wouldn't end up with a horse in town. I told him I didn't know how long I'd be gone, but I'd keep him posted by wire.

As I was getting up to leave, Charlie said, "Fetch her back, Mr. Grayson, even if it has to be at the end of a lariat."

I wrinkled my brow. "I wish it could be that simple, Charlie," I said softly. "But I greatly fear that it won't. Hold the fort."

6

Laura

I was surprised to find Phoenix waiting up for me when I got back to my rooms. She was in the bedroom sitting in a wing chair against the wall. I said, "Well, my heavens, Phoenix, are you keeping close watch on me?"

She got up to help me undress. She had a grim look on her face. "I reckon somebody better had. Sashayin' 'round this hotel with the likes of that Mr. Morgan. 'Sides that, I figured I'd need to be here to he'p you cut yo' way out that dress. My lord, I don't reckon this button gonna budge."

I turned around and gave her a look. "You have seen me in this dress before, Phoenix, and you didn't make any remark about it being too tight. Or daring."

"That," she said firmly, "was at home. Wadn't up here with that slick piece 'o work runs this here place."

I gave her a frown. "Phoenix, now stop that. Mr. Morgan is a perfect gentleman."

She was still working at the clasps along the side of my dress. She said, "Oh, he perfect ar'right, but it ain't at bein' a gen'lman. But from what I heared he could git you out this dress lot faster'n I am."

I whirled my head around. "Phoenix, what are you

talking about? How would you know anything about Mr. Morgan?"

She got the last stay loose and helped me take the dress off from the front. She was nodding her head all the time. "Oh, I knows, I knows. I taken my supper in the kitchen with some most reliable folks, folks has worked here a good while. I knows me a pocketful about Mr. Morgan. Mighty nice behind that screen 'round the table. You done forgot you a married woman, Miss Laura?"

I sat down on the end of the bed to take off my silk stockings. I said, "Well, you certainly have been making yourself free about the place. Just how did you happen to end up eating in the hotel kitchen?"

She was hanging up my gown in a big closet in a corner of the bedroom. "I gits around," she said primly. "Wadn't all that much trouble. Whole hotel is a buzzin' 'bout you and the high mucky-muck what slicks his way 'round here. I knows most of what they call de staff here. Mighty high-falutin' buncha hired hands."

"And you were spying on me from the kitchen, is that it?"

"I took a peek. Ain't gonna deny it. But I got my job an' I gonna do it. Yes, I had me a peek. You an' that Mr. Morgan havin' you a little suppah behind that screen. They tell me ain't the fust time he use that screen. Oh, that gen'lman, he got hisself a reputation."

She said it all with a great deal of satisfaction, as if she had caught me red-handed and I should immediately be contrite. I didn't know whether to laugh or be cross with her. I settled for middle ground. "Phoenix, you are not supposed to be sashaying around this hotel, to use your word, as if you were one of the paying guests. You are going to get me in trouble with Mr. Morgan if you keep up such antics." I went over to the dresser and found a nightgown and removed my chemise and slip and other undergarments and put the gown over my head, letting it slide into place. Then I sat down at the dressing table where Phoenix had laid out my combs and brushes and looked at myself in the mirror as I slowly began brushing my hair. I said, "Are you paying attention to me, Phoenix?"

"Oh, yes ma'am, I's payin' attention. Question is, who is you payin' attention to? Ain't that Mr. Morgan you better worry 'bout gettin' mad at you."

I glanced at her in the mirror. She was standing with her arms crossed under her ample bosom. "Now just what do you mean by that?"

"I reckon you knows what I means."

"Are you talking about Mr. Warner?"

"I ain't sayin', Miss Laura. I ain't sayin' a word. Only I'm beginnin' to wonder jest what we doin' here. What this all about? We runnin' here, runnin' there. I can't see where we tendin' to our main business."

I had used some light rouge to highlight my cheeks, and some face powder. Now I began to take them off with cold cream and a soft cloth. I said, as severely as I could, "Phoenix, I want you to understand that absolutely nothing happened between Mr. Morgan and me tonight. Do you understand that?"

She was still standing behind me with her arms crossed. Disapproval fairly steamed off her. She said, "Yes ma'am, I understand that. I also understand that most things start with nothin' happenin'."

I turned from the mirror and gave her a sharp look. "It's late, Phoenix, and I want to get to bed. I'm going to overlook your absolute impertinence. I expect you are missing Albert. Well, don't worry. I'll send for him in a few days."

She uncrossed her arms. "Oh, I ain't worryin' 'bout my man. I knows where my man is and what he's doin'."

I glared at her. "Go to bed, Phoenix. And since you've made yourself so comfortable in the hotel kitchen you can just get your breakfast there."

"I'm goin' along," she said, moving across the room. She put her hand on the doorknob. "I know I won't have no trouble sleepin' tonight."

I opened my mouth to say something pointed to her, but she was gone before I could get the words out. I just shook my head, finished my preparations for bed, and then climbed onto the big, luxurious mattress that was covered with silk sheets. The only gaslight left burning was close to hand and I turned that off and settled my head on the pillow. There was a long row of big windows to my left that faced onto the main street. Moonlight and the soft sounds of the night filtered through the filigreed curtains.

I shut my eyes, expecting sleep to come quickly. It had been a long day and night and a great deal had happened. I was tired, both in mind and body. I did not expect to, but I found myself thinking about Warner and wondering what he was doing and how he was faring. I wondered if, by now, he had figured out where I'd gone. I wondered whether, if he had, he would come to Jefferson. Then I wondered what I would say to him, what he would say to me. I wondered if there was anything really to say. Thinking about that disturbed me. We were still man and wife and it seemed to me we still had matters to discuss. I found myself missing him, which surprised me. It really had not been that long. We'd been separated for longer periods than five days. I supposed the gulf seemed greater between us because I had put miles between us and, more important, plans. I had already bought one house and here I was trying to lease the wing of a hotel. Such actions more than hinted that I was taking strides toward an independent life. For a moment I lay there visualizing a life without Warner. I could do it, but it felt barren and lonesome.

Barren. The word he'd called me.

With resolution I burrowed my way into the pillows and turned off my mind, willing myself to sleep.

I had hardly finished the breakfast that Phoenix brought me the next morning when the flowers started arriving. I had eaten in my bedroom, wearing just my dressing gown. Phoenix went through the sitting room to answer the summons at the hall door and returned, looking grim, carrying a basket of flowers in each hand.

Startled, I said, "My word, Phoenix, where did you get those?"

She said, "Oh, they be more." She set the baskets down and waved through the door to the parlor. "Jes' bring 'em on in here. Set 'em anywheres. I'll tend to 'em later."

I was a good deal startled to see two uniformed colored porters come in with four more baskets. There were flowers of every description, all the way from yellow roses to crimson carnations and yellow jonquils. I pulled my dressing gown around me even though I was sufficiently covered. I thought it a little presumptuous of Phoenix to bring the porters into my bed chamber.

I said, "That will quite do, Phoenix. Get those men out of here."

She waved them out and then shut the door. After that she tilted her head back and looked down her nose, first at me and then at the flowers and then back at me.

I said, "Now what is all this, Phoenix?"

She said, "They is a card with de flowers. But if you ask me what it be all about then I say it is more of this nothin' happenin' that gets things started. Course, I'm just a poor ignorant country woman don't know nothin' 'bout nothin'."

"Give me the card." I held out my hand.

She marched over to a basket of long-stemmed blushing pink roses and plucked out a small envelope. She stepped back. She said, "I reckon this be tellin' you this the way they welcome ever'body to de hotel. Even the men folks."

I gave her a short stare and opened the envelope. Inside was a small sheet of cream-colored note paper. In a neat, precise hand was a message from Charles Morgan. It began by thanking me for my company of the evening before but quickly got to the business at hand which was an invitation to a late luncheon picnic. He thought it would be a capital idea to get away from the bustle of the town for a few hours and for him to show me the attractiveness of the Jefferson countryside. He added a sentence, "I think such an informal occasion will allow us to better judge our amicability as business partners." I looked at the line a long time. It seemed very handy, very convenient to throw in as a final clincher. Business was conducted in offices and amicability could be judged there much better than over a picnic table with bees buzzing about and birds calling. My father had always said that business was business and should not be confused with anything else, especially anything involving personal feelings. But, still, Mr. Morgan had made it clear that he did not think nor act like other men and to assign him motives as I might others would be a mistake. Perhaps his motives were simply what they said in the note, to get away from town and size each other up. My proposition could hardly be considered an average one. I had been in town one day and was proposing to finish and lease a wing of his hotel. Besides, I was not afraid of Mr. Morgan. I considered him a gentleman and so long as he acted that role I would never need the small revolver I carried in my purse.

Which served to remind me that the gun was a little bulky when I used a small purse. I had once seen an elegant lady who carried a muff with a clever design inside that held a small pistol. I determined, as soon as was practical, to find a leathersmith and have such an article created. With pockets on the side it could also serve as a purse.

I looked back at the note. Mr. Morgan had stated his intention of calling at my suite at ten o'clock to receive my response. I sat there, waving the letter idly, and staring at the ceiling, thinking. Phoenix said, "Ain't no chance them flaw'rs is from Mr. Warner, be they?"

I gave her a startled look. "Phoenix, when did you ever know of Mr. Grayson sending me flowers?"

She wiped her hands on her apron. "Yes, that's right. Mr. Warner was never de man to go in fo' de lightweight stuff. He gen'lly jest sent you houses an' ranches and such truck."

"Just when did you become Mr. Grayson's champion?"

She looked around. "I guess when de water goes to gettin' too deep you go to lookin' 'round for de man got the boat."

I shook my head and laughed. "Four days ago you were disgusted with Warner. Now listen to you."

She pointed at the note. "That looks like fox tracks 'round the hen house to me. I bet I don't have to be no witch woman to figure out where all this come from, these flaw'rs and that piece of writing you holdin' there, makin' up yo' mind 'bout something."

"Now what makes you say that?"

"Miss Laura, you know the 'mount of years I been with you. You reckon I'm deef an' dumb an' blind. I seen that expression on yo' face bunches of times."

I put the note on the table. "Mr. Morgan will be calling at ten o'clock. I want you to lay out my riding clothes. I want—"

She got a horrified look on her face. "You don't mean them tight britches of yours 'bout like puttin' on another skin."

"If you'd waited—No, I want the riding pants that have the flare in the thighs, the jodhpurs. And I want a severe blouse with a black vest. And be sure the boots are shined. We're going on a picnic."

"Me and you is going out in the country to eat on the ground?"

Sometimes she tried my patience beyond my strength. "Mr. Morgan and I are going on a picnic. The note is an invitation. I have decided to accept."

She turned her head and walked toward the clothes closet mumbling something.

I said, "What?"

"Nuthin', nuthin'."

"What were you saying, Phoenix?"

"What would I be sayin'? Ignorant ol' woman like me."

"What?"

She shrugged. "I was jus' speculatin' how Mr. Warner could use that there Mr. Morgan down on de ranch."

I gave her a suspicious look. "What is that supposed to mean?"

"Oh, not a thing. We gets here late yesterday afternoon and he got you havin' suppah with him before the sun goes down. Now here it is today and you ain't drawed three good mornin' breaths and already he talkin' picnic."

"What has that got to do with the ranch?"

"Oh, I was jus' thinkin' Mr. Warner could use this Mr. Morgan for a breedin' stud. Fast as he is, Mr. Warner ought to be able to get some fine race hosses out of him."

I wanted to laugh but I managed to keep a straight face. "Phoenix, you ought to be ashamed of yourself. That is very disrespectful."

"I thought I was payin' the gen'lman a compliment." She gave me an innocent look. "Don't you be wantin' eagerness in a stallion?"

"That will do, Phoenix. By the way, you will be accompanying us."

"I know that."

"I just said it. How could you have known it?"

"Oh, they is things a body knows don't have to be said. I knowed it because I done planned for it."

"Phoenix, I think I am a little old to need a chaperone. You will be going along to serve."

"Yes ma'am. I gonna serve. The closer he gits to you the more I gonna serve. I don't know what gonna be in the picnic basket but he gonna have some of it shoved in front his face every time he move."

I received Mr. Morgan in the little sitting room, already dressed in my riding clothes. He seemed surprised at my outfit. He said, "Were you planning to ride this morning?"

We were both standing. Phoenix had let him in and I entered from the bedroom. He was wearing another lightweight linen suit of a pale blue color with a dark blue tie. On second meeting he appeared more handsome in an elegant way than I remembered him. Nevertheless, I did not ask him to sit down. I said, "No, I thought I would ask if you could furnish me a mount for our picnic. I would enjoy a ride."

It took him off guard for a moment. I thought he'd envisioned us together in a small buggy heading for some secluded spot with me wearing a very accessible dress. He recovered quickly, however, and said, "Of course. As a Virginia lady I should have known you would enjoy a ride. I will join you. Do you ride side saddle?"

I gave him a thin smile. "I grew up riding hunters and jumpers, Mr. Morgan. Do I need to answer that?"

He gave me a small bow. "Of course not. You are wearing jodhpurs. You would ride astride. I don't know what I was thinking." He nodded his head around. "Have you found your accommodations satisfactory?"

"Very comfortable. Of course I will feel more comfortable when I'm in more permanent quarters."

Now he gave me a thin smile. "That's a conversation to be had over cold chicken and a light wine."

I said, "By the way, I will be bringing my maid."

If he gave a sign of displeasure I didn't see it, unless it was a very tiny tightening around the mouth. "Of course. I had intended to bring my manservant. We can't very well carry a picnic hamper on horseback. Your maid can ride with my man in the buggy. I will see to all preparations. What time would you like to leave here?"

"How far is it to the picnic spot?"

"Oh, a pleasant hour. Of course I seldom dine before one or one-thirty."

"Then let's leave at half-past noon."

He nodded and opened the door. "Shall I call for you here? I'll have the horses out front."

I said, "I think it would be more seemly if we met in the lobby."

He bowed. "As you wish."

When he was gone I went into the bedroom and told Phoenix to get me out something to wear around town. "I want to have a little look-see. We really haven't seen the place yet." I sat down on the edge of the bed and slipped off my riding boots and began unbuttoning my blouse.

Phoenix stared at me. "You gon' change clothes now and then change again?"

"I just wanted to let Mr. Morgan have an idea what he was in for."

She shook her head. "You the beatenest lady I done ever seen. Put on yo' britches to make shore he understands you done locked up the kitchen for the night and now you gonna put on a frock and go sashaying around town. What if he sees you? What he gon' think."

I said, "Frankly, Phoenix, I don't care what he thinks."

Jefferson was an astonishingly bustling and busy town. The main commercial district was a few blocks to our left as we exited the lobby of the hotel, back two blocks from the wharves and docks. There were stores of every kind and more banks than I had ever seen concentrated in one small area in any city of any size. I took a moment to step into a leathersmith's store and describe what I had in mind to the man behind the counter. He never turned a hair, just acted as if he got orders every day for a muff-holster-purse. He said, "You want fur on the outside, rabbit or beaver is the best I can do. You want her satin lined ain't no problem, but why don't you let me do the outside in a nice chamois skin or a suede?"

I left the revolver with him to fit to its hidden pocket and he said I could have the item in two days. It was the very spirit that seemed all about the place. Walking down the sidewalk no one ambled as if time were valueless. People hurried right along, giving the impression they were busy and had places to go and people to see.

I left Phoenix, over her protests, back at the hotel. I was determined to teach her that I did not need her protective presence every step I took. I did not know what had gotten into her. Certainly she had always, even from the first, been solicitous of my welfare, as any good personal servant should be, but since we'd left the ranch she'd turned into a positive mother hen.

I walked the streets, taking in the hurried bows of the

gentlemen and the sidelong looks of the ladies, searching for a bank to my liking. It wasn't terribly important which one, so long as it had not just started up the day before. I finally settled on a correspondent bank from New Orleans, the First Federal New Orleans. It was a rather large building with an imposing lobby and a number of customers bustling about. I was not prepared to wait and did not have to, as soon as I made my business plain to a clerk. I was quickly shown into the office of the senior vice president, Mr. Clive Dupree. Mr. Dupree was getting on toward mellowness both in girth and years. Most of his head shone in the bright gaslights and his fat little cheeks were flushed from either good will or good whiskey. He took my letter of credit and said they would be pleased to have me for a customer. I got the idea, fairly quickly, that letters of credit of one hundred thousand dollars didn't raise anyone's eyebrows in Jefferson.

I opened two accounts, one with a small amount to write checks on and another that would draw six percent interest. I had never been one to let my money lie idle. Mr. Dupree gave me a fatherly pat on the shoulder as he walked me to the door. He said, "Feel free, Mrs. Grayson, to come to us for help on any matter, no matter how small."

I wanted to tell him that I was not a helpless female who would have to come running in case my checkbook didn't balance. But I said, "Thank you, Mr. Dupree. You advertise in your window that you compound interest monthly on accounts over ten thousand dollars. Be sure you put my money in the correct place." I gave him a little smile. "I'm familiar with all forms of compounding, especially where my money is concerned."

I left him with his fat little mouth open and went back to the hotel. He had asked me a surprising number of questions in a short time about who I was and what my plans were and what did I intend to do with my money. I succeeded in skirting all his queries while at the same time making it clear to him that the money I was placing under his care would be visited often. It sometimes made me shudder to think how easy it was for unscrupulous men to play upon unsuspecting and uninformed women. I thought that a good job for myself might be to start some sort of school in the town that would educate women about the ways of business and how they could best protect themselves. I felt certain that Phoenix would not approve.

She would say, "Why, Miss Laura, that ain't one bit ladylike. What would you want to be goin' an' doin' somethin' like that fo'? You let them other ladies look out fo' theyselves. You tend to yo' own business. Lawd knows you got 'nough of it in a mess."

The picnic spot was as close to perfection as I guessed was to be found within riding distance of Jefferson. It was down near a small creek of sparkling water that was lined by cottonwood and sycamore and elm trees. The grass was low and lush, almost as if it had been carefully mown. I had expected nothing less of Mr. Morgan. I was only curious how many other women had preceeded me to the same virgin spot. Even though we rode for almost an hour, Mr. Morgan had taken me on a circuitous route. I kept up with the turnings and I was fairly certain we were no more than two miles from town. Mr. Morgan sent his man, James, on ahead with the buggy containing the picnic and the other paraphernalia, along with Phoenix, who had given me a warning glare as they disappeared out of sight, leaving us on horseback by the side of the road.

Mr. Morgan cut an even better figure in his riding clothes than in a suit. He wore khaki twill riding pants with knee-high, highly polished boots and a loose silk shirt with an open throat and full sleeves. The shirt, especially, showed off his lean hard frame at its best, while making him seem elegantly dressed even while at casual pursuits. I was a little surprised to see that he wore a sidearm. Whatever the pistol was, it was in a military holster with a top flap that was secured so the pistol couldn't fall out. When I asked him about it he just smiled and said, "With such precious treasure to guard what fool wouldn't go armed?"

James and Phoenix set up a delightful little folding table and spread out the picnic on its top. There were two small, ingenious folding chairs and a large awning stretched over our heads to protect us from the afternoon sun. James and Phoenix withdrew some hundred yards or so to eat their own lunch. I expected them to stay and serve, but Mr. Morgan dismissed James with a wave of his hand and Phoenix had no choice but to follow. Now there were just the two of us and the picnic luncheon. There were cold roasted chicken and potato salad and a salad of mixed fruit. There was a wonderful chilled wine that Mr. Morgan said was a French Chablis. I didn't know. I just knew it was crisp and tasted like nothing I had ever tried before. Finally, for dessert there were eclairs filled with whipped cream. I had never had a problem with my weight, but that lunch would have frightened a woman wearing a corset.

We neither one of us talked much while we ate. One bottle of the Chablis lasted us through the food and part way through the dessert. Mr. Morgan opened a second bottle that he took from an interesting canvas bag that was filled with ice. As he opened it he said, "This wine was made four years ago. Four years ago I would have never dreamed that I would be sitting in this idyllic spot having a picnic with the most strikingly beautiful woman I have ever seen. Are you very tired of compliments about your hair?"

Up on a little hummock I could see James and Phoenix sitting in the buggy under a large, shady oak tree. The horses had been taken out of the traces and were grazing nearby. The buggy was near enough that I could see Phoenix glance my way even while she was eating. Mr. Morgan said they were having the same food as we had except for the wine. "I don't believe in giving domestics alcohol, especially when they are about their tasks. In fact I would as soon they didn't use it at all. Being of a lower order they are not as well equipped to handle it."

I hadn't answered that remark, but now I did respond to his compliment. I said, "Mr. Morgan, you surprise me. I would not have thought you'd be a man who would mix personal affairs with business."

He gave me a gallant smile. "Believe me, Mrs. Grayson, only someone like you could tempt me to do so."

I gave him a smile in return, only mine was not so pleasant. I said, "But you convict yourself out of your own mouth, Mr. Morgan. Did you not enter into a business arrangement to have another man ready for your wife to marry before she would consent to a divorce? Surely that is a mixture of the two."

It did not faze him. He shrugged. "Perhaps on the face of it. But the end of my marriage was as much a business proposition as any I have ever dealt with. There were no sentiments involved, certainly not on my part. She gave me certain conditions and I set out to meet them because the end result was to my gain. Was that not business?"

"If I am prying tell me so, but I find it an interesting situation. Are there any details you could reveal?"

He gave me a keen look. "This seems a trifle unfair to me, Mrs. Grayson. When I try to ask you about your personal life you make it clear that it is out of bounds. Now you ask me."

I lifted my wine glass and sipped at the cool, crisp liquid. "Perhaps I would be more inclined to share confidences if I had received confidences."

He leaned back in his chair and smiled a Cheshire cat smile. "I think I am being played, Mrs. Grayson, but it really doesn't matter. My wife, my ex wife, wanted to marry a man who would maintain her position in local society. She wanted someone who was presentable and had some means of his own. She wanted a smooth transition. The man I gave the twenty percent to fitted that bill of particulars."

"There was no, uh, spark of romantic interest? Just any man would do?"

"Oh, he had to be presentable, of course. But romantic interest?" He put his head back and gave a short laugh. "What he really needed was a strong arm to carry her to bed after she passed out. My wife was in love, all right, but with the bottle. She was a drunk. She was a weak drunk who could not face life sober. I cannot abide weakness." As he said the last he looked up at me with a significant glance.

"She was young, I take it."

"She was old enough. Certainly at the last. I had my way to make in the world and a certain degree of prosperity to attain. She was a hindrance."

"I would think," I said dryly, "that it would take an exceptionally strong woman to be by your side constantly."

He gave me a hard look. "Is my company such a chore?"

"Certainly not. But then we are not married. Attitudes and actions change between men and women once they become man and wife. I sometimes think that a marriage license is a license to be uncivil and hurtful."

He looked at me over his cheekbones. "Are you speaking from experience, Mrs. Grayson?"

"From observation, Mr. Morgan. I'm a great student of human nature."

He suddenly got up and went down to the little creek, kneeling to swish his hands in the water. He came back, drying them on his hankerchief. "You change your clothes a lot I notice."

"What?"

"I saw you on the street before noon wearing a very fetching frock." He nodded his head at me. "But in the hotel you received me in riding clothes. And now you are back to them."

I lifted my chin. I felt as if I were being accused of something. I said, lying, "I wanted to be sure my jodh-

130

purs would fit, Mr. Morgan. You happened to come at that time."

He sat down and laughed. "My dear lady, you haven't had to try on your clothes in your life. Your figure does not change."

I gave him a cool look. "Then what could have been my reason?"

"I think you received me in your riding clothes so as to appear less feminine and to make it clear this picnic would be just that, an outdoor eating experience. But I have to tell you, Mrs. Grayson, it would take far more than riding clothes to detract from your femininity."

I colored, I couldn't help it. "Mr. Morgan," I said forcefully, "it was my understanding we were taking this excursion to discuss my business proposition. Your opinion of why I do or don't change clothes has nothing to do with that and is damn well none of your business."

He laughed. "Pardon me, my dear lady. I see I have lifted a veil best left untouched. You are right. I did suggest in my note that this would give us an opportunity to investigate your proposal to finish the wing and lease it. But I go back to my original concern, and that is what you intend to do with it."

"I have told you. Occupy the apartment when I'm here and rent out the rest as your other rooms are let and to rent the whole of them when I am not here."

"And I have asked for some idea how often you would be in residence."

"And I have questioned you as to what that has to do with the matter. Whether I am here or not you still get your money. And it's my capital that will be used to finish the wing. I went to a bank today and deposited my letter of credit so I am ready to do business."

"I know." he said. "I saw you. Very reputable bank, though I had to laugh visualizing old Clive Dupree trying to advise you on where to put your money. I'm sure he wanted it in a two-percent account so it would be safe."

I said, "We came to a fairly quick understanding.

Which is more than I can say is happening here, Mr. Morgan."

He got up out of his chair and walked around behind it. He put his hands on its back and leaned toward me. "Mrs. Grayson, you are not making it easy for me to do business with you. I like to know something about the people I conduct affairs with. So far all I know is that you are the wife of a successful horse breeder, but you won't tell me anything beyond that."

I challenged him. "What more is there you need to know? I have the money, I have made you a proposition. Who I am or what I am has nothing to do with it."

"I think it does. I would like to know your present relationship with your husband, Mrs. Grayson."

I could feel my eyes flash. I looked up at him. "That is none of your business, Mr. Morgan."

He suddenly came around the table and stood over me. I was uncomfortably aware of his presence. He said, "I think it is, Mrs. Grayson. I think you have left your husband. I think you are available. I think you are fair game."

I rose so that we were standing in close proximity, facing each other. I raised my voice. "How dare you, sir! That is a distinctly unchivalrous remark. My personal business is my own and will remain so until such time as I choose to tell it."

He took a step backwards. "All right, Mrs. Grayson. You have made your point. Now I'll make mine." He walked back around the table and stood by his chair until I sat down. He resumed his seat. He said, "Frankly, I am a great deal more interested in you than I am in leasing you a wing in my hotel. I am a prosperous man, Mrs. Grayson, and have no need of your funds." He paused, thoughtfully, as if arranging his words. Finally he said, "However, and I pray you will not take this wrong, if leasing you the wing would place me in the forefront of your favor I would be willing to do it on whatever terms you find agreeable. All my instincts tell me that you are not happy in your marriage. I can well understand that. I will never ask you about that again. Not until you volunteer the information will I know." He locked my eyes with his. "I want you to understand this clearly. I have no interest in leasing you the wing in the hotel if you are not at liberty as a woman. I do not ask that you choose me. I only ask for an opportunity to be in what I would reckon a very spirited race for your hand." He sat back and regarded me.

It was quite a blow. That he was sincere about not leasing me the wing unless I declared myself an available woman I had no doubt. He very easily looked the part of one who would drive such a deal. But I could not, I would not, be so quickly disloyal to Warner. For all I knew he was giving me no more thought than a castoff horse who didn't meet his standards. But I would not dishonor our vows until such time as we had finalized the disposition of our marriage. Perhaps we were finished. I did not know. But I would not discuss Warner's business with another man until I was truly and fully free. I had loved him, I still loved him, and I might well go on loving him after it was obvious we couldn't live together as man and wife. But having left him I was determined to carve out as independent a niche for myself as quickly as I could and the investment in the wing had seemed made to order. Now I found myself thwarted because I was a woman that another man desired. It was all too complicated. All I knew was that one day Warner would show up. When that day came I wanted to be able to appear as independent as possible. Now this opportunity was slipping away.

I composed myself as best I could. I glanced toward the hummock and could see Phoenix out of the buggy and looking down our way, shading her eyes with her hand. I smoothed the cloth over my thighs. I said, "Strange terms, Mr. Morgan. Strange terms for a businessman."

He laughed without humor. "I am not a businessman, Mrs. Grayson. Business bores me. I am an adventurer. I would have thought you'd have recognized that by now. I warned you, if you will recollect, that I did not always act from what might seem like sensible motives."

I sat for a moment, thinking. I could easily have given him some plausible reason for my being in Jefferson with a desire to have suitable quarters available at all times. After all, my husband was in the kind of business that occupied great amounts of his time and I was not the sort of lady who thrived on the solitude of a horse farm. Mr. Morgan had made it clear that he would not lease unless I was available. It would not be difficult to claim a continuing, reasonably stable marriage, while at the same time holding out the slight hope that the situation might not be as solid as I was presenting it. It was possible that such an explanation, reluctantly given with the most subtle of shadings, might be enough to cause Mr. Morgan to give favorable thought to leasing me the wing.

But I was damned if I would do it. He was a very ruthless man, a very dominant man, a very confidant man, a very handsome man. Free, I might even have considered his suit, but I was damned if I'd be forced into it. I said, "Well, then I suppose that is it, Mr. Morgan." I stood up and brushed imaginary crumbs off my shirtwaist. "I'm sorry I can't offer the kind of booty with the deal that you seem to insist on. I'm afraid that mine will have to continue to be just a straightforward business proposition without any lagniappe."

He laughed. "You surprise me, Mrs. Grayson, knowing that word. Lagniappe, sweeting a deal. That is a Cajun word, a Louisiana word."

"I have been to Louisiana, Mr. Morgan. And I believe it is a word used throughout the South. This is not my first business venture." I glanced over to where the very ordinary roan horse I'd ridden was grazing. He was still bridled but I'd slipped the bits out of his mouth as Warner had taught me. "I take it the two mounts do not belong to you, Mr. Morgan."

He seemed reluctant to leave his chair. "No, they are livery horses. I'm afraid I don't own a horse."

"Hadn't we better go? I confess I'm fearful my husband might unexpectedly show up."

"And catch you with another man?" He'd gotten a little edge in his voice.

"No. He wouldn't mind about that. But it would be a great source of embarrassment for him to find me riding such a plug horse."

We did not talk much on the ride back to town. Phoenix and James were behind us, having had the task of cleaning up the picnic and then loading its remains in the buggy. This time I led the way and the route was much shorter. We struck the road into town after a ride of no more than half a mile. Now, as we could see town just ahead Mr. Morgan pulled up his horse. I stopped also. He said, sounding thoughtful, "I have made a mistake with you, Mrs. Grayson. I do not ordinarily make mistakes with ladies, but I have made a grievous one with you."

"How is that, Mr. Morgan?"

"I misjudged your degree of independence. You are not a woman to be pushed. In fact you are not a woman who cares for even the impression of being pushed. I gave you what sounded like an ultimatum. Or I can see how you might have misinterpreted it as that."

"Oh, really?" I said, cooly. "What part did I misinterpet? That the wing wasn't available unless I was available or that the wing couldn't be leased unless I could be leased?"

He winced visibly. "Ouch. Did it come across so crudely? Damn, you must think me a lout."

"I think you a man used to getting your way."

He nodded slowly. "Unfortunately, that last part is true. However, I had not reckoned on the skill and determination of my adversary. My admiration for you grows by the moment, Mrs. Grayson."

"And what does that mean in practical terms?"

He stared off, giving me the benefit of his striking profile. Around us birds of the autumn season chirped and called. My horse nodded his head up and down and worried his bit. He said, "Perhaps I have been hasty. Perhaps that wing might be a valuable addition if it were activated. And, God knows, I have no doubt that you would be an asset to the hotel if you were affiliated with it in any way."

I felt a little thrill of victory. "Are you saying you are willing to give favorable disposition to my proposal?"

He looked around at me, smiling faintly. "I did not say that, Mrs. Grayson. I am willing to think about it favorably. I am not at all sure I like the idea of the size of the apartment you are planning. Make that smaller and there is space for another room. Besides, the size of it alone would make it difficult to let if you weren't in attendance. I would have to put a pretty healthy price on it."

I said, crisply, "All I'm interested in for the time being is that you be willing to sit down and talk business without other considerations."

He gave me a mocking smile. "How prettily you term my attentions."

I gave him a like smile in return. "Mr. Morgan, I have seen prairie fires that were slow and less intent than your so-called attentions."

He laughed. "All right, fair enough. Shall we make a new start?"

"As you wish."

"We shall have dinner tonight and talk nothing but business. I will not make one inquiry into your private affairs."

"No screen?"

"Better than that. There is a chop house of unsurpassed quality down Front Street a short block away. I will even surrender the advantage of being on my own ground."

"Your gallantry is quite overwhelming, Mr. Morgan.

136

But tell me this, have I any hope of receiving an answer tonight?"

He regarded me for a second. "Mrs. Grayson, until I give you an answer I am almost assured of your company. What would you do in my position? Assuming you did not intend to act honorably."

I answered him promptly. "Were I in your position, Mr. Morgan, and wished for the lady's company, I would give her an immediate yes. You can well imagine the conferences that would be called for during the planning and the construction."

He pulled his head back and looked at me from a long way off. "Why, now, do I have the feeling that the reins have just passed from my hands to yours?"

I laughed and urged my pokey old horse forward. I said, "I haven't the slightest idea, Mr. Morgan. What time do we dine tonight?"

From behind me came the answer. "Eight. I'll pick you up at your rooms."

I turned to look back, to suggest that such might not be seemly, but he was already coming up with a rush and swept on by me before I could lift my horse into motion. I watched him as he loped down the road. I could not help thinking of Warner. Mr. Morgan probably considered himself, and was considered by others, to be a good rider. But once you'd seen Warner on a horse no one else could ever compare.

7

Warner

I finally got away for Jefferson on Sunday, taking the afternoon train. I did it quick, making up my mind with barely enough time to get in and catch the train. I didn't pay much attention to my clothes in spite of the way I'd been thinking. I just threw several clean shirts and an extra pair of jeans in a valise, added some clean socks, put on my best hat, and set out. I had given up worrying whether or not it might be more than a two-shirt job to get her to come back. I was going to go down there and give my opinion as to what I thought was wrong and see what she wanted to do about it. I was not going to let my pride get in the way, but then neither had I left it at home in my bureau. Wilson Young had his cardinal rule about never loaning money to strangers on trains. My new cardinal rule was that no one was ever necessarily right or wrong in a marriage. In fact, the more I thought about it, I decided that no such thing was possible between man and wife, not if they'd lived together for more than a year. By then enough of one would have rubbed off on the other that both were a part of the good and the bad.

I decided to bring Paseta with me. I was riding in the chair cars, as opposed to what I usually did, which was

138

ride in the stock car with my animals. But it was windy and dusty back there and I wanted to arrive in Jefferson looking halfway presentable. My hair was a little shaggy, but it was Sunday and there'd been no chance to get it cut. Besides, we hadn't had a falling out about the length of my hair.

I did not expect to need Paseta, or any other horse in Jefferson, and I didn't know why I'd brought him, except it was Paseta who'd brought me and Laura together in the first place and I was just superstitious enough to think that maybe he could be a help in patching us back up. God knows he'd saved my life by escaping from the Mexican horse thieves and wandering out on that forsaken alkali flat where I was near to death. It had been he that had gotten us out of there and to the Rio Grande. I sure as hell hadn't been much help. It had taken all my strength to make it up on his back. After that I'd just clung to his mane and held on for dear life. He was some horse, though I didn't know how good he was at being a good-luck charm.

As the train neared Jefferson I found myself feeling skittish. That struck me as an odd thing, that a grown man should be nervous about facing his wife. We'd had an argument and I'd left and then she'd left and now I was going to set matters straight. That seemed straightforward enough, though I still couldn't get the uneasy feeling out of my stomach. I had a good bottle of whiskey in my valise and I got it down from the overhead rack and had several pulls, but it didn't seem to help much.

Then, soon enough, we were steaming into Jefferson, with the train jolting and swaying as it slowed down and the conductor making his way through the cars calling out our next stop.

I was waiting in the vestibule as the train rolled to a stop in front of the passenger platform. I stepped out as soon as we quit moving, my valise in my hand. My intention was to get to the freight office and arrange to have my horse taken off. But before I'd made much progress toward the depot a pleasant-faced man with a badge on his chest stepped in front of me. He pointed at the sidearm I was wearing and said that it was illegal in Jefferson to carry a firearm, especially a revolver. Well, that surprised me considerably and I said so. The deputy, for that was what he was, said, "Yes, sir, I reckon you're not the first to be startled by the rule. But this is a booming town, sir, and we get quite a mix of strangers through here. Some of them are all right but some of them ain't. So we just passed us this law about guns. Now you can surrender your firearm to me and pick it up when you leave town or you can put it in your bag there. I want to warn you, though, that if you get caught carrying it on your person it will be taken away from you and you won't get it back. You might also get fined or get a few days in jail."

I shrugged. I said, "Well, if nobody else has got one then I don't reckon I'd be in need of one. Ain't that right?"

He nodded. "That's the way we got it figured."

I unbuckled my gunbelt, rolled the whole affair up, and stuffed it in my valise and then buckled the bag shut again. I said, "You can do me one service, if you are of a mind."

"If I can."

I got out the piece of paper that the banker Quince had scribbled for me. I said, "Can you make out the name of this hotel? Or do you know of it."

He glanced at the paper. He said, "Why, that's the Excelsior." Then he looked me up and down. "You going to stay there? That's a pretty high-toned establishment. They get ten, fifteen dollars a night for a room. And that's if they got one."

I said, "I think that's the place I need to go. But I'd like to stable my horse first."

He kindly gave me directions to a nearby livery stable and then further instructions on how to get to the Excelsior. It was a word I had never heard before and it seemed damned funny when attached to the word hotel. But then, as the deputy had said, this was a booming town and I'd no doubt find more than a few things a touch on the strange side.

It took almost an hour to get my horse unloaded and stabled. I gave the feed boy a dollar to make sure he didn't short Paseta on his rations and told him to give him a good currying down. After that I walked toward where I could see the stacks of the big steamboats, found Front Street, and started west along the boardwalk.

It was a bustling place, just as the deputy had said, and I reckoned a man could find just about anything he needed in the town, maybe anything he wanted. Just judging from the crowds on the street, there seemed to be considerably more men than women, though I reckoned that the streets of such a place were not quite fit for a lady and most of the respectable women would be home. The men ran the gamut from raggedy workmen to what I reckoned to be businessmen or bankers dressed to the nines, some of them even sporting high hats or derbys. I felt naked without my sidearm, but it was pretty clear that the rest of the men were in the same shape, because I didn't see any guns being worn openly. I'd have given odds, though, that there were more than a few derringers or bulldog revolvers tucked away in hip pockets or inside the vests of the better dressed.

Finally I was standing across the street from the Excelsior hotel. It was quite a sight. A fancy coach had just pulled in under the portico and was unloading a bevy of stylishly dressed ladies wearing what I could see were ruffled petticoats and carrying lace-trimmed parasols. The men with them were dressed in the best that money could buy. Seeing them made me slightly conscious of the dowdy condition of my own clothes. But then I wasn't there to impress the populace; I'd come for my wife and she'd seen me in my ordinary dress more than any other kind.

I let the crowd from the coach get inside before I started sauntering across the street. I paused a moment before the big double doors that were trimmed in gleaming brass. Whoever owned the place certainly made sure it was kept up. I pushed open one of the doors and stepped inside the lobby. It was as plush as I'd expected, though not quite as big. Chairs and tables were grouped around and little knots of folks were sitting at them, being served drinks and whatnot by colored waiters wearing some sort of monkey suits made out of short red jackets and white trousers. Beyond the lobby I could see a big dining room where another crowd of hired help was setting tables with linen and tableware and dishes. I figured it was close to four o'clock, so they must have been getting ready for the first serving of supper.

Ahead of me was the desk, manned by a young man in a high-necked collar and wearing a foulard tie. The way he had his hair slicked back made me conscious again of my own shaggy locks, but to have slicked mine back would have taken about half a pound of pomade. He looked up as I came to the desk. I couldn't be sure, but I kind of got the impression I didn't quite measure up in his eyes. But he said, stiff and formal, "May I help you, sir?"

But he said it as if he very much doubted he could possibly have anything that I'd want. I said, "I'd like to know which room Mrs. Warner Grayson is occupying."

He gave me a blank look. "Mrs. Grayson?"

"Yeah. Mrs. Warner Grayson. What room is she in?"

He cleared his throat. Apparently the question seemed a little hard for him. I saw him turn his head and glance at a door behind him. He said, "We have no Mrs. Warner Grayson here, sir."

I frowned at him. I said, "That's not what I heard. You telling me you don't have a Mrs. Grayson here? Staying at this hotel?"

He cleared his throat again. I couldn't figure out what was causing him to fidget so. He said, hesitantly, "We have a Mrs. *Laura* Grayson. But no one by the name you gave."

That was just Laura declaring her independence. I said, "That would be the one. What's her room number?"

He glanced at the door behind him again. I wondered what was in it. Maybe he had him a bottle hid back there and had been going to get a snort when I so rudely interrupted him. He said, hesitantly, "Mrs. Grayson is not in a room. Mrs. Grayson is in the Rose suite."

That sounded like her. It was probably the best the place had to offer. I nodded. "All right. Now if you'll be good enough to give me directions I'll go and hunt her up."

He pulled his head back and raised his shoulders slightly. "I'm sorry, sir, it is not the policy of the hotel to allow visitors to have access to the floors unescorted. If you will tell me who is calling I will inquire if Mrs. Grayson is in and if she will see you."

He had his hand poised over a little bell and was about to bang it when I moved it out of his reach. I said, "Just hold on, young man. I am Mr. Grayson, the lady's husband, and I reckon I'll be the one to decide if she wants to receive me or not."

He stood there looking worried. I could see him running his tongue between his teeth and his gums, worrying. I could not, for the life of me, understand what his concern was. He said, "Ah, if you will excuse me for one moment, sir. I will be right back."

I said to his back as he went through the door he'd been glancing at, "Just a damn minute. All I need is—" But by then he had slipped through the door and closed it behind him. Hell, I figured he had to have a bottle back there and needed a drink something fierce, though he looked a little young to have such a case of the trembles. I drummed my fingers on the desk for a few moments and glanced around at the lobby. It was about as plush a place as I reckoned I'd ever been in. Knowing how Laura liked such luxury I figured to have more trouble prying her loose than I'd counted on.

Just then the young man came back. Or rather he opened the door and came just to my side of it and indicated I should come around the desk. He said, "Sir, if you will step this way our manager will see you."

I frowned at him. I said, "Young man, I don't know what in hell is going on around here, but if I'd wanted to see the manager I'd have asked for him in the first place. It's my wife I'm wanting."

He got a kind of anguished look on his face. He said, "If you would, sir. Mr. Morgan is the principal owner as well as the manager. He's asked if you'd step into his office for a moment."

A little chill hardened up in my stomach. Could Laura be hurt? Or sick? I said, "Ain't nothing wrong with my wife is there?"

"No sir." He motioned at the door again. "If you'd just step through, sir. Mr. Morgan is most anxious to meet you."

I gave a little shrug. I didn't seem to have much choice. This was, after all, their damn hotel and they knew where my wife was. I didn't, which I considered a fine mare's nest.

I went through the door and into a moderate-size office. I could tell no expense had been spared in its furnishings. I did not ordinarily think in those terms but that was the thought that jumped into my head as I made a quick inventory of the office and its appointments.

A man was just standing up from behind a desk as I entered. He was not as tall as I was nor as set up in the shoulders, but he had a presence about him that struck me immediately. He put out his hand as I came up to his desk and I took it. "Charles Morgan, Mr. Grayson. I am most delighted to make your acquaintance, sir."

His grip was firm. We shook once and then I dropped his hand. He nodded at a chair. "Won't you take a seat, sir."

I didn't move to sit down. I said, "I seem to be having the devil of a time finding out if my wife is in your hotel, Mr. Morgan."

Mr. Morgan remained standing. "I can assure you she is, Mr. Grayson, though I believe she is out just now. I saw her pass through the lobby a short while ago. Now won't you sit down and have a brandy with me? Or a whiskey if you prefer. I am a devotee of the Thorough-bred racing horse and I am honored to have so illustrious a member of the breeding fraternity here in my hotel."

There was something about the man I didn't much like. Something about his eyes or around his mouth. It wasn't anything I could put my finger on or give tongue to, just a sort of wary feeling he created in me. I had known from the first second I'd laid eyes on him that he was a hard man, a dangerous man, a man whose scruples were routinely bent to fit his quest. There was no way I could have explained to anyone else why I felt all that. It was an instinct. And it was instinct you needed to stay alive if you'd been in as many tight places as I had. That instinct had saved me more than once and I had learned to listen to it. Oh, he was all dressed up in his Sunday go-to-meeting clothes, as fine and elegant looking as you please, but I had the feeling that every church pew in the country was safe from his weight, clothes or not.

But he had made me an invitation and put it so I couldn't really refuse. I sank down on a fragile looking chair and found it would bear my weight. Behind me I heard the door close as the clerk went out. Mr. Morgan got up and went to a sideboard behind him. Over his shoulder he said, "Whiskey or brandy, Mr. Grayson?"

"Either one," I said. "Both work about the same."

He came back to his desk and put a half-filled tumbler in front of me. "Well put," he said. He lifted his glass. "Cheers."

I said, "Luck," and knocked about half of mine back. It was brandy and about as smooth as any I'd ever drunk. I said, "Much obliged. That's some slick liquor."

"Napoleon," he said. "Twenty-five years old."

I nodded and took another sip. I didn't have the slightest idea what he was talking about, but I was very conscious of how grubby I must have looked compared with him and in his glittering office. I noticed there was a lot of green to the place. The chairs were gold and green and the felt pad on his desk was green, as were some drapes that hung behind him. Hell, there was even a green carpet on the floor. I wondered if he liked green because it reminded him of money.

He said, "Are you in Jefferson for a time, Mr. Grayson, or just in and out on a quick visit?"

I didn't see where it was any of his damn business how long I was in Jefferson for. But he did own the hotel that Laura was staying in and since it was probably the best in town I didn't want to get in further Dutch with her by getting her thrown out of her accommodations. I said, kind of mumbling, "I ain't real sure. Got a little business might take me a day or two. Hard to tell."

"Horse business?"

I looked up at him. Somebody needed to teach this son of a bitch some manners. Pretty soon he'd be asking me to open my mouth so he could look at my teeth to see how old I was. But for the same reason I hadn't called him down before I said, "Not exactly sure."

"The reason I ask is that you didn't seem to have any luggage. At least my clerk said you didn't come in with any."

Damn! The place was working alive with busybodies. I took another sip of the brandy and then turned the glass up and emptied it. It felt good going down. I said, "I left it over at the livery, where I stabled my horse."

He perked up. "Oh, you brought a horse then. I find it hard to believe that anyone around here would have an animal you'd be interested in so it can't be a trade. Are you selling Thoroughbred stock into this area?"

I took my hat off and looked at the sweatband. It was something to do to keep from answering him too quickly. "No," I said slowly. "I ain't trading or buying or selling. This is a riding horse, a road horse. Didn't know but what I might need him."

"Aaaah," he said. And then, without asking, he took my glass, wheeled around, poured me a good measure, and set it back in front of me before I could say if I wanted another drink or not. I was beginning to wonder if maybe he and I hadn't been old friends for a number of years and it had slipped my mind.

But I said, "Thanks," and lifted the glass and took a swallow.

He sat back down, looking mighty comfortable with himself. He said, "The reason I inquired is that Mrs. Grayson is going to dine with me this evening and I wanted you to join us if you'd brought clothes. We dress for dinner at the Excelsior."

He had hit me a quick one-two so fast I couldn't quite take it in. He'd just said a Mrs. Grayson was going to dine with him that evening. Was he talking about my wife or was there some other Mrs. Grayson floating about that I didn't know of. I said, "Are you by chance talking about my wife, Laura?"

He sat up in his chair a little straighter, though I'd have sworn he was already sitting as straight as could be. He said, "Why, yes. I thought you understood that."

I stared at him for a long half of a moment wondering when was the last time someone had announced they were going to eat supper with my wife and would I like to join them. I decided, circumstances being what they were, I'd step along very carefully until I got the lay of the land. I said, "Yeah, I saw when I came in that they were setting up for the evening meal."

Now it was his turn to stare at me, uncomprehendingly. He said, "Pardon me? I don't quite understand. Who is setting up for the evening meal?"

I jerked my head in the general direction of where I thought the dining room was. I said, "Right here. Your place. I saw some hired hands in uniforms laying out the cups and saucers and plates and silverware."

His face suddenly crinkled and he let out a high, crackling kind of laugh. After a second he said, "Oh, that was a good one, Mr. Grayson."

I frowned. "I say something funny?"

He took out a handkerchief from his sleeve and put it to his eyes. He shook his head. "No, no, no. I'm not laughing at you. I can just see how it might have looked. They were laying out for tea. Tea, Mr. Grayson, not dinner. We serve tea at four o'clock."

I did not, again, have the slightest idea what he was talking about and neither did I care to subject myself to that laugh of his again. I said, "I thought it was a little early for supper. But then I don't get to towns like Jefferson much. When you raise race horses you've got to stay where they are and that is generally not in town."

"I completely understand, Mr. Grayson. It was uncalled for, my laugh. It just struck me funny. We don't begin serving dinner until seven-thirty and very few dine at that hour. Mrs. Grayson and I will probably not go in until a few minutes after eight. So you will have plenty of time to retrieve your valise and dress."

Now he was getting just a touch too familiar where Laura was concerned. He kept calling her Mrs. Grayson as if she were not connected to me in any way. I thought it was about time to find out a few things. For all I knew Laura might have declared herself a free agent and put herself back out on the market. I said, "Mr. Morgan, would you mind my asking how you come to be having supper with my wife?"

"Mrs. Grayson?" He gave an airy wave. "Oh, we have dined together several times since she came to grace this hotel. Why we've even had a picnic. I think she enjoyed it."

I studied him for a good few seconds without blinking my eyes. Mr. Morgan was beginning to look more and more like trouble. I acutely felt the loss of my revolver. I would have liked to feel its weight on my hip. I said, evenly, "You didn't exactly answer my question, Mr. Morgan."

He frowned. "I didn't?"

I shook my head slowly. "No. I asked how it came about you were having supper with my wife. Now I reckon I need to ask how come y'all been eating together regularly. How about if I just put it like that? Why have y'all been taking so many meals together?"

"Oh, I see." he said. "Of course you'd wonder about that, wouldn't you." He gave me a quick, mighty white smile. "Well it's nothing to concern yourself about, Mr. Grayson. Mrs. Grayson is enchanting company."

"Well just how come she has decided to enchant you, Mr. Morgan?"

"Oh, I see!" he said, as if he'd suddenly understood that two and two are four. "I assumed you knew. Though why I should think that, I don't know. Mrs. Grayson and I are investigating the possibilities of a joint business venture."

"What kind of business venture?"

He looked at me intently. "I see you really don't know. That is surprising."

He said it as if I must be some kind of damn fool not to know what my own wife was up to. At least that's the way it sounded to me. I said, "All right, it's surprising. Why don't you tell me about this business venture so we can both be surprised."

He looked at me quickly. "I hope I haven't said anything you've misunderstood."

"I haven't misunderstood a word you said, Mr. Morgan. Now what's the big secret?"

He looked undecided. He said, "Well, Mr. Grayson, I mean, what if it is some sort of surprise Mrs. Grayson is organizing. Or perhaps she wants to keep it secret for the time being."

I stood up. I couldn't help myself. I was starting to get just a little hot. "Mr. Morgan, the lady is my wife. I reckon you might be taking on a little more than you are allowed when you go to deciding my wife's business. Especially when you are talking to me. Maybe I'll just skip on along and ask her. Maybe she's been in this town a day too long."

He stood up, quickly. "I'm sorry, Mr. Grayson. I didn't mean to offend you. Your wife has asked to lease a wing of the hotel. We are still discussing terms."

I stared at him. It kind of staggered me. A whole wing of the hotel? Hell, that made it sound as if she were fixing to set up residence in the damn place. I felt a cold shiver start in my stomach and run all the way up my spine until the hair on my neck stood up. I said, awkwardly, "Lease? Not buy?"

"Of course lease. I would hardly sell part of the hotel. She has asked to finish an uncompleted wing, building herself a large apartment in it."

"For how long? The lease?"

"We are presently talking ten of years." He cocked his head. "I would have thought your wife would have communicated with you about such a large undertaking. Telegraphed. I thought that was perhaps what had brought you to town, since I promised her an answer by tomorrow."

I could almost feel myself blushing in shame. The man had managed to embarrass me with my own wife. I hadn't seen him lay a finger on her and yet he was claiming closer knowledge of her than I had. I was hurt and I was bewildered. I felt betrayed and it was a terrible time for such feelings. I managed as best I could to stammer out a sort of explanation. I said, "My wife has independent means, Mr. Morgan. She leaves the horse breeding to me and I don't interfere in her other business."

He gave me what looked like a smirk. "That is very understanding of you, Mr. Grayson. Most men wouldn't be that indulgent."

Now I was being played for a sucker. Mr. Morgan was burying me deeper every time I opened my mouth. I said, "She's a good businesswoman, Laura."

He nodded, that same little self-satisfied smile on his lips. "Yes she is. I can certainly testify to that. Laura, yes."

"You call her that?"

For the first time he looked not so certain of himself. "Our relationship has been kept on a more formal basis. Business, you know. By the way, I'm sorry if I gave you cause for any confusion concerning the reasons for our meetings. It was careless of me."

He was slapping me in the face again. I figured I'd had

just about enough of it. I said, "Oh, there was never any confusion on my part, Mr. Morgan. Maybe there was a little confusion about the way you were putting out the information, but I never doubted that my wife would have a mighty good reason for taking a few meals with you. Business or some such. Laura is a mighty outgoing woman and more than a few people have misunderstood that she is just naturally friendly." I gave him a smile. "I hope she didn't cause you any confusion."

That flustered him a little bit more. His mouth got tight and a certain glint came into his eyes. He said, "I'm sure you would like to visit Mrs. Grayson as soon as possible. Just tell the clerk at the desk to have someone escort you to her suite. Possibly she is back by now. Or her maid will be there."

"I'm obliged," I said.

"As I mentioned, we will be dining at a little after eight. Would it be convenient for you to meet us in the dining room? I had planned to call for Mrs. Grayson at her door."

I looked at him. The son of a bitch was challenging me. That was it plain and simple. I had had plenty of men make a run at Laura and it didn't bother me any. Usually I just let her beat them off. But this snake was using a tactic I'd never seen before and had somehow put me in the position of being the guest at my own wife's table. I said, "We'll see how she goes, Mr. Morgan. Much obliged for the brandy."

He motioned at my glass. "But you haven't finished your drink."

I put my hat on. "That was a drink I didn't ask for, Mr. Morgan. But I didn't touch it so I reckon you can pour it back in the bottle. Some things, though, once out, are harder to get back in the bottle. Good day to you, sir."

I had my hand on the doorknob when he said, "Mr. Grayson."

I turned to look at him. He had my drink in his hand. While I watched he knocked it back and then put the empty glass down on his desk. He looked at me. "That wasn't my drink, Mr. Morgan," I said. "I still got everything I came with."

He smiled thinly. "Mrs. Grayson is a strikingly beautiful woman."

I wiggled the doorknob back and forth in my hand. Hell, he'd come right out and challenged me. I said, "You ain't the first man that has noticed that, Mr. Morgan. And I doubt you'll be the last."

Then I went through the door, pulling it closed behind me. The young man was still at the desk. I said, "Mr. Morgan said you'd have someone show me up to my wife's rooms. Why don't you go ahead and ding that bell now?" While I waited for a porter, or whatever they were called, to lead me through the maze of the hotel, I had time to reflect that I wished it had been a bottle the young man sought behind the door instead of what had actually been there.

I wanted to be angry and I wanted to challenge Laura about Charles Morgan and especially about her seeking to lease a wing of the hotel, but I knew that I had better not. In all my years of horse trading and playing poker (they are essentially the same, since both call for a cool, dispassionate eye) I'd never once let my feelings get the best of me. Many a trader will try and rile you just so you'll turn rash. None of those childish tactics had ever worked on me. Though I would say the methods employed by Mr. Morgan had come as close to lighting my fire as any ever had. But I knew that the position between Laura and me was a fragile and precarious one and, if I was smart, I would keep my emotions, especially my temper, under close rein. Dry as the tinder was around the both of us it wouldn't take many sparks to start a forest fire that would consume our marriage. I had the feeling, unfortunately, that resolving to hold my tongue was going to be a hell of a lot easier to accomplish than actually doing it in her presence. She didn't have any business taking meals with a snake like Morgan and she damn sure didn't have any business, her money or not, making large capital investments in a place to live without at least telling me. We still had a piece of paper that said we were married. Maybe she needed to have a fresh look at it. But just then what they called a bellboy came up and said, "Yes, suh," to the desk clerk. The young man directed him to guide me to the Rose suite.

Phoenix answered the door. For a second she looked startled and then flustered and then glad. "Mr. Warner!" she said. "Oh, lawd, look at you here! I been wonderin' when you was gonna show up."

"Hello, Phoenix," I said. "Is Miss Laura in?"

She nodded up and down vigorously. "Yes, suh. Yes, suh. She shore be."

But she was still standing in the door. I said, "Phoenix, you been eating too many bricks. I can't just walk right through you."

It took her a second to get it, but then she jumped out of the way, giggling and pulling the door wide. She said, "You jes' come on in here, Mr. Warner. My goodness is I glad to see you."

I stepped into what appeared to be a parlor for a fair-size house. I said, "Where is Miss Laura?"

Phoenix said, "Oh, she in de bedroom. I run quick and tell her you here."

I grabbed her arm before she could move. I said, "That's all right, Phoenix. I'll just go on in."

She said, "But she might not be dressed, Mr. Warner."

I fixed her with a look. "Phoenix, I know a lot has been going on around here, but I am still her husband."

She put her hand to her mouth. "Oh, my stars, yes. I'm mighty sorry, Mr. Warner. We been gone so long from home I reckon I done lost my senses. Yes, suh, you walk right on in."

I stepped to the door of the bed chamber and opened it and passed through and closed it softly behind me. Laura was standing in front of a six-foot-high window looking out. Of all things, she would have to be wearing one of her yellow frocks that I liked so much. As she turned to see who'd come in, the sun shining through her golden hair made an aura around her. I didn't know if it was the situation or not, but I didn't think I'd ever seen her looking quite so beautiful. I took my hat off. I said, "Hello, Laura."

There was a long pause. Perhaps she had been staring out into the sun too long and it took a time for her eyes to adjust so she could recognize me. She gave a slight start and half lifted her hand. She said, "Warner! You startled me."

I pitched my hat into a nearby chair. "Yeah, I guess you weren't expecting me. But I was close by and thought I'd drop in." I did my best to give her a little smile to show that I was joking. It was an effort because my heart, which was beating like a hummingbird's wings, was up in my throat. I said, "I figured it was about time we had a talk. What do you think?"

She turned away and looked out the window again. Her voice was hesitant when it came. "I don't know, Warner. I don't know if there is anything left to be said. It seemed as if you made your last remark when you walked out of the house."

My heart sank. I had hoped to somehow find a way to soften the words I'd flung at her before they came up. But her first bet had matched the pot and the words were out. They just lay there, chiseled in granite like the epitaph on my tombstone. I had not expected to find her waiting to welcome me joyously, but I had hoped she would be as eager to seal the breach as I was. It did not appear she was. She had turned her back on me and the line of her shoulders was stiff and firm.

8

Laura

The sight of him startled me so that I was breathless for a second. In the instant I recognized him I realized how badly I had been missing him. There he stood in the clothes that became him so well, the clothes of the working horseman. Next to him Charles Morgan looked like a fop. Having him suddenly there had addled my wits. I had expected him to come, I had even practiced what I would say in the first moment of our encounter, but he came upon me so unexpectedly that every word was driven out of my head. I heard the door open and close and assumed it was Phoenix. I turned to tell her what I'd be wearing that night and there stood Warner, holding his hat in his hand and smiling that slow, soft smile of his. "Hello, Laura," he said. Standing there with his broad shoulders and his big hands and his gentle ways. "Hello, Laura." He might as well have set off a stick of dynamite. He couldn't have startled me any more if he had.

In my uncertainty I turned back to the window and then he said something about having a talk. All I had to do was agree with him. Just that and we could have begun slowly to set matters straight. But then the words leaped out of my mouth, words I didn't even know I was going to say. Maybe they had hurt me worse than I'd thought the first time they'd been said, the words he'd flung over his shoulder about finding another woman to get a son from. It was the only explanation I could think of for my reply. As I told him I thought everything had already been said, I could see him sag. He almost wilted back against the door and, for just an instant, I was glad. I had hurt him. Good! He'd hurt me terribly and I wanted to hurt him back. Unfortunately, in doing so I made it sound as if I had taken the position that there was nothing further to talk about, that we were finished. I could have bitten my tongue off.

But the words had been said and I couldn't suddenly retreat from the position. Just as he'd boxed himself in with his words, so had I with mine. I was still so flustered by his presence that I was trembling inside. I said, still looking out the window, "This is not a good time, Warner. I have an engagement."

"I know," he said. "They got tea all set up downstairs. All them waiters in their little short red jackets."

"Tea?" I looked around at him in spite of myself. I didn't think he even knew what a tea was. I said so.

He lounged back against the door. "Oh, I get around more than you might think."

I turned away from him. The bastard could still make me weak in the knees when I looked at him and it had been over a week of doing without. Warner was the kind of lover every woman dreams of, experienced, but not too experienced, eager to learn how to give pleasure, quick to pick up on subtle hints. He was an unselfish and very generous lover, and that was just one of his lesser attributes. I so desperately wanted to sit down with him and talk about what had happened, figure out what had caused the friction and fighting to turn into a schism of such proportions that I was now in a hotel miles from our home and unwilling to bend.

"Yes," I said, turning. "You warned me you were going to do that when you walked out of the house."

I could see the pain cross his face. He said, "Oh, hell, Laura, you know I didn't mean that."

"You said it and, so far as I know, you've always prided yourself on being a man of your word."

He looked miserable. "Laura, damn it, you know I said it in anger. There's never been another woman since the day I met you. You know that as well as I do."

I wouldn't look at him. And I wanted time to sort out my feelings. I had been moving so fast and dealing so fast that my mind hadn't had time to catch up with me. In truth I had not spent enough time thinking about what was between Warner and me, both the bad and the good. Seven years before I had been attracted to him physically, but through those years I had come to love him for the kind of man he was. I not only loved him, but I respected him, something I couldn't recall doing with very many men before him. I needed a strong man and then I immediately kept forcing them to prove how strong they were. I knew that I had Warner in a position where it was extremely difficult for him to be strong, yet he could not win unless he was. There was a diffidence in his manner I was not used to seeing. It made me want to rub his nose in it. I said, "Warner, I wish you would please go."

"You don't think we ought to talk?"

I couldn't just keep staring out the window as if the street scene was more interesting than my husband. I turned away and walked to a chair at the foot of my bed. I chose it deliberately as there were no others near it. I said, "I don't know what good it would do."

"Good?" He took a step toward me, wrinkling his brow. "Good? Hell, Laura, we are talking about our marriage here." He made a motion backwards with his hand. "Or have you already thrown that off? Is it done in your eyes? If that's the case, why, just say so and I'll get on home and go to making arrangements."

I saw I had been a little hasty. He was not quite as

subdued as I'd thought. Warner was an easy man to underestimate, but you did it at your peril, whether with a gun or your wits. He was nearer to me now and I could see him much clearer with the sunlight striking us equally. He looked tired and worn and just a little shabby and shaggy haired. Unless I was there to remind him he tended to let his appearance go. He always said, "Long as you are pouring the right amount of oats the horses don't care what you are wearing." And I knew how hard and how desperately he had been working to get the first crop of colts ready for the track. And then to have to take time off to chase an errant wife. I guess if I needed proof of his regard for me I had it in his presence here when he would much rather be at the ranch.

Or had he come to see his financial partner? I said, "I'm saying this is a bad time for both of us. Shouldn't you be at home with your precious bloodstock?"

He blinked. "They're as much your precious bloodstock as mine. And you took off. I thought maybe I'd come give you a report on the condition of the stock. But I see you are too busy." His voice was even, very even, much too even.

I kept my own voice controlled. I felt my upper hand slipping slightly. I said, "That's very thoughtful of you, but completely unnecessary. Right now I am really not thinking of horses."

"Neither am I," he said. Without moving he'd somehow seemed to come closer so that he was planted right in front of me. His eyes were boring right into me. "But I am thinking about you and me."

"Please, Warner, not right now. This isn't the time."

He challenged me. I could see he was not exactly contrite. Something was bubbling right below his surface and it wouldn't take much to get it to boil over. That was the last thing I wanted to happen in the Excelsior hotel. He said, "All right, then when is the time? Tonight? Later on this evening?"

"No, not tonight."

"Listen, Laura, I realize that I'm the supplicant here.

But you don't have to make it as hard as possible. I wouldn't if it was the other way around. You say not tonight. When? Tomorrow?"

"I don't know."

"Hell, Laura, I can't hang around this god damn town at my leisure. I've got business seventy miles from here. And it's your business also. I never heard of a wife wouldn't, or couldn't, take the time to talk to her husband." He gave me a look that was growing harder by the word. "Just what the hell is going on around here?"

"Nothing," I said. "I have an engagement later on, that's all."

He stepped back. "Yeah, I know." he said. "For supper. I was invited also. But the man put it a kind of funny way. He wondered if I'd like to join him and Mrs. Grayson for dinner. Said they'd be dressing, whatever that means. But he kept talking about Mrs. Grayson as if we were no relation. Sounded kind of odd hearing another man talking about my wife like that."

I put my hand to my throat. The last man I wanted Warner to see was Charles Morgan. But, in a way, it accounted for the edge I'd perceived in him, as if he were a revolver on half cock slowly being drawn back to a firing position. I was afraid to imagine what Mr. Morgan might have insinuated to Warner in that suave but deadly way of his. "You saw Mr. Morgan?"

"I saw a Mr. Charles Morgan, the principal owner of this plantation, yes. Anything wrong with that?"

"I don't quite understand how that happened."

Before he answered he walked over to the wall by the door, where a straight-backed chair was sitting. He'd dropped his hat there. He took it up and sat down. He said, "Well, it was kind of strange. I guess it was my fault. I knew you were staying at this hotel so I came in and asked at the desk for your room number. You would have thought I'd asked for the combination to the office safe. They don't give out room numbers and they don't let strange folks go wandering around their halls. Especially folks that look so poorly dressed and desperate as I."

It took all my strength to keep from smiling. I tried to look severe, as if he'd done something against my wishes.

"Anyway," he said, "this young desk clerk figured it was way too big a job for him to handle so he ducked into this office behind and the next thing I knew I was back there talking to Charles Morgan himself. He even gave me a glass of brandy and told me he was flattered to meet a member of the Thoroughbred fraternity. Those were his exact words. After that he invited me to dinner with you and him."

I sighed. I said, "Are you planning to come? I must tell you how uncomfortable I'd be."

He leaned forward, dangling his hat in his hands. "Yes, I dare say you would be a little ill at ease. But if dressing means what I think it does I don't reckon I'd be allowed in because all I've got is some more clothes like the ones I'm wearing and these may be the best of the lot. Of course if I'd known I was going to be in competition with a big-city dandy maybe I'd have tried to dress a little better."

The last words were like the blade of a jagged knife. It cut and slashed its way completely through me. I said, "Mr. Morgan is no competition to you." But it sounded faint even in my own ears. I could imagine the possessive way he'd talked to Warner about me. He'd have looked at Warner and thought, "Ah, here's a hayseed come to town. Let's have some fun." Except the man didn't know he was playing with a loaded pistol.

Warner's nostrils flared. "No? Hell, Laura, you'd be within your rights in paying me back. Wasn't the last thing I said about going out and finding another woman?"

He had suddenly put me on the defensive. I said, "I did not take it that way, Warner. And I don't think you meant it."

"That's why I came, Laura. I figured we had to sit down and sort through this whole mess and find out what that fight was all about, find out what it was caused us both to say such hurtful things. That's what I've come for."

He was pressing me now toward the real issue and I wasn't ready for it. There wasn't enough time and I hadn't given it enough thought. When you discussed a matter with Warner you had better be sure you had thought your position through because you could be assured that he had. Instead of answering him in the vein he'd started I said, "Warner, how did you find me? How did you know where I was?"

He laughed dryly. It was a way of his when he thought I'd gotten up to something a little too smart. He said, "Hell, Laura, I found you because you intended me to. I admit you did some slick work with that little house in Tyler, hiding out like that without going to a hotel. But you told Quince and you knew I'd have to go to the bank. You knew he'd tell me."

Now that made me furious. I said, "Damn it, Warner, he was not intended to tell you. If he were here I'd twist his damn nose until he admitted it. I knew you had to have another signature on the ranch account and he was the only one I could think of. I gave him where I was going in case he had to reach me on business. But the son of a bitch was given specific orders not to tell you where I was."

He regarded me gravely and with disappointment in his eyes. "You put our business about in Tyler? You told that son of a bitch Quince that you'd left me?"

"No! Hell, no! I've got no more wish than you do to do our dirty linen in public. I told him not to tell anyone where I had gone. I assumed when you came in you'd have sense enough to go along with it and act as if you knew where I was. I guess you beat it out of him."

"Now you're the one pulling on the wrong rein. I never touched him or threatened him. I just made plans to take the money out of his bank. He like to have had a hissy fit about that."

I didn't laugh. He had expected me to, us both knowing Quince, but I didn't. He was drawing me out to talk and I'd told him I wasn't ready. I said, "So, you see, I did not intend you to find me until I was ready. And I'm not ready yet. I've made that plain enough."

"You mean you haven't finished your business yet, is that what you mean?"

"I don't know what you're talking about."

"With Morgan. Buying a wing of this hotel."

"Leasing. Did you discuss that with him?"

"No, he discussed it with me. Seemed to enjoy it. Someone listening to the conversation wouldn't have known whose wife we were talking about. He talks of you with what I'd call a proprietary air."

"It's none of your affair."

"I reckon it's not if this is where you are planning to make your new home."

"I didn't say that."

"You don't have to." He looked down at his hat. "You know, I reckon that was the first time you've told me something was none of my business since we've been married. And that includes your independent money." He looked at me. "How do you weigh up which words hurt the most? I know what I said did you harm, but what you said, that it was none of my affair what you did, that stung. They ought to have a kind of numbering system so we can be sure to keep the scales balanced."

I bit at my lip. "I only meant that it was business and nothing to do with Charles Morgan. I didn't want you thinking I viewed him in any other way."

He put his hat down on the floor. "He didn't sound to me as if he looks at it that way. He told me you were about the best looking thing he'd ever seen. He makes his intentions plain, Laura. To your husband. Contemptuously so."

Now I gave him a wry look. "Of course I believe that, Warner. I haven't heard a gunshot, so I rather doubt he's treated you contemptuously."

He shrugged. "Believe what you want to. When the remarks were passed I didn't know if I had a wife or not.

A man can't be insulted about a wife he doesn't have. Doesn't take a divorce to end a marriage. And from what he was telling me y'all became pretty thick in a short while."

"I am trying to do a piece of business, Warner. Now, please, get out of here and let me start dressing."

For answer he looked at his watch. "You got plenty of time. He ain't going to call for you until around eight. It's only a little after five now. By the way, I couldn't have shot him. They don't allow you to carry guns in this town. Deputy sheriff took mine off me when I got off the train."

It was hurting me to have him there, confusing me. I said, "Warner, if you won't leave I'll call Phoenix in. You won't be able to talk in front of her."

He stuck out his legs and leaned back in the chair. "Oh, I wouldn't be too sure of that. She just greeted me as if I were the man who'd come to guard the henhouse. I think she wanted to hug my neck. I also got the impression she ain't overly fond of Mr. Morgan."

I stood up and clenched my fists at my side. "God damn it, Warner! Will you get it through your thick head that this has nothing to do with Charles Morgan. It's between us. I am doing business with Morgan. Nothing else."

He looked up at me. "He's playing you, Laura. You must want this wing deal awful bad and you've let him know it. He's going to dangle it in front of you while he tries to get his way with you."

I could feel my eyes catch fire. "Are you calling me a whore?"

He shook his head calmly. "No. I'm calling you a not very good poker player. And I'm calling Morgan a snake. He'll slip up on your blind side while you are all confused about me. Right now you don't know which way to jump—about me or about anything. That's why I see that we need to talk. And it can't be put off too long."

I said, icily, "Mr. Morgan has already, as you call it, tried to play me. I made it clear it wouldn't work and he immediately desisted. Mr. Morgan is a gentleman. He is from Virginia."

He looked up at me calmly. "I'm from Texas, but that don't make me tall."

"Will you please leave?"

"Yes." He stood up and put on his hat. "I just realized I'm running out of time. I got to go out and buy a boiled shirt and a frock coat. Best bib and tucker. Ain't that what they mean by dressing for dinner?"

My eyes widened. "Warner, you wouldn't!" But I was not so sure. In his own calm way Warner was as audacious as any man I'd ever met and got more so the higher the stakes.

But he was shaking his head. "No, I wouldn't. But not because you don't want me to. I'm not going to accept Morgan's invitation because I know his intention would be to make me look silly. I'd be on his range. Now, I want you to tell me when you'll be willing to talk. Tonight? Later on?"

I shook my head. "I've told you I need time to think. During dinner I'll be talking business. I won't have a chance then."

"You go through with this deal we may not have anything to talk about. You will have a home right here in Jefferson. I've heard you talk about this place and I know what a bug you are on culture. Is it this place, this town? Does this suit you?"

"You are trying to make me talk now, damn it. I won't!"

"All right. Tomorrow. I'll come around after lunch."

I turned away. "No. I don't know. Don't press me, Warner. Where are you staying? I'll get word to you."

From behind me he said, "I came straight here from the depot. Don't have a place yet. But I'll get word to you in the morning."

"Fine, fine, fine. Now please go."

I heard his boots on the hardwood floor and then the sound of the door opening and closing. There was a velvet-covered wing chair in the corner and I immediately went to it and slumped down. Warner had confused me so badly, first by showing up so unexpectedly and then by knowing as much as he did. Not the least of the surprise had been the relatively easy-handed way he had accepted what I was doing with Charles Morgan. Warner was not a violent man, but he can be extremely effective when he sets his mind on a course of action. That he took the baiting that Charles Morgan must have given him and let it pass without deadly effect was amazing. He might not have had his gun, but he still had those strong hands of his and Morgan would have been no match.

Maybe it was, as he said, that he felt no claim on me until matters were clear between us. But that, somehow, left me feeling vaguely disappointed. Hell, wasn't he going to fight for me? Or did he not consider Morgan a proper suitor for me? He was right about that. No one was going to appeal to me as long as I was still tied to Warner, but Warner couldn't know that.

My thinking was interrupted by the explosive entrance of Phoenix. She took a position in the middle of the room, put her fists on her hips, and glared at me. She said, "Well I knowed you was a lot of things, Miss Laura, but I never thought you was just plain out an' out mean! Cruel!"

I really did not want to be distracted by Phoenix's histrionics. I said, tiredly, "Phoenix, what do you want?"

She said, in a pitiful voice, "Wisht you could have seen that poor man way he left here. Looked like a little rag doll somebody done pulled all de stuffin' out of. Here he come with his hat in his hands, wantin' to make it up. And den look. Come out of here whipped to a frazzle. I hate to think what you done to that fine gen'lman, Mr. Warner. No, never mind." She put up her hand. "Phoenix don't need to know. Ain't none o' Phoenix's business. Phoenix need to learn her place and stay right there. No, no. Don't tell me what you whipped that poor man with. Don't want to hear the words. You jes' keep 'em to yo'self." She turned around and went back to the door to the parlor. "I jes' be out here puttin' de lace 'round the collar dat green gown you gonna wear tonight for that man downstairs. De gown poor Mr. Warner won't get to see you in. I be out here doin' that. You jes' set an' enjoy yo' victory over that poor man."

She was gone before I could get my mouth open. I shook my head. I knew that Phoenix could not be bought but she could be appealed to. I wondered what Warner had said to her on his way out. Perhaps nothing. Phoenix had imagination enough for two and she was already dead set against Charles Morgan. That naturally put her in Warner's camp. Now I could be assured of a steady diet of thinly veiled suggestions and innuendoes and attitudes and a host of other postures and positions just short of open rebellion.

And now, in a little while, I would have Mr. Morgan to deal with. He had promised me an answer about the wing on Monday, which was the morrow. But there was still the matter of several hours of dinner to be got through with him. And now he had met Warner, and I felt sure the meeting had supplied him with fresh fuel. If he had, indeed, been so bold as to comment about my looks to my husband and to strike a tone that suggested familiarity between us, then he must have been coaxed to such rashness by something Warner said or something in his demeanor. I was fearful that Mr. Morgan, to advance his own suit, might attempt to denigrate Warner in my eyes. That, I could assure him, would have the effect opposite to what he was striving for.

I leaned my head back against the chair. What, really, did I want with the damn wing after all? In the first flush of anger and independence it had seemed like a capital idea. But now I was no longer sure. The meeting with Warner had left me blue and feeling very much alone. I found myself wishing that he knew some magic words that would suddenly make it all right and allow me to take him back and go on as we had. But going on as we had was what caused the trouble in the first place. I was damned if I knew what to think, much less do. I raised my head and my voice. "Phoenix! Phoenix! Get in here, you busybody!"

Our entree that evening was giant shrimp that had been sauteed in a mushroom sauce. Mr. Morgan had entertained me by dwelling on the story of how the shrimp were kept alive in giant barrels filled with salt water all the way from New Orleans. "Fresh," he said. "Fresh as if you were eating them right after they left the Gulf of Mexico. Tell me, Mrs. Grayson, can you get anything like that on a horse ranch in the pine woods off a mud road?"

With the meal half over he had not directly mentioned meeting Warner but he had consistently made references to the luxury of the life he was living. I finally put my fork down and said, "Tell me, Mr. Morgan, exactly what are you after?"

He looked at me with a slightly amused expression on his face. "I'm not sure, Mrs. Grayson. I have been speculating on that myself. Tell me, would your husband buy a horse without trying it first?"

I said, "I hope, Mr. Morgan, you do not mean that the way it sounds. If you do it is as crude a remark as I've heard from anyone, any time." I threw my napkin on the table.

He said, quickly, "I don't know what you thought, Mrs. Grayson. I only had reference to the fact that we had never done business before. How do you think I meant it?"

It was glib enough. I said, "Somehow the one does not fit with the other."

He made a motion with his hand. "I used the analogy of your husband and horses. Your husband is in the horse business. That should indicate I was talking about business. Isn't that what you're here for?"

Mr. Morgan seemed somewhat changed. He was looser and many of his remarks bordered on innuendo. He had not become familiar enough to, say, address me less formally, but he had the air of a man who felt as if he was playing the tune and I was obliged to dance. I had to feel that it, in some way, had to do with his meeting with Warner. Whatever it was he had certainly gained a degree of gross confidence and it was not at all becoming. For my part, I kept trying to draw him toward the business proposition I'd put to him. I tried to talk about the size of the rooms, their configurations, their decorating. But he would have none of it. Each time I would make a sally he would bring the conversation back to me or him or the two of us in Jefferson. He held Jefferson out as bait as if it were Baghdad or Paris or the lost city of Atlantis.

Then he suddenly said, "I am very much surprised that Mr. Grayson could not join us tonight. I'm surprised he would let so lovely a lady as you out free in public."

He had caught me off guard with the sudden subject shift. I said, "Oh, Mr. Grayson is convinced he can't swallow while wearing a necktie." It sounded shallow even to my own ear.

"Oh? I thought perhaps he had left town. So he is still here."

I said, hesitantly, "Yeeess. I suppose so."

He gave me a quick, narrow-eyed look. "You don't know your own husband's plans?"

I gave him the same look in return. "I have just said he remained in town."

"Ah. Then he is staying here at the hotel. With you." I didn't say anything. "He is staying with you, is he not, Mrs. Grayson?"

"What affair is that of yours, Mr. Morgan?"

He laughed and waved a hand. "Well, for one thing, it is my hotel. But I was more concerned with your comfort. Is the bed big enough for the two of you? If not I can have another brought in. Or perhaps you don't sleep in the same bed as an ordinary matter. Many modern couples don't. Some even sleep in separate bedrooms. Shall I have another bed sent up? A small one?"

There did not seem to be any escaping his relentless questioning. I put my fork down. "Mr. Grayson is not staying here, Mr. Morgan. So it really is none of your concern."

But he persisted. "Am I to understand that the two of you are staying in different hotels?"

I struggled for a plausible lie. "Mr. Grayson has business at a ranch just out of town. I believe he is staying with the rancher and his wife."

Mr. Morgan frowned and looked away toward a far corner of the busy dining room. After a time he shook his head. "That won't do, Mrs. Grayson, that won't do at all."

"What won't do?"

"I expect the truth from my business associates."

I felt myself redden. "I beg your pardon, sir."

He put up his hands. "Oh, I am not calling you untruthful, dear Mrs. Grayson. I got the distinct impression from my desk clerk that Mr. Grayson was here only to see you. In fact, during our visit—Did I mention I had the opportunity to have a talk with Mr. Grayson?"

I was becoming more and more uncomfortable. I was beginning to damn myself for becoming involved with the son of a bitch for any reason. I said, evenly, "No, but Mr. Grayson told me you had met."

"Well, that is what I assumed. That is why I did not speak of it directly. But it seemed to me that he also told me he was here only to visit with you. No!" He lifted a quick finger in the air. "No, that is not true. I asked him if he were in town on horse business. He said he wasn't. That's where I was thrown off. I didn't know Mr. Grayson had other business interests."

"Perhaps you might know that horses eat feed, Mr. Morgan, large amounts of it. And hay. Perhaps he came to buy feed and hay. They do grow that here, don't they?"

"You know, Mrs. Grayson, I never thought of that. That's the perfect explanation. What could I have been thinking of. And I was blaming my poor desk clerk for misinforming me." He smiled, a spark of cynicism in his eyes.

I picked my fork up. "Misunderstandings are easy to

come by," I said pointedly. "Someone could see us and easily get the wrong impression. Tell me, when are we going to talk about the wing?"

He didn't answer me directly. A waiter came to take away our dinner plates. Mr. Morgan inquired if I would care for dessert and, when I shook my head, instructed the waiter to bring us coffee and brandy.

I said, "You did not answer my question, Mr. Morgan."

"I have told you I'd give you an answer about the wing Monday. That's tomorrow. Tonight I'd rather talk about other matters."

"I don't see where we have other matters to discuss."

"Ah, but there you are in error. I have a great deal of curiosity about you that I'd first have to satisfy before I can make a sound judgment about you as a partner, a business partner."

I said, dryly, "Your criterion seemed to be rather lax the last time you brought someone in."

"That," he said, "was a totally different matter. Our affair is a little more complicated."

"I don't see what my personal situation has to do with a straightforward business proposition."

He was about to answer when the waiter brought the brandy and coffee. He waited until the man was finished and gone before proceeding. "I am bothered," he said, "by the fact that you will not give me truthful information concerning your personal situation."

I felt a little edge of anger, but I smothered it. I said, calmly, "I have told you time and time again that my personal business is none of yours."

He shook his head. "And I am telling you that it is. You are all that I am really interested in, Mrs. Grayson. And yet you continue to lie to me about the state of your marriage."

Now I was angry. I said, stiffly, "I am afraid I will have to leave, Mr. Morgan. For a man who styles himself a gentleman you have a peculiar way of showing it."

"Oh? I submit to you, Mrs. Grayson, that you have fled your husband. I submit that you have fled him, his bed, and your marriage. I submit that you have come to Jefferson, where you have found a cultured climate more in tune with your tastes. I submit that sitting alone on a horse ranch for months and years with no society to speak of within reach has driven you to desperation. I submit that you plan to make your new home in Jefferson and that you would like to make your headquarters an apartment of rooms at the most exclusive hotel west of New Orleans. And that, Mrs. Grayson, is what is known as the truth."

I sat a moment, organizing my thoughts. "You are wrong once again, Mr. Morgan. For instance, had I choosen Jefferson as my new home I would have bought a house, a large house."

"There are none for sale. At least not in the more desireable locations."

"Then I would have one built."

"If a town lot could be found, yes, you could do that. But where would you live in the meantime? The construction of a house that would suit you could take a year or better. I submit that you have decided on an apartment in my vacant wing. I know that you are a woman of more than ample means, and I know that you are interested in using the Excelsior and its setting as your introduction into Jefferson society."

He had not secluded us with the screen from the rest of the restaurant, but just then I wished he had. He had spoken his last speech in a rising voice, leaning toward me as he did. I was very conscious of the other diners around us. When he finished he picked up his brandy glass and emptied it in one gulp. It was instantly refilled, as if he'd left standing orders. I noticed that he'd been drinking more than on other occasions. His face was slightly flushed and now and again the brandy showed in his speech. But I didn't think that was what was making him so much bolder. I thought it had something to do with Warner. As icily as I could I said, "Mr. Morgan, you are drawing a great many more inferences about my personal life than your information warrants."

He leaned toward me and tapped his index finger on the tabletop. "Listen, Mrs. Grayson. I allowed you to bluff me at the picnic. I gave you an ultimatum there and then retracted it. But since then matters have changed. I believe, Mrs. Grayson, that your husband came here to win you back and failed. I submit to you that you have no intention of returning to him. I submit that you are fair game, that you are on the market. So I believe that your business is my business, personal or otherwise. I feel that I am within my rights to pay court to you and I intend to do just that."

I looked him over cooly. I wondered how I could ever have found him the slightest bit attractive. "Mr. Morgan, those are reckless words. I am glad, for your sake, that my husband is not here to listen to them."

He raised his hands and laughed. "Your husband. I made my intentions clear to your husband this afternoon. The man is a whipped dog. He has no fight left in him, no backbone. You apparently took it with you when you left. But I've got the steel to match yours, Mrs. Grayson. You will find that I don't give up so easily."

He was beginning to worry me, not for myself or the business deal, but for Warner. If he were foolish enough to make such remarks to Warner there might well be a killing and, with Warner a stranger, he could end up in jail. I said, "Mr. Morgan, I implore you not to speak in such a manner to Mr. Grayson. I ask it as a personal favor."

He shrugged. "I have no reason to embarrass the man. The loss of you is enough of a blow. But I won't stand for his hanging around here like a lovesick moon calf."

I looked at him in amazement. I wondered if he realized how foolish the words were that he was saying. But this new tack certainly placed me under a different set of constraints. Now I had to worry about Warner. I did not know what was to become of us, or even what I wanted to happen, but I did know that Mr. Morgan's word would carry a great deal more weight with the town law than that of a stranger.

When the meal was completely finished and Mr. Morgan had had another glass of brandy, he insisted that we go out into the courtyard and sit at one of the wrought-iron tables and smell the magnolias.

"It's a scent I never tire of," he said, taking my arm and steering me toward a side door that led out of the restaurant into the courtyard. "The perfume you were wearing when you first came into my office reminded me of magnolias. I think I shall always be reminded of you when the magnolias blossom."

It was a chilly night and even though I was wearing a heavily brocaded gown with long sleeves and a high, military collar I was feeling cold. But I hated to leave Charles Morgan before a few more things had been said and understood. I didn't want to talk in the lobby or his office and I certainly was not going to allow him inside my suite. I said, "Mr. Morgan, I think we should get a few things straight before the evening ends. But I want to do it quickly because it's a little cool out here for me."

He was wearing a black waistcoat with a boiled shirt and a broad, half-Windsor tie. He took a flask from inside his coat pocket, unscrewed the top and offered it to me. "Brandy? That might help the cold."

I shook my head and hoped he wouldn't drink any more. I was starting to believe he was a man who couldn't handle his liquor. "No thank you," I said.

He took a long pull from the flask, took it from his mouth, and then set it on the table. "What needs to be set straight, Mrs. Grayson? I thought we had all our linen out on the line and drying."

I said, evenly, "I want to be sure that you understand that my proposal of business was just that. Business. I am no part of the deal. And also, I want you to understand that you are wide of the mark about Mr. Grayson and me. That continues to be none of your business."

He put his head back and laughed. "Mrs. Grayson," he

said, "I very much appreciate your spirit and your determination to be hard to get, a prize worth pursuing. It works with me very well. I'm not going to tell you that I always get what I want. Nobody does, though some fool occasionally says it. Do you understand, Mrs. Grayson?"

He looked at me with those agate-hard eyes of his, unblinking. I shivered inside. He was, I thought, a truly dangerous man.

"I understand your words, Mr. Morgan. But words do not make reality. Now, please, I would like to go in. I'm tired and cold. If you'll just see me to the lobby I'll escort myself to my suite."

He stood up and bowed. I thought there was something mocking in it. He said, "As you wish, Mrs. Grayson. I'm sure your husband would have much preferred to hear you coming to his defense tonight than what you said to him this afternoon. I saw him as he passed back through the lobby. He did not look a happy man."

I didn't answer. There was very little I could say.

Phoenix let me in as I was about to use my key. She followed me through the parlor and into the bedroom. I slumped down on the end of the bed and sighed. I was too tired and discouraged to do much more than slip off my shoes.

Phoenix said, "Miss Laura, what in the world is we doin' here? We ain't got no business in this fas' town and you ain't got no business keepin' company with dat lizard what owns this place. Ain't no good can come of none of this."

I shook my head. "I don't know, Phoenix. And right now I'm too tired to think. Mr. Morgan may or may not be a lizard, but he is very tiring company. You have to watch your every word."

"Whilst you was out with de lizard word come from Mr. Warner 'bout where he stayin'. He at the River Hotel. You want me to rush 'round in de mornin' an' tell him to fetch hisself on over here?"

I shook my head. "I can't see him in the morning,

174

Phoenix. I can't see him until I hear from Mr. Morgan about our business. I have to know about that before I can talk to Mr. Warner."

She put her hands on her hips. "I know I ain't bein' in my place, but I got to say it, an' I gonna say you don't need to be studyin' 'bout anything with that lizard."

I said, "Phoenix, I can't talk to Mr. Warner until I know we have an option, another place to stay, another life to choose. I know it's difficult for you to understand."

She glared at me. "Ain't nothin' hard to understand. I seen hardheaded folks before. I seen folks cut off they noses to spite their face. Ain't nothin' new 'bout what you doin'. But that shore don't make it no smarter."

"Phoenix, I have to know that I'm making a free choice in my heart and not going back to Mr. Warner because I have to. Can't you see?"

She threw up her hands. "I see a lady ain't got the stren'th to undress an' get in bed. You give out, Miss Laura, cause you workin' against yo'self inside. That's what got you wore out. Person can't fight theyselves inside all the time and stand it."

I was too tired to argue. I stood up so Phoenix could help me undress. All I wanted was to go to bed and sleep for about a week. At least Warner had not left town so perhaps there was still hope in that direction. Phoenix helped me into bed and pulled the covers over me. Just as I was drifting off to sleep I said, "Don't you see, Phoenix? Mr. Warner has got to do or say something to move me. I have my dignity to think of."

She turned the gas down in the lamp by the bed. "Well, you just snuggle up to yo' dignity, Miss Laura. See how warm it keep you."

9

Warner

I figured, if nothing else came of the trip, I'd be able to
say I slept in a floating hotel. Actually it was an old
steamboat tied up at the end of the wharf. They'd ripped
out the guts, the engine and boiler and crew quarters and
whatnot, and turned it all into guest rooms. It wasn't
much and it was expensive. I was in a room that didn't
have enough space to catch a cold and there were no
private bathrooms. For that I was paying six dollars a
night and glad to get it. Jefferson was growing faster than
its accommodations and the River Hotel had been the
only place I'd been able to find that was halfway decent.
It still looked like a steamboat. The paddlewheel was still
in place and the Texas deck and pilothouse were still
there, but they'd been turned into rooms. And since a
steamboat is built light on the topside to keep it from
turning over, the walls of my room were so thin you
could nearly see through them. You could hear your
neighbor breathing and the night I'd got settled in the
man and woman in the room just aft of mine had got to
carrying on to where it had brought a sweat to my face.
Laura and I had been separated a little too long for me to

be listening to such exercises and visualizing them in my mind.

I had got word to Phoenix the night before. I hadn't bothered with the desk, but just went around to the back and caught me a waiter working in the courtyard. He knew Phoenix and where to find her so after only a few moments wait she showed up and I gave her my new address. It wasn't but about two blocks from the Excelsior and I had hopes that Laura might send for me that very evening.

Phoenix said, "Lawdy, I hopes so, Mr. Warner. You's got to do somethin', Mr. Warner. That lizard ain't up to no good. Whyn't you up and wring his neck like some old scrawny chicken?"

I'd shrugged. "Phoenix, Miss Laura might take that all wrong. She might consider that interfering in her business."

"Yes, suh, but I is here to tell you that her business needs interferin' with. Most recklessly."

I smiled. I said, "Phoenix, this is a little more complicated than a strong right arm can handle. If I thought it would work I'd jerk Miss Laura up and haul her home."

"Well I sho' wish you would. I swear, that do be the hardheadest lady what ever lived. You got to do somethin', Mr. Warner."

"You just keep me informed, Phoenix. I'll be waiting for word."

Now it was four o'clock on Monday afternoon and I was still waiting. I'd been afraid to go out for a meal, afraid word might come while I was out. The desk clerks didn't appear to be all that reliable, since they spent a great deal of their time at the water side of the boat fishing over the railing. A messenger could come and go for all they would notice.

Finally I could stand it no longer. There was a little café across the street and I went over there and had some chili and eggs and drank a couple of beers. I sat where I could watch the steamboat, but nobody approached it who looked like Phoenix or some messenger from the Excelsior hotel. I was shaved and was well dressed as I could be considering the clothes I'd brought. I reckoned I could have bought a new shirt or even a pair of twill riding pants, but that would have made it kind of obvious that I was trying to impress, and Laura (and I for that matter) never cared for that kind of behavior. I figured I didn't have much to lose by going down and trying to see Laura. The night before Phoenix had shown me how to get to the second floor by the back stairs near the courtyard and how to make my way through the unfinished wing and out the door that was almost at Laura's suite. It was a way to avoid seeing Morgan or seeing Laura dining with him or in his office. I simply did not want to see her with the man. Accordingly, as soon as I'd paid my score at the café I walked straight over to the Excelsior and went upstairs and knocked on Laura's door. No one came, so after a moment I rapped again. In a few seconds the door opened and Phoenix stood there.

"Mr. Warner," she said, "Where in the world you been?"

I shrugged. "Waiting for word. It didn't come so I came. Is Miss Laura in?"

"Yes, suh, she sho' is."

"Is she fixing to get busy or go out?"

"No, suh. She be sittin' in there waitin' fo' that lizard to let her know 'bout her business doin's. You be gettin' on in there. You talk right up to her. Tell her it be time we was goin' home!"

"Phoenix, as I tried to tell you, there are times when you got to take a gentle approach to Miss Laura. And this is one of those times for me. She ain't in much of a listening mood."

"She don' know what she is, Mr. Warner, and that be a fact. She as confused as a puppy dawg chasin' its tail. You got to jerk her up, make her see the light."

I had to smile. "Phoenix, I'm not a Baptist preacher."

"Right now that be a shame. Maybe we ought to send fo' one."

I said, "I'll see what I can do. Don't announce me. I'll just slip in quietly."

"Yes, suh."

I was halfway across the parlor when I turned and said, "Phoenix, why don't you go on down to your room and rest. Maybe she might talk a little looser if she thinks she can't be overheard."

Phoenix smiled so that her gold tooth gleamed. She said, "I hope you is gonna loosen her up the way I thinkin'. Yes, suh, I do believe I needs me a nap. I don't see how I can get back here under a hour an' a half."

I said, "I don't know what you're thinking, Phoenix, but I got an idea. You ought to be ashamed of yourself."

Her tooth was still catching light. She said, "She be mighty down. I knows what brightens me up. Yes, suh, I surely does. You get on in there now an' I be on my way."

I opened the door and stepped into the room. Laura was sitting at her dressing table staring into the mirror. She turned as I came into the room. "Oh!" she said. "You startled me. I guess I was daydreaming."

She was wearing a peach colored silk dressing gown that I knew was one of her favorites. I could see the hem of her night gown below that of the robe. She must not have left the room all day.

I took the chair that sat by the wall near the door and carried it to the middle of the room and sat down. As I did I pitched my hat on the bed. I said, "They say that is bad luck, but I don't see how mine can get any worse so I ain't afraid."

"I hope you haven't come to talk because I'm still not ready."

"You mean you haven't heard from Mr. Morgan. Is that it?"

She swiveled around on the little backless chair so that she was facing me. "I see you have been talking with Phoenix." She shrugged. "It wouldn't make any difference between you and me if I had. But, no, I haven't." She glanced over her shoulder at her reflection in the

mirror and then idly picked up a brush and gave the back
of her hair a few swipes. "I think you are right. I think he
is playing me along. I have made it clear to him that I'm
not part of the deal but he is a hard man to persuade."
She put the brush down. "You have nothing to be jealous
of Mr. Morgan about."

I said, slowly, "I'm not jealous of him. I don't own you.
Like I said yesterday, you don't need papers to get a
divorce." I tapped my chest. "And if you've already
divorced me in here then what Morgan and you do is
none of my affair."

She bit her lip. She said, "Damn it, Warner, don't get
reasonable all of a sudden. There are some hard matters
between us. You can't just come waltzing in here and
start acting halfway civilized and think I'll fall for it."

"I'm not doing anything to make you fall for anything," I said evenly. "We ain't talked yet so you don't
really know how I feel." I looked around. "You got any
whiskey in here?"

She shook her head. "I don't think so. But Phoenix
could go down and ask them to bring you some."

"Phoenix is gone to her room. She said she was wore
out and needed a nap."

She gave me a close look. "You sure the idea of a nap
didn't come from you?"

I let out a sharp breath. "Hell, Laura, put your damn
hackles down. How was your breakfast, or lunch? Not
good? Want to blame that on me, too?"

"Why don't you go down and get your whiskey. I'll be
here. I'm not going anywhere."

I shook my head. "I don't want it that bad."

"What did you mean I didn't know how you felt yet?"

"Do you?"

She looked uncertain. "I don't take your meaning."

"You seem to think that I'm up here to get you to come
home."

"Well, aren't you?"

I pondered my words for a brief moment. Finally I
said, slowly, "Yeah, if that is what is right. I'd like you to

come home if we can make it right between us. But I am not here just to take you back no matter what. I think we got some serious understanding and discussing to do. At the end of that it may be that we ought not to be together. God knows, the last six months haven't been worth saving. We've got to quit fighting and go to talking. I'm here to see if we can do that."

I had taken her by surprise. She wheeled back around on her dressing chair and picked up her hairbrush and began working at her hair with brisk strokes. She always did that when she was displeased or nervous about something. She said, "I can see now why you're not jealous of Charles Morgan. You don't care. I'm surprised you are here at all."

It was amusing to know that this strong, tough, independent, pushy, selfish, willful woman could act just like a little girl. I said, "I don't think I said that, Laura, which is what is wrong here. We got too much misunderstanding between us. I said I thought we had to talk this matter out and find out what the real cause for that fight was."

She turned back again to face me and her dressing gown fell open to reveal her lacy nightgown and a good length of bare leg. "You called me barren. You said you needed another woman. That was what the fight was about."

I gave a little short burst of laughter, though my eyes were still interested in what the open robe was revealing. "There were a few more things got said before that. You had a few remarks to make about my ability to match the right sire with the right dam."

"As I recall it you were doing a lot of moaning and aching. I simply wondered, if you were supposed to be such an expert, what you were worried about. I'd been sitting in the house all day long with no one to talk to except Phoenix and you come in carping about your damn colt crop. And that was all you'd been talking about for months. Did I match the right stud to the right mare? What if that big stallion is going to make the colt too damn ungainly to run? And then you'd get on the present colts, a crop that had been bred three years before. Could they run? Could they run in Kentucky? Could they run in the big meets? Were they going to embarrass you? Hell, Warner, I only had one pair of ears."

I nodded. "Now I see I was wrong about that. Now I can see why you said what you did."

"What did I say?"

"The most hurtful thing you could think to say. You found my most sensitive spot and went right for it. You said if I didn't know what I was doing why didn't I tell you before you put money in the enterprise."

She dropped her head and looked down. "Yes. I have to agree, that was not very nice. I know how you feel about using my money."

I shrugged. "So I came back with the remark about what did you know about breeding since you'd never been so successful yourself in that line."

She nodded and smiled wanly. "Yes, I remember now. I said you couldn't breed a mule and that you were not only as stubborn as one but had the same kind of balls."

I sighed. "We were pretty well off and running. Wasn't no stopping then. All it could do was get uglier."

"And it did." She put her arms back and stretched. It was a nice pose that let me admire her breasts.

I got up and went over and stood in front of her. She leaned her head back and looked up at me. I bent down and kissed her, a gentle, tender kiss that I hoped would convey some of what I felt for her.

When I straightened back up she had a faint smile on her face. She said, "You know it won't solve anything."

My voice was husky. "It's been a good while. It'll solve that much at least."

"Yes," she said, and her voice was thickened also. "Yes, I agree about that part." She stood up, letting her robe fall to her feet, standing before me in the filmy nightgown. I could see the nipples of her breasts through the thin lace cups of the gown.

I put my arms around her waist and pulled her to me,

lowering my head as I did. We kissed again, with mounting passion, our mouths opening. It was a long kiss and when it finished she stepped back from me and shrugged the nightgown off her shoulders. It fell at her feet and I stood there staring. I said, my heart pounding in my throat, "I—I had forgotten how beautiful you are." I swallowed. "Go lie on your back on the bed. I want to look at you while I get my clothes off."

I never took my eyes off her as I shrugged out of my shirt and stripped off my boots and then my jeans. I was sitting on the side of the bed, just at her feet. I rolled over on my belly. Her knees were at a level with my face. I looked up the golden length of her, from her milky white inner thighs through the silken patch of butter-colored hair that grew on the soft mound I knew so well; looked on past the little round of her belly to her breasts with their rounded bottoms and red, erect nipples. I began kissing her on the inside of her leg, gradually spreading her legs as I eased my way forward. By the time I reached the forest of downy hair she was beginning to make little moans and to jerk convulsively. I could feel and taste the wet warmness of her long before I entered. When I did she coiled around me with arms and legs so that we were so close nothing could have pulled us apart. I could feel the strength of her increase with the rhythmic intensity of our agreement. As we struggled to become one with mouth and thigh and arm and leg, I wished, in the brief instant I had before the fire consumed me, that we could be so together in everything.

I sat up on the side of the bed. Even with my long legs my feet were unable to reach the floor from the height of the tall mattress and bed frame. I said, "I hope you don't take to walking in your sleep. You could break your neck if you fell off this thing." I looked around at her.

She had hiked herself up until she was half sitting with a couple of pillows behind her. "Do you still deny you sent Phoenix away in anticipation of this?"

"Are you complaining?"

She shook her head and smiled wanly. "No." She looked away.

"But it still doesn't change anything?"

"No. We never had a problem with this."

"Then why did it stop a month before that last fight? I don't know if it was a month exactly. Maybe more, maybe less."

"Because you can't fight the way we were and then make love."

"We used to fight and then make up."

She looked away again. "We started fighting differently. Couldn't you tell that?"

"That's all I've been thinking about since I got over being angry at you."

"Oh, and when was that?"

I laughed a little ruefully. "After I run off and stayed away overnight so you could worry about me and be all tearful and sorry when I got back. But Lord, was that house empty when I walked in. Felt as if it had been vacant for ten years."

She smiled. "I'm glad you enjoyed it. I spent far more than my share of lonely hours and days in there."

I looked around at her again. "You didn't have to. You used to be more involved in the business. Remember how it was at the ranch in Corpus? Remember the trips we made to buy mares and stallions? Nobody shut you out of that."

She reared up on her knees and leaned toward me. "Oh, Warner, that's not fair. It all changed once we went into the Thoroughbred business. Or you went into the Thoroughbred business."

"I don't see the difference."

"When we were breeding traveling horses with the Andalusians the horses were mine and I had some idea of what we were doing. And even the quarter horses, the short-distance race horses, I could understand that. And you would work with me and show me. But all that changed. You got so serious, so terribly, terribly, horribly serious."

"There was—there is a lot at stake. And most of it is your money."

She sat back, sitting on a pillow. She made a face. "There it is again, my money. That was another point of argument. You couldn't talk five minutes without bringing up my money."

I stood up and pulled on my trousers and then rummaged in my shirt pocket until I found a cigarette. I lit it with a match from my pants pocket and then went to sit down in the chair so I could face her. "You can't ignore a fact, Laura. It is your money and I am using it. It scared the hell out of me."

"You don't have to tell me that. My God, Warner, I was scared to have anything to do with the breeding of the Thoroughbreds. You were so agonizing about it. This stallion had to go with that mare at exactly the right time and this stud had to be kept away from such and such a mare until six months after she'd dropped a colt. Do you want to know when it changed?"

I drew on my cigarette. "Yes."

"When we got our first crop of Thoroughbred colts. I feel as if I haven't seen you for two hours at a stretch after that. You had to nursemaid those colts as if they were the first horses ever born. You were gone before I woke up and sometimes you didn't come in until after supper. Hell, I'm surprised we had enough sex to know whether we could have a baby or not."

"You know that fight wasn't about that."

She nodded. "But does it really matter? If we would go far enough to say the things we did then there's something awfully wrong."

"That's what I've been trying to say since I walked in the door yesterday. I'm trying to figure out if we can't find out what that something awfully wrong is and fix it. You've been saying it's because I stayed with the horses too much. Maybe that's so, but I felt I needed every minute I could get with those animals. You don't start a bloodline just by guess and by golly. It takes time and attention to detail. I think it's because you stayed shut up in the house so much. You ain't ever exactly been one to take to quilting or crocheting, but you could have got out more, gone to town, visited around."

She gave me a droll look. "Gone to town? Tyler? And visited with whom? Whom would I have talked to, the wife of the sawmill manager?"

I shrugged. I could see we weren't getting anywhere. "You could have gone to Houston or Austin. Hell, you could have gone back to Virginia visiting your family."

"Damn it, Warner, those are temporary measures. A person doesn't live her life day by day like that. A husband and wife do things together. Otherwise what in the hell is the point of being married?"

I sighed and wished even more that I had a drink. I said, "All right. I take the blame for it. I was too busy with my work. But, damn it, it was your money invested. I couldn't stand the thought of failing you."

She rose up on her knees again and pointed a scarlet tipped finger at me. "There! There! My money! Money! I never was so sick of hearing anything in all my life. Weren't you investing your money too?"

"Not as much as yours by a long shot and I—"

She cut me off. "What about your knowledge, your experience? A lifetime of learning that few men could match? Or your instincts about horses. How many times have I heard that Warner Grayson knows more about horses than horses? Isn't that worth something? Instead all I hear about is the puny amount of money I put in. Yes, puny. I've got ten times that much. Maybe fifteen times. And there you'd be, searching for a bargain in a stallion or a mare when I had money to buy anything you wanted."

I stood up and leaned toward her. "Yes, and that's just it! I knew it and you knew I knew it. So I damn well hunted for the bargains because I was damned if I'd spend a nickel more of your money than I had to."

She sat back on the pillow and lowered her pointing finger. She sighed and shook her head. "See, Warner? It doesn't take much. How long before we would have been into hurtful remarks."

I sat back down and looked at the floor. "You're right. And it's a damn shame. I guess a man ought never to marry a woman that's got more money than he has."

"At least your kind of man. There's plenty would jump at the opportunity."

I glanced at her. "Mr. Morgan by chance?"

She gave me a look. "Don't be funny, Warner. You're not very good at it. You're also a damn fool. Texas is a community property state. Or did you not know that. Whatever I have is yours and whatever you have is mine."

I looked back down at the floor. "You didn't quite hear it right, Laura. That holds true about what you accumulate in the marriage. Whatever you brought in to the marriage is yours. It would have made a nice answer, but it just ain't so."

She eased off the side of the bed and went over to her dressing table and picked up her peach colored silk robe. Even so soon after the greatest satisfaction known to man the sight of her stirred me afresh. But she was putting the robe on and tying it closed with the sash. She said, "Well, so much for that thought."

I said, earnestly, "Laura, I hate to see this going all wrong just when matters are about to change."

"Change how?"

"Come spring the colts will be ready to race. We'll be going to race meets in Kentucky and Tennessee and Louisiana, even Virginia, maybe. You'll have the excitement of traveling and of meeting and getting to know people of your own class. You won't be stuck out on that ranch day after day and I won't be so busy with the horses."

She looked at me, contemplatively. "That sounds good, Warner, and I'm sure you believe it. Right now, anyway. But I know you. There will always be an emergency with the horses that demands your immediate attention. For the last two years I haven't felt as if I've had a husband so much as a man I'd hired to raise race horses. I have to come first."

"You do come first," I insisted. "What the hell you think I'm doing here right now? This ought to say something."

"It does. For the time being. But what happens when you get me home again?" She came the few steps to my side and put her hand on my shoulder. "I think you love me, Warner, and I think you mean the best. But right now I am very confused. I wish one of us knew some magic words that would make it suddenly all right, but I don't. Do you?"

I was silent. I realized that I had forgotten Wilson Young's lesson about having a cardinal rule to keep you on track. We were starting to argue, to get snarled up in the small change rather than keep our eyes on the prize. The prize was our marriage. Did we really want it together? I didn't want to woo Laura and take her back to the ranch. She would only leave again. And I didn't want to take her back unless I felt she was going to be happy. I sat there thinking about all that, trying to find a way to say something we both could understand.

For some time I had been staring at an object on a low bureau between the two tall windows that faced on the street. The object was about a foot and a half long and cylindrical in shape. It was a very light tan with a darker tan patch on the side I could see. I got up, for lack of something better to do, and walked over to it. Outside it was about ten inches in diameter and was hollow. I could see now that the patch on the side was actually a pouch made out of some kind of very soft and fine leather with a silver snap at the top to hold it closed. There was one on the other side too. The body of the thing appeared to be made out of suede. I could see that the inside was lined with red silk. I said, "What in the hell is this thing?"

Behind me Laura said, "That's my new muff. It was

delivered just before you came. The two pouches on the side are for use as a purse."

I said, "Hell, Laura, it ain't glove or muff weather. Rushing the season a little, ain't you?"

"It's not fur. It's perfectly acceptable at this time of year. Besides, it's not really for warmth. Put your hand inside."

I picked it up with my left hand and slid my right inside. I was surprised at its weight until my fingers felt the butt of a pistol. I pulled it out and looked at the small, blue steel revolver. I said, "What are you doing with this?"

"I'm alone in the world, remember?"

I glanced over at her. She was sitting at her bureau again. Our eyes met in the mirror. "By choice," I said. "By choice." I put the muff down and wandered back to the center of the room. I stood there a moment with my hands in the back pockets of my pants. I said, "You know I'm not trying to talk you into doing anything you don't want to do. If I have to do that then it's no good. I don't want you unless you can make me happy and I can do the same for you. It won't work any other way. I've been studying on this the past week and I've come to the conclusion that a marriage has got to be the most even horse trade in the history of horse trading. I know there are folks who stay married that ain't got an even deal, but generally one of them is limping along on a bowed tendon or a bruised frog or the other one shies at shadows. But that ain't the kind of marriage I want. I know how wrong I've been in the past, and I think you've gotten a hump or two in your back and went to bucking when you had no reason to buck other than to see if I could tame you."

She glanced in the mirror. My face was reflected just over her head. She said, "Yes, I will admit to that. That has always been one of my failings. I want a strong man, but I seem to insist that he keep on proving it."

"And you've nearly worn me out in the process."

"Maybe that's why you spent so much time in the barn."

I shook my head. "No, I've never ducked out on you. If I was in the barn it was because I needed to be."

She was putting rouge on her face, highlighting her cheeks, which I always thought was gilding the lily. I walked over to the chair and bent down and picked up my hat. She said, "Are you going?"

I nodded. "Yeah. I get the impression you are waiting for Morgan. I'd as soon not be here if he comes."

She shrugged. "He said he would let me know sometime today about the business proposition. I'm not making up my face to go anywhere. It's just something to do. I ought to get dressed and go out. Maybe I'll look at houses."

I stood there with my hat in my hand. "I take it by that remark that you are determined to stay in Jefferson. That your business with Morgan is not the deciding factor."

She turned around to face me. "Warner, you are jumping to conclusions. I can invest in property without living here. What is between us is just that, between us."

I nodded. "I still think Morgan is an influence in this matter. God knows he's everything I'm not. A Virginia gentleman. Probably spends more on his clothes than I spend to eat in a year. I can't tell you about men's looks, but I got an idea I'd come off a poor second if you were to line us up. And, of course, he's more your kind of people than I ever have been. I'm just a horseman."

She put her powder puff down and said, "Warner, honey, you don't know anything."

It startled me. I said, slowly, "You know, I believe that is the first time since I first saw you seven years ago that you've called me by a pet name."

She turned back around. "I don't hear sweetheart or darling too damn often either."

I smiled. "That's because you ain't very sweet or darlin' very often." I adjusted my hat. "I can't stay much longer, Laura."

She glanced at me in the mirror and then looked down.

Her words were a long time in coming. Finally she said, "That's up to you, Warner. I understand your pride."

"It's not pride. And it's not the ranch. If you want me as much as I want you then it won't matter whether I'm here or not. When I've said everything I have to say and heard everything you have to say then there will be no further point in lingering. I'll say goodbye now."

She turned on her little chair. "Kiss me first, Warner."

I went over, surprised, and leaned down to kiss the lips she raised to me. It was not the kiss of passion we'd experienced in the bed but the kiss that can only occur between two people who know each other very well. I straightened up. I said, "I will come over tomorrow. If you want to reach me before then Phoenix knows how to find me."

As I walked down the stairs toward the lobby I wondered if I shouldn't have suggested that we eat supper together. Maybe doing an ordinary thing like that together might have been a giant step in resolving our differences. Maybe we could even have slept together and had breakfast together and then, without having spoken any more words, have picked up where we left off.

But I doubted it. No, it was best not to crowd her. She was a filly that needed a loose lead rope, let her think she was going where she wanted on her own. I was not feeling particularly encouraged by the talk we'd had, even if we had ended up in bed. And I sure as hell hated to hear her say she might go out looking for a house. It put a knot in my stomach.

I was surprised to come off the last step and find myself in the lobby. I had not turned and gone out the back way, the way I'd come. Instead I was once again walking through a lobby full of what I considered overdressed folks. I knew I stuck out like a sore thumb and I hurried toward the front door to be rid of the place. Just as I was about to put out my hand and shove one of the heavy doors open I felt a hand tap me on the shoulder. I turned around and found Charles Morgan standing there. He was got up, as usual, in his tie and waistcoat and stiff collar. For the first time I noticed he had washed out blue eyes that were as pale as a New Mexico sky. The last time I'd seen eyes like that had been on a man who thought inflicting death was the best way to settle an argument. I'd had to kill him, but not before he'd put the only blemish on Laura's body with a chance bullet that caught her just in the side.

Morgan said, "Mr. Grayson, good evening."

I nodded. "Howdy."

"I'd like to buy you a drink."

I didn't want to drink with the man and he should have had sense enough to know it, though from the self-satisfied look he kept on his face I think he figured everybody would want to drink with him. I said, "Much obliged, Mr. Morgan, but I'm not thirsty right now."

He said, "I don't think you understand, Mr. Grayson. I think we should talk. You can drink or not drink as you please."

I studied for a half a moment. I said, "All right, put like that. But not in your office or your hotel. Is there a quiet saloon around here?"

"Just down the block. Not fifty yards. It's actually a private club made up of the business leaders of the city."

I half smiled. "Does that mean Mrs. Grayson would be invited to join if she goes in with you?"

"Certainly not. It's a men's club."

"She won't care for that."

He pushed the door open. "Shall we go?"

The place was called the Cotton Club, named, I figured, after the mountains of bales of the stuff that were stacked up on the broad wharves just across the street. The place was dim and quiet with a bunch of tables with big leather chairs surrounding them. Gentlemen sat around reading the newspaper or playing cards or just having a drink. The waiters were got up in white uniforms. It occurred to me that I had never seen so many uniforms outside of an army post in all my life. I wondered if the folks did that to be sure they didn't get the servants confused with the gentry. But, since all of the servants were Negroes, it didn't seem like a problem that should have sought long for a solution.

Morgan and I sat down in a corner at a round table with little slots around the edges that I finally figured out were for putting your chips in when you gambled. A waiter came over and I ordered whiskey and Morgan called for a brandy and soda. Then we waited until the drinks came before any talk was attempted. No effort was made at a toast and I took one swig of my drink and then set it down. I said, "You are the one wanted to talk."

"Yes," he said. He sipped at his watered-down drink and looked away for a moment. I thought he was trying to organize his thoughts. I was wrong. He must have been trying to summon his nerve, for the question he asked me took plenty. He said, "Mr. Grayson, how much do you have in your Thoroughbred breeding stables?"

I looked at him. "How much? How much what?"

"Why, money. Whatever else could I have meant?"

I smiled but not with much humor. I said, "Oh, there's time and instinct and sweat and experience and know-how and good will and about a half a dozen other items. What did you have in mind?"

"I would like to buy an interest in your operation."

Now I had to blink. Here was a man who had the same as told me he wanted my wife and now he was showing an interest in my business. Next he'd be wanting to know if I had any kinfolks I might knock down to him at a good price. I was of two minds on how to answer him. I didn't know if Laura had told him she owned half of the ranch or not. If she hadn't I sure didn't want to be the one to enlighten him. And I didn't know whether to kind of string him out a little to see how much he knew or to just laugh in his face. Finally, I decided on a middle ground. I said, "Mr. Morgan, the colts I've got that are about to enter their maiden season are unproven. I don't know if I've got a sack of gold or a sack of grits."

He tossed his head backwards. It was a womanly gesture and I was surprised. He said, "Come now, Mr. Grayson, I'm familiar with your reputation. I'm certain you know exactly what your stable is worth. Name a figure."

I shook my head slowly. "You haven't even seen my place. You sure as hell haven't seen my books. Why in hell would you be interested?"

"I don't see how my reasons have anything to do with the business at hand."

"What percentage are you interested in buying?"

"A majority interest."

The whole matter was making me curious as hell. It wasn't every day that someone just tapped you on the shoulder and asked if you'd sell your ranch. I said, "I'd reckon there are two prices. One with me and one without."

"Without."

I nodded. "I have to ask you a question, Mr. Morgan. Does this matter have anything to do with my wife?"

He ducked and dodged. "Mr. Grayson, I am a wealthy man. My reasons are my own. Name a figure."

It was the strangest way to do business I had ever run across. But perhaps the pace was such in a going concern like Jefferson that it was common. I said, "I don't reckon, Mr. Morgan. I wouldn't have anything to do with about twenty hours a day of my time."

He pursed his lips into a sour, tight little mouth. "Mr. Grayson, the ranch is the one link holding you and Mrs. Grayson together. I am trying to sever that link. Surely there is a price that will tempt you."

It was the damndest thing that I could recollect ever being said to me, especially on such short acquaintance. I didn't know if he realized just how dangerous such talk could be. But I kept myself calm. I said, "You and I need to get something squared away. You keep talking about Mrs. Grayson. Is that my wife you are talking about?"

He straightened in his chair. I could see the small bulge where he was either carrying the biggest pocket watch around or else a regular-size derringer. It was in a pocket in his vest that was revealed as his coat pulled back when he straightened up. I reckoned the law about carrying firearms didn't apply to him. Likely he was in tight with the local law. It didn't make me any difference. The reason I wasn't breaking his jaw was not for fear of jail but because I worried it might make him look sympathetic in Laura's eyes.

He said, "Mr. Grayson, I prefer to keep this on a civilized level. I am a gentleman and I'm approaching you in a gentlemanly fashion."

I looked at him thoughtfully for a good half a moment. I said, "You know, Mr. Morgan, you kind of remind me of one of the colts we got back at the ranch. This here colt is about as high bred as you can get. I mean he's got papers going back to when Moses was riding bareback. And all the papers say he is a Thoroughbred race horse. We even call him a Thoroughbred race horse. If somebody was to come up to where he was and point him out and ask what he was we'd have to answer that he was a Thoroughbred race horse. The only problem is he can't run fast enough to get out of his own way."

He sat quiet for a time. Finally he said, stiffly, "Just what are you implying by that statement?"

I didn't want to finish my drink. In fact I remembered I hadn't finished the last drink I'd had with him. Maybe he wasn't anybody I wanted to drink with. I said, "I'll leave you to figure that one out, Mr. Morgan. Maybe it means all I got is slow horses that you wouldn't want to buy."

His eyes seemed to have gotten paler. He said, "Do I understand that you will not name a price?"

"You are a quick study, Mr. Morgan."

His eyes narrowed. "I have a strong feeling that Mrs. Grayson owns a considerable part of your ranch. What if I were to approach her about buying her part?"

"You approach her all you want about the ranch," I said. "She makes her own decisions." I didn't add that without Laura I didn't want the ranch. "You can approach her all you want to about business."

He said, stiffly, "Mr. Grayson, I would think you would appreciate the forthright approach I am taking. I have given you fair warning that I am interested in Mrs.

Grayson. And I can assure you that whatever connection I am trying to make with the lady in question is honorable."

I stood up. I said, "Listen, Morgan, let's get something straight. You go on talking about being a gentleman and doing the honorable thing all you want. But get it straight that you are talking about another man's wife and there ain't no honorable connection so long as they are man and wife." I shoved my half drunk glass of whiskey across at him. "I don't have anything I want to sell you and the only thing I'm willing to give you is the dregs in my glass." I reached in my pocket and took out a few dollars and threw them on the table. "That ought to cover the refreshments. The advice was free."

"You didn't give me any advice."

"Maybe you didn't listen close enough."

With that I turned on my heel and walked out of the Cotton Club. Outside it was coming dusk but the sidewalks were still thronged with people hurrying this way and that. I felt pretty low. I couldn't think of anything of any weight that I had to say to Laura, not anything that might swing the tide. It appeared to me that she was being taken in by Morgan's flash and sophistication. Well, that was one department I couldn't match him in, that and money. And the culture of Jefferson. If that was what she wanted it looked as if I were going to be the loser. I made my way across the street, dodging through the traffic of buggies and wagons and carriages, and stepped up on the big planks of the huge wharf. I didn't really know how I was going to get through the balance of the evening. Eat some supper and then drink myself silly, I reckoned. The way things were looking I couldn't see much reason for sticking around. Maybe the best idea would be to head on back to the ranch the next day. At least I'd have work to keep me busy.

But I hated like hell to leave the field wide open for Morgan. I had never met a man with more gall in all my life. If I had heard him right he was proposing to buy my share of the ranch just to get me out of the picture. It made me feel sure that Laura must have told him how much she cared about horses. Likely he wanted to buy her a present that would really impress her.

I said, "Damn!" out loud. Nobody in the bunch that was hurrying by me even glanced my way. Obviously, yelling out damn on a busy street was nothing new. I was working up a fine hatred for this town.

10

Laura

I was not only confused about what I was doing and what I was thinking, I was even confused about what I really wanted and that made for a very unpleasant quandary. I was very much enjoying having Warner pay court to me. He might say he would not woo me to win me back, but it seemed to me that was exactly what he was doing. The Warner I had left a short nine days before would never have displayed the patience of the one who was lingering in a town, away from his work, waiting for me to reach a decision. And certainly that previous Warner would not have stood by and allowed a dandy and a fop like Charles Morgan to try and seduce me with the possibility of being in the center of the appealing society of Jefferson.

Everything that Warner had said made a great deal of sense, especially the part about the worst of the ranch time being over. We would be going to race meets and I would be part of the work and it would be exciting. I found it all particularly amazing because I had never suspected Warner could be so thoughtful. He had evidently given a great deal of thought to our circumstances before he'd ever come to find me. That in itself was

198

miraculous. Warner was a man who acted rapidly when he considered something amiss. When he first walked in on me I expected him to take a come-home-right-now-or-else attitude. I had been most pleasantly surprised to find him quiet and understanding, advancing gentle arguments for our continued marriage and even having the good sense to dig well beneath the surface for the cause of the fatal fight we'd had.

When I talked it over with Phoenix she thought the matter was settled and was all ready to begin packing. When I said that, no, I was still not clear in my mind about what was right and what I wanted to do, she rolled her eyes in her head and said, "Missy, I don' know what you wants! That gen'lman, an' I talkin' 'bout a real gen'lman, not that gussied up fool, done come all this way an' made his 'pology an' talked sense an' throwed the door wide open fo' you to have yo' way anyway you wants it an' you settin' there tellin' me that ain't enough?" She lifted her face toward heaven. "You better git down on yo' knees tonight an' thank the good Lord he allowed you another chance at that good man. What you want to try his patience for? Ain't he done nearly ever'thing a man can do to make it up?"

I reminded her that it hadn't been so long ago that she was all for dragging Mr. Warner behind the wagon. She'd said, "Huh! That was then, this here is now." She folded her arms. "Ain't no good you sayin' nothin' 'gainst Mr. Warner to me. Naw, ma'am. I wisht he'd take that critter and strip him naked of them fancy clothes an' run him through the streets fo' 'bout an hour and then maybe we could get out of here and get home where we belongs. I ain't got no idea, fo' instance, what Albert has done got hisself up to. That man can't be trusted alone fo' ten minutes an' we been gone better'n a week. How much longer this foolishness goin' to go on? You can fool other folks, even Mr. Warner, but you ain't got no interest in that worm and you ain't got no interest in no business dealin's with him."

I had said, "What makes you so sure of that?"

"Cause you wouldn't let me put the bad mouth on him if you was serious."

There was a great deal of truth in what Phoenix said and I did not know why I was dilly-dallying around with Charles Morgan. I had begun to find his company distasteful and, since it was obvious that to be in business with him was to be in his company, I had begun to lose interest in leasing the wing.

But the son of a bitch wasn't giving me the opportunity, on my terms, to reject him and his proposal. He had promised me word on Monday, word of some kind. Either he was definitely interested or somewhat interested or not at all. I knew what his delay was all about. He was making sure that I understood that I wouldn't be paying with just money for the lease. He was hoping to keep me dangling long enough that my own position might weaken. He was wrong if he expected that.

So Monday passed without word from him. I took breakfast and lunch in my rooms and then Warner came in the afternoon. When he left, I was more confused and not just a little regretful that I hadn't asked him to stay the night, or at least to take me out somewhere for dinner. I dressed and then, accompanied by Phoenix, strolled out through the better neighborhoods of Jefferson. I saw homes and houses that, except for their small grounds, would have equaled some of the mansions I had seen in Virginia. I estimated that fully fifty thousand dollars had been spent on some of the larger ones. The beauty of their location was that they were just a street or two removed from downtown and from the wharves. It would have been a very pleasant stroll to leave the quiet and comfort of your home and arrive, a few moments later, right in the middle of bustling commerce.

Phoenix was not impressed. She said, "These folks puttin' on the dawg, that's all they be doin'. Spendin' money don't be quality. Po' white trash is still po' white trash even if they got a bushel basket o' money. You don't want to be havin' no truck with these folk, Miss Laura. We best be gettin' on back to our own."

I asked her if Mr. Warner had bribed her by chance to be such a naysayer about Jefferson. The suggestion scandalized her. She said, in a huff, "Mr. Warner too fine a gen'lman fo' such carryin' ons. Besides, he don't have to give me no money to see the right of the matter."

I wondered, as I dressed Tuesday morning, if I was dallying to punish Warner or if I sincerely did not want to go back to Tyler and live on a ranch. I could not deny that the vibrance of Jefferson had a strong pull on me. I wanted to be in the midst of its excitement. I wanted to be involved in the trading of the goods that piled up on its docks every day. In a way, I still wanted to finish and decorate the wing. I couldn't think of a better location to dip my fingers into all sorts of pots. If only, I thought, the bargain didn't include the attentions of Charles Morgan. But then, I thought, if I couldn't handle Charles Morgan I wasn't the woman I thought I was. Once I had a duly legalized deal with him I could fend off his attentions as easily as I might swat a pesky fly.

But getting him to arrive at a decision was proving much harder than I had ever thought. I intended to take lunch in the dining room. I would not make it a point to be seen by him, but, if our paths should cross, what would be more natural than to have a business talk. Besides, I was getting tired of taking my meals in my rooms. I had waited up the night before until almost eleven before I changed into my sleeping clothes. Still he had not come. And the morning was half over and not a sign of him. Well, besides having lunch in the dining room, which was perfectly normal for a guest of the hotel, I wasn't going out of my way one iota to further the discussion. The man had said Monday and he had broken his word. It made me furious to be kept dangling in such a cavalier fashion.

I dressed in a light green frock perfectly tailored to show me off to the best advantage while remaining well within the bounds of decorum. To make sure I wouldn't be kept waiting I sent Phoenix ahead of me to reserve a table. As I walked off the stairs and past the desk I didn't so much as glance toward the door to the office behind the desk. Mr. Morgan owed me an explanation for his tardiness and it was up to him to seek me out.

I was given a small table near the front of the restaurant. The waiters were deferential and prompt, a result, I was sure, of their having seen me dining with the hotel owner. I ordered chicken breasts stewed in a wine sauce and a green salad. The waiter wondered what wine I would take, but I asked for iced tea. I knew the room was almost full, but I did not look around. As my courses began to arrive I went about the business of eating, paying no mind to those around me. It was only when a bottle of white wine arrived at my table that I was aware I would shortly have a visitor.

He was not long in coming, sliding into the chair opposite me. I had finished eating and was looking at the dessert menu. Without glancing up I said, "I assume you ordered the wine for yourself, Mr. Morgan, because I don't care for any."

"I hope you don't mind if I join you."

I put the dessert menu down. "You seem to do as you please, Mr. Morgan. Besides, I've finished." I made as if to get up but he put his hand out.

"Please don't go so quickly. I'd like a few words with you. And why not have dessert. I'm advised that the pastry chef has made cheesecake fresh."

"No, thanks." I said. I sat back and stared straight at him. "I think I was given cheesecake Sunday when you said I'd have your answer Monday. That was yesterday. Unless I've gone deaf I don't believe I heard from you."

He appeared freshly barbered, at least he smelled like a barber shop with his eau de cologne. He sat up straighter in his chair, throwing his shoulders back. He said, "I have not broken my word, Mrs. Grayson, if that is what you are implying. Different circumstances arose that had to be taken into consideration."

"And what would those be?" I had already decided that Warner was right. Morgan was going to play me along as far as he could while he tried to get my body as part of the deal. Of course he was too much of a gentleman to say it in so many words, but the implication was clear and unmistakable. I found myself looking over his shoulder at a fashionable lady who had just come in. She was wearing a wide silk-beribboned hat that looked very good on her. I wondered if big hats were on their way back. I had always preferred them to the demitasse version that had come into vogue.

Mr. Morgan said, his little pale blue eyes snapping, "Mr. Grayson insulted me."

He brought my attention back quickly. I said, in disbelief, "My husband did what?"

"Insulted me."

"That is a first." I said. "Warner generally doesn't bother with that sort of thing. If you cross him he takes immediate physical action. If he doesn't like you or care for your company he avoids you. I can't recall a single incident of Warner ever taking the time to insult anyone. He kids pretty rough sometimes. It's a habit he picked up from a pardoned ex bank robber who holds nothing sacred. You sure he wasn't just joshing you?"

"I believe I can be relied upon to be the judge of that. First he obliquely compared my background to the breeding of a Thoroughbred race horse that could not run fast. I called him on it, but he declined to elaborate. Then, when I made him a straightforward business proposition, he shoved his half-finished drink toward me and said all I would receive from him were his dregs."

I wanted to laugh, but I was more interested in what sort of business proposition he had made to Warner. I asked him.

He delayed long enough to pour himself a glass of wine and to offer me one. I shook my head no. He set the bottle down and took a long sip of the wine. Then he poured the glass full again. He said, "I asked him to put a figure on the value of his horse farm."

I blinked. I couldn't have been more surprised if he'd asked Warner to put a price on me. I said, "I would imagine that fairly startled him. What did he say?"

"Nothing that would advance the discussion, I can assure you of that."

"May I inquire what your interest is in the horse ranch?"

"I am a wealthy man, Mrs. Grayson. I can afford to interest myself in many pursuits. As a gentleman and a Virginian, horse racing is in my blood. Have you not seen Mr. Grayson?"

"That is neither here nor there. But this is the first I have heard about this offer of yours. I would imagine Warner was curious about your reasons."

"Why is it you will refer to him by his given name, but refuse to call me Charles?"

"The man is my husband, Mr. Morgan."

"On paper, Mrs. Grayson. I don't see why you keep up this charade about your marriage when it is perfectly obvious what state it is in."

"Never mind my marriage Mr. Morgan." I said sharply. "You have not yet given me the answer you promised Monday."

He poured himself more wine and drank half a glass deliberately. He put it down, blotted his lips with a napkin, and said, "I believe you have been given an answer. Mr. Grayson continues to cloud the picture. On my own initiative I attempted to negate his involvement by buying out his ranch. All I got for my trouble was an insult."

I wondered if he really believed what he was saying. No one in his right mind could have put forth such a flimsy excuse for not following through on a promise. I said, "Mr. Morgan, surely you are aware that I own half of the horse farm. The arrangement was made prior to our marriage. It still stands as a business proposition."

He nodded. "I thought something like that was the case. For that reason it would have made perfect sense for me to own the half Mr. Grayson presently possesses.

Even he must be aware that you have no intention of going back to that life."

I could scarcely credit what my ears were hearing. The man had actually approached Warner and as much as said, I've got your wife, you might as well sell me your ranch in the bargain. Or your half of the ranch. I was finding a whole new world of admiration for Warner. I found it difficult to believe that he had merely insulted Mr. Morgan. I said, "First of all, Mr. Morgan, the ranch is not worth very much without Warner. The horses don't train themselves, you know. And, secondly, you somehow continue to think there is more on the table than my wish to lease and finish the General Grant wing."

I had called it that on purpose, just to get his goat. His face darkened and his eyes snapped. He said, "It is not the General Grant wing and I wish you would never refer to it in such a fashion. As for what I think is on the bargaining table, it is what I choose to place there. I have been doing business for quite a number of years, Mrs. Grayson, and I am seldom disappointed. I fancy myself a rather good judge of human nature. I don't think I have read you wrong. I think once the distractions are out of the way and we have come to know each other on a more informal basis that our dealings will reach a level of satisfaction for each of us."

I studied him, wondering how I could have ever found him the slightest bit attractive. The only excuse I could find for myself was that I had been dazed and not quite myself in the first forty-eight hours of our acquaintanceship. "Fine," I said flatly, "make up whatever you like in your mind. Since the words I have been saying don't seem to register I will simply save my breath. Now, when can I expect an answer from you? Yesterday I went out and began looking at houses. Today I am going to do more of the same. If I find a house that suits me before I have a satisfactory answer from you then I will withdraw my offer. Is that plain enough?"

He said, stiffly, "I was ready to give you an answer

yesterday until the unfortunate meeting with Mr. Grayson. I encountered him passing through the lobby and invited him next door for a drink and a talk. I assumed he had been up to speak with you. He did not act like a man in a very pleased state of mind so I assumed his suit had met with no good result."

"You are saying that your answer depends on what Warner does? Whether he is here or not?"

"I am saying that the question of Mr. Grayson has to be resolved." He lifted his hand and slapped it down on the tabletop. I looked around to see if any of the other diners had noticed and was surprised to see the place almost empty. The waiters, all in a row, were standing at the kitchen end in their white coats with the white napkins folded over their forearms.

I said, "I don't understand."

"You must make it clear to him that he is not wanted. He is a hindrance, an annoyance, a burden to our discussions. As long as he is here you will continue to be formal with me and you will continue to resist the inevitable. He makes you shy, he causes you to moderate your behavior."

I stood up. I said, "You are an amazing man, Mr. Morgan. I don't believe I have ever met anyone like you." I took the silk scarf I had been wearing off the back of the chair and hung it around my neck. "Please tell the waiter to bill my lunch ticket to my lodging." Then I was past him before he could answer a word. I walked rapidly through the lobby and up the stairs. The lizard was probably still sitting there drinking wine and feeling certain that I had been complimentary when I called him an "amazing man." The idiot.

I was certain now that I no longer wanted the wing or any other deal that would involve me with Charles Morgan. But I also knew the state of accommodations in the town and I didn't want to get thrown out of my suite until I had somewhere else to go.

I had unfortunately, out of loneliness or some other female weakness, been giving Phoenix reports of my encounters with Charles Morgan. I should have learned better, but each time I told her just a bit more than was useful for my own sanity. As I was undressing I told her about my lunchtime encounter with Mr. Morgan and the gist of what had happened. When I finished she put both her hands to her face in a gesture of despair. "Oh, my," she said, "Oh my, oh my, oh my. Lawdy, Miss Laura, I don' know what all this gonna lead to. Mr. Warner gets word of de way that man truckin' 'round with you they gonna have to bury him in half dozen graveyards, Mr. Warner gon' bust him up so bad. I gonna start gettin' out de luggage. We ain't gonna be heah no more. They a train goin' back to Tyler leaves eleven o'clock in de mornin'. We gonna be on that train!"

It was all I could do to keep her from hauling out all the luggage and starting in to pack. I said, "Phoenix, you are just being silly. I can handle Mr. Morgan."

She gave a horrified look. "Handle him? Handle him? Missy, you ought not to be touchin' that varmint with a pair o' blacksmith's tongs. Yo' mamma must not've tol' you bout folks like that Morgan. He tryin' to get holt the hem o' yo' dress an' jerk it ovah yo' head! I tell you, that man scares me most nearly to death. I gonna go down to the kitchen an' get me a butcha knife an' carry it up my sleeve. That what I'm gon' do. I tell you Miss Laura, you can't be too careful with a scorpion like that Mr. Morgan."

I had taken off my dress and hose and pumps and put on an emerald green silk dressing gown over my undergarments. I was half expecting and half hoping that Warner would come by sometime in the afternoon. If he did I intended to send Phoenix on some sort of errand. The memory of our tryst the previous afternoon was still in my mind. I said, "That will do, Phoenix. That's quite enough on the subject. When I'm ready to leave here I'll tell you in plenty of time for you to pack."

She gave me her dignified, hurt look. "Oh, yes ma'am, Miss Laura. Yes ma'am indeed. Phoenix know her place. She ain't one to get uppity and go to runnin' white folk's business. No, ma'am. I de one can keep my mouth shut when I tol' to. If Miss Laura got her mind made up to let that lizard run up her laig, why, it don' matter to me. Huh! I gonna stand by an' watch. And when Mr. Warner come by an' want to know what happened to his wife I gonna say I don' know. Last I seen of de lady she was bein' drug off in a black carriage o' some kind pulled by de blackest lookin' horses you ever did see. An' when Mr. Warner ask me why I didn't take better care o' de lady I gonna say she slap me in de mouf an' tol' me to jes' shut up an' stay that way. Oh, I knows my place, all right, yes indeedy. Land o' Goshen, I knows what my business an' what ain't. Yes, I does."

I said, "Oh, shut up, Phoenix."

"Yes, ma'am, yes ma'am. Phoenix know when to shut her mouf. She de one can keep her mouf shut jes' fine. Phoenix Franklin be a woman can keep to herself."

I said, absently, "Franklin was your maiden name. You married Albert, remember? Your last name is now Pelcher. Seems as if you could remember it after four years."

She drew herself up. "That poor man Albert pro'bly daid by now, it been so long. Might as well get used to my old name again. Leavin' a husband that long. Course, I may not be de main lady what forgot her last name."

I laughed. "Phoenix, if you don't stop this I'll send you down to fetch Mr. Morgan. Albert is hardly a boy. He's forty-five if he's a day."

"He don' admit to no more than forty-three. Myself, I has as yet not turned thirty-two."

I gave her an amazed look. "Not turned thirty-two? Phoenix, you were damn near thirty when you came to work for me."

"Huh," she said. "Well, this be the thanks I git. But I knows my place. That one thing you can't 'cuse me of, gettin' out of my place."

I was beginning to think the whole adventure was wearing us both down to the point we could no longer think straight. I got a small, straight-backed chair and pulled it over to the window and sat down and stared out at the street scene below me. I had to admit I enjoyed the vigor of the place. There was money changing hands right before my eyes, deals being made, intrigue, daring, gambling, chances taken and given. I did not consider myself a woman of business, but I had to admit I enjoyed the parry and thrust of human commerce. I had thought it was going to be that way when Warner first proposed we go into the Thoroughbred horse racing business. I had envisioned colorful race meets and Southern mansions and dances and becoming a name recognized among breeders. It had sounded so exciting and so, well, high class. Then it had come down to two and a half years of watching colts grow up with the agonizing slowness of wash drying on the line. But maybe Warner was right, maybe the worst was over, maybe the exciting times were almost upon us. Over my shoulder I told Phoenix to go downstairs somewhere and buy a good bottle of whiskey. "Take ten dollars out of my purse. That should be enough."

I heard her mumbling to herself as she moved around behind me. I said, "What?"

"Nothin', nothin'. Phoenix ain't said nothin'. Ol' fool black woman, what she know?"

I turned my head all the way around. "What did you say, Phoenix?"

She straightened up from my purse, a bill in her hand. "I said maybe git you drunk on whiskey we get Mr. Warner an' get you on a train and go home. That's what I say."

"We haven't got a home right now."

"Yeah, they that little house in town. Place you left Albert at. Poor man prob'ly starved to death by now."

I shook my head slowly. "Go along, Phoenix. I swear, I believe you are dedicated to driving me crazy."

She didn't say anything until she was at the door. "You stay 'round here much longer you gonna do more'n go crazy." Then she skipped through the door into the parlor and shut it behind her before I could answer.

After she was gone I got up and walked around restlessly for a moment. Finally I took off my undergarments and then put the robe back on and cinched it with the sash. The smooth material of the silk felt good against my skin.

Phoenix hadn't been gone five minutes when I heard the door between the bedroom and the parlor open. I looked around quickly, suddenly fearful that it might be Charles Morgan. After our conversation at lunch I was not sure what he was capable of. But it was, I saw with relief, Warner. He came in, taking off his hat as he did. He shut the door behind him and then lounged against the wall, his hat dangling in one hand, looking not quite certain if he was going to stay or go. He said, "I saw Phoenix as she was coming down the back stairs. She said to just go on in that you'd never hear me knock on account of you just wouldn't listen. You got an earache or something?"

I smiled ruefully. "That's just Phoenix's idea of a smart remark. She's going to buy a bottle of whiskey."

"Yeah, she said. You taken to drinking?"

"Oh, I like a little pick-me-up every once in a while. Are you keeping that wall in place?"

He pushed away from the wall with a little laugh, picking up the chair that sat by the door as he did and moving it to the foot of the bed. He said, "Naw, I was just checking on my welcome. Man never knows with a tamale like you."

"We are still married," I said. "The whiskey is for you in case you came by."

"Mighty thoughtful," he said. He pitched his hat on the bed and sat down in the chair facing me.

I said, nodding toward his hat. "I thought that was supposed to be unlucky, hat on the bed."

He gave me the smile of his that I loved, a kind of sly little devil-may-care look, that I suddenly discovered I had been missing. He said, "If I remember correctly last time I put that hat on that bed I got more than just a little lucky."

I colored slightly so as not to disappoint him. I said, "Luck had nothing to do with it."

"I see you are wearing that green silk robe I like so much."

"Oh, this?" I looked down at it as if I were surprised myself at what I was wearing. I said, lying, "Oh, I never heard you mention this. I think you just like me in green." Of course I didn't want him to think I'd put it on for him specially.

"Yeah," he said. He reached in his pocket and got out one of the little cigarillos he sometimes smoked. I could sense a certain tenseness behind his usual calm. I didn't know what it was, but something more was bothering him than had been the day before. He glanced at the door between the parlor and the bedroom. "Phoenix coming straight back?"

"She should be." I crossed my legs unconsciously and was instantly aware that Warner's eyes had gone straight to the movement. I was seated, not quite facing him. I glanced down and saw I'd exposed a good bit of thigh but I made no attempt to cover it up. I had my arms crossed under my breasts, but the upper folds of my robe were loose and I was sure I was showing cleavage. I knew that I wasn't doing it deliberately, but I did *hate* to be distracting Warner so.

He lit his cigarillo with a match he dug out of his pocket, striking it on his boot heel. He said, "Had quite a little talk with your Mr. Morgan yesterday."

I said, dryly, "Don't try that on me, Warner. He's not *my* Mr. Morgan."

"I didn't mean anything by it. I only meant that it's you who are the main topic every time we have a visit. I ain't going to call him *my* Mr. Morgan."

"From what I heard at lunch, the ranch was the main topic."

He raised his eyebrows, which, for Warner, was an exclamation as loud as a shout. "You had lunch with him?"

"No. He slipped in late as I was finishing to explain why he hadn't given me an answer on the proposition."

"I told you he would play you, Laura. He'll string you along until he gradually gets you to agree to everything he's after."

"He said the reason was because you had insulted him."

Warner smiled and looked at the ceiling. "Insulted him? How the hell would that arrogant son of a bitch know he's been insulted? The world don't exist outside of his skin. Hell, I don't think enough of the bastard to insult him. I did, however, do my dead level best to let him know I thought he deserved the same amount of attention as anything else that lived under a rock." He laughed shortly. "Insulted him? Why that self-centered snake. He don't draw enough of my notice to insult him. I reckon I better set him straight."

"No!" I said quickly. "Don't do that. Leave him alone, Warner."

He cocked his head at me. "You protecting him? Or your deal?"

"Neither one," I said. I couldn't very well tell Warner my fear that he would lose in any quarrel with Morgan because of Morgan's standing in the town. He wasn't the sort of man who would seek advice on such a score from anyone, much less a woman, and especially a woman he was in an awkward position with.

"Has to be one or the other," he said. "Otherwise you wouldn't care what I did to him."

"I promise you it's neither."

He shrugged. "Well, as I've said before, the situation between us means a lot of what you are up to is none of my business. Right now what's between us only concerns the two of us. We've got to figure out if we can live as man and wife. I guess, what's more important, is do we want to be man and wife."

It was suddenly frightening to hear him characterize it so bluntly and concisely. Two lives reduced to less than two dozen words. But he was right. That was what it came down to. I wished, though, that he didn't feel the need to rush the situation so fast. I felt I needed more time to cool out, as horsemen said after they'd rode a horse hard, before I started making decisions. It had been two and a half years building up. It seemed wrong to rush to a conclusion in a matter of days. But I said, "Yes, that is true."

He was silent for a moment, drawing on his cigarillo. I studied him as he thought. He looked drawn to me, as if he had not been sleeping or eating right. I could see the hint of a scab along his jaw where he'd cut himself shaving. His poor face was probably suffering from shaving every day. It touched me that he would go to so much trouble on my account. Finally he looked at me. He said, "I got to ask you something that may not be any of my business but I got to ask it anyway. I got to know if there is anything else in your head other than what I know about. The reason I need to ask you this is that it will affect the way I think and what I do. It embarrasses me to ask my own wife this question, but I got to. Besides, if you answer yes there ain't no point in my going on."

I felt myself trembling inside. Even though I was still undecided I knew I did not want Warner to give up, not yet. I said, as calmly as I could, "What's your question?"

"You understand I don't ask it out of jealousy?"

"I haven't heard the question yet."

He heaved a breath and said, "I need to know if there is anything between you and Morgan besides this business proposition you've been talking about."

I don't know what I had been expecting but the question was a relief. "No," I answered promptly. "Not at all."

He got up, carrying his cigarillo carefully because of the long ash, looking around for an ashtray. I said, "There's a cup and saucer on the dressing table."

He walked to it and knocked off the ash, took one more drag, and then put the cigarillo out in the cup. He looked around at me with a smile. "I used to catch hell from you when I did that at home. You claimed it stained your good china."

"This is Morgan's china," I said. "I'm not quite as careful of it."

He went back to the straight-backed chair, flipped it around and straddled it backward, looking at me. He said, "Well, there may not be anything on your part besides the business deal, but Morgan sure as hell thinks there is."

"I know. I have told him everything possible to the contrary but he still persists." At that moment I was strongly tempted to tell Warner I no longer had any interest in leasing the wing of the hotel. But I held my tongue. He would have seen no further reason for me staying in Jefferson and would have put it on an either-come-back-to-me-now-or-don't-come-at-all basis. I didn't want that, not then.

He said, "I want you to know that I ain't doubting your word, but he come at me about buying me out of the ranch. He made it sound as if it was your idea. That's how come I had to ask you that question."

I nodded slowly. "Yes," I said. "I got that impression when he talked to me at lunch. I was amused, but I didn't realize he had told you that. I promise you, Warner, that I had nothing to do with his approaching you in such a manner. I even laughed at him. I told him that without you the ranch was nothing."

He nodded again and looked thoughtful. I could almost see his mind working. At last he said, "Well, let's throw out this Morgan business for the time being. It ain't doing nothing but muddying the water. If there ain't nothing between you two then all that has got be figured out here is me and you."

"Yes," I said.

He paused again and stared off into the distance.

Somewhat hesitantly he said, "I reckon you know I love you." His voice came out gruff, as if he were embarrassed.

I smiled. "Yes, but it's nice to hear it every now and then."

He looked uncomfortable. "I never been much of a one for that kind of talk and I never figured you needed that kind of fence mending. You know me well enough to know that when I say a thing it stays said until I say otherwise. And I ain't never done that. Not with all the ugly words I said." He reached in his pocket and found a match and then searched his shirt pocket for another cigarillo.

Over his shoulder I saw the door open and Phoenix look in. Warner was not aware of her. He was staring intently at his cigarillo. Phoenix set the bottle of whiskey just inside the door and then straightened up. She made little walking movements with her fingers and then pointed toward the street. I nodded and she closed the door softly behind her.

Warner said, "And, since you ain't told me otherwise, I reckon you still love me."

"Yes. I do. I'm not saying I can live with you, but, yes, Warner, I still love you."

I could tell that he was leading up to a point. I knew how Warner thought. He liked to get all of his boundaries lined up, the way you'd funnel a herd of horses into a corral with narrowing fences. I could see it was difficult for him. He fumbled with the cigarillo for a second or two more and then finally lit it. He blew out a cloud of blue smoke and then tugged at his collar as if it were binding him. But since it was unbuttoned enough to show the hair of his chest curling up I didn't think it was the material of his shirt that was stifling him.

He said, "I wish to hell I had a drink. I meant to get a bottle of whiskey before I came up here. But I had so much on my mind."

I said, "There's a bottle right behind you."

"Where?" He took a quick look over his shoulder, stopped, and then looked again. He said, "I'll be damned. Where did that come from?"

"You wished for it, didn't you?" He had obviously forgotten what I'd said.

He got up and went to the door and picked up the bottle. He worked the cork loose and gave it a smell. "Got a good aroma to it. Good whiskey." He looked around. "I don't see a glass."

I gestured. "There is one in the bathroom."

"Do you want a drink?"

I shrugged. "I think so."

He came back with two empty glasses and handed me one. I held it while he poured me a generous drink. He did likewise for himself and then hefted his glass, "Luck," he said.

I said, "Luck," and took a sip.

He went back to his chair and looked at me. "I hope all my wishes come true so easy."

I smiled faintly. "I guess that depends on what you wish for."

He nodded slowly and took another drink of whiskey. He put the bottle on the floor and wiped his mouth with his sleeve. He said, "I want it to work, Laura. I hope we can figure out a way to make it work."

I didn't say anything, just watched him.

11

Warner

I had been doing considerable thinking about what I might offer Laura as an act of good faith that would set things straight between us. In fact, I had been doing so much thinking that I had not been getting in much sleep, or eating either, for that matter. I knew it was going to have to be something significant, something that would get her attention. I'd figured out pretty quickly from our other talks that just promising to make some changes wouldn't do it. She wanted something concrete, some big concession on my part that would give her cause to trust me. We had the same as agreed that it was going to take some kind of eye-opener to rebuild the bridge between us. For my part I was content to just understand what had caused that mean and ugly fight, but I think she needed that act of penance on my part to allow her to save her pride and come back to me. I didn't know if all women were like that, but I damn well knew that Laura was. She set a great deal of store on her pride and she could be sitting right in front of me, dying to make it up, but her pride wasn't going to let her unless I gave her a good enough excuse.

But, lord, I was nervous about coming out with it. I didn't know if it was going to be enough, but it was the best I could think of. I thought it was a hell of a concession, but Laura and I didn't always agree, especially when it came to matters of money.

I stalled. I said, "I didn't tell you. I brought Paseta with me."

She looked surprised. I couldn't tell if it was because I'd brought the horse or because I'd decided to talk about the horse when I'd so obviously been leading up to something. She said, "Oh? Really? I wouldn't have thought you'd have any use for a horse around here."

I shrugged and tried to make a joke. "I thought I needed at least one friend in town."

"Aren't you the one who always made fun of me naming horses or being fond of them? Now you are using the horse's name and talking about being friendly with it. My, my, Warner. That doesn't sound like you."

I said, with a little irritation, "I didn't do it to butter you up. I never feel quite right when I'm completely afoot. And I called him by that name you gave him to avoid trying to explain which horse I meant."

"You couldn't have just said the Andalusian that was yours?"

"I suppose so." I said. I reached down and got the bottle and poured myself a little more whiskey. She sure as hell wasn't making it easy on me. I said, "Laura, you know that I will be lonely without you. And you know that all my future plans were based on us two."

She nodded. "So were mine," she said softly.

"I can make it on my own if I have to. I don't want to, but I can."

She said, "Warner, I know you well enough to know you are trying to lead up to something. You are about to leave it on the stove too long."

"It's the best I can think of, Laura. On the one hand I've shown how it is going to get better for you as soon as we start racing. Won't be all that lonely business stuck at the ranch by yourself. Can you see that part?"

She studied a few seconds and then said a grudging yes. "I guess so. But that won't start until the spring."

Damn it, I thought, but didn't say. What is it going to take to please the woman? Aloud I said, "I'm only pointing out there were two bones of contention. That was one. The other, the one that put the burr under my saddle, was your money. Do you agree to that?"

She frowned. "Yes. I suppose so."

"You got to do more than suppose. Did it or did it not come up in every fight we had?"

She nodded. "Yes. Yes, I guess it did."

I let the guess pass. She wasn't going to come out firm with anything. I said, "I think I have figured out a way around that." I stopped and watched her.

After a moment she said, "Well?"

I said, "I don't know how much money you got. I never wanted to know. But I have the strong impression from a number of things you said, especially when we were on breeding stock trips, that you got quite a bit socked away."

"Some people might think that. To others it wouldn't be much."

"How about to me?"

She shrugged. "You're different. You don't think of money the way most people do. You think of it as something you use to get the kind of horses you want. But, yes, I guess you'd think it was a lot."

There wasn't much point in waiting, though I hated like hell to actually say the words. It almost made me shrivel up inside to even think them. I said, as evenly as I could, "What I'm willing to do, Laura, is for you to gather up all your money and bring it down and put it all in together, and I will do my best to act as if I ain't done something dishonorable by making use of what was your money. I've studied on this and thought on it and I see it as the only way around the problem of you having all that money. It come to me that if I thought of it as our money it wouldn't bother me. I wouldn't be making this offer if I weren't pretty sure I could hold up my end of the deal. I know you want to say that first time I lose my temper I'll get mad at both of us for making such an unusual arrangement, but I'm pretty sure I won't. I see it as the only solution to the problem that has bothered me the most." I took a drag off my cigarillo and immediately got up and got the cup and saucer off her dressing table. She was sitting there, her hands resting in her lap, frowning. "Well? What do you think?"

She thought a moment. "Well," she said slowly, "I know this is a big step for you. Right now you've caught me so off guard that I don't know what to say. It was the last thing I expected out of you."

I was a shade disappointed at her reaction. I had expected her to be surprised, all right, but in a kind of thunderstruck way, as if she could see it was the perfect answer. But all she was doing was sitting there with a small frown on her face, mulling it over. I didn't see where there was that much to think about. It appeared to me I had solved the two most contentious issues between us. I poured some more whiskey in my glass and tossed it back. Finally I couldn't stand it any longer. If it hadn't been for the whiskey my heart would have been going like sixty. I said, "Well?"

The frown deepened. She sighed. She said, "I know you mean well by this, Warner, but I don't think it will work."

"Won't work? What do you mean by that? Hell, Laura, strikes me this is a pretty handsome offer for a man like me. Yet you are sitting there as if I said something every day along these lines. Hell, I laid awake many an hour to come up with this idea. Why don't you think it will work?"

She shrugged. "Because I don't think you would ever touch the money. I could bring it and put it in a joint account, but you'd keep figures in your own head and you'd be careful to never touch a penny of it."

I sighed disgustedly. "Hell, Laura, there is no pleasing you. I said I could handle it and I can. But I can see you are sitting over there finding fault. I don't know if that is because you don't like or trust the idea or because it wouldn't make any difference what I proposed."

"All right," she said, "tell me this. Could you have made such an offer a week ago?"

"Hell, I didn't even know where you were a week ago."

"All right, a month ago then."

I thought it over. I said, "I don't know. What difference does it make?"

"A lot. I think you are making this proposal right now because you'd do anything to patch our marriage up. I know you love me and I think you feel I'm slipping away, going my own direction. I think that is why you are willing to take such drastic action. But I think that once we were back to normal, once I was settled in back at the ranch and you felt secure, that it would just come up again. And again. And again."

I could feel myself getting a little hot. "Damn it, Laura, now you are questioning my word. If I say I'll do a thing, I'll do it. You would never hear another peep out of me about your money, mainly because it would be our money."

She shook her head slowly from side to side. Her robe was falling loose across her breasts and, in a gesture that was like a slap in the face to me, she pulled it closed and tightened the sash around her waist. She needn't have bothered. The use of her body was the last thing on my mind. She said, "I don't know what to say, Warner. Obviously you feel as if you've fixed the main bones of contention between us. I don't know how I feel. I don't know how to answer."

"Answer the way you want to." I could feel my chest getting tight, the way it did when I was in a dangerous situation. I put my cigarillo out in the coffee cup that already held one butt. "It's up to you, Laura." I couldn't look at her.

"Obviously, the way you have it calculated, I should immediately call Phoenix and tell her to start packing, that we are going back to the ranch." She looked directly at me. "But I don't feel like doing that. Not right now. I don't know what is holding me back, but somehow, it just doesn't seem right."

I nodded slowly. There was a little whiskey left in my glass and I drained that and then set the glass on the floor by the bottle. "I'm not going to try and talk you into anything, Laura. You have got to want it the same way I do."

She put out her hand as I started to rise. "Wait, Warner. You don't understand. I'm not certain of anything right now. I still need some time. I can't explain it."

I shrugged. "I don't know what else to do, Laura. Maybe it was a mistake for us to get married. You've always been your own woman. Even when you married John Pico you did it under a contract that left you pretty much a free agent. Maybe our being married made you feel hemmed in. You look back on it maybe neither one of us was ready for marriage. God knows we argued about it enough."

"It just doesn't feel right yet."

I shrugged. I felt sick inside, but I was trying not to let it show. "I took my best shot, Laura. I thought of all I could do, what kind of a gesture I could make and what I said about the money seemed about the biggest thing I could do. And it didn't turn out to be enough. I ain't got anything else to offer." Now I did rise and stand by my chair.

She put her hands together as if she were praying. "It was a magnificent gesture, Warner. I think I'm the only person in the world who can realize what a sacrifice it was for you and your principles to make such an offer. I am really touched by it."

I nodded. There didn't seem to be anything else to say. I thought I would like to be gone before Phoenix returned. And there was always the chance that Morgan might put in an appearance. I had hoped to take her to dinner at some place where I didn't have to dress, as they called it. But, even if she had been willing, I found I didn't have the stomach for it. I needed to be out of her company and get started practicing doing without her. I said, "I guess I better get along." I tried to make it sound light. "Still parts of this town I ain't seen."

She said, "You don't have to rush off."

She had a kind of funny tone in her voice when she said it, but it still hit me in the face as if I'd been slapped. Here was my wife saying something to me you said to a casual accquaintance or a neighbor who had dropped in. The casualness of it hurt like hell. I said, "No, I reckon I'd better get on." I near about couldn't take it, standing there watching her slip through my grasp. It seemed as if she had been part of my life forever. I could not imagine living without her, but I didn't know what else to say to her. She'd become a stranger to me. I was aware that she wasn't wearing anything under her robe, but all it made me feel was as if I were intruding where I didn't belong. My chest felt tight and I had a hard time taking my breathing slow and easy. The sooner I was out of there the better. I walked the few steps over to her side and looked down. "Do I still rate a good-bye kiss?"

She looked strained. She stood up. "Of course."

She turned her face up to me and I gave her a little soft kiss on the lips. I could feel her hands start up my back as if she were going to put her arms around my neck. I backed off quickly, putting on my hat as I did. I said, "Well, you take it easy, Laura. Tell Phoenix she might want to go into the bootlegging business the quiet way she snuck that whiskey into the room."

Then I turned around and was through the door before we got to saying the kind of things that are meant well but don't make good-byes any easier. When you part you ought to part and not hang around and unravel.

I went through the parlor and opened the door and stepped out into the hall. My intention had been to go out through the lobby, but as I turned in that direction, I saw Charles Morgan standing near the stairs, not more than twenty feet away. I figured he was on his way to see Laura. I wondered if she was going to receive him in her emerald green silk robe with nothing on underneath. The thought cut me like a rusty knife, but I stifled it down. It was no longer my business and I couldn't allow myself to think on such matters or I'd go crazy.

I turned away from Morgan and started out the back way. I could not trust myself to get near him. I did not believe I was capable of getting near the man and not doing him some severe physical harm.

Once I was out of the hotel I stood on the boardwalk and watched the people hurrying by. I envied every one of them. They had places to go and loved ones to see. Their lives had not just been deposited in a jumbled heap down around their feet. But I could not let myself go on thinking like that, I had not lost Laura today; she had left my life several months before, while I was out in the corral working colts and she was moping around a big, empty house. I'd lost Laura because I was blind and deaf. As I'd thought back of the last few weeks, I could recall hint after hint that she had given me, both by word and deed. But I had not heeded. I had been too busy, too involved. Now she was gone.

And it didn't really matter about Morgan. I knew Laura too well to believe she could ever be attracted to a phony, lightweight like him. She'd left me for herself, not another man. Another man might come along, but I didn't think he'd shown up. I'd taken my best shot and I'd missed. That was that. There was no point in cogitating on it. I believed that you didn't feed a dead horse anymore than you whipped it, and it was pretty clear that Laura and I as an entry were no longer in the race. It was time to put it out of my head.

It was coming on dusk and I figured I might as well get an early supper. I had a few things to tend to and then I was going to go buy a ticket and take the morning train back to Tyler.

There was a little café a few blocks down from my floating hotel and I went there and settled in at a table. I did not understand how ordinary folks lived in Jefferson. Even at the little café I was in, a steak dinner cost you two dollars and fifty cents. Other places it was higher. And I had never been able to eat breakfast for less than six bits or a dollar. What with the price of my hotel and the stable rent on Paseta, plus grub, it was costing me twelve dollars a day to stay in Jefferson. Add to that the price of whiskey and beer and you were up around thirteen or fourteen dollars a day. That came to better than four hundred dollars a month. Of course it was no strain on me, but I couldn't see how an ordinary hired hand could afford to visit the place even for a night or two. Yet the town was full to bursting and growing every day and everywhere you looked you saw folks with a pocketful of cash. It was the damndest place I'd ever seen.

I had a second-rate fried steak along with canned vegetables and stale bread and washed it down with a lukewarm beer. When I paid out of the place I consoled myself with the thought that I was heading for better groceries even though I doubted I'd have much appetite.

I went down to see Paseta at the stable. He'd been standing in a stall a good deal longer than he liked. I rubbed his ears and looked in his feed trough. He had grain he hadn't even eaten. I said, "Days might be coming you'll wish you had that feed."

He didn't answer me back.

I gave him a final pat and then got my saddle and slung it over my shoulder and started down the road to the depot. I planned to check the saddle with the ticket agent and get myself ready to make that morning train. I'd been in Jefferson long enough. As if to confirm that I stopped in at a saloon on the way back to my six-dollar-a-night room in a floating hotel and paid a bartender wearing a bow tie and a vest a quarter for a nickel beer and a dollar for a two-bit shot of whiskey. I reckoned it was a good thing Laura had turned down my offer to take her money and care for it. It was clear I didn't know anything about money.

I sat in my room until late that night, sitting at the window that faced out on the water of the big landing. All kinds of boats, all lit up, were still scurrying back and forth even as late as it was. I'd gotten a sheet of writing paper and pen and ink and an envelope from the desk clerk. They all lay on the tiny table along with a bottle of whiskey and a glass. I poured the glass full and then went to the window to sit and stare out and smoke cigarillos and try to think what I wanted to say to the woman, the only woman I'd ever loved. I had decided, almost as soon as I'd seen her reaction to my plan about her money, that I couldn't accomplish a damn thing by seeing her again. But I couldn't just go without some sort of *adios*, some sort of summing up, some statement to let her know I was sad the way it had ended but I wouldn't take the world for the years we'd had together. The difficulty with that was that I wasn't a man given to sentimental phrasing and I knew it was going to be a hard task to get it set down just right on paper. But I figured it would be a hell of a lot easier, here in the solitude of my room, than facing her.

After a time there wasn't anything left to see on the river. All of the boats had either quit whatever they'd been doing and tied up for the night or else had put out their lights. There finally wasn't anything left to do but get at the letter, or the message, or the thank-you note, or whatever it was. I picked up the pen and dipped it in the ink and wrote, "Tuesday night, 9 PM," in the upper right-hand corner. Then I wrote "Dear Laura," and dipped my pen again. From then on it got hard. I took a drink of whiskey and forced myself to concentrate on what I wanted to say.

Two hours later I was finished. I was surprised to see that I had barely covered one side of the sheet of paper. I felt as if I had written a volume. I sat there letting the ink dry and had one more drink. It had been a question whether the whiskey or the letter would get finished first. I figured I'd averaged about a drink per line and could have used more.

But it was done. It was a pretty pitiful document to show for eight years, but it was the best I could produce. I folded the letter and put it in the envelope and sealed it. Then, when I took up the pen to address it, I ran into another stump. I didn't want to address it to Laura Grayson and I wasn't about to put it to Mrs. Warner Grayson, which was her legal name. In the end I just labeled it Mrs. Laura Grayson and added Rose Suite in case whoever was on duty at the hotel didn't know where she was rooming. After that I had another drink, carefully saving one or two for the morning, and then I undressed and went to bed. I was just enough drunk so that I went off to sleep pretty quick. I knew I was going to have a lot of nights in my future when I'd lie awake, unable to sleep, thinking about her. But I was in no rush to start.

I got right up when I awoke the next morning. By my watch it was a little after seven. I brushed my teeth and shaved with cold water. The shave only hurt a little less than losing Laura, but I figured I might run into Gentleman Charlie Morgan and I didn't want him high-hatting me over some beard stubble. After that I went out and had some coffee and a quick breakfast at a little greasy spoon café that was next door on the wharf. The place was full of river riffraff but they didn't bother with me so I didn't pay them no mind.

When I was back in my room I slowly packed my valise, leaving my gun belt on top. I'd brought four shirts and had ended up not needing all of them. For all the good I had done I'd have been just as well off with one shirt. Actually, it had been a no-shirt job. I could have accomplished just as much if I'd never left the ranch. No, that wasn't true. At least I'd been able to take back the ugly words I'd said to Laura. I hadn't wanted to see us part angry. I was glad we'd parted with a kiss.

Finally there was nothing left to do. I picked up my valise and went around to the office and paid my score and then started for the Excelsior hotel. I was going to leave the letter at the desk and I was hoping that I did not run into Charles Morgan. If he said anything to me I felt I wouldn't be accountable for my actions. It was about eight-thirty. I was hoping he wouldn't be on duty that early. Maybe he was out somewhere telling people what a gentleman he was, or having a new suit tailored or whatever he did for recreation besides chase my wife.

But I had to put that kind of thinking behind me. She wasn't my wife any more. I went into the resplendent lobby, stopping just inside the door to make sure I didn't run into anyone I knew. The place was quiet. There were a few gentlemen and ladies going in to breakfast, but apart from them, no one was around. I walked up to the desk. I couldn't tell if the same clerk was on duty or not. It didn't matter, they all looked alike. I had thought to warn the one I'd first encountered that he'd be wise not to go out into the rain. The way he had his nose turned up there was a good chance he'd drown.

I said to the young man, putting the letter on the desk top, "Wonder if you could help me?"

"Yes? What is it?"

I slid the letter over to him. "Would you put this in Mrs. Laura Grayson's box, please?"

He looked at the envelope and then at me. Finally he picked it up and turned around and shoved it into one of the pigeon holes. He turned back to me. "Anything else? Any message?"

"She will get that?"

He gave me a lofty look. "Of course."

I nodded. It was done. "Much obliged."

I had to stop in at the stables on my way to the depot. I was going to leave Paseta for Laura. I figured she'd need a good horse while she was in Jefferson and she ought to be able to cut a finer figure than anyone else on the high-stepping Andalusian.

I went into the office at the stables and found the manager. I explained that I would be leaving the horse for a little longer. I gave him a twenty-dollar bill and said that someone else would be stopping by to make further arrangements with him. He was quite glad to take my money.

I went on down to the depot, there being no other business to delay me. I got my saddle from the passenger agent and then sat down in the waiting room with it and my valise to await the train.

I wasn't feeling much. I guessed it was too soon. I reckoned it would take me pretty sharply once I got back to the ranch and felt her absence and knew she wouldn't be coming back. Laura wasn't a weed who blew back and forth with the wind. Once she made up her mind, wasn't much going to change it.

Leaving Paseta meant I'd have to hire someone to take me out to the ranch. That or rent a nag from the livery. I reminded myself to send Albert to Jefferson as quick as I could. I'd send him with the carriage and the span of horses that fit it. At least Laura would be able to get around in style. And I reckoned Phoenix, though she'd protest to the contrary, would be glad to see her husband. At least she'd have somebody to boss around and bully-rag. Thinking of Phoenix made me smile. She'd been on my side. It was a pity she didn't have more influence with Laura, but then nobody did. I reminded myself to send her a gift of money in care of Albert. She'd earned it for her kindness to me in Jefferson.

Pretty soon I heard the train blowing way off in the distance. I stood up and moved myself and my gear out onto the platform. I thought about Charlie Stanton and wondered what I was going to tell him. Mine wasn't the only life that was fixing to undergo a big change.

12

Laura

I was surprised and not a little disappointed when
Warner took his leave so unexpectedly and abruptly. It
seemed he had no more finished explaining his gallant
gesture when, the next thing I knew, he was giving me the
most passionless of kisses and was out the door. It left me
stunned and bewildered. I had had other plans for that
evening with Warner besides watching him go out the
door. I had expected, outside of what we would do in
bed, that we would parade through the lobby so that Mr.
Morgan could have a look and that later we would eat
supper at some good restaurant that was not so strict
about a gentleman's attire.

But he left. Afterward, reconstructing the way the
conversation had gone, I suppose that I could have been
more encouraging about his grand plan to put my money
into his name. Looking back at it, I suppose I did not
make as much over his offer as I should have. The
moment the words were out of his lips I was impressed
that he would bring me such a gift. Someone, someone
who didn't know him, hearing him make such an offer,
might have laughed and said, "Oh, my! And that is what
you call a sacrifice? Accepting all this money is your idea

of giving in in the give and take of marriage?" But for Warner, it was a magnificent effort. He must have been in agony to actually offer it to me. It was directly opposed to everything he thought a man should be and do. It was absolutely against his code.

And he had done it for me, for me and our marriage. I realized it must have seemed to him that I had dismissed it out of hand. In truth I had been very impressed and had intended to bring it up later in the discussion or later in the evening. But, for purposes of strategy, I had not wanted to seem too taken with the offer too quickly. I was rather enjoying having Warner as a supplicant and I had no plans to rush the reconciliation. But then he left so abruptly, giving me very little warning and leaving me with no clear-cut reason to ask him to stay without weakening my position.

It was stupid, really. I could see that later, after he was gone. I resolved not to be quite so coy in future. Warner was an honest man. He didn't know much about feminine wiles and subterfuge. If you said something to him, and you were someone he trusted to be honest, he took it at face value. It was one of the traits he had that made me love him.

For a time I thought he might go out, walk around, and then come back. For that reason I kept the silk robe on. But as time passed, I begin to doubt that he would be back that night. When the door finally opened it was Phoenix, coming back an hour after Warner left. She found me striding up and down in my robe with a glass of whiskey in my hand. She said, "My, my, Miss Laura, if you can't catch no bee in dat honeycomb then de world is done turned upside down!"

I gave her a grim smile. "No bees caught today. Phoenix, I may have done something not very wise. I may have made a blunder."

Naturally she had to hear all about it so she could give her opinion. But she was strangely silent and uncharacteristically subdued. She said, "Miss Laura, I greatly a-feared no good gon' come of this. Mr. Warner be a mighty proud gen'lman. Maybe you done pushed him a mite hard."

I snapped at her. "Damn it, Phoenix, what do you think I've been telling myself since he left? I don't need you to come in here and make me feel worse."

She immediately changed her tone. She said, "Now, now, Missy, don't you go to flusterin' yo'self. What you say Phoenix run on over to where he be stayin' an' see if he don't want to come over heah an' join you fo' some suppah?"

I shook my head. "No, it's too soon."

She frowned. "Miss Laura, I don' know how much money ya'll be talkin' 'bout, but if that done been the problem, look like Mr. Warner fix it jes' right."

I frowned and took a sip of the whiskey and shuddered. I had always hated the taste of the stuff. I was sorry now that I had told Phoenix as much as I had and I hadn't really told her about the money. I had just mentioned that he was willing to swallow his pride about some property and money I had and make use of it for the benefit of the marriage. Naturally, that was what she picked up on. It was also the last subject I wanted dwelt on. I said, "Phoenix, I don't want to talk about that and I don't want to listen to you talking about it. The whole matter is very complicated and is going to take time to work out."

She gave me one of her rolling-eye looks. "Onliest thing I see 'round here is complicated is a hardheaded lady in a silk dressin' gown 'thout no underwear on. I can't b'l'eve Mr. Warner done walk out of here with you ungot up like that."

I said, grimly, "Well he did. I feel as if I've been left waiting at the altar."

That alarmed Phoenix. She said, "Don' be talkin' like that, Miss Laura. This here marriage of your'n shaky 'nough without you throwin' no hexin' at it. Keep yo' mouf off that noble estate. Miss Laura, I wisht you would let me go see Mr. Warner. I got a feelin' he be feelin' pretty bad right now. Maybe I can lead him on back heah without sayin' much of nothing."

"No, I said." I sat down at my dressing table. "Now, damn it, what am I going to do for dinner? I had expected to go out with Warner, but he left so quickly I never had a chance to open my mouth." I looked around at Phoenix. "None of this went according to the way I planned."

Phoenix folded her arms in that gesture that implied somebody needed a good talking to. She said, with an air, "I 'spect somebody tried to get too cute. Anybody that know Mr. Warner know he ain't a gen'lman you gets cute with. He ain't like some folks 'round this hotel who is always talkin' 'bout what a gen'lman they is an' doin' damn little to prove it. Folks what know knows you don't mess with Mr. Warner. No, ma'am. That gen'lman be all business. He do what he say. Yes, ma'am. Land 'o Goshen, Missy, what you want to be prankin' 'round with a gen'lman of Mr. Warner's temperature?"

"That's temperament, Phoenix, not temperature." She had learned a great many words she ordinarily wouldn't come in contact with because I talked to her as I would anyone else. She sometimes got them confused because she didn't know what all of them meant.

But this time she was shaking her head. "Naw, ma'am. I say temperature cause that what I mean. Mr. Warner can get mighty warm when he feel he ain't bein' treated right. Sounds to me like you raised his *temperature* till he had to get out of here an' cool off. Ain't sayin' he ain't got no temperament, but he only show that 'round horses."

I glanced back at her, wondering if she knew what she was saying. I started to ask, but then thought better of it. I said, "Well, that still doesn't satisfy my problem of dinner. I can't go out somewhere unescorted and I'm not going to the dining room since I don't want to run into Mr. Morgan there."

"The lizard."

"Mr. Warner calls him a snake."

"Snake. Lizard. They both live under a rock. I reckon I gonna have to fetch you something from the kitchen."

I looked around. I said, "I am about to get damn tired of this hotel. When was the last time I was out of it?"

"Yesterday when we went out walkin'."

I made a face. "And now it's getting dark outside so it's too late to do that. And I can't go anywhere because I'm alone." I picked up my hairbrush and slammed it down. "Sometimes I hate being a woman."

"You hates bein' a woman what don' always get her way."

I said, with a little edge in my voice, "It's not that simple, Phoenix."

"It be as simple as me goin' to fetch Mr. Warner an' y'all get in that bed yonder and patch things up."

I turned around and glared at her. "Mr. Warner did not want to get in the bed. I gave him everything but a written invitation."

"Maybe he catch on slow. Maybe the best idea is to give him another try."

"Stop that, Phoenix."

"That's fine with me, Missy. I got *my* man. I can't lay my hand on him right now, but I know where he be. An' I know I ain't gonna have to coax him toward de bed. He know the way."

I glared at her. "You can remember everything else that goes on, Phoenix. How come you can't remember you're my maid?"

She put up her hands. "Dat's right, dat's right. Phoenix done forgot her place. Hope lightnin' strike me dead before I open my mouf 'bout yo' affairs in future. Yes, ma'am. This one colored woman knows to keep her mouf shut! Ain't 'nother word comin' out this mouf on the subject at hand. No, ma'am! No, ma'am!"

"Please shut up, Phoenix," I said crossly. I picked up my hairbrush and began to dig savagely at my hair. "Damn it, damn it, damn it! Damn it to hell!"

She said, "Reckon you want me to go fetch Mr.

Morgan? He be mor'n happy to escort you. Or anything else fo' that matter."

I turned around and gave her a look that was intended to straighten her hair. I said, "I better not hear that man's name again. Or it better not come out of your 'mouf'. Not unless you want to be an unemployed maid, and I don't know who else would put up with you."

She assumed her hurt but dignified posture. "What I 'spose to do he come to de door? Come in heah and tell you they's a man outside? Then you ask who an' I can't tell you cause I get taken off de job."

"What you do," I said carefully, "is you tell him I am not in and you don't know when I'll be back. Or you tell him I'm sleeping or I'm sick or I'm with Mr. Warner. I don't care what you tell him. Don't let him in. You think you can remember that?"

Her eyes and her gold tooth gleamed in spite of herself. She said, "Now you be talkin'. Next thing we be on that train headin' home. When Mr. Warner be comin' back?"

I brushed at my hair, feeling calmer. "Tomorrow, I would think."

"Mawnin' or evenin'?"

"I don't know, Phoenix! Will you stop picking at a body?"

In the end I sent Phoenix down to the kitchen to fetch us up some supper. We ate together at a table in the parlor. I was still wearing the emerald green silk dressing gown, but I had it sashed up tight. That night, as I was dressing to get ready for bed I took off the robe and pitched it to Phoenix. I said, "Here, take this. It's been bad luck for me."

She caught the robe and looked pleased. "Ain't nothin' wrong with this robe. Robe ain't got no bad luck. Course I ain't sayin' nothin' 'bout the party wearin' it, but that wadn't bad luck neither."

"That's enough, Phoenix."

"I be glad wear this robe. Plenty good luck left in this here garment. Wait'll I gets back to my man Albert. I show you de luck in dis robe. I gonna wear that man out."

"Damn it, Phoenix, *shut up!*"

I had a very difficult time going to sleep. Once I lay down and composed myself for sleep my mind suddenly jolted me awake with the sudden, rude news that, for the first time in my life, I was without a man at my beck and call. It was a very disconcerting thought. Even though I considered myself an emancipated woman I was only too well aware that there were certain restrictions on where I could go unescorted. It had hit me fully when I'd realized I could not seek out a restaurant on the street and enter unaccompanied by a man. True, I could have gone down to the restaurant in the hotel. That would have been perfectly seemly, but, unfortunately, it would have meant an excellent chance of encountering Mr. Morgan, a chore I had no wish to undergo.

But it was not just that one single instance. I would be faced with the same situation the next day and the day after that and the day after that. It would go on until I united with a man, whether it was Warner or someone else. I had talked of the society in Jefferson. There was no society available for a single woman. Every wife in the town would decline to have her husband near me. I could well imagine just how quickly I would be welcomed into polite society. I did not know what I had been thinking of when I had spoken so glibly of the so-called cultural benefits of this city.

I stared at the ceiling. I felt very alone and very vulnerable. If Warner had been there at that moment I would have agreed to anything to put our marriage back together. It made me curse myself for being so weak. Not only would that have been unfair to Warner, it would have been unfair to the marriage, and never mind what it said about me. I knew it wasn't the ugly words in the last fight that had put me on the road; it was the better than two years I had sat in the ranch house accomplishing nothing. Even if that particular fight hadn't started I would have started one over something else just to have a reason to leave. I had gone looking for something to do on my own. In a way I had found it. What I found was a man with much greater depth than I thought he had when I married him. I was never going to do better than Warner Grayson and I knew it. I only hoped he would be patient a little while longer while I played at being an independent, grown up lady. I felt as if there had to be one more little something to put us back together whole again. I didn't know what it was, but I'd know it when it happened or I saw it or it got said. Meanwhile, I wanted to buy something. Of course I no longer had any interest in the wing of the hotel, but I thought it would be nice to own a home in Jefferson. It would be a place to come, to relax, to watch the hustle and bustle. I was not planning on a mansion, but something nice that I wouldn't be ashamed to invite the elite of the town to. Perhaps, I thought, I would have a home built. It would be fun to watch it being constructed. That had been the only part of the building of the Tyler ranch I had enjoyed, watching the home I had designed being constructed and making as many last-minute changes as I liked. But then it had been built and furnished and there was nothing to do but live in it. We had never entertained, except for a few business people that Warner was dealing with. Mostly it had been just he and I in that big house. So much waste, and I included myself in that inventory.

Gradually I began to relax and look at matters in a better light. Surely things would work out fine. However, I didn't exactly know what I meant by that. Finally I slept.

I was up quickly the next morning and had an early breakfast. I did not know exactly what time to expect Warner. Previously he had come in the afternoon but, just to be on the safe side, I dressed casually, but knowingly, in a lightweight cotton frock with a square bodice that showed plenty of skin. It had short, puffy sleeves and a flounced skirt that I knew showed off my figure to good effect. As soon as she saw me Phoenix said, "Uh huh, settin' de trap. Only hope de fox come along."

He did not come that morning. It didn't bother me as I had not really expected him. I didn't, however, want to

eat another meal in my suite so, Mr. Morgan notwith-
standing, I went down to the dining room just before
they were to quit serving. He was nowhere in sight and I
was able to enjoy a luncheon of stewed chicken and rice
with fresh vegetables. It was a great relief to see something besides the same four walls while I dined. I made
sure that Phoenix stayed in the suite while I was out just
in case Warner should happen by.

Two o'clock came and went and then three. I was
determined I was not going to sit there all day waiting for
any man. At half-past three I sent Phoenix out to fetch
me a hack. I intended to ride around through the better
sections of the town, as well as some of the outlying
districts. I was not, at that point, interested in visiting
estate agents. I preferred to see what might be available
on my own. Real estate agents, as a general group,
seemed far too pushy to me. They insisted on telling a
person what they themselves wanted. They usually
ended up trying my patience.

I went down and took the hack with its Negro driver,
but I left Phoenix with strict instructions to stay in the
suite and to hold Warner there if he should come by
before I returned. I said, "But you are not to tell him I
wanted him to wait."

Her mouth fell open. "Then jes' how am I supposed to
hold him here?"

"Use your wits. You've always got enough advice for
me. But you better not make it sound as if I'm eager to
see him or I'll skin you alive."

"Well, you got a careless 'mount of nerve, Missy. I say
that fo' you. You got a careless amount. Land 'o Goshen!
Hol' Mr. Warner? I soon get holt of a old Brahma bull an'
try an' make up its mind fo' it. Laws!"

I drove around for longer than I expected. I was
enchanted by the look of some of the houses and by what
appeared to be available building sites. I was disturbed,
however, by the unevenness of the neighborhood prosperity. There would be a virtual mansion, with well tended,
extensive grounds, and to its left and right might be two

residences that could be considered nothing but shacks. Of course that was a condition to be found in all boom towns, but it gave a body pause when they were considering where to buy a building site. All of the better neighborhoods were packed solid with proper residences and no lots were for sale there, nor indeed were any houses.

Driving around a person with an experienced enough eye could see, like the growth rings on a tree, the spurts in the town's prosperity from the widening semicircle of elegant homes working back from the wharves and the center of town. It was clear that the town, so far as money went, was very new. I guessed the ages of the first rim of prosperous homes as no older than five years and the hack driver, if he were to be believed, confirmed it. What it signalled to me was that a person should be very cautious investing in the growth of a boom town, especially one like Jefferson that based its wealth on its use and access as a port. The day would come when railroads would fill in the gaps that the steamboats were supplying and then Jefferson would become just another sleepy plantation town and all the frantic activity at the wharves would cease and the big mansions could be had for a song. I came from a country of old money and, therefore, had an instinctive distrust of hurried money that rushed to throw up monuments to its own prosperity. I had seen too many turn into decaying tombstones as the money dried up and the entrepreneurs moved on to new pickings.

In fact, the more I looked at Jefferson the more suspicious I was becoming. It reminded me of a chicken coop that had been enlarged and painted. It might look good from the outside, but inside it was still a chicken coop. I was rapidly deciding that the cultural aspects and the genteel society of Jefferson were, like Mr. Morgan's insistent title of gentleman, largely a matter of self-invention. I had no doubt that there were people in the town who knew how to make money and recognized opportunity when they saw it, but just because a man struck gold didn't mean you invited him onto your parlor carpet and best chairs dripping of mud and slurry.

But my opinion about Jefferson in no way was coloring my thinking about Warner and our marriage. I was still not ready to recommit, not until we could come to some better understanding. I wanted a greater measure of freedom, I wanted a greater say in affairs that concerned both of us. I wanted to be a partner more than just in money and name. I knew that Warner would instantly agree to such terms to put the marriage back together. My concern was how to assure myself they would be put into practice, not just at first, but in the years to come. I could never hope to match Warner in horse instincts, but there were many areas in finance and land acquisition where I could play a capable hand.

Then the lateness of the hour suddenly struck me and I directed the driver to hurry me back to the Excelsior. Once he stopped under the portico I pressed a five-dollar bill in his hands and hurried inside. A clock in the lobby told me it was almost six o'clock. As I rushed across the lobby I saw Charles Morgan out of the corner of my eye. He was standing near the entrance to the dining room. I saw him put up his hand and call my name, but I was much too rushed to dally with him.

I hurried up the stairs and then to my suite. I burst through the door to find Phoenix sitting, sewing. I gave her a look that had only one question in it. She shook her head. "He ain't come, Miss Laura. And I ain't left this spot since yo' departure."

"Are you sure?"

"Missy, my back teeth am floatin' right now. No, ma'am. Ain't nobody knocked on de doah except the lizard an' I tol' him I ain't had no idea where you was."

I sighed. "Damn it!"

"They is still de matter of my back teeth."

"Oh, go along if you have to."

"Yes, ma'am. I has to."

I sat down as she hurried out the door, slumping in a big, overstuffed wing chair. "Damn it," I said aloud, "where are you, Warner? The damn lizard is knocking at the door and you are not here to run him off." I felt troubled and worried by his absence, but I told myself he was only doing what I had asked him to do, which was give me more time. There was, however a limit. We had matters to discuss and business to settle. Was I going to have to lead him by the hand?

Phoenix came back in. She said, "Miss Laura, I don' like the way affairs are turning out, heah. I don't be likin' them at all. No, ma'am. You runnin' round lookin' at houses you ain't got no intentions o' buyin' when de main affair of business is with Mr. Warner."

I was afraid she was off on another tirade. "Don't start, Phoenix. I can't think with that non-stop nagging of yours going on in my ear."

She put her hands on her hips. "Doan you reckon it be time for me to go hunt up de party in question?"

I shook my head. "These matters can't be rushed. He has to come to me."

"You gonna play de cute one too many a time, Miss Laura. You may be winnin' de cakewalk wid yo' fancy steppin', but you sho' can't sleep wid no cake. Mark my words."

I could only look at her in amazement. I badly needed a sane person to talk to, someone other than Phoenix or Charles Morgan. One thing you could say about Warner, he was down to earth and a man who could go right to the heart of the problem. But where was the son of a bitch?

13

Warner

It was a long, lonesome ride home. I willed myself not to think about Laura, but she kept rising, unbidden, to the surface of my mind. Every mile the train clicked off from Jefferson felt like a barrier being raised between us. I sat in my seat in the chair car, a bottle of whiskey to hand, and listened to the wheels going over the joints in the rail, distinctly hearing each *click* and seeing it as another fence raised between us. With my whole heart I longed to turn around and speed back to her side and try, once again, to find some way that we could patch it up.

But I knew it was hopeless and the most hopeless aspect of the matter was that Laura's decision to remain away really didn't involve me. I had slowly come to see, as we talked, that what she really wanted to be was independent and she felt she couldn't do that within the framework of a marriage. I had no defense against that argument and no attack philosophy to reverse her position. If a woman doesn't want to be in a marriage it's no good coming to her with promises and inducements of how you are going to be a better husband and how much better the marriage will work. You may have the best price in town on sidesaddles, but if she doesn't ride sidesaddle you are not going to sell her one no matter how cheap you make it.

About the only consolation I could find in the affair was that sooner or later, that being her bent, she would have wanted out anyway. It was about the same as filling up on water when you are starving to death, but I could console myself with the thought that the last fight had not caused her to flee. It sure as hell didn't make it hurt any less, but I knew from the way she had talked in that goddam suite in that goddam Charles Morgan hotel, that she wanted her freedom. There wasn't a damn thing I could do about that and maybe, viewed on the whole, it was better that it had happened sooner rather than later. Every day I'd spent with Laura was probably going to take two mourning days to get over. So it was just as well she'd left when she did. The trip hadn't been wasted; at least I would no longer have to castigate myself for running her off with ugly, untrue words.

What I did castigate myself for was ever falling in love with her in the first place. From the very first I had been leery of her. Hell, for that matter, I had always been leery of becoming too fond of anyone. As soon as you did they up and left you. I knew that the attitude was silly. My parents hadn't left me, they'd died. And the same went for my grandfather. But when you keep getting put in that situation you get cautious. I'd never had no great struggle with any other woman before and there had been more than several. But none of them had been a Laura and they had been just as easy to leave and forget as a broken pocketknife. But I'd known from the very first that Laura was different and, if I was wise I'd build a wall around my feelings. And, at first, I'd succeeded very well. When I had the ranch ten miles out of Corpus and she'd come out to visit for a few days and then leave early over some spat, I just laughed and didn't let it bother me. Even after we'd gone to living together on a regular basis I still had some of my armor left. However, once we got married it seemed as if I was caught by some force stronger than myself and I gradually, little by little, came to love her and depend on her and to seek comfort and aid in her mind and her heart and her body. After a while, the love became second nature and I grew so used to having her around I took her for granted. I had done it mostly because of the new work, but nevertheless, I still expected affairs to go on as they had. I had been a blind fool. And now it was too late to rectify matters.

A few minutes after noon the conductor came through the car, swaying in rhythm with the train, to announce that the next stop was Tyler. I got my valise and saddle down from the overhead rack and then took one last drink of whiskey before putting the bottle away in my bag. I wondered if Laura had read my letter yet. I figured she ought to have. I had delivered it early that morning, and surely it would have been sent to her or picked up by her. I looked out the window at the familiar piney woods countryside and wondered what she would think of the letter. I wondered if she would read it more than once or just glance through it and cast it aside as she got on with her other business. I had put a good deal in the letter, but I hadn't spelled it out as well as I might have. Not that it mattered. The letter wasn't going to change anything. But at least I got my feelings on record so she'd never again be able to say that I hadn't cared.

I was never much of a letter writer, but even if I had been it would have all been the same. What was knocked all cockeyed between me and Laura wasn't going to get set straight by a letter or by ten thousand letters. I'd lost her a long time past; I just hadn't noticed she was gone because she was still there.

But what seemed to hurt the worst inside my chest was the way we'd been almost like two strangers. There she was, my wife, and yet I was seeing her almost by appointment. Protest as I would that I was not there to woo her, that I didn't want the marriage unless she did and that it must be on equal terms, I was nevertheless the supplicant who was received so his pleas could be heard and was dismissed when they weren't sufficient. I had been in the town three nights and three days and never once did we so much as eat a sandwich together. We'd had one drink of whiskey in common, but hell, I could say that about strangers. The rememberance of seeing her like that, under such demeaning circumstances, made me wish again that I had never gone to Jefferson in the first place.

The train finally pulled into the Tyler depot. I slung my saddle over my shoulder and took my valise and walked into the town. After the frantic pace of Jefferson the little town looked as if a cold wind had blown in off the North Pole and frozen everybody into slow motion. The whole place seemed to be just dawdling along, loitering. Even the shabby town buildings looked small and practically empty.

I walked down to the livery and hired one of the stable boys to drive me out to the ranch for two dollars. At least I was back in a world where folks didn't figure to make their month's overhead off you in one transaction.

I didn't see anyone around as we drove into the big backyard. I had the boy drop me off at the kitchen door. I left my saddle outside and opened the door and went in. The place was as empty and lonely as a whore's heart. I walked through the kitchen, my boots sounding like bass drums on the wooden floor. I called out for Jambalaya, but silence was my only answer. I went through the swinging kitchen door and glanced over at the table where Laura and I had staged our last fight. It didn't look much like a graveyard but that was what it was.

I stopped for a moment at the foot of the stairs. From that point I could see into the parlor and the dining room. They both looked immense. I had not realized how big the house was until I became its sole occupant.

I mounted the stairs as I had done many times before, only this time they seemed much steeper. The door to our bedroom was open. I walked in and dropped my valise on a patch of bare wood floor. In the echoing silence it sounded as if I'd let go of an anvil. Lord, was that place deserted. Closets and cabinet doors stood open. Bureau drawers were still pulled out. It all still looked as it had when I had returned to find Laura gone. Jambalaya would never come up and straighten the place out. She was the cook and that's what she did, cook.

The bottle of whiskey I'd left on the bedside table still stood there, half full. There was a glass beside it. I walked over and poured myself a stiff drink. As I drank it down I looked out the back window that faced on the barns and the training rings and corrals. Now I could see a few men working here and there. It was just after one o'clock and I reckoned the men had been taking their noon hour.

There was still Charlie Stanton to talk to and I wasn't sure what I was going to say to him. The loss of Laura was going to affect him, too, and in ways that might not be for the good. There were going to be a lot of changes around the place and I reckoned I was going to be the first change. I had to figure out some way to go on with my business and my life. I had been living and functioning before I met Laura. I was going to have to learn to do it all over again without her.

I wanted to feel despair, but I couldn't let myself. I had a lot of work ahead of me and if I threw myself into it, it just might be the saving of me. But whether it saved me or not it had to be done. Laura was gone. I had to make up my mind to that and get on with matters.

I finished my drink and turned around and went down the stairs and out the door. Off in the distance near the mares' barn I could see the unmistakable figure of Charlie Stanton, looking slim and straight and well shaded by a hat that always looked too big for his slight build. There had been smoke coming out of the cookhouse chimney when I came into the yard. Now it was reduced to a thin whisp. I figured Jambalaya was helping out the crew cook with no one to cook for in the big house. I kept walking and when I was near enough I called out, "Charlie! Yo, Charlie."

Charlie's young face was troubled. We were sitting in his cabin because I'd wanted a quiet place where we could talk at some length in private. Normally I would have had him come up to the house, but I couldn't stand to be in the place. Laura had more or less designed it and seen to its construction and there was still a whole lot of her left in its rooms. Charlie said, "Mr. Grayson, I can't hardly believe this. You and Mrs. Grayson splittin' the blanket. Lordy! I mean, I always thought y'all was about as well matched a team as there was."

I said, "Yeah, Charlie, but you know how it is with matched teams. You hook them up because they look the same and are the same size, but they don't always pull together in harness. One gees and one haws."

He looked down at the floor. His cabin was of a comfortable size. Laura had had a hand in the building of it, too, and she had made it bigger than necessary in case Charlie got married. It was big enough for two or three more hands but Charlie, because he was foreman, had it all to himself. He said, "Lordy, Mr. Grayson, this done knocked me for a loop. I knew there was a little trouble, but I didn't figure you'd have much of a problem fetching her back. I know women sometimes get a hump in their back and want to pitch around and buck a little, but . . . Hell, I don't know what to say."

I had not told him all the details by any means. None of the personal details. He had only heard what he needed to hear and that simply came down to the fact that Laura wasn't coming back and there would have to be a divorce. I said, "Don't worry about it. We've got some work getting an inventory of all the stock and whatnot. I need to take a hard look at the colts and—"

His face suddenly brightened and he sat up straight in his chair. We were sitting at his kitchen table drinking coffee, which he had insisted on making on his little cast-iron coal stove. He said, "Mr. Grayson, I got some news for you along those lines. You know the blaze-faced black that's out of the Virginia mare, that great big mare?"

"And that Kentucky stud we thought might be too small?"

"Yessir. And you thought that colt might be too small

too? Well, we have been working that little gentleman, Mr. Grayson, and I reckon he is gonna give you a right nice surprise."

"Yeah? What distance have you been working him at?" We had a mile oval track laid out that we used to build up endurance. It was too soft to give an accurate reflection of a horse's speed. But we wanted it that way since the soft track reduced the chance of injury to muscles and tendons.

Charlie said, his face beaming, "Half mile to a mile. Near as I can figure we could work him at two miles. Mr. Grayson, we are going to have one hell of a time finding that horse's bottom. I put the workout boy up on him yesterday and the kid asked him for a little something after a half-mile gallop and the horse liked to have jumped out from under him."

"That sounds good," I said slowly. Such matters were a lot more fun if you had someone to share them with. "Anything else?"

He said, "Mr. Grayson, you know how I hate to go out on a limb."

I nodded. Maybe, from Charlie, was wild enthusiasm.

"But I got to say the whole crop is looking pretty good. Of course I ain't seen many of those bluegrass racers, but I've read up on them and I've memorized their times at a furlong and the quarter and so on. I'd say we wouldn't embarrass ourselves if we showed up with this batch of colts. And we still got until spring."

"I'm real happy about this, Charlie."

He glanced at me. "You don't look real happy about anything, Mr. Grayson."

I finished my coffee and set the cup back on the table top. "Charlie, our business is training horses to run faster than they think they can. Anything else is just a distraction."

He ran his hand through his hair and looked worried. "I guess, Mr. Grayson. But here I am fixing to get married and then you and Mrs. . . ." He paused and stared at the wall. "Hell, if y'all break up what chance have *I* got?"

I stood up. "Charlie, you know what makes a matched pair finally get straightened out and pulling together?"

He looked up at me. "Shore. They get it figured out which one is the leader."

I nodded. "And what happens if they can't get that settled?"

"They never pull in harness. They never make a pair."

I said, "Get that part straightened out as quick as you can."

He stared at me. I knew he wanted to ask if that was what had happened between me and Laura but he was too well mannered. Finally he just nodded his head. "I reckon maybe that's good advice."

"Most folks don't get it settled until it's too late and they have to get unharnessed. Sometimes they don't get it figured out until they've broke the traces and kicked the wagon to pieces."

He ran his hand through his short, sandy hair again, looking worried. "There appears to be considerably more to this man and woman stuff than first meets the eye."

"You can pass that one along, Charlie. Now let's get outside. I want to see every coming colt we got and see how they're working. And I also want a full report on what mares we want to bring in season this fall. Lot of work to do, Charlie. And don't let me forget about Albert. I need to send him and the carriage and that matched span to Jefferson."

He nodded, but I could see him playing with the matched span idea in his head. I hated to see Charlie learning the hard facts of life so soon. They had to be learned, but sometimes a man was better off ignorant.

I arrived back at the ranch on a Wednesday and fully intented to take Albert and the carriage and horses into Tyler and have him on the train and on his way. But

Thursday came and went and it never entered my head. I felt a press of time to get my surveying of the inventory done, so I worked with the horses almost from dawn until dusk. The same thing happened on Friday and Saturday afternoon, and when I remembered the errand, it was too late to catch the train. I jumped Charlie about the matter, reminding him that I had asked him not to let me forget. He got a little smile on his face and kind of looked past me. He said, "Well, Mr. Grayson, I have reminded you every breakfast since you got back. We've sat there eating breakfast and I've mentioned about Albert and you've said you would see to it. Ain't no use mentioning it at lunch because by then it's too late to get into town to catch the train."

I said, "Well, I've got to get it done and don't let me forget."

He was right about the colt crop. I had worried myself sick about the bunch of them and it had all been for nothing. Hell, there wasn't a one of them I'd've taken five thousand dollars for. And the blaze-faced black had run written all over him. I could not believe it was the same bunch of horses I'd despaired of only two weeks before. They had simply bloomed overnight. I had seen other breeds do that, but I'd never figured it to be a trait of the Thoroughbred. It made me sad that Laura couldn't be there to see the sight. But, as it turned out, she'd made a good investment after all. The horses from Grayson Farms were going to win some money and then they were going to command some very respectable stud fees.

I wondered if I was forgetting to take Albert in on purpose because he was kind of my last link with Laura. When I'd first told him he'd gotten very excited because he'd never ridden a train before. I reminded him he was going to be seeing his wife again and his face got immediately serious. He said, "Lawd, that be a good woman, but she sho' death on whiskey. I reckon I bettah gits ready to mend mah ways."

I started us on the road Sunday in what I considered ample time to get to the depot and get Albert and the carriage and the team settled in a stock car before the train pulled in. But halfway there a hub nut on the front axle came loose and we spent the better part of forty-five minutes getting it fixed with some smooth wire I borrowed from a fence line beside the road. As it was, we barely got to the depot before the train pulled in. It was fortunate indeed that the train, which got made up in Dallas for its eastern run, had an empty stock car in its string. But it was still a tight fit. Engineers and train crews are awful touchy about having their schedules interfered with for much less than a head of state. One Negro coachman and a carriage and a span of horses didn't rate much leeway with them even though I was paying for the whole car. Two roustabouts from the freight dock helped us load the big carriage and the horses. I thought the worst was over, but then, all of a sudden, Albert got a bad case of the trembles. He'd been all excited about riding his first train, but now that the belching and smoking and steaming monster was right in front of him his nerve failed. The engineer had his steam built up and was impatiently blowing his whistle and ding-donging his bell. It was nearly too much for Albert. He stood there, right beside the open door, visibly shaking all over. One of the roustabouts suggested we physically force him on and tie him to the coach. He said Albert wouldn't get loose until the train would be running too fast for him to jump off. I didn't think that was going to work. I figured if he could get the door open he'd jump anyway.

So there we were, the horses loaded and secured, the carriage loaded and tied down, and Albert a foot from the car door but refusing to go any farther. I had an idea. With the whistle blowing incessantly and the conductor starting down the line to see what the holdup was, I talked Albert into entering the stock car and getting up on the seat of the carriage. He looked mighty nervous when he took his first hesitant step into the car, but when he'd crawled up on the driver's seat of the carriage he seemed to relax. As quickly as I could I grabbed up the harness from where it was piled in the corner and hung the traces over a hook at the forward end of the car. Then I took the reins and walked back to Albert and put them in his hands. "There," I said, "now you can drive the train to Jefferson. Nothing to be afraid of now, Albert. I've seen you handle a team of four and this old train ain't nothing to that."

He beamed. "Why, dog my cats, Mr. Warner, I do believe you is right as rain." He gave the reins a tentative little shake. "Git up, you!"

I said as I backed out of the car, "A railroad train has got a hard mouth, Albert, so you'd want to keep a pretty tight rein on it."

He nodded vigorously and pulled back on the slack in the harness. "Yessuh. I ain't gonna have no troubles. This heah train gonna know who be the boss 'fore we gone a mile."

I stepped back onto the platform as one of the roustabouts pushed the door shut and latched it. I walked along beside the car as the train started to moving out, bumping and jolting. Albert said, sternly, setting back on the reins. "Heah, you square-jawed cuss! Settle yo' seff down, you heah? I take de whip to you."

I called through the slats of the door, "Now remember, Albert, as soon as you get unloaded take that note to the passenger agent and he'll direct you from there. Ask for the passenger agent until you find him. And be sure and give that envelope to Phoenix."

But he was too busy bringing the "team" under control to bother with me. All he could spare me was a vague, "Yessuh, yessuh, Mr. Warner."

The note to the passenger agent asked that the bearer of the note be directed to the Excelsior hotel. I knew that Albert could handle the team with no trouble, even on the crowded streets of Jefferson. Once he got to the

Excelsior and asked around at the back for either Laura or Phoenix he would be all right. In my letter to Laura I had mentioned the stable where I'd put Paseta and suggested she use the same one for the team and carriage.

I stood on the platform watching the train disappear down the tracks. I had also given Albert a gift of one hundred dollars in a sealed envelope to give to Phoenix. I had sent nothing further to Laura. There wasn't any more to say.

Standing there, watching the caboose of the train recede, I was glad we'd got there too late. I had feared temptation as we drove in. It would have been very easy for me to get aboard to keep Albert from being too afraid. Too easy. Fortunately, I hadn't had time to think about it as a logical alternative. If I'd had the time to work it out I probably would have climbed aboard and been in Jefferson in less than two hours.

Less than two hours. It made me shake my head as I went back to where I'd tied my horse and mounted up. As I wheeled him around I could see that the Baptist church was just letting out. They'd been at it since eleven that morning. I figured the Baptists like their money's worth when it came to preaching. I liked mine, too, when it came to marriage, but I didn't figure I'd gotten it, not if you counted coin in peace and contentment. But I felt sure Laura could say the same thing herself. I looked at my watch. It was about ten after one. My intention had been to head straight back to the ranch and get to work. Somehow, suddenly, my heart wasn't in it. I was passing through the main part of town, if there was such, and I saw that one of the saloons was open.

I pulled my horse up and stared at its inviting open door. What the hell difference would a few drinks or a few hours make. I didn't really have anywhere to go that was all that demanding of my time. I wheeled my horse and turned in toward the saloon. I got down and tied the reins to a post there and went on into the cool dark. A bartender who wasn't wearing a bow tie and a vest asked me what I'd have. I said straight whiskey and he poured me out a shot and asked for twenty-five cents. I was only too happy to pay him. I said, "Leave the bottle. Save you some effort."

He nodded. "These here Sundays can get a mite tedious."

"More than you'd ever guess," I said.

14

Laura

Wednesday had come and gone and there had been no sign of Warner. The same held true for Thursday. By Friday afternoon I was becoming frantic. Phoenix was full of self-righteous, I-told-you-so smugness, "As ye sow so shall ye reap." She had a biblical quotation for every occasion, though I had never seen her wearing out the road to church. She said, "I done tol' you you be treatin' that good man wrong. You been settin' over heah waitin' an' 'spectin' him to come to you. I reckon you jus' gon' have to swaller the bitter cup o' pride an' go to him."

Friday, at about four o'clock, I relented and sent her to his hotel to find out what she could. I was halfway afraid to be there without her to intercept Charles Morgan should he come to call. He had made several attempts to see me, but I had been unwilling. Only once had we had an encounter. I had become sick of staying in my rooms and taking every meal there, so Thursday evening I dressed as well and as inconspicuously as I could in a dark blue gown that was so deep in color it was almost black. I hoped people in the dining room would take me for a widow in mourning, thus explaining why I was alone and also guaranteeing my privacy. But Mr. Morgan chose to come to my table in the middle of my meal. He couldn't sit down because I'd had the waiter take the other chair away from my small table. But he stood there, speaking low and earnestly, requesting that we have a talk as soon as possible. I told him that I felt we had nothing to discuss and, frankly, felt that he had treated me in a cavalier fashion concerning my business proposal. He hissed at me that there was a great deal more between us than the leasing of an unfinished wing in a hotel and that he had information that, once I knew, would cause me to view our relationship in an altogether different light. I assured him that no such information existed and that I had him in as good a light as I wanted. He stalked away, the back of his neck reddening and his jaw working. The man became more unappetizing and obnoxious each time I saw him.

But that one encounter did not deter him. That morning, shortly before noon, he called at my suite and insisted Phoenix call me to the door. Phoenix said I was in my bath and likely to remain there the balance of the day.

She came into the bedroom once Morgan was gone, and said, "Missy, we can't stay in dis place no longer! Dat lizard gonna come slitherin' under de door 'fore long. I don' care where we goes, but we's got to get outta here!"

I answered that I understood but I feared to leave without Warner knowing where I'd gone. I also said I doubted there was another hotel of quality that would have proper accommodations.

She said, "Huh! You and dem accommodations! Day comin' you might wish we was accommodated back on de ranch. I know I already does. I got me a man an' I ain't got no quarrel wid him. But here I sit while you worries 'bout 'commodations!"

Looking back, I knew I had no one to blame but myself. When she was hired in Corpus Christi she was sassy and now it was too late to change her. She'd once explained, earnestly, that it was her light skin that caused it. She'd said, "All us high coloreds is like that. Why, Miss Laura, was I as light skinned as you wouldn't nobody be able to stand me."

I'd looked at her, knowing there was a good deal more behind the remark than an explanation for her scandalous mouth. But I'd let it go. Now there was nothing to be done about her. I had a sister I wished I could palm her off on, but even Lauren, testy as she was, didn't deserve such a turn.

I waited impatiently in the bedroom for her to return. She was gone so long I even considered drawing a bath and taking a soak to calm myself down. I didn't do that but I did have another drink of the whiskey. It was getting easier to drink and the effect was much faster than a hot bath.

Finally the door from the parlor opened and Phoenix came in. She looked grim and less than happy. I said, "Well?"

She shook her head slowly from side to side. "He ain't there."

"Well, where is he?"

"He be gone."

"What do you mean gone?"

She made a motion with her hand. "I mean he done flew de coop. Left. Quit de place."

I stood up, alarmed. "You mean he's left his hotel?"

She put her fists on her hips. "Ain't dat what I been tryin' to tell you?"

I couldn't take it in. I said, "When did he go?"

"Done quit de place Wednesday mawnin'. Paid his bill an' took off."

My head was reeling and Phoenix was giving me her grim look. "I don't understand."

"Ah reckon you don't. Wasn't I tellin' you, in dis very room Tuesday evenin', dat you had better let me go fetch him? You was goin' on 'bout you couldn't go out without no escort an' I was sayin', Let me run fetch Mr. Warner. But would you have it? No. No, ma'am. Said you'd jes' sit heah and wait fo' him to come to you. Well, you don't see him 'bout de place nowhere, does you?" She turned around on her heels, holding out her arms, surveying the room. "No, no, he ain't heah. Guess he ain't comin'. Wonder who we can get to escort you to yo' suppah. How 'bout de lizard?"

"Enough, Phoenix!" I slumped down on the bed. I couldn't believe he had left without a word or a note or a good-bye of some kind. Of course he had told me good-bye. He'd said good-bye and given me the kiss to go with it. I just hadn't realized what he meant. I said, "Damn, damn, damn, damn it to hell!"

Phoenix said, in her self-righteous voice, "Oh, now we gonna feel sorry fo' ourselves. Yes, ma'am. Yes, indeedy. We been done wrong. That mean ol' man done us wrong. Wouldn't stick around while we rubbed his face in de mud. Shame on dat man!"

I walked over to the window and looked out on the street. It was as busy as ever. I looked around at Phoenix. "They had no idea at his hotel where he'd gone? He left no word?"

She had her arms folded under her bosom. "Miss Laura, dat ain't de kind of place takes much interest in the comin' and goin' of de guests. Place is an ol' boat. It floats."

I bit my lower lip in agitation. "Did you think to go down to the depot and inquire there?"

She rolled her eyes. "You seen de crowd at the depot?"

I nodded. It was all too true. All a person had to do was step out into the swirl of humanity to be lost forever. I sighed. "I can't believe he didn't leave a note. Something."

Phoenix said, earnestly, "Miss Laura, what we gonna do?"

I shook my head. "I don't know, Phoenix. I don't know what we can do."

"I do be knowin' what we can do. We can pack them bags and trunks tonight an' get ourselves on that train tomorrow mawnin an' get on home! That's what we can do."

"I can't," I said.

"Yes, ma'am, you can. I show you. I'll put all the clothes in de luggage and den you follow me an' that luggage down to the depot. That be the way to do it."

I laughed weakly. "You know what I'm talking about. I can't go crawling back, Phoenix. I can't. Warner would never respect me again."

"We can go to de little house in Tyler. Maybe he stumble across you there. At least we be out of this Sodom an' Gomorrah."

I gave her a look, but I only shook my head. Phoenix meant well and she was a good maid, but I wasn't going to take her marital advice. Of course she did, as she said, still have her man. I felt very tired. I went over and sat down on the bed. I said, "I think I'll take a nap, Phoenix. I'm not feeling very well."

"You heart sick, that what you be. Heart sick."

"All right. Be quiet now. I want to close my eyes for a few minutes." I felt very alone, suddenly, and very unprotected. I wanted to curl up like a little girl and pull the covers over my head.

Phoenix came over to the bed. She pulled the covers up and patted me on the shoulder. Her voice had gone soft. She said, "Rest yo'self, honey. It all be aw'right. You wait an' see. It gon' be fine."

I didn't so much sleep as fall into a worried drowse. At some point I heard voices. When a man's voice turned loud and angry I tried to raise my head to see or hear better, but I was too tired. Later, when I was up, Phoenix said that Morgan had come by and insisted on seeing me. He had threatened that we'd be turned out if I didn't come to the door. Phoenix said she had "stared at de man 'till he slunk off."

We made some kind of a late supper and then I sent Phoenix away and put on the peach colored dressing gown and sat in the parlor, drinking a bottle of wine that Phoenix had fetched and trying to think of what to do. The game had turned serious. Warner had quit playing and it was not a game you could play with one person. It appeared I had taken the courting demand one step too far. I didn't know exactly what my next move should be but it appeared obvious that we could no longer stay at the Excelsior hotel.

It was getting late at night. I had a little clock on my bedside table. I wandered into the bedroom and saw that it was half-past ten. I was carrying a glass of wine. I sipped at it and thought. There was pen and ink and stationery in the little desk in the parlor. I didn't know what I could say but I could always write a letter to Warner. The problem was, I wasn't sure if I was ready to try the marriage again or if I was just very lonely. Was I lonely for Warner or lonely for my marriage or feeling sorry for myself. I sighed and went back into the parlor and sat down at the desk. I opened the lid and took out pen and ink and a few sheets of letter paper. I could always write something and, if I didn't like it, I didn't have to mail it. At the very least I could let Warner know I was leaving the Excelsior and possibly Jefferson. I knew he was worried about me being under the influence of Charles Morgan. I could at least reassure him on that count. And I could say, once I had moved, that I would get my new address to him. After that it would be up to him.

But did I want to do that, be that cold and distant? Phoenix would read me the riot act if she'd thought I was contemplating such a thing. Perhaps I should tell him my true feelings. Except I wasn't sure what they were. Earlier, I was hurt and bewildered that he'd left without a word, but now—and it could have been the wine—I was feeling a little better. With a sigh I picked up the pen and dipped it into the inkwell and held it poised over the paper.

Some time later, quite some time later if judged by the long pauses when I stared at the wall, I became aware of a slight noise. The desk was backed against a side wall. The door to the entrance to my rooms was to my right and behind me. At first I merely raised my head, trying to think what the noise sounded like. It was very faint.

Then some sense alerted me and I wheeled in my chair and looked behind me and to my right. Charles Morgan was in the room. In his right hand I saw a key. His eyes were fixed directly on me. There was a gleam in them and an odd, slack smile on his face. With a quick movement he shut the door behind him and I heard the key turn as he locked it. He took two unsteady steps toward me and said, hoarsely, "There's nothing between us now. That's what I've been wanting to tell you."

For a second I was so shocked by his intrusion into my chamber that I sat frozen. Then, as he neared, I jumped to my feet and put the chair between us. I said, loudly, "Mr. Morgan! Have you taken leave of your senses? *Get out of here!*"

He came a step closer. He was fumbling inside his coat. He said, still in that same hoarse voice, "I've got something to show you."

Even though I had had several glasses of wine I could smell the reek of much stronger spirits on his breath. He was drunk. That was what had given him the nerve to invade my privacy. In a way it was a sort of relief. Given the choice between that and insanity I much preferred the alcohol. He was closer now, almost to me, still fumbling at his jacket. I put out my foot and shoved the chair into his shins. "Get out of here! *Get out of here!*" I reached out my hands to push him back since he'd barely noticed the chair. As I did he reached for me, grabbing me by the lapels of my robe. I felt his grasp tighten and, in a panic, I jerked back, flailing at him with my fists. I heard the sound of my robe tearing as I jerked and pulled backwards. Suddenly the fabric ripped and I staggered away, suddenly free. I did not pause. So far as I was concerned he was beyond reason and was to be treated as dangerous. From what I had seen so far, he had rape or worse on his mind. I had no intention of being a pliant victim. If he managed to take me he would pay more dearly than he'd ever dreamed.

When I was freed I immediately ran for the door into the bedroom, clutching my ruined dressing gown around my body. Fortunately, I was wearing a camisole and a full slip underneath so he was not going to satisfy any of his lusts by what he was able to see. As quickly as I could I opened the door into the bedroom and slammed it behind me, frantically trying to turn the key. He was too quick. He got to the door faster than I expected and was pushing his weight against it, making it impossible for me to shut it far enough to turn the lock. I could feel his superior physical strength winning out. I suddenly released it and ran frantically for my dressing table, which was to the left of the big bed, hoping to find a weapon of some kind. The sudden release of the door brought him skidding off balance into the room. It gave me an extra few seconds to search for a nail file or a hat pin or any kind of weapon. I glanced over my shoulder and saw him starting my way. He lunged and I barely eluded his grasp. I had picked up a rat-tailed comb and I stabbed at him with the sharp end. It was a futile gesture. With no room to maneuver I was boxed in between the bed and the two walls. He was coming after me, disregarding the comb. I threw it at his face and took two steps and jumped up on the bed and then skipped across and jumped off on the far side. I now had the bed between us, but I knew it was only a temporary respite. In another moment he would come around the bed and have me trapped. I looked wildly around and my eyes lit on my muff, lying on the low table beside the window. It seemed a century since Warner had walked over and picked it up asking curiously, "What's this?" Oh, how I missed him at that instant.

But with a quick step I reached the table and slid my hand inside the muff, feeling the comforting weight and solidity of the grip of the revolver in its little pocket.

Morgan was winded. He was starting around the bed but he stopped, swaying a little, and said, each word coming out between pants, "I only wanted—wanted to—tell you that there is nothing between us now."

I said, meaning it, "Stay right where you are, Morgan. You son of a bitch, don't you come near me."

He was either deaf or did not perceive any danger. He

said, "I have something you will be very interested in." And started around the foot of the bed.

I did not want to shoot him. I wanted him to stop, to leave, to allow Phoenix and me to leave. And I wanted Warner. I wanted Warner, right then, more than I had ever wanted anything in my life.

Morgan came on. He passed the post of the foot board. He was only six or seven feet away. Inside the muff, with my thumb, I cocked the small revolver. It made no sound in the muff. I must have looked absurd with a muff on my right hand, but he made no comment. I was aware my robe was in tatters on the left side. He started to take one more step and I shot him. I aimed low. I didn't want to kill the man, but I wanted to stop him. I felt the gun buck against my hand and then he stopped and jumped back, surprised. The shot made very little sound. He stared at me and then he looked down at his left thigh. There was a hole in his pants a foot and a half up his thigh from his knee. The cloth around the hole was rapidly turning crimson. He looked at it and then at me. His mouth fell open. He said, in a strangled voice, "You shot me!"

I could see smoke rising from the end of the muff. I guessed that the shot had set the silk lining on fire. But, for the moment, I couldn't worry about it.

Morgan had clamped his hand over the wound. He began hopping around on his good leg, holding his wounded leg off the floor. His face was suffused with such rage that it had turned a beet red. I had never seen such a sight. As he hopped he cursed. He yelled at me, "You stupid bitch! I only wanted to show you something. If you'd have stopped and listened you'd have been glad. Crazy bitch, you shot me!"

With his right hand he was pawing around inside his coat. For a second I raised the muff and pointed it at him, thinking he was reaching for a weapon. But then he came out of his pocket with a long white envelope and threw it at me. It landed on the bed. He screamed, "Look at that you crazy bitch! Look what you ruined!" He was starting to drip blood on the floor.

I wanted to get at the envelope, but I didn't want to take my eyes off him. The muff was continuing to smoke and I knew I'd have to do something about it. I wanted to see the contents of the envelope even though I was fairly sure I knew what they were. Still watching him while he hopped and cursed I took a quick step and took up the envelope. It had been torn open so that the contents were easy to get at. I expected it to be some sort of legal conveyance giving me the wing of the hotel somehow. Instead, when I shook open the single folded piece of paper, Warner's handwriting jumped right out at me. I gasped. I looked at Morgan, who was still hopping and cursing. I glanced at the top of the page. The letter was dated Tuesday night, obviously written not too many hours after he had left me. I said to Morgan, my voice shaking with rage, "How long have you had this?" I shook the letter at him.

"What difference does it make." He was screaming. "You've shot me and I'll kill you for it." He took a hop toward me and fumbled at his vest.

"Tell me!" I screamed back at him. "When was this brought to the hotel?"

He was still trying to fumble at a pocket of his vest, but he was off balance. He grabbed at one of the posts at the foot of the bed, trying to steady himself. "Several days ago. What do you care? If you'd seen me, talked to me, I'd have shown you. Don't you see? That cleared the field for us. He's gone, cleared out. Left town. But now you've shot me. You'll by God beg my forgiveness!"

I glanced down at the letter. So eager was I to read a few words of what Warner had written that I took my eyes off the madman Morgan. But as I tried to read I became aware of just how hot my hand was getting inside the muff. I knew I had to get it off my hand before it burst into flame and burned me. I began trying to throw the muff off while I still held on to the revolver, but it wouldn't come free and I was holding the letter with my left hand. Then I suddenly realized that Morgan had succeeded in getting at a derringer he had concealed in a pocket of his vest. He would have drawn it if it, too, hadn't caught on the material of his vest. I realized he was the greater danger. I dropped the letter and tried to jerk the muff off with my left hand. It still was snagged on some part of the pistol. I could not take my eyes off of Charles Morgan. Blood was dripping steadily down his pants leg and pooling on the floor. He was holding himself erect with his left hand on the bedpost, having taken his hand away from the wound. His right hand was still tugging at the derringer. There was now so much smoke coming from my muff that he was becoming obscured. I could feel the inside getting hotter and hotter. I was about to decide to let go of the pistol, jerk my hand out of the muff, and rush at Morgan before he could draw the derringer, when Phoenix suddenly came running into the room from the parlor. For a moment I was vaguely startled because she was wearing my emerald green silk robe and I couldn't imagine what she was doing in it. But before I could figure it out, she sized up the situation and suddenly made a rush at Morgan and gave him a great push with her hands. The force of the shove sent him stumbling backwards for a few steps before his momentum overcame him and he fell sprawling on the floor, his derringer falling harmlessly at his feet. In a motion Phoenix had scooped up the deadly little gun and then skipped backwards away from the wildly flailing arms of Charles Morgan.

But I was preoccupied with my own business. I finally got the revolver out of my muff and threw the article to the floor and stamped on it with both feet until the smoke began to abate and sparks no longer flew out the end. I was not doing the purse any good, but I imagined it was only the inside and the lining that had been damaged.

Right then, however, I was not at all concerned about anything except the letter. I wanted Mr. Morgan out of the place so I could read Warner's message in quiet and solitude. I picked the letter up and refolded it and stuck it down inside my bodice. Phoenix was holding the derringer and staring first at me, holding a revolver, and then at Mr. Morgan, cursing and trying to get to his feet. She said, "Miss Laura, what in de world been goin' on heah?"

I shook my head. I said, nodding at Morgan, "Let's get rid of the trash first." I walked to the foot of the bed and looked at Morgan where he lay on the floor near the wall. I said, "Get up, you snake, and get out of here."

He pulled himself to his hands and knees. He said, "You, you—you evil woman. You shot me, you cursed bitch!" His face was alive with fury.

I cocked the hammer of the revolver, though I was careful to keep my finger off the trigger. I said, "Yes. And I'll do it again the next time you break into my room. Now get up and get out or we'll see how you like being shot in the other leg."

"You wouldn't dare."

Phoenix said, "Oh, Mr. Lizard, that ain't de right thing to say to Miss Laura. She be a woman what will take a dare. Naw, suh, you sho' don't want to be sayin' that. Not 'less you wants to get shot 'gain."

He looked at Phoenix and then at me. He was up and leaning against the bedroom wall. There was venom in his eyes and his mouth. He said, spitting the words, "Your nigger ever puts so much as a finger on me again I'll have her neck stretched."

Before I could reply, Phoenix fairly screamed, "Say what? Ain't no white trash gon' be callin' me that!" She fumbled around with the derringer even though I could see she didn't know how to work it. "I blow yo' damn head off wid you own gun."

"Phoenix," I said. "Get back. Let him get by."

"You heah what he call me? I get up-side his head wid a club he talk to me like that! I be a ladies' maid, I don' have to take no such talk."

"Get back." I watched Morgan as he made his slow way along the wall. He was leaving blood marks everywhere, with each step and with his hand along the walls. I said, "Hurry up and get out of here you bastard. You held my letter. That is against the law."

He was finally turning the corner to the other wall that separated the parlor from the bedroom. The door was only a few feet from him. He said, his lip curling, "There was no stamp on it."

"That makes no difference."

"It fell down a crack."

"You're a liar."

"You and that manure farmer deserve each other. You're not a lady. You're a whore."

"Uh oh," Phoenix said, and rolled her eyes. "And she got a gun in her hand."

I smiled without humor. "Then how does that make you feel, Morgan? You didn't have the price."

He stumbled into the parlor and began to hop toward the hall door. Over his shoulder he said, "I wonder if you are even smart enough to know what you gave up."

"I know what I almost lost. With a little help from you and your desk clerk. But were I you, Mr. Morgan, I would hurry along. You appear to be bleeding to death."

At the door he paused to look back. "You get out of my hotel. Get out and stay out. You have not heard the last of this from me."

"You get out, you snake!" Phoenix was holding the door when he made his exit speech. She suddenly yelled at him and then slammed the door. He was not quite all the way through and we heard the door hit him, heard him give a moan, and then heard him fall to the floor of the hall. Phoenix didn't bother to open it to see how Morgan had fared. Instead she looked at me with a question in her eyes. "Does you know enough now?"

"Oh, yes," I said. "We'll get a few hours' sleep and then get up early and start packing. But right now I want to read Warner's letter. You stay in here and keep the door locked." I started to turn away and then I suddenly remembered how surprised I had been to see her come charging through the door. I asked her what had summoned her to my aid. I knew the walls were thick and I had only screamed once. I doubted if she could have heard me and I knew she couldn't have heard the one gunshot.

She stared at me. A frown came over her face. She said, looking a little worried, "I don't be knowin', Miss Laura. Was a thing come in my head woke me up, said you bettah go see 'bout Miss Laura." She gave me an awed look. "You reckon it was de spirits?"

"Is this the first time you've ever come down here in the night?"

"No, ma'am. I comes ever' night. Sometimes twicet. But this was de first time anything happenin'."

"I see," I said. "No, I don't think it was spirits. I know it was in Mr. Morgan's case. But those spirits come in a bottle. I'm going to read the letter now."

I read Warner's letter slowly all the way through. Then I held it to my breast, my eyes filling with tears. It frightened me to think how close I'd come to letting such a man get away. After I'd had a little cry I read the letter again and then again. Each time the words came across so strong and honest and thoughtful that I started crying again. What a miserable bitch I'd been to put him through such a time. I'd be lucky if he'd have me back. Finally, when I'd read the letter four times I folded it carefully, got off the bed, and put it in my jewelry case.

I went into the parlor and sent Phoenix back to her room to collect her things and bring them into the suite. After that she made herself up a bed on the divan in the parlor and I set the alarm on my clock for us both to wake up at five o'clock. We had a great deal of packing to get done in order to catch the ten o'clock train the next morning.

"We really be goin', Miss Laura?"

"Yes, we are really going."

"Shoulda gone befo'."

"I know that. Now be quiet and let's both get what sleep we can. We'll have to do without coffee or breakfast in the morning."

"Alls I wants is outta dis place."

I got into bed and curled up, hugging my pillow to me and wishing for the moment when it would be Warner. I was going to make it up to him. Oh, how I was going to make it up to him.

We were up with the ringing of the alarm. I had said we would do without coffee or breakfast but further thought convinced me we'd save time if we had a cup or two. I sent Phoenix, with my heart in my mouth, to the kitchen to see what she could achieve with a little ladylike soliciting. Not only did she return with a pot of coffee and cream and sugar, but she also managed some bacon and toast. And all of it done, I was sure, against the orders of Charles Morgan. I did not know how much time he had had to render me persona non grata in his hotel, but I felt sure that the net would be drawn tight as soon as he could accomplish it. It was just as well that we were intending to leave the hotel, for I felt sure he would have us forced out, by law if necessary.

By now Phoenix knew the whole story of Morgan's intrusion and how he or his desk clerk had withheld Warner's letter from me, Morgan considering it a sign that I was now free to be his. His *what,* he had never gotten around to saying. Phoenix had grossly resented his tearing my peach dressing gown. She had said, "That be Mr. Warner's favorite."

I'd given her a look. "No, his favorite is the emerald green one, the one you were wearing last night. But I'm more interested in how you would come to a conclusion as to which of my dressing gowns is Mr. Warner's favorite."

She gave me a blank look on that one. Finally she said, primly, "Well, I do believe he done tol' me 'bout the matter."

She was outrageous. I shook my head slowly. "You do not expect me to believe that. But you had best quit listening at keyholes."

Now she said, "See what come o' not listenin' to Phoenix? You listened to me we'd've nearly beaten Mr. Warner home. But, no, ain't goin' to listen to no colored maid. No, ma'am! Got our own ideas. Gonna punish Mr. Warner. That right, look away, but dat was what you was doin'. Now ain't it?"

I couldn't very well tell her to mind her own business. By now she was so immersed in my affairs there was little she didn't know. But she said, "That man come at you an' tore yo' pretty gown. How come you jus' wound de bastard? I knows what kind o' shot you be, Miss Laura. You shot de snake in the laig on purpose."

I got up from the table, much refreshed. I said, "We had better get busy. It is nearing six o'clock and we have Lord only knows how much packing to do. But I don't have to tell you. I'm sure there's a little voice comes in your head to tell you."

She looked outraged. "Well, land o' Goshen. I come down heah and nearly get shot and you up and make fun of me. Why, I nevah!"

We started packing and it seemed to go on and on and on. I vowed if we ever got out of this mess I was going to cut my wardrobe in half. Nobody needed as many clothes as I had nor as many shoes nor as much lingerie nor as many pairs of stockings.

We packed away while Phoenix kept up her incessant reminder that all of this could have been avoided if only I had heeded her counsel and either made up with Warner on the spot or else gone to him the minute we found out he had left.

It did not help my mood one bit. Warner's letter was precious and beautiful, but what Phoenix didn't know was that it was predicated on the assumption that our marriage was finished. For all I knew I might have to do some tall talking to get myself back in his good graces.

So it was with no small amount of trepidation that I sped to finish the packing, hoping to rush to Warner in confirmation of what I felt.

At around eight o'clock there came the sound of someone knocking on the door to the parlor. I glanced at Phoenix. "I don't think that can be Charles Morgan, but if it is someone telling us we have to leave, inform them that we will be out within the hour."

She was gone for a few moments. I could hear a subdued buzz of talk. She came back looking worried. She said, "It's de sheriff."

I sighed. I couldn't believe that Morgan had felt the need to call the law to have us evicted. I said, "Go tell him we are leaving as fast as we can."

She said, "I done did that. He say it about another matter."

"What other matter?"

She looked at the floor. "He say som'thin' 'bout de shootin'."

"Oh, hell," I said. "Not now. Damn that Charles Morgan." I looked in the mirror to make sure that my hair was in place. Because I was expecting to be traveling I had put on a simple blue frock that was comfortable and wouldn't be too hot.

A tall, spare gray-haired man was standing just inside the door to the parlor. I would have known that he was a lawman even without the badge on his chest or the big revolver on his hip. He was holding a pearl gray cattleman's hat in his hands. He bowed slightly as I entered and came to the middle of the room. He said, "Mrs. Grayson?"

"Yes. What may I do for you?"

He looked uncomfortable. He said, "Mrs. Grayson, I have had a complaint lodged about you from Mr. Charles Morgan. Mrs. Grayson, I don't know how to tell you this, but I might have to arrest you."

I put my hand to my mouth. I said, "Why, that low cur. This is despicable even for him."

He nodded. "Yes, ma'am." He motioned with his hat. "Reckon we could sit down where I could hear your side of the business?"

15

Laura

My only thought as I seated the sheriff on the divan and took a chair across from him was I hope he doesn't go on too long and make us miss the train. I did not think I could abide another twenty-four hours without seeing Warner and talking to him and putting matters right. All I wanted now was to be his wife and help him raise racing horses. I'd seen enough culture and society and hustle and bustle to last me the rest of my life.

The sheriff looked uncomfortable as he introduced himself. He sat on the very edge of the divan, running a hand through his thinning hair. He cleared his throat. "I shore hate to bother a fine lady like you, Mrs. Grayson, and I wouldn't if they was anyway around it. I been sheriff here for nearly twenty-five years and this is a considerably different town from when I first put on the badge. Lots of money 'round here that thinks it gives them priv'leges. It don't with me, but it shore as hell allows them to hire high-priced lawyers and get around the law anyway they can."

I said, "What is this all about, Sheriff Long?"

He fiddled with his hat. "Charles Morgan, whom I'm sure you know owns this establishment, has brought a charge against you. He says that you tried to murder him and that you did shoot him. In the leg."

I laughed, but not heartily. I could see a web of trouble opening before me. I was as innocent as the day, but Morgan was an influential man in the town and it would be my word against his about exactly what had happened and how I had come to shoot him. I felt sick inside. How long, I wondered, would it be before I could take that train to Tyler. Why hadn't I listened to Phoenix? Why hadn't I sent her to Warner's hotel on Thursday? If I had we would have left Friday before the awful business with Morgan could have occurred. And so far as that went, why hadn't I been available to Morgan when he'd persisted in calling? He'd only wanted to show me the letter, show me that my husband was gone, show me that there was nothing to stop him. It made me nearly ill to think of what might have been. But I summoned my strength and said, "It is true, Sheriff Long, that I shot Charles Morgan. However, it was done with more than ample provocation. I think when you hear what my maid and I have to say and see the evidence we have you'll realize I acted the only way I could and that if anyone needs to be in jail it is Charles Morgan. In fact I am going to enter a charge against him right now for forcibly entering my rooms and for attempted rape."

He grimaced. "Mrs. Grayson, one charge right now is about all I can handle. If you wouldn't mind letting me know what happened I'd be much obliged."

"Very well," I said. I stood up. "I will conduct you through the affair from its beginning to its end and give you the details in between. Believe me, every second is frighteningly imprinted on my memory."

With Phoenix trailing along behind the sheriff I showed him how Mr. Morgan had entered from the hall with a hotel key. I showed him the letter I was composing when Morgan came in, showed him how I had broken off in mid word, raising my pen as Mr. Morgan startled me. I was about to go on, showing how I tried to flee to the bedroom, when Sheriff Long interrupted me. He said,

"Now, that is the part that has got me flummoxed. His claim is that you lured him up here in order to get him to make you some sort of a deal on a wing of the hotel. He says that you were, uh, uh——" He turned slightly red, looking more and more uncomfortable. "I don't know how to put this, Mrs. Grayson."

"I can imagine," I said grimly. "Did Mr. Morgan say that I was willing to be his consort if I could have the wing?"

He looked even more uncomfortable. "Well, I don't know what consort means, but if it means what I think it does, then, yes'm, that's what he says. He said your husband had been here and he felt, as a gentleman, he couldn't work out nothing with you until your business with your husband was finished."

Phoenix let out a whoop and rolled her eyes to the ceiling. I said, "That will do, Phoenix. You will get a chance to talk." I turned to the sheriff. "No, that is not true." I then carefully explained, in detail and in truth to the best of my recollection, exactly how matters had transpired. I said, "Yes, my husband and I had been having some difficulties, which is the reason I was in Jefferson. But they had absolutely nothing to do with Charles Morgan. I have rebuffed his advances at every occasion and would have done so whether I was married or not."

"Man is a lizard," Phoenix said.

I gave her a look. I said to the sheriff, "The only part that is true is that I made him an offer to lease the General Grant wing and have it finished and decorated. I offered twenty thousand dollars in return for a ten-year lease. Mr. Morgan was to have given me an answer last Monday, but he kept delaying, insisting that I get rid of my husband and that I be part of the deal. I had assured him in plain and simple and detailed language that I was in no way a part of the business bargain and that my husband was my business."

He nodded. "Why don't you go ahead to the end of the matter and then we'll sit down and talk."

I nodded. With Phoenix standing anxiously by I described how I put the chair between me and Mr. Morgan and how he had lunged for me and torn my dressing gown. After I finished that part we went into the bedroom so that Phoenix could retrieve the torn article. In the bedroom the sheriff looked around at the masses of luggage and said, with a little laugh, "Was they many more in your party, Mrs. Grayson?"

I could understand. I said, "As I told you, Sheriff Long, when I left the ranch I was expecting to be gone for some time. I have an extensive wardrobe."

Phoenix said, "Miss Laura got more clothes than a chu'ch full o' women."

Sheriff Long fingered the dressing gown. "This was what you were wearing?"

"Yes. And that was what Charles Morgan tore as he lunged to stop me from escaping in here from the parlor."

He looked around, noting the blood on the floor. "He done quite a bit of bleeding. Looks as if he moved around a lot. Got bloody hand prints on the wall and blood here on the bed post."

"He could have left at any time. We were urging him to leave."

The sheriff looked around at Phoenix. "He said your maid assaulted him. That was the word he used."

I said, "She rushed at him and knocked him over to keep him from drawing a derringer and shooting me."

"But you still had the gun?"

"Yes, but I was reluctant to shoot him again. I didn't want to kill him. But if he'd succeeded in freeing the derringer from where it was caught in his vest I would have had no choice. Fortunately my maid came in at that moment and toppled him over. He fell more because of his wounded leg than because of any action on her part."

Phoenix's eyes got big and round. "Miss Laura! You know I give that snake a bodacious shove."

The sheriff smiled slightly. His attention wandered to my muff. It was lying on the low bureau where it had been before. The revolver I'd bought in Tyler was beside it. He went over and looked at the pistol and then examined the muff. He turned around to me. "This where you had the pistol concealed?"

"It was not concealed." I said, drawing myself up. "I had that apparatus constructed for the purpose of carrying a gun in concealment, but Mr. Morgan rushed me so quickly I did not have time to remove it."

"You know we got a gun law here?"

"Yes. But the gun has never been out of this room."

He nodded. I could not tell what he was thinking behind that leathery, impassive face. "And you say that Morgan had a weapon also?"

"Yes. Now if we can go back into the parlor I'd like to show you all my proof at once."

After we were seated I asked the extent of Morgan's injuries. The sheriff pulled a face. "I'd say his pride is hurt worse than anything. Your bullet went through the fleshy part of his thigh and lodged just under the skin. Wasn't no more than a second's work for the surgeon to get it out. He bled quite a bit but I can see that came mostly from his hopping around all over the place. He claims he collapsed the minute you shot him and then your maid jumped on him and kicked and hit him."

Phoenix said, "Land o' Goshen! Dat man wouldn't know de troot' 'f it come wrapped in a ribbon."

The sheriff smiled. "I can see that. He was all over the place back there in the bedroom. I can see where he had you hemmed up on that far side of the bed so you had no choice."

I said, "He was warned any number of times. I must tell you, sheriff, that I was still in some shock from his sudden appearance. As I say, I had been composing a letter to my husband in the parlor. The next I knew he was in the door, and I was in a condition of flight from that point on. He has brought the charges because he is a low cur and a coward and has no other way to explain how he received the wound."

The sheriff searched my face. He said, "Morgan claims

it was common knowledge around the hotel that you and he were more than, uh, friendly. He claims y'all had supper more than once and went on a picnic and that you, ah, encouraged him."

I said as severely as I could, "Mr. Morgan is the type who would claim being in the same city with a lady is encouragement. Yes, I had dinner with him in a public place on two occasions. The first time, in the dining room, he had a screen up separating us from the rest of the diners. I requested it be taken down before I consented to dine with him again. Yes, we went on a picnic, which was chaperoned by my maid and his valet. I deliberately wore jodhpurs."

He gave me a questioning look.

"Ladies' riding pants that are not particularly becoming."

Phoenix said, "That do be right."

"So you didn't lure him and you don't feel you gave him any encouragement."

"On the contrary. My maid had orders, if he came to the door, that I was not in or that I was sick or asleep or anything else she could think of. He approached me in the dining room, I think it was Thursday night, trying to tell me he had something I would be greatly interested in. I'm certain it was the letter from my husband. He had intercepted it and read it and interpreted it to mean that my husband was no longer in the picture." My face felt angry. "That is the sort of man we are dealing with, sheriff."

"Why do you suppose he didn't tell you about the letter Thursday night?"

"I suppose he wanted to keep me here until he could talk to me."

"You say you have his derringer?"

"Yes." I turned around and Phoenix took it out of her apron pocket and handed it to me. It was a beautiful little thing. I calculated it to be .38 caliber by looking at the chambers. It was gold and silver chased, with ivory grips on the butt. Mr. Morgan's initials, C.A.M., were on the ivory in gold letters. I handed it to the sheriff. "He was as well armed as I was."

He looked at the gun for a second and then laid it beside him on the divan. "What do you reckon caused him to make such a fool play?"

I shrugged. "I don't know. I became alarmed by the way the man talked within two or three meetings. I think he got the courage to break in on me out of a bottle. He certainly appeared the worse for drink."

The sheriff nodded thoughtfully. "Yes, the doctor said he was drunk. Drunk and raving. But he shore didn't waste no time sending word to me and filing charges. Do you have anything else to show me, Mrs. Grayson?"

"Just this," I said. I went into the bedroom and came back with Warner's letter and the envelope it had come in. There was the trace of a bloody fingerprint on the envelope, which must have got there when Morgan flung the letter at me. I opened the page and showed the sheriff the date that was written on it. I said, "I would rather you didn't read the letter because it is personal. But if it is necessary, so be it. But you can see at the top that the letter was written Tuesday night. I imagine that my husband left it at the desk that night or the next morning. He left town Wednesday to return home. Mr. Morgan appropriated it and saw, to his glee, that it indicated my husband and I were through. Such is not the case. Had I received that letter promptly I would have been on the next train in pursuit of my husband. I treated him badly and unfairly and all I want to do is go home and make things right between us."

The sheriff looked at the letter without touching it. He said, "Your name is Grayson. You wouldn't happen to be any kin to Warner Grayson, the horse trainer?"

"I would be his wife," I said. "At least I hope I still am."

"Owns Grayson Farms, the Thoroughbred stables?"

"Yes."

The sheriff whistled. "Boy, howdy. That's the best horseman in Texas. Ain't he a friend of Wilson Young?"

"The ex bank robber? Yes. They are very close."

The sheriff laughed slightly. "I wonder if Morgan knows what he's got holt of here."

I said, grimly, "Right now he has hold of me and apparently intends to use his influence to my disadvantage."

The sheriff sobered at once. He sighed. "Right now is when I wish I'd followed my daddy into cotton farming." He looked at me. "Mrs. Grayson, I want you to know that I ain't got the slightest doubt but what you say is exactly the way it happened. I don't think enough of Charles Morgan to give him the sweat off a pig's snout, but that ain't got nothing to do with the way things could fall out. As I said, this town has changed considerably in the last few years and most of it for the worse. There are a lot of folks here ain't too particular how they make their money and Morgan is one of them. He's got a lot of influence and a lot of money to buy more with. This town is full of swindlers and cheats and plain out-and-out crooks who will do anything for a dollar, and a good many of them are in city and county jobs—laywers and judges." He looked away and shook his head. "I could take your charge on him breaking in here and molesting you, but it is his hotel and he'll say he let himself in because he heard trouble or yelling or whatnot. And it'll be hard to disprove. So far as your letter, he can claim it got hidden under some papers or fell down a crack or something."

"That's what he said."

"And that he was trying to deliver it. And so far as it being open, well, you done that yourself."

I grimaced. I said, "I see."

"What it comes down to, Mrs. Grayson, so far as law goes, is your word against his and he's got the influence and a hole in his leg."

Behind me Phoenix said, "Damn my cats!"

I looked at the sheriff frankly. "What do you advise, Sheriff Long?"

He looked at the floor for a moment. After that he

looked at his watch. He said, "You still got a little better than a half an hour to catch that westbound train for Tyler. If you were willing to leave all your luggage and gear, why, there is a back way out of here and I ain't going to be nowhere near the train depot for at least an hour, maybe more."

Phoenix said, "That's de ticket."

I thought a moment and then I shook my head. "No. I thank you sheriff, but no. And it's not the leaving of my belongings. I won't let a little snake like Morgan run me from anything, even a viper's nest."

The sheriff sighed. "I was afraid you were going to say that, Mrs. Grayson. I don't know what else to tell you."

"Are you going to arrest me?"

He shook his head. "Not until I get an order from a magistrate to do so. And I ain't got it yet." He looked at me. "But don't be too sure that one won't be forthcoming. All I've done is investigate a charge from one citizen about another one. I found it groundless. But Morgan may well go to a magistrate. Or send for one. Then, if I get an order, I got no choice. I wish you'd reconsider and get out of this place."

Behind me I could feel Phoenix writhing with a desire to hurry out the door and rush for the depot with just the clothes on our back. But I was trying to visualize Charles Morgan in my mind. He had stacked the deck against me, as Wilson Young would say, and I was looking for a way to cut the deck and his neck at the same time. I kept looking at the overdressed, dandified, strutting little peacock with the high opinion of himself, seeing him in my mind's eye and looking for a line of attack. Where was his most vulnerable weakness? As I thought about it an idea came to me and I began to smile slightly. It would involve, perhaps, my risking public scrutiny but I doubted if it would ever come to that. Besides, I had nothing to hide. I was now, more than ever, convinced that Charles A. Morgan did. I wondered what the A stood for, but I didn't really care. I turned to the lawman.

"Sheriff Long, do you think you could arrange for a meeting between me and Mr. Morgan?"

He pulled his head back in a gesture of surprise. "Well, I don't know, Mrs. Grayson. I guess I could ask him. He's downstairs in his office right now."

"Oh. I thought he would be in the hospital."

A little smile tugged at the sheriff's mouth. "Well, truth be told, he ain't hurt all that bad. But you reckon it's wise to get around him? I don't think you ought to be stirrin' him up no more'n he already is."

I smiled again. "I think that Mr. Morgan and I would both find a conversation profitable. Tell him that we'll discuss Virginia and old family ties. Who has the roots and who doesn't. Tell him he might be surprised at what would come out in open court."

He looked blank. "What's this about Virginia?"

"Mr. Morgan will understand. Just make it clear to him that it is to his advantage to have an interview with me before he proceeds any further with his present course of action. Mention that he is vulnerable in some areas he might not want to become public."

The sheriff was looking at me intently. "You got something on the man?"

"Sheriff, I couldn't really say. If Mr. Morgan is what I think he is he will be easily exposed."

"What do you think he is?"

I smiled slightly. "I think he is traveling under false colors. He insists on calling himself a gentleman. I think we might call that into question."

The sheriff looked disappointed. "If that's all, you ain't got much of a hand, Mrs. Grayson, you don't mind my saying so. Even I know he ain't no gentleman."

"We are speaking with different connotations, Sheriff Long. Mr. Morgan will understand what I mean."

He got up unwillingly. "Well, I'll go and ask him to have a talk with you. I can't make him do it, however, I can hint like hell, excuse me, that it will weaken his case if he ain't willing." He put his hat on. "I aim to mention also that he is fooling with the wife of a friend of Wilson Young's."

"That is not the way to get at Mr. Morgan."

He gave me a grim look. "I'll try it anyway."

When he was out the door and it had closed behind him I stepped immediately to the divan where he had been sitting and picked up Morgan's derringer. I said, "Phoenix, is there a bucket in the bathroom?"

She stared at me blankly for a second. "Why, yes, I reckon there is."

"Good deep bucket?"

She nodded uncertainly. "Yes, ma'am. I reckon. What that got to do with us gettin' outta here?"

"Go fill it full with water."

She stared at me. "What?"

I stamped my foot. "The bucket! Go fill it with water. And hurry. We don't have a lot of time."

"Aw'right, aw'right." She went out of the room mumbling about crazy people that didn't leave when the high sheriff said they could go. It beat anything she'd ever heard and she'd once been married to a gen'lman from N'Awleans. Gamblin' man, fancy man. Got his throat cut in a card game. Didn't leave her a penny and now all this.

I followed her into the bathroom carrying the derringer. I had checked. It was the same caliber as my revolver, both were .38s. She had the tall bucket of water standing in the middle of the bathroom, full to the brim. I got a towel from the rack, a thick one, and wrapped it around my hand and the derringer, being careful not to let the towel extend to the extreme end of the barrel. I didn't want to repeat what had happened with my muff. Phoenix was standing by, watching me with a puzzled frown on her face. I lowered the derringer until the muzzle was just touching the water and then fired. The towel did a very satisfactory job of muffling the sound. I straightened up and looked in the bucket. When the water had stilled I could see that the bullet had not reached the bottom, but had spent itself against the density of the water. I unwrapped the towel and put it back on the rack. As I started out of the bathroom I told Phoenix to empty the bucket and get rid of the slug that was still at the bottom. She was staring at me. She said, "What in the world?"

I said, with a little smile, "I am stacking the deck, Phoenix. Now do what I say. The sheriff will be back in a moment and I want this gun back on the divan when he comes in, just as if it had never moved."

I myself wasn't sure how I would use the derringer. I simply thought that it would be a good idea if both the guns that had been in the suite at the time were fired. Who was to say just when one or the other was fired. I had told the sheriff a story that was the truth. If, however, the charges were pressed, I was going to tell an entirely different one. I had an idea the sheriff would have forgotten my original honesty. You did not play fair when you were dealing with men such as Charles Morgan. I sat down in a chair in the parlor, facing the door and composed myself, trying to look as serene and respectable as possible.

Mr. Morgan was brought in in a rattan wheeled chair. I wanted to laugh at the ludicrous display, but I controlled my mirth. I didn't know whose sympathy he was trying to solicit, but it certainly wasn't going to be mine. He was pushed by one of the Negro uniformed men that did various jobs around the hotel. He carried a gold-headed ebony walking stick in his lap. The sheriff was right behind the little party, looking a little surprised, as was I. I had expected that if Morgan was willing to talk I would be summoned to his office. I wondered how the poor porter had managed to get Morgan in the wheelchair up the stairs. Probably he had got out and walked and then got back in so he could be wheeled down to my room to make his pitiful entrance. But of course he couldn't do that, not in front of the sheriff.

My question was answered as soon as they were in the parlor. Charles Morgan, giving me a black look, said, "I have chosen to come here. I did not want you in my office and I do not want to be seen with you in front of society of the quality that frequents my hotel. I do not know what you want to converse about, but if you want to beg my sympathy or my pardon you are wasting your time."

I gave him my sunniest smile. "After this conversation it may well be you who are doing the begging, *Mister* Morgan."

He poured hate out of his eyes at me. They say that hell hath no fury like a woman scorned. Whoever wrote that should have had a view of a hotel keeper scorned. He said, viciously, "Keep your remarks to yourself. What do you wish to talk about?"

I nodded at the liveried porter and the sheriff. "I think you might want to conduct this conversation in private, Mr. Morgan. I believe some things I may want to say are private."

He said, recklessly, "I have no secrets."

"Oh?" I looked at him questioningly. "Then your background in Virginia is an open book? Is that the case?"

If looks could kill I would have been dead on the spot. He glared at me for a full moment and then turned to his servant and told him he could go. The sheriff had come into the room and Morgan looked at him. He said, "Is this woman unarmed, Sheriff Long? I don't want to give her the opportunity to finish the job."

The sheriff tried not to smile. He said, "The only gun that I know is in this room is yours." He nodded at the derringer on the divan. "And I reckon I'll hold that for the time being." He picked up the derringer and was about to put it in his shirt pocket when he stopped and sniffed at the barrel and glanced at me. I gave him a smile.

I said, over my shoulder, "Phoenix, go into the bedroom and close the door."

Morgan almost sprang up. "Oh, no! I'll not be left alone with the two of them." He pointed a trembling finger at Phoenix. "She goes outside."

I nodded. "Go along, Phoenix, with the sheriff."

She was glowering at Morgan. "Aw'right. I go 'long. But I bettah not heah no commotion in heah or I gonna wring de neck of some white trash same as I would a ol' scrawny chicken."

Morgan pointed at her. "See, sheriff? See?"

I sighed. "Mr. Morgan, must you be melodramatic?"

When they were all outside in the hall and the door was closed Morgan got a sneering expression on his face. "Didn't expect the sheriff, did you, you venomous slut."

"How nice you wear that expression, Mr. Morgan. It goes well with your character. No, I didn't expect the sheriff. I didn't expect you would want to parade your shame so freely."

With his lip still curled he said, "I am a gentleman. What's more, I am a Virginia gentleman. I am above shame."

I said, "I do not believe I have ever met anyone who claims an honor so frequently and then does so little to justify it."

He leaned forward and put out his hand, slowly making a fist. "Yes, but I've got you, madam. And I intend to squeeze you to a pulp."

I shook my head in admiration. "You are quite without conscience. You are completely amoral. We were both here last night. We both know what happened."

He got a sneaky smile on his face. "Indeed we do. I am here to see what sort of offer you propose to make in return for my dropping the charges. And don't think that a pound of flesh will satisfy me." He ran an eye over my figure. "I would say you weigh slightly in excess of a hundred pounds. That is what I want and that is what I will get."

I shrugged. "Fine. If that is what you insist on."

His eyes widened slightly. With too much haste he said, "You agree?"

I shrugged again. "It's nothing to me. It will be the same as last night. You will still be impotent. Only this time you could do yourself serious damage with your pistol. If I hadn't wrestled it out of your hands you would have hit yourself in the breast rather than the leg."

He stared at me, his mouth partly open. Finally he said in a strangled voice, "What in hell are you talking about, you damn whore?"

I had noticed before how his voice went guttural and coarse when he lost his temper. It was hardly a trait found in someone who had grown up in Virginia aristocracy. And, too, he had never had the right accent. It had always been too hard, like that of someone from north of Virginia, maybe Pennsylvania or even Ohio. I said, mildly, "Surely you remember, Mr. Morgan. You came into my room late at night and were going to force yourself on me, threatening me with your derringer. And then when I was forced to submit you discovered you were impotent. I well remember your words. You said, 'It can't be! Violence is my aphrodisiac.' After that you were going to shoot me and then you were going to shoot yourself. I wrestled with you for the gun and that is when you shot yourself in the thigh."

He had gone deathly pale. The word would hardly leave his mouth. It trickled out. "Impotence? Impotence. Impotence!" He gathered strength. *"Impotence!* You low, vile slut!"

I smiled sweetly. "I would be disappointed if you had any other opinion of me."

His voice was still hoarse. "That is a lie! A slanderous lie!"

I kept smiling. "But it will sound so nice in court."

His look was becoming murderous. He was fingering his walking stick. Only a few feet separated us, he in his wheeled chair and I in a simple straight-backed chair I'd brought from the bedroom. He said, "I will *ruin* you in court. I am an important man in this town."

I nodded. I said, "Perhaps. But then I will appeal. And appeal again and again. I have a great deal of money, Mr. Morgan. I will be a hard bird to cage. And at each trial the word impotent will float through the air in the courtroom like a foul odor."

His face was choked with rage. All traces of any Virginia accent were long since gone. "You shot me with your gun. Mine was not fired."

"On the contrary. The sheriff noticed it immediately." I smiled. "Our guns are of the same caliber. But it is the impotence I think you'll enjoy the most."

His hand was sliding down the length of his cane, away from the heavy, knobbed end. He was almost choking on his rage when he said, "I will bring witnesses, women."

"And which women will those be, Mr. Morgan? Women of the town or women of the night? Women of the town would have to be married ladies. I don't think they will care to testify to your sexual prowess. As to ladies of the night, well, I doubt that they will be believed." I shook my head. "It will be really sad to see a gentleman of Virginia defamed in such a manner. But they say that those who lie are often caught in their own deceit."

Spittle was flying from his lips. "You are the liar!"

"Of course. It's my best defense. But you were the first to lie. And I'm not talking about last night. Really, Mr. Morgan, you should not claim a genteel background in Virginia when you are talking to someone who really has one."

If possible it made him even more furious, which was what I had expected. In all his pretentious vanity I had decided that his role as a Virginia gentleman was his most precious and his most vulnerable.

He stared at me. His eyes had suddenly narrowed and the fury had suddenly left his face. I felt uneasy, but I intended to go through with it. He said, almost in a whisper, "What do you mean, my claim to a background as a Virginia gentleman? The sheriff said you kept talking about that. Explain yourself." His words were menacing, deadly quiet.

I pulled a face. "Oh, nothing, Mr. Morgan, except you are a fraud. If you persist against me I will hire the

Pinkertons to explore your background. I don't think they will find any Virginia heritage in your lineage or any Virginia Military Institute in your background."

His hand gripped the end of the stout-looking walking stick. "You go too far, woman."

I said, "I think the reason you profess to hate Yankees so much is because you are one. Probably a Yankee deserter. No wonder you didn't want General Grant here."

He gave a wild cry and stood up, raising his stick over his head as he did. As he started toward me I jumped up and ran around my little chair and shoved it at his feet, screaming as I did so. The chair caught him neatly in the shins and he stumbled forward, falling full length on top of the light chair, breaking it with his weight. His right arm was still outthrust, the walking stick in his hand.

At that instant the door opened and Sheriff Long stood there. He took in the scene in an instant. He looked at me. "Did he try to attack you, Mrs. Grayson?"

I said, "It should be obvious."

It took a few moments to get matters arranged, Mr. Morgan back in his chair and the question of the charges settled. Morgan played his part with poor grace. He shook his finger at me and shouted, "That woman is a goddam lying bitch!"

Sheriff Long said, "That sounds a little scandalous to me, Mr. Morgan. That sort of slander is actionable, you know."

Morgan still glared at me. "I want her and her nigger out of this hotel and this town immediately!"

Before I could stop her Phoenix had stepped around me and spit directly in Morgan's face. The act shocked us all. Morgan went stiff, staring, stunned to the very soles of his feet. He slowly reached a hand up toward the spittle that was hanging from his nose.

Phoenix said, "Bettah not rub it in, honey. That's de way you get to be a nigger."

Both the sheriff and the porter, who was standing behind Mr. Morgan's chair, were trying to stifle a laugh.

Finally Morgan spoke. "Out," he said hoarsely. "Out, out, *out, out,* OUT!"

I said, sweetly, "You have caused us to miss the train, Mr. Morgan. We will have to stay over until Sunday. And I do not intend to hide here in my rooms. So, until we are gone tomorrow morning, I don't want you in this hotel. I do not want to ever lay eyes on you again. Is that clear?"

Through gritted teeth Morgan said to the porter behind him, "Get me out of here. Get me away from this she-devil."

We watched as the porter backed Morgan in his wheeled chair out into the hall. Just as he was about to wheel him away I said, still sweetly, "Oh, Charles, I don't expect to receive any sort of bill when we leave. Do you understand? There are always the Pinkertons."

He shot me one last venomous glance and then shouted at the porter, "Push, damn it, push!"

The sheriff lingered long enough to tip his hat. He said, "You sure *you* ain't Wilson Young, Mrs. Grayson?"

"He's a better shot, sheriff."

"But I would reckon no more audacious."

I smiled.

He said, "Why didn't you tell me Mr. Morgan shot himself with his own gun?"

"I guessed it slipped my mind. Things were all of a jumble."

He tipped his hat again and closed the door.

I turned and Phoenix was literally jumping up and down. She said, "Oh, Miss Laura, you is de berries! De absolute berries!"

I said, "Really, Phoenix, I am ashamed of you."

She stopped jumping and looked crestfallen. She said, "I done wrong, didn't I?"

"You certainly did," I said. "I would have thought you had more spit in your mouth than that."

16

Laura

It seemed to be the longest train trip of my life, even though we actually arrived early. When I stepped out onto the platform I looked at the little watch I carried in my purse and was greatly surprised to see that it was just a quarter of noon. I had expected it to be late in the afternoon, the miles and the time had passed so slowly.

The town seemed very peaceful and composed on a Sunday morning. Across the way was the Baptist church with its big steeple pointing toward the sky. I thought I could almost hear them singing hymns. My luggage had been unloaded out of the baggage car by a couple of roustabouts who worked on the passenger platform. To make sure they handled the bags and trunks carefully I gave them each a dollar. The moment we were off the train I sent Phoenix flying to the little house to roust out Albert and get him over to the depot with the carriage. It was about a mile, I knew, but I fully expected her to make good time.

In the interim I went into the depot and settled myself down for the wait. The passenger agent glanced at me and there were a few hangers-on about, but no one took much notice. I had changed from the blue frock in which I had done battle to a gay, yellow gown that bore no traces of Morgan's presence. Actually, I thought, it had all worked out for the best. Phoenix and I needed the extra day to pack, and I had a lovely dinner in the dining room and, that morning, I marched triumphantly out of the hotel without paying a red cent.

I wanted Phoenix to hurry back with Albert. I was in a burning hurry to get to the ranch and see how matters stood between Warner and me. But even as I was thinking that I noticed a small stain on the skirt of my gown. I cast my mind back, trying to think of what clothes I had left in the little house. Perhaps there was something there that I could change into out of my travel-worn outfit. I knew that it was silly, that Warner wouldn't even notice, but I wanted to look my best for him. If it was going to be a close question I wanted to be dressed for the occasion in clothes that might tip the balance in my direction.

I grew impatient. By the clock on the wall it was twenty after twelve. I walked outside and, in the distance, saw Phoenix hurrying along on foot. I could not imagine what had happened. Where was Albert? And the carriage? How were we going to get to the ranch?

I descended the steps of the platform and hurried through the dust of the street to meet her. When we came together I asked about Albert.

She shook her head, looking worried and said, "He ain't deah, Miss Laura."

"Not there? Where is he?"

"I don' be knowin'. Ain't hide nor hair o' him or de carriage or de horses." She looked all around as if expecting Albert to suddenly pop into view.

I bit my lip in agitation. I could not imagine a time where a delay was so unwelcome. I said, "Was the house broken into? Did you look inside?"

"Place looked peaceful enough. I opened de back doah and hollered in case he was sleepin'. I shouted de roof down and he wadn't there. And, course, they wadn't no horses and no carriage. I wouldn't o' missed dat carriage, big as it is."

I was uncertain what to do. I didn't want to walk all the way to the house to investigate the matter myself, not in the shoes I was wearing. I stared down the main street. I knew there was a livery stable next to the hotel. I pointed. I said, "I want you to go down to the livery and hire a buckboard and team with a driver." I pulled a ten-dollar bill out of my purse. "And don't take no for an answer just because it's Sunday. Bring him right back here so we can load the luggage. Now hurry."

I climbed back up on the platform and watched anxiously as she hurried toward the livery stable. I had given Albert strict instructions not to move out of that house. I could have believed he was at church or visiting neighbors or buying groceries, except he wouldn't take the carriage for such errands. Had Warner told me something about Albert? Something had been said, but I couldn't remember what it was. Or had I only imagined it? Our conversations had been so intense, so important, that I had blocked all else out of my mind.

Finally, I saw a buckboard with Phoenix sitting up on the seat beside the Negro driver come out of the livery stable and start down the street toward the depot. I went in search of the two roustabouts to enlist their help in loading my luggage.

Phoenix was right. There was no Albert nor carriage nor horses. I even looked in the feed bin in the carriage house. It was empty. Only a few moldy bales of hay remained to show the place had ever been in use.

The house had not been broken into, although a considerable portion of the clothes I'd left were missing. Only a few had been overlooked, but that was probably because they'd been hung in a small closet off the kitchen. One of the frocks was a coral green shantung silk with an exaggerated vee neck that I knew Warner especially liked. I took the time to change into it and to freshen my makeup and remove any other traces of the train trip. Outside, Phoenix and the livery driver were waiting. I sank into a chair at the last moment, suddenly hesitant to face Warner. If he did not want me back I didn't know what I was going to do. In the distance I could hear the northeast-bound train tolling its bell and blowing its steam whistle impatiently. The sound made me shudder. It was the very train I'd taken almost two weeks before. I wished the engineer would quit blowing his whistle, stop reminding me of the mistake I had made.

For consolation I opened my purse and took out Warner's letter. I had read it a half a dozen times, but I thought a refresher would strengthen me. I looked at his kind, simple, bold handwriting and tears almost came to my eyes. I had been a damn fool and I could only hope I didn't have to pay for it. I smoothed the page and began to read.

My dear Laura:

Well, it appears that I am out of aces and will have to fold my hand. I took my best shot with the proposition about your money but it didn't seem to carry much weight. I guess when a man offers to use his wife's money it don't sound like much of a sacrifice and might even be considered some kind of joke by most folks, but I feel sure that you knew I meant serious business by the gesture.

Looking at the whole situation I can see that it is not you and not me. I take the blame for leaving you hemmed up and tied down for over two years. If I'd been the caring husband I ought to have been I would have noticed and taken steps to correct it. You were too good a wife and too good a person to complain when you had every right to. I guess it doesn't matter, not really. I guess it would have happened sooner or later. I can't expect a high-bred filly like you to live my kind of life and I don't know no other. I hope I have made it plain that I love you and you are going to leave a large hole in my life. I feel as if I'll have a permanent cavity in my chest where you used to fit exactly when we were hugging. I will miss you for a long time.

Like everything else in the affairs of men and women, our situation needs some washing up and putting away. I will be leaving the ranch as quickly as I can. It is going to be painful to be there without you. I am going to take what little I put into it and the rest is yours. Aside from some Morgan and quarter-horse stock I had, I'm going to take that Thoroughbred Louisiana stud and the two Kentucky mares. I calculate I put about twenty thousand dollars into the place. I calculate the worth of those three Thoroughbreds at about fifteen thousand dollars. I'll take five thousand out of the bank to help me get started. I hope you feel that this is fair.

The only lawyer I know in Tyler is a man named Brown. I intend to go by and see him and sign divorce papers, listing what I am taking. You can go in and fill in the rest of it and give as the cause of the divorce any reason you care to. My advice is to list me as a sorry son of a bitch who cared more about horses than what really counted. I guess if you come right down to it, blindness was the cause of the divorce.

I am leaving you Charlie Stanton. He is a very good man, Laura, and knows nearly as much about horses as I do. I guess you could say that if I was any kind of man I'd stay there and operate the business for you, since I'm the cause of your investing so much money in the idea. I'd do it, but I can't. It would tear the heart out of me. That was why I left Jefferson with nothing but this poor letter to mark my going. I could no longer see you and talk to you as if we were casual acquaintances.

As soon as I get back to the ranch I will put Albert and the carriage and the span of horses on the train to you. I want you to be able to get around that town in style and I guarantee you, won't nobody have a smarter looking team than yours. I have also left you Paseta. I want you to have a good horse to ride. He is stabled at Bailey's Livery, I know you don't have your English saddle there, but I expect one can be found. If not, telegraph here and I am sure Charlie will send it.

I believe that I am leaving you in good shape so far as the stable of Thoroughbreds goes. I think you should have an exciting time racing them. I recommend that you give Charlie a pretty substantial raise. He is loyal to me and might buck and pitch a little about staying there, but it is an opportunity for him, especially with him marrying, and I will see that he stays.

There is no more I can think of to be said except I count our years together as the best I ever had. I didn't realize that until lately, but it's like the old story about not missing the water until the well runs dry.

I don't know where I'm going, but when I get settled I will drop that lawyer a letter how to reach me. If you ever need me all you have to do is let me know.

You know that I wish you the best of luck and happiness in whatever you do.

It was signed, "Love, Warner." I put the letter down in my lap, staring through the window at the scrubby pines outside. I thought to myself that if Morgan had lost me that man by keeping the letter from me I was going back to Jefferson and shoot the bastard again. Only this time I would kill him.

I got up and went outside, closing the door behind me. The team and the driver and Phoenix were all waiting patiently. I climbed into the back of the buckboard, assisted by the driver, and took a seat on one of the trunks. Phoenix had thoughtfully provided me with a cushion from somewhere.

As we wheeled out of the driveway one of the women who had visited me when I spent the few nights in the house came out of her front door and waved. I waved back. I don't know why I thought so little of those neighborhood women. But then, I was a snob. It took the real frauds in Jefferson to show me what was real and what wasn't.

It was a long, bumpy, anxious ride, but finally we were turning into the yard area of the ranch. Phoenix cast a glance back at me, rolling her eyes. I tried to smile.

As we pulled in I saw a man come out of the barn nearest to the house. Since it was a half hour after one o'clock, I expected Warner to be out working somewhere. If he was there.

The man was the only one in sight and I bade the driver steer for him. As we came up to him he touched his hat. I vaguely recognized him, but since I had so little to do with the day-to-day management of the ranch, I didn't know his name. I asked him where Mr. Grayson was.

He took off his hat. "He's not here, ma'am."

My heart sank. "When will he be back?"

He said, "Well, I couldn't say, ma'am, since I don't know where he be."

I nodded numbly. I motioned for the driver to go on up to the house. I glanced backwards all the way to the kitchen door, where the driver pulled up. There was very little stirring. But then it was Sunday and no real work was done except the feeding and care of the horses.

The driver came around and helped me down. I told Phoenix to see to the unloading of the luggage. I raced up the back steps, opened the kitchen door, and stepped inside. The house was silent. I went through the swinging door and stood in the morning room. The house was as desolate and empty as if it had never been lived in. I glanced over at the table near the big windows that looked out toward the barns and the training rings. It was Warner's place to sit so he could keep an eye on matters when he was having coffee or breakfast or even lunch. I fancied the only way I ever got him to the dining room for dinner was because it was too dark to see out by the evening meal.

I could feel his absence all around me. It made my heart sob.

When I could, I moved out of the morning room, glancing in other empty rooms as I went, until I came to the stairs. I went up them slowly, knowing what I was going to find when I entered our bedroom.

The bed was as neatly made as if no one had ever slept in it. Beside the bed was Warner's bedside table. There was a bottle of whiskey, a quarter full, and a glass with a hint of brown liquid in the bottom. I went over and put my finger in the glass. The whiskey had evaporated, all that was left was a sticky, gooey film. Warner hadn't been in the room in a long time.

At last I went to his closet and opened the door. With the exception of the dress suits I had made him buy, all of his clothes were gone. I looked in his bureau drawers. They were empty. He was gone.

I walked slowly over to the bed and sank down on his side. How long I was there I didn't know. Finally I became aware of Phoenix calling me from downstairs. "Miss Laura! Miss Laura! Where you at?"

I got up and left the bedroom and went down the stairs. Phoenix met me at the bottom with a question on her face. I shook my head. "He's gone. His clothes are all gone. All he left were those damn suits I made him buy."

She put her arm around me and patted my back and steered me into the morning room. She said, "You set down at the table an' I'll fix you a cup of coffee."

I said, "I'd rather have a drink."

"I put a little in de coffee. Be bettah fo' you that way."

I sat down, aware I was sitting in the end chair, the one that faced the kitchen and gave the best view out the window. It had always been Warner's chair. We only kept two chairs at the table. The others were against the wall. I guessed it was our way of saying the table was private, just for Warner and me. Husband and wife.

Phoenix came in with the coffee and set it in front of me. "You drink some o' that. Make you feel better."

"What time is it? I left my watch and purse upstairs."

"Kitchen clock say a little after three. I wonder where ever'body is? Ain't many folks churnin' around."

"It's Sunday, Phoenix. Have you seen Albert?"

"Ain't no sign of the man."

"Why don't you go look for him? Maybe he's in the cook house."

"He bettah not be in no cook house. I ketch him shinin' 'round that damn Jambalaya I gon' have some o' his hide."

"Pour yourself a cup and come sit down with me."

She gave me a long look. "Ain't my company you need, Missy. Don't fret, it gon' be all right by and by."

I looked at her and shook my head. I raised the coffee cup to my lips and took a sip. The fumes of the whiskey ran straight up my nose and I was taken with a fit of coughing. When I recovered I frowned at Phoenix. "How much whiskey did you put in this coffee? Or, should I say, how much coffee did you put in this whiskey?"

"I bring de pot," she said. She went through the swinging door. In a moment I heard her hollering. She was making such a commotion that I almost got up to see what the trouble was. But before I could, she stuck her head around the door and said, "Miss Laura, you better look out de window."

"What?"

"Look out de window! Look out an' see who jes' ridin' through de gate."

I leaned forward, peering through the windowpane. There, distinctly, was Warner Grayson heading toward the barn on a stylish quarter horse. There was no mistaking him. No one, ever, sat a horse like Warner Grayson. I said, "Quick, Phoenix! Get out on the back porch. Wave your apron or something."

She gave me a blank look. "What I want to do dat fo'? Mr. Warner ain't lookin' for me."

"You ninny! If he sees you he'll know I'm here. Get out there!"

She ducked back through the door and I concentrated my attention on the barn Warner had ridden into.

He seemed to stay in the barn forever. But then, I knew that Warner would see to the horse's feed and water and curry him down and maybe even polish his saddle. He was meticulous about the tools of his trade. Finally, however, he emerged. For a horrible second I thought he was going to turn away from the house. But then he stopped and stared, even putting his hand to his brow to shade his eyes. After a hesitation he finally started walking toward the house. He was still a good hundred yards away. I heard the back door slam and then Phoenix was sticking her head around the swinging door. "He comin', Miss Laura! He do be comin'! See, he ain't gone nowhere."

I pointed a finger at her. "You stay out of the way. *And keep your mouth shut!*"

She looked indignant. "Keep my mouf shut? I one of de people most nearly always keeps dere mouf shut. Land o' Goshen." She glanced back inside the kitchen. "Look out, here he come!"

I watched him walk slowly toward the house. The closer he got and the better I could see him the more my heart fluttered. He went out of sight a little before he reached the kitchen steps, the angle of the window not permitting a view. I heard the kitchen door open and shut and then a little conversation as he and Phoenix talked. I couldn't make out the words, but I heard Phoenix giggle excitedly. A moment more and the swinging door opened. Warner came in and stopped. He looked at me and smiled slightly. He didn't look so much surprised as uncomfortable. I guessed that Phoenix had told him I was in the morning room.

He took his hat off and turned it around in his hand, holding it by the brim. He said, "Hello, Laura."

I smiled. I said, "Hello yourself."

He looked uneasy. Of course he didn't know what was in my mind. For all he knew I was coming to protest the property settlement he'd mentioned in his letter. He said, "You kind of took me by surprise. I meant to be cleared out and out of your way."

I smiled. "Are you going to stand there?"

"I reckon I could sit down." He moved to the opposite end of the table and sat in the chair I usually occupied. He put his hat on the table, brim up so the luck wouldn't run out. He gave me a level look. "You get my letter?"

I was feeling a little ill at ease myself. I didn't quite know how to describe my presence. I patted my purse. I said, "Yes. Got it right here."

He jerked his thumb toward the kitchen. "Looks from all the trunks and luggage that you kind of moved back."

"I have," I said. "Kind of."

He rubbed his jaw. There was a little beard stubble and it made a rasping sound. He gave a half laugh. "That letter was kind of sappy. I don't generally come out so—so, oh, kind of strong like that. Guess I might have had one drink too many."

I said, softly, "Don't you dare say that. It was a beautiful letter."

He lifted his hand and let it fall on the table. He shrugged. "Well, whatever it was I meant it all." He made as if to rise. "I better get out of your way."

I put out my hand to stay him. "Where are you staying?"

"With Charlie," he said.

"Charlie Stanton? Here on the ranch?"

He nodded slowly. "Yeah, I was trying to get everything shaped up for you. Charlie had room."

"Why didn't you stay in the house?"

He gave me an odd look. "I guess you didn't read my letter very close."

"But I did. Over and over again."

"Then you ought not to have to ask that. I couldn't stay here. I couldn't sleep in the bed we'd once occupied. Hell, Laura, what do you think I'm made out of?"

It was not going at all the way I had imagined. I had thought there would be some sort of tumultuous reunion but all that was happening was we were sitting there, both ill at ease, talking all around the matter at hand. Someone was going to have to declare his or her position and it appeared I would have to be the one. Warner could not know that I had undergone a complete change of heart and had come home to him. I said, "I suppose you're made out of the same stuff I am. I got quite a shock when I saw your clothes were gone."

He ran his hand over his face. "Yeah, I know what that feels like." He looked down at the table. He had looked everywhere in the room since he'd come in except into my eyes. "You make your deal on that part of the hotel?"

I shook my head. "No. That was really only a passing fancy. Jefferson can get to be very tiring."

"Pretty busy place."

I hesitated. But I knew we could not sit there like that much longer. I would burst if we did. I said, "I didn't get your letter until Friday night. Otherwise we would have been here sooner."

He nodded. "That's only right. There's a ton of details you got to get familiar with. Even though Charlie will be running the ranch, he won't be making a lot of the decisions. You've got to understand the business side of it."

I stared at him in amazement. The damn fool thought I had come home for the horse farm and not him. I said, "I don't think you take my meaning about the letter."

He nodded. "Yeah. You didn't get it until Friday night. When did y'all get to Tyler? Yesterday? You must have stayed in that little house you bought."

Was he deliberately obtuse or was he afraid of taking

anything for granted. I said, "We came in today. On the noon train."

It surprised him. He said, "Why, I was in town today. As a matter of fact I was putting—"

But he got no further because Phoenix suddenly came barging in and plunked a cup of coffee in front of him. She said, "Whiskey in there."

"Thank you, Phoenix."

Then, as she was turning away, she said, "Miss Laura shot de lizard."

Warner was about to lift the cup to his lips. He set it down immediately, shock on his face. "Whaaat?"

I said, severely, "Phoenix!"

She was halfway through the door. Without looking back she said, "Y'all be takin' too long. Get on wid de business at hand."

Warner was staring at me. "You shot Morgan?"

I shrugged. "She's exaggerating. You know how Phoenix is."

He leaned toward me. "Laura, you either have shot someone or you ain't. There's no in between and there's no exaggeration. Which is it?"

I tossed my head. "All right, I shot him in the leg."

He cocked his head at me. "Well, it ain't none of my business. But—"

That was one too many. I slammed my hand down on the top of the table. "How dare you say that! Your wife shoots someone and it's none of your business? What kind of man are you?"

He was a long moment in answering. He said, slowly, "I know what kind of man I am. What I don't know is what kind of husband I am."

"Have you been to see that lawyer?"

He shook his head. "I guess I been kind of putting it off."

"Then you are the same kind of husband you were before all this nonsense started."

He narrowed his eyes. "Wait a minute. Wait a minute. I want to know about this Morgan business. Is that what drove you home? Did you have a falling out with Morgan and shoot him and then come here?"

I stared at him. I was damned if I was going to answer such an insulting question.

Phoenix suddenly stuck her head back into the room. "Mr. Warner, she done shucked off de lizard days 'fore she shot him. Wouldn't see him, wouldn't let him in de rooms. Didn't want no part o' him or his blamed hotel. He broke in on her late dat Friday night and she shot de snake. All she be doin' last few days is mournin' 'bout you. Den when she found he been holdin' yore letter she good and sorry she only shot him in de leg."

Warner was smiling his long, slow smile. I looked over at Phoenix. I said, "Wouldn't you be able to hear better if you came on in here?"

She wagged her head. She said, "I is one lady knows my place. I don' interfere in other folks' business."

Warner said, "I'm scared to get too presumptuous here. Is there any chance you've come back to me and not to the ranch?"

"I never really left." I picked up the coffee cup loaded with whiskey and had a long draught. My heart was going like a trip-hammer and my hands were shaking slightly. It was all out on the table.

He leaned back in his chair and looked at me as if from a long way off. He said, "Well, you could have fooled me, the way you acted when I came to Jefferson with my hat in my hand."

I said, with a little force, "Well, if you'd waited one more day and been a little stronger about the matter we could have come home together. I was confused."

"Hell, I was trying to be understanding."

"You didn't have to be that goddamn understanding. Couldn't you see I was in a strange place and not thinking right?"

He frowned, "Well, maybe I was at fault." Then he glanced up at me. "Oh, no. You ain't laying this one off on me. I have taken all the pounding I'm going to take."

I said, "Fine." My heart was trembling. "I have

declared myself. You have not. And that letter sounded pretty final."

He looked at me, working his mouth. He said, "Laura, I never went back on a horse trade in my life."

I made a face. "How romantic."

"It's the best way I know to put it. You never really know what you're getting when you trade horses. You'd have to know the horse inside out and you never do. So whatever you get you try and make it work. You and I traded horses. We both gave up the single life to pull in double harness. Sometimes it takes a team awhile to get comfortable. You know I ain't all that good with words."

I wanted to laugh out loud I felt so happy. He was such an honest, certain, good man. It frightened me how close I'd come to losing him. I said, "Well, I guess I take that to mean you want me back."

"I never stopped."

We sat a moment staring at each other. Finally he said, "We back together?"

"As far as I'm concerned."

He stood up. "Then get out of my chair. I've been uncomfortable in this position ever since. What do you mean sitting in my chair?"

As we passed each other at about the middle of the table he caught me with one arm and spun me around and leaned me back and kissed me the way I'd been wanting to be kissed for a long time.

After that we both sat down, having switched places, as if nothing had happened. Except I could feel a wave of emotion rising in me and I could tell that Warner was having trouble keeping his breathing regular. He said, "Now I want to know about this shooting business. And I want the details."

I had gotten to where Morgan tore my dressing gown when Warner interrupted and said, "That wasn't that green silk one I like, was it?"

"No, it was a peach colored one. I gave the green one to Phoenix."

His mouth opened, but before he could say anything, I

plowed on ahead and finished the story. When I was done he sat a moment, sipping at the remains of the coffee and whiskey I'd left. He shook his head slowly. "You warned me about that town and then you up and done it. That was slick, Laura, but it scares me sitting here listening. That sheriff didn't have to be that good a man. A thousand things could have gone wrong. I'm with Phoenix. You should have lit out of there when the sheriff gave you leave. I'd've gone back and got your clothes."

"And let that weasel scare me off?"

He played with the cup for a moment, staring down at it. Finally he said, reluctantly, "Yeah, I can see your point. But none of this happens if—" He stopped. "Hell, I'm about to start another fight. We better stay away from this table."

"You're going to have to get some men to move my luggage upstairs."

"I don't know if we got anybody that stout. We'll have to pay them extra."

I said, firmly, "And be sure they pick up your clothes and move them back in the bedroom."

He leaned back in his chair and smiled a sly little smile. He said, "That last day in Jefferson. You were wearing that green dressing gown with nothing on underneath."

"And you didn't do anything about it."

"Well it ain't been out of my mind, I can tell you that." He looked down. "Reckon Phoenix would loan you that back?"

I gave him a flat stare. "What for?"

He was about to answer me when he suddenly slapped his brow with the flat of his hand. He said, "Oh, hell! I put Albert and the carriage and the horses on the one o'clock train!"

"When?"

"Today. Lord, I gave him a note to the livery stable. But you won't be there and he's going to be walking around lost as a goose. And it'll be tomorrow before I can send someone to bring him back."

"The sheriff is a good man. If you sent him a wire he'd see about Albert. I have to go back to Jefferson anyway."

He gave me a quick look. "Why?"

I told him about the money I had left there.

He said, "You'll have to get Robert Quince to write or telegraph after that. You ain't going back to Jefferson anytime soon and then only in my company." He got up. "I better send someone in to wire to that sheriff. What'd you say his name was?"

"Long. Sheriff Long. Buford Long, I think. Sign my name to the telegram. No, wait. He's an admirer of yours. He'd be thrilled to get a telegram from the famous horse trainer, Warner Grayson."

He pulled a wry face at me, but when he was almost at the door he looked around. "I want you to know something."

"What?"

"When I came back here from Jefferson and walked into this house it felt like a tomb. I never expected to see you again. It was as if you had died. I didn't know if I was going to be able to stand it or not."

"Is that your way of saying you love me?"

He shrugged. "Love, like, lust, long for. Whatever the word is at the time. What I'm trying to tell you is that neither one of us is ever going to try and welch on this horse trade again."

"I believe a bargain is a bargain."

"Good." He went out the door.

It was about two minutes before Phoenix stuck her head around the door again. She said, "Well, you sho' taken yo' own sweet time 'bout that, Missy."

"Go draw me a bath and get out my lotions and perfumes and such. And dig out that green silk dressing gown I gave you and take it upstairs."

"Thought I jus' heard you say a bargain be a bargain. That be my silk robe."

"Not today it's not. Now hurry up."

I sat back and let out a long sigh. I felt as if I had finally brought a team of runaway horses to a stop. I relaxed slowly back into the chair. It seemed that I had been tensed up forever. The strange thing was that neither Warner nor I had brought up any conditions for our reconciliation. I guessed we neither one felt they were necessary. I think we both knew what had to be done and both were willing. It was a good feeling.

Epilogue

It was a little over two years since the occasion that Warner liked to refer to as The Time Laura Went Loco. It was November and cold and we had a fire going in the fireplace in the parlor. Warner was sitting in a big leather wing chair and I was sitting across from him on the small divan. He was reading a horse breeders' magazine and I was reading a week-old newspaper. In the time that had passed since my Jefferson adventure matters had gone very nicely. Just as Warner had promised we had gone racing and I had had more than my share of excitement and things to do. In fact, it had gotten to where I looked forward to a few quiet days at home. Our colts had done even better than Warner had expected and we were rapidly making a name with our stable.

As I looked at the paper a sizable article caught my eye. I read it swiftly. It said that at the beginning of the summer the Army Corps of Engineers had begun blasting loose the large log jam that had caused Gaddo Lake to back up into the bayou in front of Jefferson. The engineers had explained this was necessary to deepen the channel of the Red River at Shreveport. But as a result of the slow breakup of the five-mile log jam that had formed a natural dam, the bayou in front of Jefferson had flooded back into Gaddo Lake and that water had flowed back into the Red River. The result was that Jefferson, once a boom town, once again became a sleepy plantation town. I got Warner's attention and read him the article. I said, "What do you think of that?"

Without looking up from his magazine he said, "I imagine you could get a pretty good price on that hotel wing you were going to lease. Shows you that patience generally pays off."

I said, sarcastically, "Yes, sweetheart."

Still without looking away from his reading he said, "I believe that is the second time in ten years you have called me by a pet name."

"Are you going to reciprocate?"

"I don't know what that means, but I might name a horse after you."

"What would you call it?"

He thought a moment. "Laura's Sweetheart, I guess."

I said, "That wouldn't tell much, would it."

There was a long pause before he looked around the edge of his magazine. He said, "Now exactly what do you mean by that?"

"Nothing," I said. "Nothing. Not unless you feel you are taking me for granted again."

He stared at me. "All right. We'll name the damn colt Charles Morgan's Folly."

I threw the paper at him.

ZANE GREY

The U.P. Trail
☐ 50672-2/$4.99

Wildfire
☐ 52631-6/$4.99

The Border Legion
☐ 52640-5/$4.99

The Desert of Wheat
☐ 5264-X/$4.99

*Completely repackaged for 1995
Published by Pocket Books*

POCKET
BOOKS